Where the
WINGS RISE

CLIMBING HIGHER

When the Ice Melts

Where the Wings Rise

Why the Mountains Stand

Where the

WINGS RISE

CLIMBING HIGHER

BOOK 2

ASHLYN McKAYLA OHM

Words from the Wilderness

© 2023 by Ashlyn McKayla Ohm

I forgot to fly. My fall from grace
Shot me from the sky, grim gravity—
My failures weighed my wings. No second chance
To once more catch the clouds. And so I sought
To hide the sinking shame—but still I wept
Alone with wounded wings. But then I saw
That healing often hurts, but hope-filled hands
Reach with grip of grace toward shattered souls.
Now I choose
To offer up my dark, let in the light.
I am not earthbound now; I spread my wings
And soar once more upon the wondrous wind.

CHAPTER 1

September.

For as long as Addisyn Miles could remember, the meaning of the month had been condensed to only one thing: the Mid-Atlantic Regional Figure Skating Championships.

Let others gush over the promise of fall and the start of school and the reappearance of pumpkin spice lattes at chic coffee shops. For Addisyn, September was the month when she emerged from the obscure cocoon of summer training and local events. September was the month she stood again on ice with the best competitors in the nation, all vying for the same honor—a pass to Sectionals and Nationals and, maybe, a route to the U.S. Olympic Team. September was the birthplace of dreams, possibility swirling through the air with the floating leaves.

But not this year.

This year, September held no competition-crammed rinks, no freshly sharpened skate blades. This year, the month meant nothing more than cooler weather and gilded aspens in the Colorado mountains where Addisyn now lived with her sister Avery.

Don't go there. Addisyn shook her head slightly and stretched her arms over her head, easing both the stiffness in her back and the gloom in her mind. She turned her attention back to the jumble of bags and suitcases scattered across the closet floor. She'd rather not have her room resembling the aftermath of a laundromat explosion when Avery returned from work, so she had—she stretched to see the clock—a little over an hour to finish unpacking everything.

She reached for the next layer of clothes in a pull-behind luggage and shook out her favorite green blouse, wincing at the creases that sliced through the fabric. Well, what had she expected, leaving it crammed in her bag as long as she had? She'd moved in with her older sister a month ago, for crying out loud. She should have emptied her luggage and arranged her belongings during the first few days.

Another *should*. Her life had been full of them.

She tapped the blouse. What could she do for the creases? The silky fabric didn't exactly look as if it would make friends with an iron. Maybe Avery would know what to do. Then again, maybe not. Walking the straight and narrow as she did, Avery had probably never had to learn how to undo damage caused by carelessness. It was Addisyn who had stumbled along a more zigzag course.

She reached back into the suitcase, and a glittery evening gown spilled into her lap like a river of silk. Now here was something she wouldn't need—not in the simple life built by Avery, whom she couldn't possibly envision in a dress like that. A wry grin tugged at Addisyn's face at the very idea. Her sister had never been one to study styles, but now that she lived in the Rocky Mountains, she'd taken her aversion to fashion to a whole new level. Her entire wardrobe seemed to consist of hiking pants, muddy boots, and shirts in a palette of earth tones.

Yes, Avery had found her groove here, transforming completely to her new identity as a mountain girl. But for Addisyn, the seams between her old life and her new one still didn't quite match.

Addisyn sighed and glanced around the room she still couldn't think of as hers. It was beautiful, of course, but it was saturated with her sister's personality—from the wooden four-poster bed, to the pinecone-patterned rug, to the lamp that was, according to Avery, made from real elk antlers. Nestled in the trees, the whole house was in contented harmony with itself, like a purring cat who'd loyally befriended her sister yet held itself distrustfully aloof from her.

Of course she was imagining things, and regardless of her feelings about the house, Addisyn had met only open-armed welcome from Avery. Her sister had forgiven her for years of rejection, supported her through the disastrous end of her skating career, and offered her a second chance with unreserved grace. And she was grateful—overwhelmingly so.

The dress was still splashed over her lap, the glitter seeming to clash with the very air in the room. Addisyn frowned and shoved the dress aside. She wouldn't need it again.

The next item in the bag was an old hand mirror, the reflective surface warped slightly. An odd snippet of memory flashed to mind—herself as a little kid, when she'd peered into mirrors with a hungry hope, always searching for Avery's face in her own. And in those days, she'd often been able to find it. But over time, the resemblance had blurred. Addisyn's features were softer, and her eyes were dark brown instead of Avery's hazel. They'd both had the same cocoa-colored hair, but now that Avery had gone and cut hers short, even that last trait no longer matched.

She'd stared at her distorted reflection long enough. Addisyn flipped the mirror over and dug through a few more items. A jacket not nearly heavy enough for Colorado weather. A dog-eared novel—yikes, was that a library book? And then, at the very bottom—a folded red sweatshirt.

The smile was coming even before she unfolded the shirt to reveal the design on the front. WHISTLER, CANADA. White letter-jacket font over an understated maple leaf.

Of all the items she'd unpacked so far, this was the most precious—her souvenir from the Canadian mountain town where she'd found herself again after—well, after everything had happened. Darius had given it to her, a parting gift at the airport before her flight to Avery.

Just so you don't forget. That's what he'd said. She rubbed the embroidery. Sweatshirt or no, she'd never forget. Not when she could still hear his gentle voice, still see the light in his ocean-colored eyes.

She tugged the sweatshirt on over her clothes and relaxed into its warmth, as soothing as an embrace. A wave of longing crashed over her. Darius was a true friend, strong and steady. And if she had stayed in Whistler, they might have been more than—

She slammed the brakes on her thoughts and pushed the empty luggage aside. There, all the clothes were done, and she only had one more bag to unpack. Evidence that she was moving forward, ticking off the mile markers on her journey toward tomorrow. She was fine. Of course. All she needed was a little more time. All she felt was the usual strangeness of adjusting to any new routine.

Right?

She dragged the last bag toward her and heard the clink of contents shifting. If she recalled correctly, it held mostly mementos and souvenirs—salvaged pieces of her past that hadn't been swept downstream by her turbulent life. There were some cute knickknacks in there too. Maybe she could set them on the shelves—finally put her own fingerprints on the room.

But when she unzipped the bag, a gleam of light flashed forth, and her breath snagged on itself. Her medal. Right there on top. A single shining disc on a royal-blue ribbon. Addisyn looped her finger through the ribbon, watching what had once been a circle of possibility spin from her hand.

Some kind of paper rustled underneath—a program. She glanced at the elegant script. *U.S. Figure Skating Junior Championships.*

No need to look inside. The day had been four years ago, but the memories were still Polaroid-permanent. It had been the fulcrum of her existence—her first professional skating victory, catapulting her at the age of seventeen into the world she'd always dreamed of.

A world for which she had been totally unprepared.

What else was in the bag? She set the medal carefully aside and sifted through a layer of crumbling dried roses until her hands bumped a heavy square. Her photo album.

She leaned against the closet wall and flipped slowly through the stiff pages. The highlight reel of her life bloomed bittersweet in her soul. Practicing, performing, making silly faces with skating friends after a competition in Chicago.

September was still calling. She closed her eyes for a moment to block the ache.

Another page, and then a vise clamped over her ribs. In these photos, she wasn't alone. Instead, she was with the man who had been much more than her coach.

Brian was smiling in every picture, but now she had the painful perspective of hindsight—like looking through the wrong end of a telescope. How could she have ever believed he was her Prince Charming? How had she never seen the darkness in his smile—the same darkness her sister had warned her about? And how the *devil* had she let him separate her and Avery?

And who was she in these pictures? Nausea curled in her stomach as she stared at the girl she must have been. Snuggled against his chest. Arms entwined around his neck. Shadows stiffening her smile.

Who was she angrier with? Him, for deceiving her? Or her, for being deceived? A frenzy of frustration ripped at her. With unsteady fingers, she snatched the corner of the first photo and tugged. The photo released from the page with no more protest than a faint snap. The glue must have been weaker than she realized.

Instead of looking at the blank square left behind, she plowed on through the pages, yanking out all the photos that featured Brian. Then she slapped them into an untidy stack and thrust them into the cavernous bag.

There. Her exorcism fueled her with a rebellious sort of strength. She unfolded her cramped legs and carried the album out to her desk. She might like to look through it again, sometime.

The closet looked good now. She stashed the luggage on the shelf and glanced around the room with satisfaction. Yes, she'd completed all the tasks—except one.

Forgetting what September had meant.

△△　△△　△△

SEPTEMBER WAS THE most mystical season in the mountains.

It was the time of wandering winds and silver streams and aspens dipped in a glowing gold. And this particular autumn day was a prism of perfection—the kind of day that made Avery feel thrillingly alive.

Pinecones crunched under her hiking boots with every step upward, the narrow trail winding between the trees from which the cones had dropped. Sun slanted through the trunks in a hazy sort of blessing.

El Shaddai…God of the mountains…thank You.

Could Avery ever pray those words enough? Ever fully express her gratitude to Him? She inhaled the incense of the High Country—the fragrant breath of the evergreens and the spicy aroma of the falling leaves and the wild, exciting tang that only came with altitude. *Thank You that I'm alive and I'm in Your country.*

The trail tore itself from the trees, skirting an eyebrow track around the edge of the mountain. Below her to the left, Moraine Park—the meadow from where they'd started—unrolled like a verdant carpet, trees and fields juxtaposed in fascinating textures. From up here, the river looked like an unspooling ribbon, losing its looping way across the valley. The brown smudges dotting the banks had to be an elk herd.

The joy was a spiraling song from her heart, swirling upward like autumn's dry leaves in the mountain winds. She glanced over her shoulder at Addisyn, trudging up the trail an ever-increasing distance behind her.

And thank You that I have my sister with me again.

How much El Shaddai had lavished upon her—the chance to dwell in this beautiful place, the chance to enjoy a perfect day like this, and most of all, the chance to rebuild a relationship with her sister. After three years of misunderstandings and hostility, Addisyn was finally back in her life—for good.

A few more steps, sand scrunching under boots, and there was the overlook on the point of the ridge. Lacing her fingers, Avery stretched her arms over her head and sank into the scenery. The rugged line of the High Peaks scraped against the sky, chiseled from the same stuff as eternity. Her gaze wandered over their familiar faces—rocks like unspoken secrets, hillsides furry with forests, the majestic crown of Longs Peak rising above the stenciled shoulders of his brothers. Clouds rubbed against the fourteen-thousand-foot peaks. No snow on them yet, but it could be any day.

The moment broke as Addisyn stumbled up beside her. "Whoa." Her younger sister sagged forward without even a cursory glance at the view. "That's—that's a climb."

"But you did great." Avery shrugged off her backpack and slung it over the weather-beaten hitch rack designed to accommodate horse riders. "We can take a few minutes here."

"O—okay." Addisyn's breathing was still jagged. She plopped down on a fallen log and shook her head. "I don't know how—you—you make it look so—so easy."

"Just because I have more experience." Avery joined her sister on the log. "The thinner air at high altitude takes some getting used to."

Addisyn was watching a cloud moving overhead, the shadow drifting across the valley beneath them. "Sometimes I wonder if I'll ever get used to it."

"You will. Of course you will." Yes, Addisyn would get used to the altitude. To everything about Colorado. She'd become a mountain girl—just as Avery had.

Uncertainty still peered from her sister's expression. "How long did it take you to get used to it?"

Avery paused. She could tell Addisyn that from the moment she'd crammed her belongings into her battered pickup and started driving west, she'd known she was a mountain girl. Seeing the mountains for the first time hadn't been an introduction—it had been a homecoming. And the altitude hadn't stolen her breath. Instead, it had allowed her to take her first deep breath in far too long.

But Addisyn looked discouraged enough already. "Well, Ads, I've been here a lot longer."

"Right. A whole year today." Addisyn's tone lightened again. "And you wanted to celebrate your one-year anniversary in the mountains by trying to kill me."

Avery joined her sister's laughter. She didn't mention that she'd purposely chosen a trail that she'd expected to be easy for Addisyn. "No way. Just giving you the chance to develop mental toughness."

"Oh, sure. More mental toughness, that's what I need." Addisyn grinned ruefully and shook her head. "I'm the one who spends two hours at the gym every day, and hiking with you still hurts muscles I didn't know I had." Her expression softened as she finally gazed at the carved profile of the mountains. "But this is beautiful."

"Wait till we get to the top." Avery's heart soared once more.

Addisyn turned paler. "This—is not the top?"

"Uh—no." Avery smiled sheepishly. "But it's not too much higher up. And the view is breathtaking."

"Breathtaking." Addisyn's eyebrows rose. "I bet."

Avery tried to slacken her pace somewhat on the next leg of the climb, but Addisyn still lagged. At the crest, they paused for photos, and Avery patted her sister on the back. "Good job. And now we start heading down the other side."

"Oh, thank goodness." Addisyn laughed. "I might survive after all."

Just as the trail plunged downward toward a copse of graceful aspens, the muffled strains of John Denver's "Rocky Mountain High" broke the quiet. "What? I never have cell service here." Avery fumbled with the zipper on her backpack and snatched her phone. Laz Jobe. She answered just in time. "Hello?"

"Miz Avery?" As usual, her boss's drawl was in no hurry. "Can't believe I gotcha, girl. You told me you was going up in the mountains today."

"I am, but somehow I have service." Avery grinned and leaned against an aspen. "Please tell me you're not calling to let me know the store fell apart just because I had one day off."

His hearty laughter rumbled through the line. "No, ma'am. But I will say that some city slicker came in here askin' me"—Laz's tone shifted in imitation—"'what time of year the elk turn into moose.'"

"Again?" The question was as common as it was ridiculous. "And you said—?"

"What I always say!" His voice was almost a roar now. "'Same time of year them sparrows turn into hawks, son!'"

Avery laughed and shook her head. Laz could be uncompromisingly blunt, but he'd been an understanding employer and a loyal friend. If not for his encouragement and guidance, she might not be celebrating a year in Colorado today.

"Anyhow—" He cleared his throat. "I'm needin' some help."

"What happened? Are you okay?"

"Yeah, yeah, of course." His sigh was gusty with irritation. "I gotta friend comin' over Monday mornin.' Chayton Wingo, ya know?"

"Right." Chayton was a regular customer at the store. "What's up?"

"He needs some help with a project."

"What kind of project?"

"I'm not tellin' you now. But it's gonna take us both."

What on earth? Avery shook her head. Knowing Laz and the outdoors store, the *project* could be anything. "I guess questions would be useless."

"Yep." His laugh held an obvious enjoyment. "I can't tell ya; I've gotta show ya. But, listen, I've got more news too. About that sister of yers."

"Addisyn? What about her?" Avery glanced at her sister, who'd now jerked toward the conversation.

"I think I've found her a job finally."

Addisyn leaned closer. "Avery? What's going on?"

Avery waved her off with a *wait-a-minute* gesture and pressed the phone closer to her ear. "Really? Where?"

"Workin' for Miz Skyla. Chayton's wife."

"Oh…yes." Avery pictured the tall, stone-quiet woman who'd been in the store a few times with Chayton. "She's looking to hire someone?"

"Yeah. You know she runs that little gift shop downtown." Avery hadn't known, but Laz kept going. "Well, Chay was sayin' as how the gal she had working there went on maternity leave. They need somebody temporary for a couple months. I told him I thought yer sister would do a good job, and if she didn't, I was sure you'd yank her up yerself."

Avery laughed. "You know it. That sounds perfect, Laz." Even better that the owners were people he knew. She'd feel more comfortable if Addisyn weren't working for total strangers. "I'll tell her now."

Laz gave her a few additional details, and by the time she ended the call, Addisyn was bouncing in place insistently. "So? What'd he say?"

"A project, first of all." Avery slipped her phone back into her bag. "He wants me there to help him."

"A project?" Addisyn tipped her head to the side. "Something at the store?"

Avery chuckled. "It could be anything. But here's the best news. He found you a job."

"Oh! Great!" Addisyn gave a fist pump. "Where?"

"A gift shop downtown."

"A gift shop?" Her sister's expression drooped.

"Yes." Avery narrowed her eyes. "Something wrong with that?"

"No—" Addisyn shrugged and gazed toward the mountains. "I was just hoping for, you know, something more challenging."

Avery blinked with a quick flare of irritation. Here Laz had bent over backwards to find Addisyn a job, and she wasn't even thankful? "It's a good opportunity, Addisyn. And it's just a temp position anyway."

"Oh." Addisyn's face cleared some.

"The store owner is Skyla Wingo. She's a friend of Laz's." No need to mention the woman's personality, or rather lack thereof. "You'll go to the store on Tuesday and meet her, and if everything's good, you'll start that day."

"If I want to, you mean."

Avery blinked. Hadn't she said that? "Well—yes. Obviously."

"Okay. Good." Addisyn's smile was still hesitant, but at least it was there. She hoisted her backpack. "Thank Laz for me."

As the hike continued, Avery's spirits lifted. Wasn't this a good sign? See, Addisyn was adjusting. She was. She'd assimilate into Colorado just the way Avery had. And with a job, even a temporary one—well, that only increased the chances that she really was here to stay.

"It will be nice to be working again." Addisyn's voice broke the stillness of the mountains. "Then I can help you with the bills."

"Ads." Avery squeezed her sister's shoulder. "We've had this discussion. I'm not worried about that."

"But I am."

Overhead, a Steller's Jay scraped its jarring cry. Avery watched it float into the crown of a ponderosa pine before Addisyn spoke again. "I had a lot of money in the accounts I shared with Brian."

"I know." Avery's fingers tightened on her backpack straps. Just the mention of Brian was a shadow suspended over the trail. "Did you call the bank again?"

"Yes. There's nothing they can do. He closed those accounts, and he was the primary accountholder, so…"

Just beneath Addisyn's words was something as hard as the stones underfoot. The same granite grudge Avery had to deliberately set aside whenever she considered the jerk who'd nearly wrecked her sister's life. "At least you're away from him."

"I know." Addisyn trailed her hand through the tall, papery grasses that lined the path. "That's what matters, right?"

"Right." Of course, if Addisyn had only listened to her from the beginning, she would never have— Avery shoved the thought away and pointed at a weathered trail sign. "About two more miles back to the trailhead, Ads. And then there's something I want you to see."

The trail had curved around the mountain now, meandering down to Moraine Park. By the time they reached the meadow once more, the sun was barely suspended above the horizon, the afternoon floating weightlessly in September serenity.

In the gravel parking area, Avery's dilapidated green truck waited like a patient old dog. "We're not leaving, are we?" Addisyn watched as Avery pulled down the creaky tailgate. "You said you had something to show me."

"I do." Avery pointed into the meadow. "See the elk herd? Way out there?"

Addisyn peered that way. "Yeah—"

"Okay." Avery hopped onto the tailgate and patted the space next to her. "Sit down right here and listen." She closed her eyes, sorting out the sounds—bubble of the little stream, rustle and whisper of the bronze meadow grass, last chirps of sparrows in the treetops. And then she heard it—part roar, part screech, part growl, rising from the tree line and filtering through the valley.

Addisyn's grip snapped onto her wrist. Avery opened her eyes to see shock scribbled over her sister's face. "Whoa! What is *that*?"

"Elk." Avery grinned. "It's the big bulls making that noise. It's called bugling."

"Seriously?" Addisyn shook her head, awe shining through her smile. "That's—I've never heard anything like it."

"This is the rut. Mating season. They're gathering in the valleys." A second bugle broke the silence. "Rival bull, trying to steal the herd." Avery scanned the hillside, then pointed. "There he is."

The newcomer trotted into the valley, a hefty bull with silver-tipped antlers. He paused for a moment, front leg churning the ground, and gave another bugle. Then he stretched out his dark, shaggy neck and galloped toward the herd.

"They're so far over there." Addisyn squinted. "We need binoculars."

"I know. I should have grabbed some. But they'll do this for several weeks, so we'll have time to watch them again."

Addisyn was obviously transfixed by the scene. "It's amazing." She swung her legs from the tailgate like a small child. "The whole world in your backyard, A."

A. The nickname squeezed at Avery's heart. Nearly two decades peeled away, and once again she could see her sister as a toddler, shortening the name she couldn't fit through her little-girl lisp. She smiled and scooted closer to Addisyn. "I'm glad you like it."

"It's awesome." Addisyn cocked her knee, resting her foot on the tailgate, and played with her shoelace. "I need to send some pictures of this to Darius. He'd love it."

"Oh…yes." The moment deflated slightly.

Her sister must have felt it too. She slid narrowed eyes to Avery. "Why don't you like Darius?"

"Ads." Avery's laugh sounded nervous, but she couldn't help it. "That's not it. I don't even know him."

"Exactly." Addisyn's words were snipped short. "So don't pass judgment till you do."

The elk cows bunched together, shuffling restlessly while the bull trotted a circle around them and bugled. As the sound died away, Addisyn cleared her throat. "I'm sorry. That came out kind of rude."

The words had stung, but Avery just shrugged. "It's okay. And I'm not passing judgment. Really."

"You would like him."

Was Addisyn trying to convince Avery or herself? Either way, Avery could go along. For now. "I'm sure I would." Actually, from Addisyn's description, he sounded like a decent guy. But Addisyn's discernment had always been clouded when it came to men.

Brian was the proof.

The conversation veered to easier things, like how many elk were in the park and how impressive the bugles sounded and where the most bulls could be seen, and Avery felt herself relaxing back into the magic of the mountains. A few more cars were arriving in the lot now, people watching the elk and snapping photos. Just as dusk began to settle over the landscape, Avery slid off the tailgate and grabbed Addisyn's hand. "Come on."

Still towing Addisyn, she stepped up to another visitor and handed him her phone. "Sir, could you please take our picture?"

"Of course!" The man tucked the water bottle he'd been holding under his arm and nodded approvingly. "Perfect backdrop there, with the mountains."

"Yes." Avery glanced over her shoulder, where Longs Peak surveyed the meadow like a watchful sentinel. Then she gave her best smile and wrapped her arm tightly around Addisyn. Her little sister—her best friend. The one person she had most wanted to share her mountains with.

The man studied the screen as the moment dragged out, and Addisyn leaned a little closer to Avery, whispering through her frozen smile. "Is it a bad sign if smiling this long hurts my face?"

Avery couldn't contain her laugh, and Addisyn joined in, the joke tickling them both. The man looked confused, but he still smiled as he held out the phone. "I was just snapping it when you laughed. Do you want me to retake it?"

Avery studied the screen. Addisyn and her, laughing into each other's eyes. September wind tangled in their hair, elk in the background, the mountains wrapping protective arms around them both.

"No, sir." She caught Addisyn's eye, and they both smiled. "It's perfect."

△△ △△ △△

ONE, TWO. THREE, four. Five, six. Breathe. Breathe.

Fire shot through Darius's arms and shoulders. He gritted his teeth and focused on his breathing.

Seven, eight.

The burn was only to be expected. He was benching almost three hundred pounds and had increased his sets and reps this week. *C'mon, Payne.* The bar was slick in his sweaty palms.

One more rep, and the bar clanged back into its holder. Whew. Time for a breather. He sat up, stretching his burning arms over his head and gazing out the window of the gym, where Whistler Mountain glowed in the early morning sun.

The mountain was his motivation—his focal point during reps, his inspiration through the pain, and in practical terms, his reason to keep himself in top shape. His job as a Whistler climbing guide demanded nothing less.

But still, the gym was more than his training ground; it was his sanctuary. His years as a professional athlete had been spent in spaces just like this one—where strength was built in mind and body, where battles were won inside and out. The salty smell of the equipment and the humming of the machines and even the blaring power-song mixes brought him a calm clarity. And the disciplined routines gave him something to think about.

Something besides Addisyn Miles.

As always, the thought of her clutched at his soul with an agonizing kind of longing. If he closed his eyes, he could still hear the music of her laughter, still see the way her hair sparkled in the sun, still remember—

Enough. He stood. The break was over. Treadmill next. He dialed up the speed and gradient on the machine, but even as he ran, Addisyn's face and voice wandered through his mind. No wonder, really. After all, their first real conversation had taken place when he'd driven her home from this very gym.

Every detail was tucked into his heart, where it would always stay. It had been a bleak night, saturated with a heavy darkness and a drenching rain. During the drive back to her hotel, they'd talked about deep, soulful things—second chances and new beginnings and the many questions and answers that floated around in the world.

Such a difference between then and now. Oh, they still talked, occasionally on the phone but more often by text. Somehow, though, the distance between their homes was gradually settling into their conversations. The closeness they'd shared during Addisyn's time in Whistler was melting to nothing more than casual friendship.

But maybe that was how Addisyn had always seen him. As just a good friend who'd helped her through a rough patch. She'd kissed him in the airport, before she left. But that didn't have to mean anything, did it? It could have been the emotional overflow of the moment. Or a possibility that she'd later decided not to explore.

If only she were still in Canada. But during their infrequent talks, she seemed content in Colorado. And he was happy for her, certainly. He was glad she'd rekindled her relationship with her sister, proud that she was working hard to move forward into a new future. It was nothing more than selfish to want her here with him. Even if his life was an echo in an empty hallway without her.

He gritted his teeth and bumped the difficulty up higher. Thirty minutes later, he gave up and stepped off the machine in disgust. Running gave his mind too much blank space to fill. Maybe more strength training would be better.

Just as he began the weights, his phone vibrated in the pocket of his exercise shorts. An irrational hope was squelched when he saw the caller ID—an unknown number, but a local prefix. Could it be someone from work with a new number?

He swiped the call and set the phone to speaker, laying it on the bench while he reached for a pair of dumbbells. "Hello."

"Hello, is this Andrew Payne?"

Andrew.

The word froze his thoughts, and the dumbbells clattered back to the floor. He winced. "Sorry. Um—yes. This is—that's me."

At no point during his run had his heart hammered this fast. Only someone from his past would call him Andrew. Only someone who still remembered him as the gold-medal skater who'd competed in the Olympics under his middle name.

"Mr. Payne, I'm Bob Worski, calling from the Whistler Area Figure Skating Club."

Figure skating? Nothing about this made sense. He hadn't been a figure skater in years. Not since he'd switched to short track at age seventeen. And he hadn't been on the ice since his career-ending accident the next year. He forced himself to focus on the man's words.

"—holding a benefit program in January." The man's voice was calm, cultured. No hint that this was a scam or a joke. "It would be our honor to have you as one of our performers."

"I—I'm sorry." The noise of the gym pelted him from all angles. Darius took the phone off speaker and pressed it to his ear. "Are you asking me to—to skate?"

"Yes, forgive me if I was unclear. We hold an annual benefit program at our skating club to raise money for the British Columbia Children's Fund. You know, scholarships for disadvantaged youth, afterschool programs, that sort of thing. Each year, our committee selects a number of retired or current skaters to perform." There was a smile in the man's voice. "The vote this year was unanimous for you, Mr. Payne. It would be our honor to have you."

Darius sank onto the weight bench. He was still sweating, but no longer from the workout. "For figure skating?"

"Well, pairs skating actually, but yes."

"I can't." The words rushed out, fear chasing hope. "I mean—I had an injury. Perhaps you weren't—"

"Yes, sir, we do recall that, certainly." The man paused. "However, our technical standards are not rigid. Your performance can be as simple as need be. And, forgive me, but it was our conclusion that given your current profession, the injury was not so severe as to affect your daily life."

The man had a point. Addisyn had said much the same thing when she was in Whistler. Was it possible the injury had indeed healed? That he could safely skate?

"Oh, and of course for pairs skating you would need a partner. Is there a fellow skater you could invite to perform with you, Mr. Payne?"

A fellow skater.

A fellow skater. Of course. This was it. The chance he'd never expected. And suddenly, all his objections seemed small. Compared to the opportunity to skate with—

"Yes. There is." Darius drew in a deep breath. "Thank you so much for the invitation—uh—" What had the man said his name was? "Thank you, sir. There are a few things I would need to check on first. Is that okay?"

"Absolutely." The man gave him a few more details. The date and time of the event, the website where he could find additional information, the number to call back if he decided to participate. "And please let us know your decision as soon as possible."

"Yes, sir." Darius needed to end the conversation before the impossibility of the whole incident knocked him right off the bench. "Thank you again."

When the call ended, Darius sagged forward under the disbelief. Was this for real? He glanced at his recent calls again. Yes, there was the number. He wasn't dreaming or going crazy or hallucinating from the oxygen deficit of exercising. Even though any of those would be more plausible than the notion that someone would call him out of the blue and invite him to skate. The whole possibility was too big to absorb yet—the idea that he would be able to not only skate again but also perform with the only other skater he'd consider inviting.

Addisyn's face filled his mind, and this time he didn't attempt to banish the image. He pulled up a long-unused number in his contacts. Three rings, and Lenny's always-upbeat voice boomed over the line. "Payne! Long time, man!"

"Hi, Lenny." Darius smiled. The guy had been a friend of his father's and still worked as a trainer at the Whistler Olympic Centre. "Hey—as you might guess, I need a favor."

"Of course you do." Lenny had an easy, rolling laugh. "Happy to help. What's on your mind? Let me guess—you need a wingman for a cocktail party."

"Ha. No." Darius wasn't in a joking mood. "Lenny, do you still have connections with that doctor—uh—the one you recommended after my accident, you know—"

"Arjun Patel? Yeah."

"Can you—do you think you could get me in to see him? Soon?"

"Don't tell me something's wrong." Lenny's voice frayed with concern.

"No, Lenny." Darius relaxed against the bench and looked out the window, where Whistler was perfectly framed. A peak of possibility, waiting for him. "Actually, I think something's right."

CHAPTER 2

Silver mist shimmered over the mountains like the first breaths of the new day. The gold ribbons of September aspens threaded their way along the bristling green hillsides. Avery rolled the truck window down slightly as she turned onto Marys Lake Road. The morning air rushed in—bracingly cold, yet exhilarating.

"So today we find out what the project is." In the passenger seat, Addisyn raised her eyebrows. She'd been so curious over Laz's phone call on Friday that she'd asked to come with Avery to work this morning.

"Yeah." The truck groaned slightly on a hill, and Avery shoved the gearshift harder—it had always tended to stick in cooler weather.

"What do you think it will be?"

Avery slowed to navigate a curve and smiled. "With Laz involved, it could be anything. But we'll see." Something nudged her elbow, and she glanced toward the backseat to see her black Lab leaning over the console. "Mercy, you're excited too, aren't you? Ready for work?" The dog had been accompanying her to the outdoors store for almost a year now.

"She's a sweetheart." Addisyn rubbed Mercy's ears, and the dog squinted in rapturous enjoyment. "And I've finally recovered from my shock that you adopted a dog the size of a horse."

Avery grinned. "Yeah, I'll never forget the look on your face when you opened the door to the cabin for the first time."

"And this giant bear hurtles out, and you're like, 'Oh, did I mention I got a dog while you were gone?'" Addisyn pulled a mock exasperated face, but her eyes glinted with fun. "You know, I could have had a heart attack, A."

"I know." The laughter was like a cleansing burst of joy. This was something Avery had missed more than she'd realized—the banter they'd always shared. "At first, I thought you had."

Five minutes later, they pulled into the gravel parking lot beneath the carved wooden LIVE BIGGER sign. With Addisyn and Mercy at her heels, Avery opened the creaky door and stepped into the maze of display racks, which featured everything from walking sticks and trail maps to hiking boots and fishing rods.

"Laz?" The lights were on, and John Denver was crooning from the sound system. But there was no movement except for the lazy spinning of the taxidermied ducks suspended from the ceiling.

Addisyn glanced into the back room and shook her head. "Could he be at his house?"

"Hmm…maybe." Laz lived in a small cabin not more than a hundred yards from the store. Perhaps the *project* was over there. "Let's put Mercy in the back room and find out."

Sure enough, Laz was behind the shop, talking to someone in the driver's seat of a mud-splashed SUV. Avery waved. "Laz!"

"Howdy, gals!" He gestured to the driver, a deeply tanned man with chiseled features beneath thick black hair. "Miz Avery, you 'member my buddy, Chayton Wingo."

"Of course." Avery offered her hand. "How are you?"

"Wonderful!" Chayton's smile was as bright as a sun-dazzled mountain lake. He turned off the ignition and swung out of the SUV, then tipped his head toward Addisyn. "And you are—"

"This is my sister, Addisyn." As soon as the words sprang out, Avery winced inwardly. She'd always had a bad habit of answering for her younger sister.

Addisyn pinched her lips together but shook hands with Chayton. "It's a pleasure to meet you."

"Addisyn will be helping your wife in the store." Avery smiled at Addisyn, but her sister wouldn't meet her gaze.

"The Bluefeather Boutique!" Chayton shoved a hand through his bristle-brush hair. "Thanks for helping Skyla out, Addisyn."

"Well." Addisyn tossed an unreadable glance at Avery. "I haven't actually agreed yet."

Why was Addisyn being so stubborn? The moment itched with awkwardness, but before Avery could smooth over her sister's odd response, Laz broke in. "This is why I needed you, Miz Avery. Chay dumped a big ole headache on me—" he glared darkly at Chayton—"an' it's gonna take more than me to manage it."

Whatever reason Addisyn had for her unfriendly behavior would have to wait. Avery took a deep breath and focused on Laz. "So what is it?"

Chayton had already turned toward the SUV and opened the hatch. He slipped on a pair of leather gloves and then retrieved a large box that somewhat resembled a pet carrier, gently settling it on the dusty ground.

A box? What could possibly— Avery's thoughts scattered when she heard a soft rustling from inside the crate.

Addisyn jerked back. "There's something alive in there!"

"Yep." Laz didn't sound happy about the fact. He tipped his head at Chayton. "Go ahead. Do the honors."

His movements still gentle, Chayton knelt beside the box, reached inside...and pulled out the most magnificent bird.

Avery gasped. The bird was as tall as her forearm, with a splendid shimmer of mahogany feathers and the proud profile of a raptor. He rustled his wings slightly, the golden eyes under his bold brows seeming to gaze far beyond the small crowd.

"That's—that's a hawk." Her laugh was an exhale of shock. Of all the possibilities she could have envisioned inside that box, this would never have crossed her mind. "What—"

"Where did he come from?" Judging from the hushed tone in Addisyn's voice, she was as impressed as Avery was.

Laz folded his arms, an odd mixture of emotions tugging at his expression. "Chay runs a raptor rehab center here in Estes. Him and his folks get birds that've been hurt. Shot, hit by cars, poisoned, you name it. Then they fix 'em up and send 'em back out there."

Cradling the bird expertly, Chayton took up the story. "This poor guy was hit by a car about a month ago. When he was brought to our center, he had multiple injuries, including a broken wing."

Avery had already noticed the stark white patch of bandage on the bird's side.

"Anyhow, he's had surgery for that, but now he just needs a quiet place to rest up and keep healing."

Laz scowled. "An' for some reason Chay wants to pawn him off on me 'stead of keepin' him in that world-class center of his."

Chayton raised his eyebrows. "As I mentioned, Laz, that 'world-class center' is filling up more each day." He sighed. "We simply don't have room to accommodate the birds that are just in need of a resting place. Which is where volunteers like you come in."

"Volunteers. As if." Laz snorted. "I didn't 'zactly offer my services. You jes' called me up an'—"

"Because I trust you." A quiet intensity filled Chayton's voice. "And you're still one of the finest raptor rehabbers around."

Raptor rehabbers? Avery pivoted toward Laz. She'd seen him help stray dogs and last summer a sick squirrel, but she hadn't known— "You're a rehabber?"

Laz grimaced. "No. Not anymore. Jes' 'cause I still got a license—"

Chayton bent and returned the hawk to the box. "He's still a rehabber, Avery." He kept his eyes on Laz with a pointed gaze. "He's got the touch in his hands and his heart. He knows more about birds than—"

"That's enough." Laz held up both his hands and spun on his heel. "If yer really gonna make me do this, then let's get started. Don't have all day to waste bickerin'."

With Addisyn behind her, Avery fell into step next to Chayton as they followed Laz across the backyard toward a small structure. "How long have you been a rehabber, Chayton?"

"Over ten years." Chayton's voice was easy, kind. "It's the best job around. Skyla helps too, but mainly she runs the store."

"A gift shop, I understand." Addisyn's voice still sounded wary, but at least she was talking about the prospect.

"Yes, it's right downtown on the River Walk. It's a really great concept. The proceeds help us keep the lights on at the center, and local artisans have a place to sell their wares. And I personally think handmade items from the mountains are the best souvenirs." He laughed. "It was Skyla's idea. I guess you can see I'm pretty proud of her."

Avery smiled. "You should be." The system sounded like a win-win. Why wouldn't Addisyn be thrilled to work at a place like that?

Before the conversation could continue, they reached the small structure, about the size of a closet with only one tiny window. Chayton opened the box and withdrew the hawk again.

"He's so beautiful." Addisyn leaned closer.

"Yeah." The bird began to squirm, and Chayton stroked his feathers gently. "I think so too."

"What kind of hawk is he?"

"Red-tailed Hawk."

"I thought so." Avery had often seen the majestic hawks swirling in the sky. "That's wonderful."

"How long will he be here?" Addisyn hadn't sounded this interested in anything the whole time she'd been in Estes.

Chayton shrugged. "It will depend on a lot of factors. His wing has to heal, of course, and then he'll have to reengage the muscles that atrophy during the healing process. And he has to prove to us that he can fly well and catch prey for himself before he can be released. It could be a long road. The other possibility is—"

The wings will rise.

The words crackled against Avery's spirit like splitting lightning and shaking earth and howling wind. She jerked, her breath a gasp against the grip. A knowing. Here?

The wings will rise.

A spin of sky, for a single snap—translucent blue, shredded clouds swirling, and somehow, around and over and within the clouds, wings whirled. Vertigo whipped at her, and she stumbled.

Peace. The wings will rise.

The sky blazed suddenly to sunset glory, and then the vision dissolved. And she was back in the autumn day, gentle sun on her face and the reassuring ring of mountains around her.

"A, are you okay?"

Avery pressed a hand over her thudding heart and glanced at

Addisyn. Chayton and Laz were busy unlocking the enclosure door, but her sister was staring at her with concern.

"I—yes." She shoved her trembling hands into her pockets. She wouldn't mention the knowing to Addisyn. The messages she received—the words and images and feelings El Shaddai sometimes laid on her heart—had always made her sister uncomfortable. She swallowed the last of the dizziness. "I'm fine."

The guys had the door open now, and Chayton gently reached into the small shed and placed the hawk on the floor. "There you go, buddy." He stepped back as Laz shut the door.

"That's it?" Addisyn looked confused.

"Yep." Laz was still wearing that unreadable expression. "He needs to be nice and quiet-like while his wounds are still healin.' He'll rest in there for a few weeks 'til he can try the flight cage." He jerked his thumb vaguely into the woods.

A flight cage? Avery shook her head. She was still too distracted to ask right now.

Addisyn craned her neck to peer into the narrow window. "Won't he get lonely in there?"

Chayton peeled off his gloves. "Actually, he needs to be left alone as much as possible. Too much human contact, and he might forget how to survive in the wild. Or start to become accustomed to interaction, which is a terrible thing for wild birds."

"An' you'll be helpin' me, Miz Avery." Laz gave her a pointed look.

"Really?" Avery grinned. She was finding the rhythm once more, the earth finally feeling firm beneath her. She forced herself to tuck aside the knowing for later. "I'd love to."

"Of course." Laz made an exasperated sound. "I'm not takin' full responsibility for this critter."

Chay ignored the comment and focused on Avery. "So what you and Laz will need to do, at least at first, is just keep an eye on him and take care of him. Visit him once a day—no more than that. You'll need to take him out of the enclosure and clean it, then put him back in, feed him, give him some water for drinking and bathing. Once a week, assess his injury and weigh him." He smiled. "Laz can give you more details, of course. He says you're always careful with wild things."

"She is." Addisyn slung her arm around Avery's shoulders. "A, this is awesome! You'll do great."

Avery didn't have time to respond to the compliment before Chayton handed Laz a small package. "Here. The antibiotics and the extra bandages. I'll bring the food over on my way home from work. He's already eaten today."

"Fine." Laz glanced warily at the bird. "Chay, I wish ya could've found somebody else to—"

"Laz." Chayton gripped Laz's broad shoulders, drilling him with an unwavering gaze. "I picked you particularly for this bird."

"Why?" Laz hurled the word with all his signature stubbornness. "Ya think he needs me or somethin' sentimental like that?"

"No." The piercing intensity in Chayton's eyes reminded Avery of the hawk himself. "I think you need him."

Laz frowned, but something shifted ever so slightly behind his expression. As though the statement had penetrated some wall in his heart.

"Don't live in that place, my friend." Chayton stepped back. His tone was lighter, but the plea in his eyes was still strong. "I mean it. I trust you." He nodded toward the hawk. "And so does he."

"Oh…" Laz coughed and swiped a hand hard over his beard. "Waalll…fine." He stomped toward the store. "C'mon, gals. Cain't stand there moonin' over that bird all day."

Avery laughed and hurried after him, Addisyn on her heels. But even as she said goodbye to Chayton and returned to the regular business of ordering fishing poles and helping customers choose the best brand of hiking boots, she couldn't stop thinking about the hawk.

And the knowing.

The wings will rise. What could it mean? The knowings were always cryptic, but this—this was different. The swirling sky, the repetition—how was she supposed to patchwork the pieces? And why had she felt so— disoriented?

It had to be about the hawk. There was no other possibility. But why would she receive a word about him? Up to this point, every message she'd heard had been about her own soul—or Addisyn's.

No matter how she puzzled over it, she couldn't unravel the thread. After her lunch break, when she returned from driving Addisyn back to the house, she finally released. *Okay, El Shaddai. You will show me in Your time.*

She glanced out the store window at the enclosure. From this angle, it almost looked like a cocoon—a protective shelter where the beautiful wild creature could heal.

Yes. The wings would rise.

◬ ◬ ◬

"LET ME KNOW how it goes today." Avery hovered as Addisyn tossed her purse into the passenger seat of the car.

"I will." Addisyn peered at her older sister. "You said you knew this lady. What's she like?"

The same guardedness that appeared whenever Addisyn mentioned Skyla crept across Avery's face. "Um, I mean—I don't know her that well. I've just seen her come into the store sometimes."

So Avery wasn't going to give any more details than that. Addisyn shrugged. "Well, I guess we'll see if she likes me."

"How could she not?" Avery wrapped Addisyn in a hug. "Sis, I'm proud of you."

Avery was proud of her? After she'd left such a shameful trail through the last three years? Instead of inspiring her, the undeserved grace simply clambered on top of the guilt she was already staggering under. "Well, uh, thanks." She squeezed Avery quickly and stepped back.

"You'll do great!" Avery gave a single confident nod and straightened the collar of Addisyn's shirt. "This will be the perfect job for you."

There Avery went again, assuming she was going to take the job. Addisyn bit back the snappy reply she felt coming. Hadn't she promised herself to be better this time around?

She slid into the driver's seat of the car she'd bought in Estes Park, a twelve-year-old Honda Accord the color of a dusty dirt road. Avery had helped her choose it—obviously. When it came to vehicles, her sister's eye was for function, not beauty. Her own battered truck was proof: the clunky thing was probably older than Addisyn.

"Is the car still making that weird sound?"

Addisyn turned the key, and her sister's brows came together. "There it is. That clicking."

Oh, not this conversation again. "Avery, I just don't hear anything."

"No, there's a definite tapping. Or clicking. Laz heard it too when you drove up to the store the other day. He said something about it."

Addisyn glanced at the flickering green numbers on the dashboard clock. If she didn't leave, she'd be late. And dragged into an argument to boot. "Look, I've got to go. Maybe I can go somewhere next week and get the motor checked out." Without giving Avery an opportunity to respond, she put the car in gear.

"Bye!" Avery waved after her. "Have a great first day!"

Addisyn pretended not to hear. She took a deep breath as she reached the end of Avery's driveway, trying to shake off her irritation. It was just that the whole car thing grated on her. And the way Avery was kind of forcing her into this job. Always so sure she knew what was best for her reckless younger sister, wasn't she?

But by the time she turned onto Elkhorn Avenue, her annoyance was subsiding. After all, Avery was only trying to help. Laz too. She should be grateful—and she was—that they'd found her this job. Her nervousness was just making her overreact, that was all.

She parked in the little lot beside the Bluefeather Boutique and sat for a moment in the car, her palms sweaty on the wheel. Would this really be a good fit for her, as Avery kept insisting? What if she didn't like it? Or what if this woman didn't want her help after all?

Come on. She forced herself out of the car and slung her purse over her shoulder. The store looked inviting from the outside at least, with large show windows and a trim brick walkway. A pot of chrysanthemums the color of sunset glowed beneath every window. When Addisyn pushed open the glass door, a copper bell attached to a feathered ornament tinkled.

The haunting lilt of Native American flutes quavered from a sound system. The back door was open, and a breeze lightly ruffled some papers on the counter. Addisyn blinked as her eyes adjusted to the soft ambient lighting. Given Chayton's description of the store as a *gift shop*, she'd expected a repository of tacky T-shirts and overpriced keychains. But this place had the nobility of an elegant showroom, with paintings and crafts and even furniture.

The only thing it didn't seem to have was an owner. "Hello?" Addisyn waited, but there was no response. Now what? Should she go back to her car? Or call Avery, or—

A silent figure flicked into her peripheral vision. Addisyn yelped and jerked away, banging her foot on a cabinet. The lamp on top clattered to the floor. "Oh! I'm sorry." She cringed as she stared at the person who'd startled her—a tall woman with dark hair that rippled halfway down her back. She couldn't bear to look at the lamp. "Did I break it?"

"It is fine." Copper bracelets jingling, the woman scooped up the lamp and settled it on the cabinet, then adjusted it a millimeter to the left. "Please do be careful, though. Everything in here is a unique creation."

Hello to you too. Addisyn studied the woman's face—resolute features and veiled dark eyes without the hint of a smile. She swallowed a sinking feeling. "Are you Skyla Wingo?"

"Yes." The woman didn't offer her hand. "But the store is not open for business yet."

"Um, actually, I'm here to—to maybe work." She'd almost said *to help*, but something told her Skyla Wingo did not need or want *help*. "Laz—Mr. Jobe—he recommended me to you, I think—or at least to your husband—he said—"

"Oh, yes." Skyla nodded regally. "He spoke of you." She tipped her head and studied Addisyn. "Well. I trust that if you work here, you'll be more careful with the merchandise?"

The whole thing was sort of Skyla's fault for having some kind of ninja stealth skills, but she'd let that pass. "Yes, ma'am."

"Very well." Skyla fingered the necklace she wore—a silver locket engraved with a howling wolf. "I can give you some details."

As Skyla shared more about the position, Addisyn had to admit the possibility was rather appealing. She'd work Saturdays, but she'd have Sundays and Mondays off. The pay was generous—more than she'd expected. "Your duties would involve ringing up transactions and dealing with new inventory. Could you manage that?"

There was doubt in Skyla's question, but Addisyn ignored it. "Yes, ma'am. Do you place orders for new inventory, or—"

"We sell unique items made by local artisans." Skyla's face relaxed some. "As I'm sure my husband mentioned, the proceeds fund the Estes Valley Raptor Center, where our team rehabilitates injured birds." She swept her reddish-black hair over one shoulder. "But as for this place— local artisans bring their items here to sell on consignment. It is a good arrangement for both us and them."

"I'm sure." The articles in here were truly lovely, in a simple, rustic style that reminded Addisyn of Avery's cabin.

"Our goal with every piece is to evoke the mountain culture for our customers." Skyla brushed her hands along the sides of her crinkled flowing skirt. "Everything we sell should carry the peace of this place."

The mountain culture? Skyla was speaking Avery's language now. Addisyn just nodded vaguely. How could she admit that she'd only been in Colorado a month and had no idea what the elusive "mountain culture" was?

"Take these soaps, for example." Skyla reached into a wicker basket atop a low table and held out a couple of paper-wrapped bars. "The woman who brings these has a goat farm just outside Loveland. She makes soaps and lotions from the milk, using crushed herbs for different scents. Her products are always popular."

"Wow." Addisyn's intimidation was growing every second. "That's—very nice."

"Yes. It is an honor to sell her offerings for her." Skyla gestured around the store. "Let me show you some of the other pieces."

She led Addisyn around the perimeter of the shop, pointing out pottery creations and intricate quilts and wood carvings and cast-iron bookends. The art was widely varied, and Skyla evidently knew the story of every piece.

"And of course we have paintings too." Skyla waved toward a separate wall, where special sconces illuminated a checkerboard of canvases.

"They're beautiful." Addisyn took a step closer to inspect a painting of a chick bursting from a shell. She noticed the name at the bottom and blinked. "This is yours?"

Amazingly, Skyla actually smiled—a small smile, but still enough to make her look far less formidable. "Yes." She nodded toward a closed door in the corner of the shop. "That leads to my studio. I work in the afternoons, when the lighting is right."

"That's really cool. The painting is lovely." Addisyn studied Skyla with a sudden respect. The woman could stand to improve her interpersonal skills, but clearly she had an artistic gift. Addisyn turned back to the painting, noticing the words across the top of the canvas. "What does that mean? Two Cor—Corinth—"

"Corinthians." Skyla cleared her throat. "It is a Scripture."

Rustic decor, mountain culture, and now Bible verses. Avery should have been the one to take this job. "Oh." The single syllable sounded rude even to her. She sighed and tried again. "What's it say?"

Skyla gazed at the painting as if it were a window to a reality only she could see. "It says that those who hold out hearts to God are new creations." Her words were slow, measured. "They are broken down and built back up as He changes them."

There was a certain intrigue about the idea. "Do you believe that?"

"Yes." The word was quiet, but it held a bedrock certainty. "I believe it like I believe in the wind and the waters. Like I believe in the rivers that flow from the heart of the mountains. Like I believe in the snows that fall and the suns that melt and the great wheels that spin the stars."

The music of the words, the intensity of Skyla's faith, caught Addisyn off guard. "That's neat." The statement sounded weak.

Skyla fixed Addisyn with her gaze. "What about you?"

An uncertain laugh caught in her throat. "What about me?"

"You do not believe?"

"It's—well—" Discomfort crept up her spine. "I just think—I mean, that's great—but I don't know much about all that spiritual stuff."

"Really?" Skyla said the word as if Addisyn's stuttered answer was an admission of guilt. "You have never lived that verse?"

Embarrassment blurred into indignation. This was getting way too personal. Addisyn bristled. "I'm sorry?"

"Forgive me. But I have never met someone who did not want a second chance at some time or another."

A second chance. Wasn't that what she'd come to the mountains for? "Well—yes." Addisyn sighed, her irritation fading. "That's why I'm here. I came for a new start. To—to make some things right. Things I messed up when—" *Stop.* She clamped her mouth shut. Skyla didn't need to know her whole biography.

Skyla nodded deliberately. "I see."

Was this part of the interview, or what? If her employment hung on a spiritual confession, she was doomed. "Do I have to be a—a believer to work here?"

"Of course not." Skyla dismissed the idea with a flick of her hand. "My husband and I have worked with the birds for years. We understand that healing takes time, and it is a long journey. I merely wanted to know if you were on it."

Addisyn gave up. In just a moment, Skyla would quit talking in riddles and simply tell her that her help wasn't needed. And then she'd go to the outdoors store and tell Avery and Laz that she'd lost her one chance at a job, and Avery would say—

"Addisyn."

"Ma'am?"

"Would you like to work here?"

Addisyn waited a heartbeat, but Skyla's unreadable expression didn't change. "Yes, ma'am."

"Sometimes the wings are folded at first, but they always open." Skyla seemed to be speaking to herself.

"What was that?"

But Skyla simply shook her head and clapped her hands softly. "Very well. You are hired. Come to the back room, and you may begin."

HE WAS BEING a coward, but he couldn't bring himself to go inside yet.

Darius gripped his steering wheel and studied the sleek modern building behind the parking lot—a wing of the Whistler Area Medical Centre. He was amazed by how quickly Lenny had been able to arrange for him to see the specialist. This morning, he'd gone for tests—X-rays and simple range-of-motion exercises to complete. He'd also had an MRI to measure the damage in his spinal discs; the radiologist had explained that the soft tissue wouldn't show up on an X-ray.

And now, he was back at the center for an appointment with Dr. Patel. He'd asked for his results this morning, but the staff had informed him that the doctor wanted to discuss the findings in person. That could be really good or really bad.

Probably the second option. After all, when Dr. Patel had first treated him, the specialist had labeled the injuries as permanent. And while Darius had definitely noticed improvement since then, it might not be enough. Some of those exercises this morning had been impossible. After a certain point, he couldn't bend any farther, at least not without that familiar zing in his spine.

Until he knew for sure, there was no sense in letting his hopes soar, only to have the wind sucked from beneath them. There was no reason to imagine how great it would feel to be back on the ice. There was no reason to continually replay his conversation with Mr. Worski. And there was certainly no reason to dream about what it would be like to perform with Addisyn.

His eyes found the faded photograph taped to his dashboard—a selfie of Addisyn and him, the day they went mountain biking around Lost Lake. He closed his eyes, savoring the memory—the melody of her voice, the sparkle of her smile, the way her every move held a sweet, elusive grace.

Yes. He could do this. He opened his eyes, brushed his finger over the photo, then headed for the clinic.

First was a thirty-minute interlude in the waiting room—half an hour of studying the ugly carpeting and watching the boring cycle of medication ads on the TV. Finally, Darius found himself in a sterile-looking white exam room, face-to-face with Dr. Patel.

"Mr. Payne." The doctor nodded and flipped through his charts.

"It's good to have the chance to assess your case again. Your situation is—ah—unique."

Unique? Darius's palms were slick with sweat. He swiped them on his pants and cleared his throat. "Umm...I'm not sure I understand."

Dr. Patel tossed the chart onto the counter and perched on the black swivel stool, cocking his head with an odd smile. "Me neither."

"What are you saying, sir?" Darius's voice sounded strange to him.

"Well, let me show you." The doctor's tone was still matter-of-fact. He made a few quick swipes on his tablet, then showed the screen to Darius as a series of X-ray photos appeared. "Immediately following your accident, you were treated for a broken wrist and a laceration to the lower leg. You also had a flexion fracture and disc herniation, which contributed to your nerve pain and other symptoms." He reached for Darius's chart and squinted at some notes. "Post-surgery, you were cautioned to avoid heavy lifting or intense exertion and to refrain from complex movements for a period of time to avoid reinjuring the area. Your ankle healed well, but your ACL remained problematic. You were instructed to take NSAID medication as needed to help you cope with any back pain, and I believe you were equipped with a TENS unit as well."

Darius nodded. The NSAIDs and the TENS unit together had helped him manage the pain without opioids—which he'd been determined to avoid.

"And—" The doctor's expression made him feel like a specimen under a microscope. "I offered you the chance to undergo additional restorative surgery—and you refused."

The memory crashed over his soul like a tidal wave. "Uh—yes." Darius studied his shoes. He'd been a wreck after the accident—physically and spiritually. Drowning in guilt and regret and a sense of failure deeper than anything he'd known, he'd simply lacked the energy to fight his way back to health.

He'd been warned that forgoing surgery could make his injuries more permanent, more difficult to overcome later. But he'd still shaken his head and checked out of the hospital. He'd been too overcome by his spiritual wounds to consider his physical ones.

Now he swallowed hard. "Sir, I understand—I mean—if I can't do anything. I had my chance. And if it's bad news now—"

"Oh, not bad news. Not at all. Actually—it seems to be the opposite." For the first time, the doctor's facade cracked into a smile. "Your injuries appear to have improved dramatically. Much more than what we could have hoped for."

There wasn't enough air in the room. "You mean—"

"Your scans from the time of your injury and now look dramatically different. Actually, the pressure on your nerves has relaxed a good bit. You do show some narrowing of the invertebral spaces, which will most likely need to be addressed later on, but it's not an issue right now. Amazingly, you've also maintained your physical strength, even without ongoing therapy. All in all, you've healed well." He shrugged. "I don't fully understand it. But your injuries are no longer considered debilitating."

No longer debilitating… A miracle. It had to be. God had been at work, breathing new life into Darius's broken body just as He had into his scarred soul. Darius worked to slip his next words past the lump in his throat. "You mean—I'm okay?"

"Better than okay, I'd say. Now, we discussed the fact that you were considering a skating invitation." The doctor adjusted his glasses. "As long as your routine wasn't technically demanding, I believe you could attempt it. Of course"—he held up a warning finger—"there will be challenges ahead. I'd recommend physical therapy to strengthen your leg and your back to avoid further injury. Lenny is top-notch; I'll write you a referral to him. Even with the therapy, it may be an uphill battle. Of course, we can't rule out the possibility of reinjury, but I do think that with the proper training and—"

Dr. Patel was still talking, still discussing how Darius would need to undergo physical therapy and maintain an anti-inflammatory diet and commit to regular check-ins. But Darius couldn't focus on that yet.

All he could imagine was standing on the ice again. A figure skater once more. And this time alongside Addisyn.

"Now beyond that, you must understand, a great deal will depend on how your body responds to the first steps." The doctor shook his head with a smile. "Again, I'm amazed by your healing, Mr. Payne. Though I should have expected no less from an athlete with your level of determination."

The rest of the appointment passed in a blur. Darius didn't remember what else Dr. Patel said or how he even made it out of the clinic at all. He barely registered Lenny's unbridled enthusiasm or their plans to meet for Darius's first training session the next day. He felt detached even when he called Mr. Worski to accept the invitation.

All he could think about during the phone calls was the call he'd make tonight. The one to the only other skater he could imagine sharing this invitation with.

Addisyn Miles.

CHAPTER 3

The Bluefeather Boutique closed half an hour later than the outdoors store, so by the time Addisyn drove up to the cabin, Avery's truck was already parked outside. As she opened the door to the house, a warm, yeasty aroma puffed out.

"Ads!" Avery was grating cheese with a no-holds-barred approach when Addisyn entered the kitchen. She looked up expectantly. "So? How was it?"

"Good, actually." Addisyn peeled off her jacket and tossed it in the corner. "I took the job."

"That's great." The unspoken *of course* in Avery's voice was maddening. Her sister's gaze shifted to the jacket. "Ads, hang that up, please."

Addisyn grabbed the jacket and crammed it on one of the hooks a little more forcefully than necessary. She drew in a deliberate breath. "Something smells great."

Avery shrugged. "It's supposed to be pasta primavera."

"Supposed to be?" Addisyn laughed and swiped a piece of cheese.

Avery flicked her hand away with a playful warning look. "Hey! Get out of that." She glanced uncertainly between the oven and a pot on the stovetop. "The problem is, it's not working quite right. The pasta is almost ready to go in the pan, but the vegetables aren't tender yet. I've already been roasting them fifteen minutes, but they're not browned."

"Hmm." The kitchen wasn't her sister's element, but Avery was a better cook than she let on. Addisyn, on the other hand, couldn't cook to save her life. Another failing. "Well, maybe they need—more heat? Or something?"

"Maybe." Doubt colored Avery's tone. She opened the oven door slightly and peered through the shimmering heat. "You know, I think they might finally be ready. Why don't you set the table, and I'll hear all about the job while we eat."

Ten minutes later, they were sitting at the rustic wood table, ready to enjoy the pasta and the delicious, although still slightly crunchy, vegetables. Addisyn started with the broad strokes of her new responsibilities, describing the store. "You should check it out some time, Avery. I think you'd like it. It's got all these handmade things. Like, wood carvings and stuff like soap and candles. Even furniture. Really cool. And all of it's local."

"That's so neat." Avery sprinkled some pepper on her food. "I'll have to swing by there sometime. So how did you get along with Skyla?"

"Uh, well—" Addisyn shrugged. "I mean, she seems—nice. She's just kind of—well, not very talkative."

Avery smiled. "Yeah, she's always struck me that way."

"But, A, guess what?" Addisyn pictured the paintings, the way the colors swam on the canvases. "She's an artist. Did you know that? She paints birds and Bible verses."

"Wow, that's awesome! I had no clue." Avery glanced thoughtfully around the room. "I should get one of her paintings to hang in here. If you see one you really like, let me know."

The conversation continued until they finished eating and began cleanup and chores. Washing dishes, Addisyn was lost in her thoughts when she heard Avery's voice from the other room. She turned off the faucet and glanced toward the doorway. "I couldn't hear you."

"Your phone was ringing. Just now." Her sister hurried through the kitchen doorway, twirling the broom in her hands.

"Well, I don't know who would be calling, but I better check." Was it Skyla? Maybe rethinking the job offer? Addisyn rinsed the soapy water from her hands, tossed her dishrag onto the countertop, and found her phone on the coffee table in the living room. She tapped the screen.

Missed call, 6:54 p.m. Darius Payne.

Her heart rate doubled. She spun away from the phone and hurried back to the kitchen.

"Who was it?" Avery was flipping the broom around in the corners.

"It was, um, Darius." Addisyn turned the water on full blast and busied herself scrubbing an invisible stain on the glass pan.

"Really?" Avery's eyes were suddenly veiled. She leaned on the broom and studied Addisyn.

"Yeah." Addisyn hated the heat in her face, hated knowing that Avery was doubtless reading her emotions, the way she always had. She cleared her throat. "I'll—I'll call him back. When I finish these dishes."

"Ah, tell you what." Avery plucked the dishrag from her fingers. "You deserve a break. I'll finish these. You go call him."

Addisyn blinked. Avery was telling her to call Darius? "Are you sure? I don't mind if—"

"I am the older sister. I make the rules." Avery held up a finger with a mock stern expression. "If your conscience won't let you sleep, you can finish the sweeping for me. After you get off the phone, of course."

"Well—okay." Addisyn hesitated. "Hey—thanks."

But Avery was already splashing the dishes around and gave no sign she'd heard. Addisyn bit her lip. It was a start, anyway. Maybe in time, Avery would soften where Darius was concerned.

She'd consider it more later. For now…Addisyn raced back to the living room and punched the number. One ring…two rings. Maybe he'd lost cell service. Maybe he'd gotten another call. Three rings. Just as the fourth ring was beginning, Darius's voice cut over the line. "Well, there she is, all the way from Colorado. Hey, Addisyn."

Warmth glowed within her at the music of his voice. "Darius." Just saying his name released invisible knots in her spirit. "Sorry I missed your call. I was washing dishes. Avery took over for me so I could call you back."

"What a pal." Darius's West Coast accent was even more adorable over the phone. "She must be an incredible sister, Ads. I'm so glad you two have made your peace."

"So am I." Guilt needled at her. For so many years, she'd let her selfish choices tear them in two. "I can't imagine how I ever got along without her."

"So how are you liking life as a mountain girl?"

This was one of the best things about Darius, the way he always prioritized her concerns. Avery was still clattering dishes in the kitchen, so Addisyn wandered upstairs to her bedroom and flopped across the buffalo plaid quilt on her bed as the conversation meandered. Darius congratulated her on her new job, and she asked about the climbing center. Things were quiet there now, apparently. "But of course that will all change in a few weeks when the ski bums show up." He laughed.

"I bet it's beautiful there this time of year." She didn't have to close her eyes to picture the quaint mountain town.

"Yeah, it's nice. Kind of a slow season. I'm just working and hitting the gym and—" His voice dwindled.

She blinked. "Darius?"

His laugh halted with hesitation. "It's nothing. I—well, I was just gonna say that I still go by the coffee shop every morning, but Chelsea doesn't make my Cubans like you did."

The compliment tugged strangely at her heart. "That's—that's really sweet."

"It's true."

Again, an awkward pause wedged between them. Addisyn narrowed her eyes. "Darius, is everything okay?"

"Well—" His voice was suddenly strained. Was he anxious? Nervous? "Well, I—I had something to tell you. Some news."

News? What did he mean, unless—

He's dating someone. Fear slammed Addisyn in the stomach. *He's met someone there, and he doesn't want to tell me. I bet she's beautiful and sweet and—*

"Addisyn? Are you there?"

"Yes." Her heart was pounding in a painfully irregular rhythm. She dug her fingers into the quilt. What was the matter with her? They were only friends, after all. If he'd met someone, she'd be happy for him. She would.

"Well, um, I'm—I've got the chance to skate again."

She'd been underwater, but now she had oxygen once more. "Darius—that's amazing!" She squeezed her eyes shut, relief replacing tension. Only then did she consider the full impact of what he'd said. "Wait. What about your injuries?"

"That's the awesome thing." Darius's voice was upbeat again. "Guess what? All those injuries years ago—they don't hold me back anymore. Seems like my spine did some healing on its own. At least that's what the doctors say. I'd say the Lord just touched my back. Same way He touched my heart." His words radiated a holy kind of joy. "And I have to have some physical therapy, so I'm working with the most incredible guy at the Olympic Centre, name's Lenny. I knew him from back in the day. He was a great pal of my dad's."

"Oh, Darius! That's terrific." The news was beyond amazing. Addisyn glanced out the north-facing window. If only he weren't fifteen hundred miles away. "So—you said you had an opportunity. What is it?"

"It's a benefit." Darius's voice was uneasy again. "Just—an exhibition skate. The first part of January." He cleared his throat. "They hold the event every year, raise money for the British Columbia Children's Fund. Afterschool programs, mentoring, stuff like that. Every year they invite retired or current skaters to perform. And, well, this year they asked me."

"Wow. That's great." It was the sort of event she would have loved to perform at, back when— Envy tried to peer above the surface of her heart, but she squashed it down.

"And—and—I want you to do it with me."

What? She blinked and gripped the phone tighter. "Darius—what did you say?"

"I want you to come skate with me." The shyness in his voice was new. "It's a pairs event. And—and—well, of course, I thought of you."

"Darius—" Addisyn had been through too many emotions in the last few minutes. She stood and began pacing the room, ignoring the familiar creak of the floorboards. "I'm not a skater anymore."

"But—I bet you get lonely for it every now and then."

Darius had always seemed to have a window to her heart. Addisyn sighed. "Of course. I miss it fiercely sometimes. It was my everything, and it's hard to—to detach from that part of me." She squinted against the sudden sting of tears. "But it's behind me now. This is my new life." She looked around the room, shame surging at her discontent. "And it's wonderful. I mean, I can't complain. Avery is awesome and the cabin is great and the mountains are really—"

"But it's not the ice."

Her exhale was a whoosh of defeat. "Yeah."

"So come skate with me."

It was far from that simple. "Pairs skating? I've only done that a couple of times."

"I did it a bit myself, way back. But most of the moves are the same as figure skating." The strange shyness was back in his tone. "It'd be fun performing together. Don't you think?"

Together. Addisyn took a breath. "Yes."

By the time Darius had explained the details again, her objections were dwindling. "I—I would love to, Darius. Truly. But—I need to think it over—I would have to talk to Avery, you know—"

"Of course." Darius's tone was still calm. "I don't need an answer tonight, girl. I want you to think it over. Talk to Avery, check on everything, then let me know. Okay?"

"Okay."

After they finished the conversation, Addisyn still sat on the bed, her thoughts whirling faster than a combination spin. Go to Canada and skate with Darius? The possibility was larger than life. Far too big to fully examine right now. Warring emotions seized her. One part of her wanted to call him back, squeal her excitement, and be on the next plane to Whistler. The other part wished he'd never called at all.

And there was the matter of Avery.

How would Avery react? Would she see this as yet another reason to distrust Darius? Or would she think that Addisyn was ungrateful, that she didn't appreciate all Avery had done to welcome her to Estes Park? The last thing Addisyn wanted to do was hurt her sister again. After all the rocky roads of their relationship, she couldn't jeopardize the fragile common ground they'd finally found.

What if—what if she didn't tell Avery right away? It couldn't hurt to wait a day or two, could it? Just long enough for her to settle her own heart, think through the options? It wasn't as if she were keeping anything from her sister. Obviously, she'd have to tell Avery if she decided to accept the invitation. But until she was sure—

"Addisyn?" Avery's voice floated up the stairs, and Addisyn jumped.

"Coming!" She hopped off the bed. A wave of guilt splashed over her. For a moment she felt uneasily like a rebellious teenager again.

Avery was waiting by the foot of the stairs. "There you are. You've got to see this!" She grabbed Addisyn's arm and towed her toward the window, pointing into the dusk. "Right on the deck, see?"

"Whoa!" Addisyn gasped at the shadow on the railing. "Is that an owl?"

"Yeah. Great Horned."

The owl was a ghostly smudge in the twilight. He swiveled his head and peered at them with a dignified gaze, then unfurled silent wings and floated gently toward the pines.

"Can you believe that? So close!" Avery was whispering, caught up in the awe of the moment.

"That was incredible." Her sister looked so happy, so at peace. How could Addisyn tell her that—

"I'm glad you got to see it." Avery glanced toward the pine trees again, then turned to face Addisyn. "So what did Darius have to say?"

When Avery knew, would it ruin all the moments like this? Addisyn cleared her throat and watched the deepening dusk out the window.

"Nothing much."

◬　◬　◬

FOR A MOMENT after the call ended, Darius closed his eyes and sat still. Clinging to the lingering magic of Addisyn's voice.

The longing slammed him all over again, and he opened his eyes. Even with all the lights on, his parents' house seemed dim and gloomy in the twilight. Funny how he still called it his parents' house. Even five years after the car crash that had taken them both, the house remained more theirs than his.

The only time the shadows scattered was while he talked to Addisyn. He'd never known a more magical girl. She had a heart as endless as the Pacific Ocean, a spirit as brave as the autumn winds, a smile that glowed like the sunrise over the mountains.

If only he were brave enough to tell her so.

41

He'd been yearning for the chance for so long now. While she was still in Whistler, he'd wanted to hold out his heart and let her read his feelings. But the timing had been all wrong. At first, she'd just escaped that jerk Brian. Later, she was searching desperately for Avery. His confession then would have only added to the chaos of her life.

But maybe—maybe now would be his time. Now, when she was coming to Whistler.

Sure, she hadn't formally agreed yet, but she'd come, right? She'd sounded excited on the phone—a little hesitant, of course, but that was no more than a natural reaction to the surprise. He'd heard the smile in her words, sensed the longing in her tone.

Maybe he could call her back tomorrow. Just to see if she'd—

No. Don't push it, Payne. She needed to make this decision without him tilting her judgment or pressuring her choice. And she certainly needed the chance to discuss things with Avery.

Avery would be okay with the idea, right? Darius hadn't really considered the possibility until now, but what if she was opposed? He certainly didn't want to become a bone of contention between the sisters. That could get a guy in trouble fast.

But surely Avery would be in favor. Why wouldn't she be? And then Addisyn would come. And once she was in Whistler, he'd find the perfect moment to let her know how much she meant to him.

He headed into his kitchen and pulled out a cup for his Keurig. He'd been drinking more coffee lately—needing the link to Addisyn even more than the jolt of caffeine. He hadn't been trying to flatter her—no coffee he could find anywhere compared to the Cuban lattes she'd made during her stint as a barista at his favorite coffee shop. However, the Keurig was a decent substitute. When the brewing finished, he splashed some almond milk into his mug and took a sip.

Confessing his feelings to a girl as extraordinary as Addisyn would require the perfect setup, so he needed to start planning now. He'd ask her to be his girlfriend in the most romantic way he could contrive. Something straight out of those tearjerker movies girls always loved.

A fancy restaurant? Nah. Too predictable. A park or a garden? Well, autumn probably wasn't the best time for that.

He took another gulp of his coffee, willing the caffeine to stimulate his imagination. *Think outside the box.* Maybe he could take her down to the pier. The view of the snowcapped mountains had always stolen his breath. Or how about that gorgeous overlook on the Sea-to-Sky Road? Yeah, that could be good.

And he'd have roses for her. No, not roses. She might think that was too much, too fast. But carnations, maybe. His mom always liked those. Yeah, carnations. Pink, like her fingernail polish.

So he'd hold out the flowers, and he'd say something like, *Addisyn, I love you, and you are the only—*

No. At this stage, an *I love you* was bound to scare her away. If he moved too quickly, she'd run for sure.

Addisyn, I care deeply for you, and—

Care deeply? Yuck.

Addisyn, I think about you every moment. You're written on my heart. How do you feel about me?

Good grief, he sounded like a sappy greeting card. A prickle of doubt crawled over him. What if he couldn't find the right place, or the right flowers, or most importantly, the right words?

All his life, he'd been a quiet guy, a guy who struggled to make words work for him. When he felt deeply about something, it seemed as if everything just clogged in his soul and wouldn't break loose.

Looking back now, he could recognize the same pattern in his father. A coach through and through, he'd treated emotions as a taboo subject. Darius was the opposite of his father in terms of personality, but he'd acquired that same awkwardness around matters of the heart.

But obviously things had worked out for Dad and Mom. So at some point, the words must have come to even his taciturn father. Right?

Darius sighed. This was one of those many times when he longed for his dad or his granddad. The two men he had respected the most could have given him the guidance he was desperate for.

The coffee was cold by now, and anyway, tonight it just made missing Addisyn that much worse. Darius dumped it into the sink and glanced out the window, where Whistler still glowed against the indigo twilight. He was up for the challenge ahead. Of course he was. And it wasn't as if he had to decide everything right now. He could settle the details once Addisyn arrived. Maybe the perfect moment would simply present itself.

It would all work out. At least he hoped it would. Because he needed one more thing besides the flowers, and the location, and even the words. One thing he wasn't sure he could find.

A dash of plain old cold-water courage.

△△ △△ △△

"MIZ AVERY!" LAZ'S greeting boomed as Avery stepped inside Live Bigger. "Yer here early." Mercy trotted to him, and he bent to scratch her ears. "Waalll, hello, puppy."

"I couldn't wait to check on the hawk." Avery grinned as Laz rummaged in a familiar jar on the counter.

"Eh, he's okay. Matter o' fact, I was fixin' to go weigh him and check his wound. It's time." Laz tossed Mercy a dog biscuit and cocked an eyebrow at Avery. "Guess I don't hafta ask if you wanna go. Leave this darn dog here, though."

As they made their way to the enclosure, Avery breathed in the crisp air. Mist rose from the bronzed fields, and the mountains basked in the early sunshine. The perfect September morning.

Laz poked a paper bag into her hand. "Hold this for me."

A damp cold soaked through the bag. "What is it?"

"His frozen mice. I've already put the medicine in 'em."

Frozen mice. Resisting the urge to drop the bag, Avery darted a glance at Laz. "Where do you keep these mice, anyway?"

"Where d'ya think?" He rolled his eyes. "In my freezer."

"You keep frozen dead mice in your freezer with your food and—"

"Yep, and don't lecture me on it." He opened the enclosure door. "G'mornin,' Isaiah."

"Isaiah?"

The hawk's wings unfurled, arching in a splendid canopy of russet and bronze and onyx. Avery caught her breath at the intricate beauty of his patterning, the way each feather seemed lovingly hand-painted. "He seems to like his name."

"Bible name." Laz's smile had an undertone of sadness. "I always gave my birds Bible names. Helped 'em. An' me."

The hawk tilted his head warily, wings still poised. Laz slid on thick leather gloves and gripped the hawk's ankles with one hand, tucking the other around the bird's chest. "Courage. That's what the Lakota believe hawks stand for." His words were soft, maybe more for himself than Avery.

"Really?"

"Hawks are real important birds to Native people." Laz brushed his hand over Isaiah's feathers. "The Lakota say hawks are messengers from the other world."

Messengers from the other world. The legend felt right, and Avery smiled. "I think all of creation carries a message. If you know how to read it."

"Yep. I'd hafta agree." Laz squinted at the sky. "The Lakota say the hawks are always there, ya know? Jes' right above our heads. Warnin' and guidin' and teachin' people."

He'd never talked this way before. "How do you know all that?"

Laz's expression suddenly closed off. "I learnt it from a pal. A long time ago." He shrugged and tucked Isaiah into the carrier, the fragile moment shattered. "Used to think about it with all my birds."

"So…all your birds." Avery glanced sideways at Laz. "Chayton said you did lots of rehab work at one time."

"Chayton don't always know when to keep his trap shut."

"But is he right?"

Laz sighed and tucked his thumbs into his belt loops. "Yep."

"So what happened?"

A scowl carved through his expression. "We tellin' stories or we takin' care of this bird?"

Avery held up her hands. She'd learned long ago not to trespass on the unknown land of Laz's past. "Sorry."

Laz hefted the carrier, and they made their way up the hill to his small house and the adjacent structure. Avery had always assumed it was a freestanding garage, but stepping inside for the first time today, she blinked in surprise. A long counter ran the length of one wall, scattered with bandages and bottles and a scale. An assortment of other supplies peeked through the glass doors on the cabinets. "Laz, this is a small rehab center."

"Yep. Who needs a garage, anyhow?" Laz scooped the bird from the box, cradling him with the ease of familiarity. "Hmm. Looks pretty healthy. Gotta little damage here." He gently brushed his calloused thumb over two feathers with notched tips. "Broke plumb off."

"Is that serious?"

Laz shook his head. "Not bad enough to mess him up flyin'. And he'll regrow 'em."

This close, Avery could notice details about the bird she'd overlooked the other day. "Chayton said he's a Red-tailed Hawk. But his tail is brown."

Laz chuckled. "He's a young 'un. His tail won't turn red 'til he's at least a year old. Next spring, mebbe." He jerked his head toward a flat postal scale on the counter. "Let's get a weight on this guy."

Laz laid a towel on the counter, then expertly bundled the bird in it until only his feet showed. "Set that board on top there." Avery placed a small board on the scale, and Laz laid the bird on top, squinting at the screen. "I already weighed the board. Six tenths of a pound. So this is sayin' 1.87, so our bird is…" He glanced at Avery.

The math flickered in her head. "Um—1.27?"

"Yep." He jerked his head toward a notepad. "Write that down an' today's date." He frowned at the bundled bird. "Underweight. I'd like to see him closer to 1.9, 2.0."

Avery grabbed the notepad and noticed a pencil in a nearby cup. "Why is he underweight?"

"Eh, he's prob'ly had a hard time for a while now. First tryin' to catch prey with jes' one wing. Then surgery and recovery." Laz loosened the towel, and Isaiah flapped free indignantly. "Plus now he's lost some muscle mass 'cause he hasn't been flyin'."

"That's a lot to contend with." Empathy twisted in her chest. Isaiah had to be scared and confused and uncertain. He'd been wounded by a roaring metal beast, confined in an unfamiliar building, poked and prodded by strangers, and now relocated to yet another new environment. "Look, Laz. He's shaking."

"He's nervous. That's why we don't go through this more'n once a week." Laz had removed the bandage from Isaiah's wing and was probing with expert fingers. "So the fracture was here—an' here—mid-shaft, right humerus—hmm—"

"Laz?"

"Mm?" He was closed off by concentration, his fingers seeking, searching.

"Chayton said he got hit by a car. How does that happen?"

Laz parted the feathers and peered at the bird's fragile-looking skin. Then he sighed and met her gaze. "'Cause people are dumb. Lotsa times people litter on the roadways, right? So you end up with chip bags an' Styrofoam cups an' all kinds of trash from food. An' that brings in rodents—rats an' mice an' such—an' then the rodents bring the raptors. Next thing you know, they're huntin' right there in the ditch, and then it's easy for cars to hit 'em. 'Specially if the drivers ain't payin' attention." He frowned. "So people cause the problem. Same as always."

Avery considered that for a moment. "But people can help the problem, too."

"Sometimes." Laz's voice held a weary weight. "Sometimes they jes' stick their clumsy hands in an' make it all worse."

There was a helpless kind of frustration in his voice, but then he abruptly changed the subject. "Hand me those mice, will ya?"

Avery watched as Laz held the hawk's beak open with his thumb and poked the food into his mouth. Isaiah gulped it down, and Avery smiled. "He'll put that weight back on if he keeps eating like that."

"Yep." Laz lowered him into the carrier and gave a satisfied nod. "It's important he keep eatin' like that. He's gotta have some body fat by the time we let him go. 'Specially this time of year." His brows came together. "Now. We gotta get that enclosure clean."

Isaiah waited in the box while Avery helped Laz scrub down the enclosure. Laz talked a bit about hawk rehab, but he didn't share any more Native legends. Finally the conversation drifted to Chayton and Skyla and how much work they had done at the center.

"How's yer sister like workin' for Skyla?" Laz's voice was muffled from his stooped position.

"I think she likes her." Avery slid the bucket closer. "She says Skyla's a little hard to get to know."

Laz chuckled softly and reached for the brush. "Yeah, that sounds like Miz Skyla." He sat back on his heels and peered at Avery. "So—yer sister. She plannin' to stick around?"

The question poked at the most fragile corner of her heart. She stared at Laz. "Why—why would you ask that?"

"Jes' wonderin'."

She'd give him the same answer she always gave herself when the question peered over her shoulder. "Well, I'm sure she is."

"But you two haven't 'zactly talked about it?"

"Um…no." Avery had been far too nervous to bring up the topic. Too afraid of what Addisyn would say. Or wouldn't say.

Laz swiped his hands on his jeans. "She ever mention skatin'?"

"That's far behind her." This consideration, at least, brought certain relief. "She never talks about it."

Laz made a sound of disbelief. "Never talks about it?" He stared at Avery. "Then I'd bring it up, girl. Folks talk about everythin'—'cept what's gnawin' at 'em."

The conversation was taking her heart to shadowed places. She narrowed her eyes at Laz. "Like you never talk about what happened when you had more birds?"

"That's different." He huffed, but as she expected, he let the topic go. He transferred Isaiah from the crate to the enclosure, but the hawk just huddled on the freshly scrubbed floor.

Avery frowned. "Shouldn't he want to fly by now?"

"Nope. Not even close. He's restin' and catchin' his breath and settlin' some." Laz gathered up their equipment. "Comin' back to the store?"

"Can I have just a couple more minutes?"

Laz's lip twitched with a small smile. "Yeah. Talk to him a bit, if you want. You did good today. Next time you can do some of that yerself."

"Great!" Avery flashed him a thumbs-up as he turned away. But when he was out of sight, she slumped against the wall of the enclosure.

Was Laz right? That Addisyn was harboring some secret hurt where skating was concerned? Of course not. She was Addisyn's sister, after all. She knew Ads's heart better than Laz did.

Or did she?

She'd missed three years of Addisyn's past. Three pivotal years of hopes and heartbreaks, dreams and disasters. And no matter how hard she tried, she'd never retrieve that time. Her view of that chapter of her sister's life would always be secondhand.

So was she really able to see into Addisyn's heart now? What if Laz was right, and what if Addisyn was planning to leave, planning to walk out of Avery's life again, just like—

Stop. Don't go there. Addisyn was fine. She was happy, wasn't she? Didn't she like her life here? Mostly, anyway? Okay, so she had some adjustment to do still, but she'd get there. She'd fall into the rhythm of the mountains just the way Avery had.

And her broken past would lose any pull it might still have.

Avery took a deep breath. She was only borrowing trouble. This was nothing more than her fear talking. She forced herself to refocus on Isaiah. There was something haunting about him. The way he was so broken, but still so brave. Even in the midst of his pain, he held promise.

Courage, Laz had said. Yes. It was in the weave of his wings and the glint in his eyes. If only she could reassure him, help him know he didn't have to be so scared anymore.

"Hey." He didn't look up, but she somehow felt he was listening. "You're safe now." She gripped the bars of the enclosure as Addisyn's face floated in her mind. "You'll heal, and you'll be happy. I promise you."

CHAPTER 4

Avery understood Addisyn's work schedule—after all, a gift shop had to be open for weekend tourists—but spending her Saturday alone hadn't been very fun.

Household chores had consumed the morning, and in the afternoon, she'd headed out for a long hike on the Glacier Gorge Trail. The aspens were simply breathtaking at that altitude, like glowing candles along the path. Addisyn had already mentioned she'd be heading to the gym after work, so Avery had been in no hurry to return to her empty house. Lights were sparking across the valley by the time she drove back into Estes Park.

It was a crackling chilly night, even with a fire snapping in the fireplace. That first snow was getting closer, for sure. Avery had taken a hot shower and snuggled into her favorite flannel lounge pants and an oversized sweatshirt with the Colorado flag across the front. Then she'd turned on her indie folk playlist for ambience. Silence at night was too loud.

Of course, Addisyn would be back before long. And then they'd have a nice evening of food and laughter and maybe a card game. In the meantime, instead of brooding over the hollowness of the house, she needed to get busy on dinner. Tonight she was going to surprise Addisyn with her favorite.

She plucked a can of pizza dough from her neatly ordered refrigerator, holding her breath as she unwound the wrapping. The pop of the can as it sprang open made her flinch—just as it did every time. She shook her head with a rueful grin and glanced at Mercy, whose ears had perked up. "It's all right, girl. It's just future pizza, okay?"

The squish of the dough under her fingers as she shaped the crust would always usher her back to the first time she'd ever concocted this meal. She could see the girl she'd been, seventeen and scared to death, struggling desperately to scratch up a cheap meal in the cramped kitchen of the one-bedroom apartment she and Addisyn had shared in New York City.

She'd been so naive then that she'd never noticed the impossibility of what she'd done, but now, she could only marvel at how El Shaddai had gripped her hands and led her through. She'd taken Addisyn away from their affluent home in Syracuse, fleeing the shadow of their mother's abandonment and their father's abuse. And while she'd known the road would be hard, the crazy maelstrom of New York City had been like a slap in the face. For every night of the first few weeks, she'd lain awake next to her sleeping sister with terrified tears trickling into the pillow. She'd been sure she'd drown in it all—balancing a litany of jobs, fretting over finances, and defusing Addisyn's teenage angst, all while trying to tame her own trauma.

The memories of that time still made her shudder. Especially here and now, in this empty house on this cold night. She suddenly realized she was pinching the edge of the crust so tightly that she'd poked a hole. She released a calming breath and smoothed the dough, running her finger along the curve of the pizza stone.

That was something else she hadn't had that first time. She hadn't even owned a cookie sheet or a pan the right size, so she'd resorted to cooking the pizza on a square of aluminum foil. In every way, she'd had no idea what she was doing. No recipe. No experience. No real plan.

So she'd followed the same strategy she used in every other area of their lives: she'd taken the ingredients she'd been given and moved forward on guesswork and faith. And once the pizza was baking, she'd peered through the cloudy oven door with low expectations—the dread of yet another disaster, when she already spent her days struggling to stay one step ahead of failure.

But the pizza had been shockingly perfect.

Avery stared out the window above the sink, watching the memories replay against the sky. She could still recall how astonished she'd been that the cheap sauce and the canned dough and the questionable "cheese product" had all come together to make something remarkably satisfying. And if she was surprised, Addisyn was nothing less than awestruck. She'd never forget her sister's excitement. "Avery! You made pizza!" The clouds that had hovered over her expression since they'd left home had lifted, finally revealing the childlike joy that Avery had worried their circumstances had extinguished. "You're the best sister ever."

Avery had laughed and pulled her close, and the yeasty aroma had blossomed like a blessing in the stark kitchen. And Avery had finally dared to believe that maybe, just maybe, they would be okay.

"Avery? I'm back." Addisyn's voice jerked her into the present once more.

"There you are!" Avery shook off the last traces of the memory and gestured to the countertop as Addisyn peeked into the kitchen, her face still flushed from the gym. "Guess what? I'm making pizza."

"Pizza!" Addisyn squealed. "My favorite!" She tilted her head. "Did you use the canned stuff?"

"I knew you would ask." Avery smiled and brandished the empty dough canister. "Of course."

Addisyn laughed and shook her head. "We're not broke anymore, Avery. We could try real vegetables and homemade sauce now, you know."

"Nope." Avery reached for her can of store-bought sauce. "We're not changing a thing about that recipe, Ads."

"If you insist." Addisyn shrugged. "How much longer till it's ready?"

"Well, I'm almost done with the toppings, and then it has to cook. Twenty minutes or so."

"Great. Gives me time for a quick shower." Addisyn scurried down the hall. "I'll be right back."

Once the pizza was in the oven, Avery turned her attention to the table, setting out the salt and pepper shakers and arranging the plates. She reached into the refrigerator and pulled out a package of bacon bits—she didn't care for them, but she kept them on hand because Addisyn liked them.

She grimaced as she caught sight of Addisyn's gym bag, slung haphazardly against the doorway. Again? No matter how many times

Avery reminded her, Addisyn would never shed the habit of leaving her things lying about. She'd always been that way, though. Even in New York.

Avery began shredding spinach into a bowl and considered the bag. She'd never admit it to Addisyn, but her sister's world of competitions and workouts and who knew what else had always felt like an enemy. Avery had suffered through all the menial jobs, all the frantic fear, all the heartache and hurt, to keep Addisyn with her. But in the end, Addisyn had left anyway—drawn away by skating and Brian and the allure of the glamorous world. And the embedded scars from that time throbbed every time Avery considered the possibility that Addisyn might abandon her again.

But what she'd told Laz today had been right. Addisyn never mentioned skating anymore.

Folks talk about everythin' 'cept what's gnawin' at 'em.

Avery brushed off her hands, crossed to the sideboard, and studied the photo there. The glass was a little filmy now, and the corners of the cheap white frame were nicked, but the picture inside was still one of her most treasured possessions.

It had been taken during one of the rare moments of normalcy in their turbulent childhood. Addisyn was perched on a swing set at the local playground, grinning ear-to-ear—goodness, she couldn't have been older than seven or eight. Avery was standing behind her.

Avery brushed a finger reverently over the top of the frame. She'd carried this picture for years—through the fears and the friction and the fighting and the failures. Even after Addisyn had walked away from her, trampling her heart, she'd held onto that picture, begging El Shaddai for just what she had now—a restored relationship with the sister who meant more to her than life. And He'd given that to her, right? So why couldn't she shake the fear that Addisyn would be drawn away again?

Folks talk about everythin' 'cept what's gnawin' at 'em.

She squared her shoulders. Fine. Instead of wasting time worrying over this, analyzing what Ads did or didn't say, she should just ask outright. But would Addisyn be honest with her? Last time she had—

No. Stop. She'd made the decision to trust her sister again. She would stick by that decision. And surely Addisyn would never lie to her again.

Not this time around.

Just then Addisyn bounced into the room, her thin frame lost in Avery's old gray sweatsuit. She sniffed and grinned. "Mm. Pizza smells amazing."

"Grab the olive oil, will you?" Avery would ease into the topic gently. "It's in the pantry."

"Got it." Addisyn flung open the pantry door and began rifling through the drawers with her characteristic haphazardness. Avery bit her lip. It was okay. She could straighten everything later.

"I got pizza once in Whistler. It was awful." Addisyn handed her the green glass bottle. "Your pizza spoiled me for any of the restaurants."

Avery laughed. "So if the outdoors store goes under, I should start my own pizza place?"

"For sure." Addisyn plucked an olive from the bowl on the counter and popped it into her mouth. "I told Darius that day that your pizza made theirs taste like cardboard."

Why did every road lead back to Darius?

Fortunately, Addisyn kept talking instead of waiting for a response. "Have you talked to Laz today? How's the bird?"

"Laz says he's still doing great." Avery relaxed slightly at the thought. "I meant to tell you that Laz named him Isaiah."

"Isaiah?" Addisyn reached for another olive.

"Yeah." Avery glanced at the kitchen timer. Five more minutes. "It's a Bible name."

"Oh." Addisyn's voice turned taut, her expression tightening with the same wariness she always wore whenever Avery mentioned faith.

"Isaiah was a prophet." Avery kept her tone light. "His book of Scripture is really beautiful. You can read it in my Bible, if you ever want to."

"Okay. Thanks." Addisyn rubbed at an invisible stain on the countertop. "So, what else is happening with the hawk?"

So much for the faith discussion. "Well, I helped Laz weigh him and check his injuries and all that stuff yesterday. It was neat."

"Do you ever think of doing wildlife rehab? Like, as a job?" Addisyn pulled out another olive.

"Ads, if you keep eating those, we won't have any for the pizza. And I don't know. I'd have to have special training for that." And, for all she knew, a college education, which she'd sacrificed to care for Addisyn, but she wasn't going to mention that. "Right now, I'm happy with the outdoors store." Maybe this was her opening. "What about you? Any long-term career dreams?"

Addisyn gave an uncomfortable half-smile. "Well, I don't know." She looked down. "I could—I could always skate again."

"What?" Alarm bells clanged in Avery's soul. "You would—are you serious?"

Addisyn blinked. "A, whoa. Calm down." She held up her hands in a mock surrender. "I was just—you know, I was just thinking out loud."

If she overreacted, Addisyn would shut down, and things would get ugly. Avery turned and busied herself chopping the green onions. "Okay." She kept her tone level, thankful Addisyn couldn't see her face. "I thought you—I don't know, lost your scholarship or something."

"Sponsorship. And I did. Because I got hurt. But there are other options." Addisyn's voice was matter-of-fact, as if she were discussing the weather instead of a completely ridiculous career option. "There's even a sponsorship program that deals specifically with returning athletes. I think they call it Rise Up or something like that."

She'd really been considering this, hadn't she? Avery put the knife down and turned to face her. "But Brian—"

Addisyn's expression froze over. "There are more coaches out there than Brian, A. It wouldn't have to be the way it was before."

"I know, but when I think of all that happened—I don't want you to get hurt again. In any way."

Addisyn folded her arms. "So, I'm guessing you wouldn't be in favor."

She didn't want to fight, didn't want to push her sister away, but she needed Addisyn to hear this loud and clear. "Well—no. Definitely not."

"Okay. Then never mind." Addisyn's expression clouded over with something darker than defeat. "Forget I ever brought it up."

This had gone all wrong. Avery swallowed hard. "I didn't mean—"

"No, I get it." Addisyn's smile was bright and brittle, but at least she was trying to back away from the tension. "I see how you feel. I just—"

Avery waited, but the rest of the sentence didn't come. "Just what?"

"Nothing."

Uncertainty crinkled along her spine. "Addisyn, are you—is there something you're not telling me?"

Addisyn opened her mouth, but no words came. Then she suddenly sniffed. "Uh—Avery—what's that smell?"

Avery suddenly became aware of an acrid burning stench. She shrieked. "The pizza!" She flung open the oven door. Sure enough, the edge of the pizza had blackened.

"Please tell me you did not ruin our food." Addisyn hovered as Avery rushed the pizza stone to a trivet.

"You're not hoping any harder than I am." Avery brushed her hair out of her eyes and examined the pizza. The edges were most definitely burned, and the bottom was a bit browner than she would have liked, but to her relief, most of it would still be edible. "We're good." She laughed as Addisyn sagged in melodramatic relief.

After the mishap, the evening proceeded peacefully. They enjoyed the pizza and exchanged stories about their days. Then they sat on the living room rug in front of the fireplace and played a dozen games of Go Fish. The night was full of laughter and joy, and it wasn't until Avery was in bed that she realized something.

Addisyn had never answered her question.

⋀⋀　⋀⋀　⋀⋀

ADDISYN COULDN'T CONCENTRATE.

They'd been walking in the woods behind Avery's house for nearly an hour in the slow September dusk, and the whole time, her sister hadn't stopped talking about that hawk she was caring for. It sounded exciting, and normally Addisyn would have hung on every word, but today it took all her concentration just to smile and nod at the right times.

Already it had been a week since Darius's invitation. She had to let him know something soon, but the whole decision had wadded itself into a complicated knot.

"Skyla came out to see Isaiah yesterday." Avery swished through the tall dry grasses with a stride so brisk Addisyn could barely keep up. "She helped take care of him when he was at Chayton's center."

"Really." Hopefully Avery didn't notice the distraction in her tone. "I wondered where she went during lunch."

"Yeah, I think she helps Chayton a lot. So anyway, Chayton says that for these first few days, we have to keep the hawk quiet. He can't get too—"

Skyla. There was another complication—her job. She couldn't exactly abscond to Whistler in the middle of her work. Would Darius be willing to wait until November when her position ended?

Avery paused under an evergreen tree and scooped a pinecone off the ground. She spiraled it in her hands and smiled. "I'm going to collect a lot of these to use as decorations this winter."

"Sounds nice." Oh, and what about the expense? Of course, she could use some of her salary for plane tickets and hotel fees, but she'd really hoped to be able to pay Avery back for—

"Ads, are you okay?" Avery slipped the pinecone in her coat pocket and regarded Addisyn suspiciously. "You're awfully quiet."

"Oh. No, I'm fine." The words were a reflex. She exhaled, watching the cloud of her breath swirl against the last embers of the dying sunset. "Just tired."

Avery's face relaxed. "You've had a busy few days. I'm sure you're tired." She gestured through the trees. "Let's head on back to the house."

Addisyn stifled a yawn as they crossed the fields behind the cabin. Yes, she was tired, but not from work or hiking or any other physical activity. She was tired from hope and fear chasing each other around her mind. Tired from days of trying to sort through her emotions to find her path.

Only one thing was clear—she couldn't talk to Avery about any of this. She'd planned to bring it up the other night, but her sister's resistance to even the idea of skating had been shockingly strong.

She glanced sideways at Avery, noticing the glow on her sister's face—the peace Avery wore when she talked about the hawk and the mountains and the God she called El Shaddai. In New York City, Avery had never looked that content—not with a thousand worries attacking her from every direction. Most of them wrapped around Addisyn.

Addisyn clenched her jaw. No, she couldn't ruin Avery's peace until she was absolutely sure this was something she wanted to pursue. Until then, she had no choice but to delay the confrontation.

She glanced toward the northwest, where Longs Peak stood against the sky, and clouds scurried on the wind, and Darius waited over a thousand miles away to hear her *yes*. On one hand, the invitation sounded like a dream. She didn't have to close her eyes to remember everything she'd always loved about skating. The intricate artistry. The song of skate blades on perfect ice. The meditative serenity she always felt on the rink. Even the perfectionist edge, the constant competition against herself.

And to skate with Darius?

She glanced up and blinked. They were already back at the cabin. How had that happened?

"—so now that he's spreading his wings some more, that will be perfect, I think."

So for the last ten minutes, she'd been so zoned out that her sister's voice had simply been part of the background. Addisyn tensed as they stepped inside. If a response was required, she was doomed.

But Avery just patted her shoulder and headed for the stairs. "I'm going to go start reading that book and see if it says anything about the feather breakage."

Addisyn nodded vaguely and sank onto the couch. She didn't know what Avery was talking about, but that was her own fault.

She leaned back, closed her eyes, and pictured the bag of skating stuff in her closet. All that she'd told Darius was true. She did miss the ice. She did long for it. But at the same time, the shadows were falling, crowding out the light of those memories, shaping themselves into a single form.

Brian.

His face taunted her mind—utterly handsome and utterly hateful. Just the thought of him made her want to hide under the couch—like when she was a little girl dashing to Avery's bed during thunderstorms. Even now the memory of his kisses and caresses made her feel sick and stained. How could she have ever believed he loved her?

Baby, I just want the best for you—somebody has to watch out for you—

She hated that she could still hear his voice. She shuddered and opened her eyes. The skating dreams she'd cherished were now clouded by his filthy handprints. How could she return to the ice, even in this new way, without reliving all the evil he'd brought to her?

But then the thought of Darius's face and voice swung the pendulum the other way. Addisyn groaned and sank forward over her knees. How was she supposed to make a decision like this? The longer she thought about it, the more confusing it became. She'd never decide, unless—

Wait.

The idea zinged with a lightning-flash of illumination. That was it, wasn't it? The only true test. A practice skate.

Yes! Addisyn sat up, the relief of clarity replacing the confusion. Of course! A few minutes on the ice, and she'd know one way or another. She'd be able to feel it. And then she'd have the courage to tell Avery she was going—or to tell Darius she wasn't.

She pulled out her phone and did a quick search for professional ice rinks in Colorado, sagging slightly when she discovered the closest one was the skating center in Denver—an hour and a half away. She didn't mind the distance, but there was no way she could make a trip like that without Avery knowing.

Okay, but there had to be a way. Could she just tell Avery she wanted to go see Denver? Skip work? Maybe go on a Monday, when she was off and Avery wasn't?

None of the options felt quite right. Addisyn winced. She hated the idea of deceiving her sister. She'd promised herself that this time, she wouldn't keep secrets from Avery. Everything open and aboveboard. But this wasn't deception; it was just delaying. Nothing like before.

Right?

She glanced again at the website for the Denver skating center. She'd been there before, actually—for a series of training sessions two summers ago. Something Brian had set up for her.

Once again, his face hovered before her eyes, but she shoved the image away. The past was behind her, and he was too. There was no way he could hurt her now.

△△　△△　△△

THE MORNING WAS still hazy and half-asleep, the crispy autumn grass fringed with frost. Avery was just stepping out of her truck at Live Bigger when an elk bugle rang out. She sucked in a breath as the eerie sound floated through the valley.

It was a dominant bull elk, and a big one, judging by the strength that resonated in the bugle. Avery shielded her eyes from the slanting morning sun and peered at the fields across the road from Laz's store. Sure enough, there was the bull—majestic and mighty, strutting through the mists. He tipped his head back until his silver antlers nearly brushed his shoulders and bugled again just as a rival bull answered him from the tree line.

Mercy perked up her ears and shifted her weight to her toes. Avery recognized the posture just in time to snag her collar. "Mercy. No, no." She steered the dog toward the store. "You're not supposed to chase the elk, girl. You know that."

The delight of the morning shivered through her. This was her home—here in the shadow of the mountains, where the air smelled like courage and the sun shone freedom. When Mercy glanced back over her shoulder at the elk, Avery caught herself doing the same thing.

With the mountains offering moments like these, it was no wonder that autumn was even more hectic than summer at the store. The tourists wouldn't trickle out until the end of November.

"Miz Avery! Ready for a busy day?" Laz grinned at her as he unloaded a new shipment of trekking poles.

"You bet." Avery tucked a pencil behind her ear and studied Laz's inventory list. "But more ready for my four-day weekend."

Laz's laugh boomed out. "What, ya won't worry about me? All by myself down in La Junta?"

Avery smiled and shook her head. "You were going every year to that outdoors expo long before I showed up here."

What she didn't tell Laz was that his trip out of town would give her some much-needed time with Addisyn. Her sister would have to work Friday and Saturday, but not Sunday or Monday. Which meant they'd have two days to hike and laugh and watch the bugling elk.

And talk. That most of all.

Avery frowned as she rearranged the knives in the glass case. For the last few days, Addisyn had seemed—different. No specific incident or comment, just a shadow on her smile. A hesitancy in her laugh. A strain on her face when she didn't know Avery was watching.

She was just—distant. Or maybe *worried* was the word. No, not worried. Distracted? Preoccupied?

Fear's fist gripped tighter, and Avery bit her lip. She was doing it again, imagining conflict where none existed. Her concerns were ridiculous, but she'd still feel better if they could have a good conversation when neither of them was dashing to or from work. And while surely Addisyn hadn't been serious about her skating comments the other night, Avery needed to ask about that again.

A wave of customers swelled into the shop right at eight thirty, and the chaotic pace of the store chased further worries from Avery's mind. In the afternoon lull, Laz tossed her another of the frozen packages. "Time for Isaiah's check-in, an' you've got a good handle on things. I'm gonna let you take care of it today."

"Really?" So far, she hadn't been more than an observer.

"Sure."

Laz held the door for Avery as they entered the converted garage, Isaiah's crate tucked under his arm. "Any special plans for yer weekend?"

Avery blinked in the dim light. "I need to talk to Addisyn."

He shot her a glance. "Sounds serious."

Avery just nodded. "What will we need today?"

"The board an' the scale an' that towel." He dipped his finger at each one as he listed them. "Now, why are you worryin' about yer sister?"

Avery's hands stilled over the supplies. "Oh, Laz, I don't know. She seems—distracted. She's just not been herself the last few days."

"So mebbe she's worryin' or thinkin' 'bout somethin'."

"Well, maybe, but she hasn't told me."

Laz cocked an eyebrow. "Mebbe it's somethin' she's gotta work out on her own."

"Maybe." The answer was simply the path of least resistance. Laz didn't understand how fragile her relationship with her sister felt, how her fear of losing Addisyn again was never more than a heartbeat away.

Laz's probing gaze rested on her for a long moment, then he jerked his head toward a pair of leather hand protectors that looked like oversized oven mitts. "Let's see the bird."

Avery slipped on the specialized gloves. Then she reached into the box and carefully grasped Isaiah's ankles, just as she'd seen Laz do. She drew the bird toward the entrance, and he emerged in a fling of feathers. "Easy." Was the whisper for him or herself?

"That's it." Laz gave a thumbs-up.

"Now what?" Isaiah's squirming weight felt foreign.

Laz put his hands over hers to demonstrate. "Keep holdin' him by the ankles so's he can't scratch you—yep, jes' like that—and hold his chest—there you go."

Avery mimicked Laz's motions, squeezing Isaiah's legs together and cradling his head against her torso. Once he was secure in her grip, he was surprisingly still, his only motion the cock and twist of his head as he scanned the surroundings.

"Good." Laz nodded approvingly. He flicked his finger at the edge of the bird's peripheral vision and made a sound of satisfaction when Isaiah turned his head. "Checkin' his sight. All good."

Even through the gloves, Avery could feel Isaiah's heart fluttering. Her own pulse was probably even faster than his. "Am I doing okay?"

"Yep. Now we're gonna check his wing. Jes' grab it by that top edge and pull it straight out, kind of like a curtain."

"I'll hurt him."

"No, you won't. Go on now."

Avery drew a deep breath and gently tugged on the upper edge of the bird's wing. She gasped with relief and delight when his wing unfurled. "I did it!"

"See?" Laz grinned. "Yer a natural."

That was going a bit far, but she did manage to navigate through the rest of the checks and swaddle Isaiah in the blanket without too much trouble. "Is it really okay to cover him completely like this?" The only visible part of the bird was his feet.

"Easier for him, really. He ain't so scared thataway." Laz squinted at the readout on the scale. "His weight's holdin' steady."

"That's good." Avery unwrapped the towel. "At least he hasn't lost any." The words were barely out of her mouth when Isaiah began thrashing wildly. "Laz!" She clung to the bird's ankles, but he was wriggling from her grasp. "What's wrong?"

"Relax your hold, girl." Laz laid his hand over Avery's. "Yer grippin' him awful tight, and he don't like it."

Avery loosened her hands, and oddly enough, the bird settled. Confusion mixed with her relief. "I was only trying to hold onto him."

Laz's look drilled into her soul. "If there's one thing you gotta remember, it's this. Don't grip wild things too tight."

What did that mean? She was about to ask when some old Rascal Flatts tune began blaring. Both she and Isaiah jumped.

"Darn thing." Laz fished out his cell phone. "Probably some joker tellin' me I need to renew the extended warranty I don't have—" He glanced at the screen, and his face changed. He shoved the phone to his ear and took a step back. "Hello?"

His eyes clouded as he listened in utter silence. Then he gave a low moan. "Oh, no. Is it bad?"

Another heartbeat, and he tucked his face into one big palm and walked past Avery. Straight out of the garage, across the field, and toward his house.

Isaiah squawked slightly. Avery hesitated, glancing from the bird to the door. Concern prodded at her. She wouldn't invade Laz's privacy, but she'd never seen him so undone.

She loaded Isaiah back into the crate, jotted down his weight and Laz's observations, then took him to the enclosure and returned to the store. It was over half an hour before Laz came back. He set his phone down on the counter and faced her. "I'm sorry for leavin' like that."

"That's fine." Avery searched his red-rimmed eyes. "Is everything okay?"

"No." He looked down for a long moment and scuffed his boot across the floor. "Forrest—a buddy of mine—he's got cancer." He sniffed and looked away. "He's only forty-two. Got a wife and four kids. Runs a ranch."

"Oh, Laz." Avery winced. "I'm so, so sorry."

He brushed off her sympathy. "Anyway—" His voice was stronger now, his tough facade sliding back into place. "This sorta changes some things."

An undefined anxiety sidled up to her. "What do you mean?"

Laz jammed his hands into his pockets. "I'm gonna have to leave for a while. His ranch is a full-time job. I promised him that I'd come help oversee things."

He was leaving during the busy season? The next moment Avery chastised herself for the selfish thought. Of course he needed to go. "Do they live close to here?"

He made an uncomfortable face. "No. North Dakota."

Avery stared at him. "How do you know someone in North Dakota?"

He scrubbed at his beard. "I lived there. A lifetime ago." He held up his hand before she could ask any more questions. "This ain't the time for my life story, girl. The important thing is I've gotta go. I'll leave tomorrow." He took a deep breath. "Miz Avery, I hate to ask you, but…"

Avery could see the question coming, the same way she could sometimes watch a curtain of rain slide across the mountains for a few sinking seconds before the clouds opened above her head.

"Can you handle things here? Jes' for three, four weeks?"

"Of course." Avery's stomach clenched, but she kept her voice firm. "I can do that."

Apology mingled with gratitude in his face. "If you could—I'd be truly thankful. Of course there'd be extra pay—"

Avery waved his words away. "Just tell me what to do."

"Waalll." He scratched his head. "Store, you got down. You know more 'bout it than I do now."

What made him think that? And how on earth could she keep up with it alone? This time of year, it was almost too much for both of them together.

"For the expo—you'll have to go 'stead of me."

The expo. Oh, she'd forgotten that. Goodbye, four-day weekend.

"I'll give you a crash course." Laz grabbed a notepad and started jotting things down. "We'll pack up what you'll need before I leave—an' I'll get you the info—tell you where the hotel is—"

A new worry grabbed her. "Oh, Laz, what about Isaiah?"

He sighed. "You'll have to take care of him too. But that's nothin' serious. Jes' his feedin' and his water an' his weigh-in. Cleanin' the enclosure, that sort of thing. You already know."

The store. The expo. The hawk. Each one was another layer in an avalanche of responsibility. Avery couldn't manage more than a nod.

"Miz Avery?" Laz set the pencil down and peered at her. "Are you sure 'bout this?"

No, she definitely wasn't sure, but Laz had done so much for her. How could she let him down? "Of course." She swallowed the panic threatening to choke her. "I'll take care of everything."

△△ △△ △△

WEIRD THAT AVERY wasn't home yet. Addisyn unlocked the cabin door and glanced at her watch. Her sister should have been off work almost an hour ago.

After waiting a few minutes, she punched Avery's number, but the call went straight to voicemail. Typical. Half the time, Avery's phone was lost. The other half, it was dead.

Maybe she could try Laz. She had his number somewhere, didn't she? She was scrolling through her contacts when the door opened. "Ads? I'm back."

"Avery, thank goodness." She hurried down the hall and cringed when she almost tripped over her jacket. She'd forgotten to hang it up again. "I was worried."

"I'm sorry."

Avery walked right past the jacket with no comment, and Addisyn blinked. Whoa. Something had to be wrong. "What's going on?"

Avery rubbed her eyes. "It was a rough day. I didn't even have time for lunch, so I'm starving." She wandered into the kitchen and glanced around as if expecting food to spring from the countertops. "Did you—did you not start supper?"

Why hadn't she thought of that? "I haven't been here that long." Defensiveness uncoiled in her tone. "Anyway, you know I can't cook."

"That's right." Avery ran a hand over her face. "Okay. Um—I froze the leftover pasta from the other night. Let's just microwave some of it, and

I'll explain everything to you while we're eating."

As they ate the lukewarm pasta dish, Addisyn couldn't believe what Avery was saying. Apparently, Laz was leaving, and Avery was going to be in charge of the store, even that hawk. "But Avery, can you even do that? Don't you have to have a license or something?"

"I asked Laz that same question." Avery had said she was hungry, but now she was just staring at her pasta as if it were a riddle to be solved. "He called Chayton, and Chayton said it was fine because I would be under his supervision, and I'm not actually doing any work. I'm basically just feeding and monitoring. Plus, Chayton will come out if I run into any problems."

Avery was taking on way too much. Addisyn could see it, even if her sister couldn't. "So why can't Chayton take care of the bird?"

"Because he's running out of room at the center, and he's overwhelmed anyway." Avery's look hardened to stubbornness. "I can do it, Addisyn."

"Okay." Addisyn didn't point out that there weren't enough hours in the day for Avery to manage all this stuff. Or that her sister was too kind and helpful for her own good. A thought struck her. "So—I'm guessing you're not still off this weekend."

"No." Avery propped her head on her hand. "Obviously, Laz can't attend the expo now. I'm going in his place."

For just a moment, Addisyn was back in their New York City apartment, watching Avery come in at ten o'clock from her job at Burger King, knowing she'd be back up at six in the morning for her receptionist job at the law firm. Struggling for even five minutes of her sister's time. She blinked. Unfair, to compare the two situations. The context couldn't have been more different, and anyway, Laz's leaving was far from her sister's fault. "So—where is the expo? Denver?"

"La Junta." Avery laid her fork down.

"La Junta?" Addisyn stared at her sister. "Where is that?"

"Southeast." Avery didn't sound sure. "Laz said it was four, maybe four and a half hours from here. So, I'm driving down on Friday and won't be back till Monday. Chayton is going to feed Isaiah those days."

So that meant—

Addisyn held her breath as the pieces clicked together. Avery would be gone for a whole weekend. Of course, Addisyn would be working Saturday, but she'd have all day Sunday. If she wanted to go to Denver…

"So anyway." The weariness in Avery's eyes lifted some. "I thought, you know, maybe you'd want to go with me."

"Go—with you? To the expo?"

"Sure." Hope hung on Avery's smile. "It could be fun. We can stay in a hotel…check out some of the sights…"

It did sound like fun. The options clashed against each other. Addisyn bit her lip. If not for Denver…but if this was her only chance… "I'm sorry, Avery. You know I have to work Saturday."

"Oh. Right." Avery lowered her head, but not in time to hide the disappointment that drooped in her expression. "No problem, then."

Guilt draped itself along Addisyn's shoulders. "I mean, it's not that I wouldn't want to go, it's just—"

"Addisyn, I get it." Avery's tone had sharpened slightly. She picked up her fork and stabbed at the pasta. "I said it's fine."

A knot twisted in Addisyn's stomach. She picked at her pasta for a few more minutes until the clinking of their forks on their plates was too loud. Then she gathered her dishes and headed to the kitchen. Part of her expected Avery to follow.

But by the time Addisyn finished washing the dishes, Avery still hadn't come. Addisyn turned the faucet off and peeked into the dining room again. Avery was still slumped at the table, her plate pushed away, her head buried in her folded arms.

Addisyn hovered awkwardly in the doorway for a moment, then reluctantly retreated to her room and flopped onto her bed. She closed her eyes again, picturing the strain on her sister's face. She hadn't seen Avery wear that scrunched-up look since—well, since New York.

Part of her wanted to call Laz and jump down his throat for putting her sister in this position. Didn't he know that Avery was conscientious to a fault? Didn't he realize that expecting her to carry all the weight was downright unfair?

But Addisyn was just as guilty. Or more so. At least Laz had a legitimate reason to abandon Avery. But as for her—

Remorse burrowed through her. She was fairly certain that Skyla would give her the weekend off, if she explained the circumstances. She should call Skyla now, receive her approval, then go downstairs and tell her sister she'd love a trip to La Junta. Better yet, she should just tell Avery everything—Darius's invitation, her own confusion.

But now that Avery was overwhelmed, wouldn't spilling the situation just add more stress to her sister's plate? And wouldn't it be better to go to Denver first? If the practice skate didn't feel right, then case closed. There'd be no need to broach the explosive subject to Avery.

She took a deep breath. No. She couldn't back down. She had to take this chance. Had to go to Denver. Had to get clarity.

But as soon as Avery came back from La Junta, she'd tell her everything.

Absolutely.

CHAPTER 5

Idiots! Why was it always his misfortune to be surrounded by idiots?

Brian grimaced at his secretary as she hurriedly collected the papers scattered across the floor. "I've told you before to be careful."

"I'm sorry, sir." The girl was a mousy little shadow with two left feet and the personality of a jellyfish. "I didn't mean to bump into them."

Her chin was quivering now, as if she might start sobbing right here in his office. That was the last thing he needed. Why were women always sniveling over the littlest things? Brian rolled his eyes and waved his hand. "Forget it." He glowered at the girl as she fumbled the papers into an uneven stack on the corner of his desk. "Do you have the report yet on the Hamley file?"

"No, sir. I'm working on it."

Working on it. Brian narrowed his eyes. What was the girl's name? Betty or Betsy…he couldn't remember. "I have to have that this afternoon."

"I know." The girl bit her lip. "We're behind, sir."

We? Brian cursed under his breath. "No, *you're* behind." He jabbed a finger at her. "I gave you everything you needed to have that done on time. It had better be on my desk this afternoon, even if you have to work through lunch. Is that clear?"

The girl wilted even further. "Yes, sir. I'll get it done."

"Fine."

"Sir?"

Why didn't she scuttle back to her little hole and leave him alone? "What?"

"I was coming to tell you—before the papers fell—Mr. Barmilli wants to see you."

Barmilli. Brian's heart rate doubled. "What? Now?" He sprang from his chair. "Why didn't you tell me that when you first came in?"

"The papers—"

He cursed again, louder this time. "Forget the papers!" He wrenched his suit jacket on, struggling with the sleeves. "Get Barmilli on the intercom. Tell him I'm on the way."

He was out the door before Beth or Bridget or whatever her name was could respond. What had she been thinking, to delay such an important message? Barmilli rarely sent for him, but when he did—

The elevator wasn't descending. "Come on!" Brian's frustration boiled over, and he kicked the metal frame. He couldn't wait any longer for the elevator. Even though his alternative was five flights of stairs.

As he raced upward through the dim stairwell, he mentally scanned his recent conduct. What had he done this time? There had been that little incident with the maintenance man last week, but everybody got upset now and then, right? Especially when some fool had just thrown away an important paper? The maintenance guy was a timid sort, anyway. Surely he wouldn't have complained.

Or was it the thing with the girl down at the rink? Everybody had tried to make a much bigger deal out of that than it deserved. He hadn't been hitting on her anyway, just analyzing her skating. How was he to know she was just sixteen? With all that makeup, she looked a lot older.

Nineteenth floor. Brian snatched for his breath as he stepped into the lobby area.

"Everything okay, sir?" Barmilli's secretary was alert and competent. Far more professional than Bethany. Prettier, too.

"Yes." Brian yanked at his sleeves. Under his jacket, sweat was making his shirt cling to him. "Mr. Barmilli sent for me." He hated the way the words sounded. Like he was a genie who could be summoned with a flick of the finger, ready to kowtow to the master. But for the next few minutes, a dose of humility would be required.

"Yes, he's been waiting for you." Was there an ominous undertone to her words? "Go on back."

Brian swallowed back his panting and ran a hand through his hair. He couldn't look like a raving madman when he went in to see the only man at the firm he was afraid of. He nodded again to the secretary—she really was cute—and headed back.

Everything was nicer up here. Real wood floors instead of laminate, crown molding around the ceiling, decorative light fixtures. It even smelled more important—like money and authority and a respect that would be demanded. Reclined in his overstuffed desk chair, Barmilli raised his eyebrows as Brian entered. "Mr. Felding. At last."

"Yes, sir." Brian hovered awkwardly.

"Have a seat."

He lowered himself to the edge of one of the slick leather chairs. "Is there a problem, sir?"

The deep lines on Barmilli's face were etched more firmly than usual. "I would say so." He sighed and leaned forward. "Felding, you're one of our best coaches and agents. Your ability to fulfill both roles is truly impressive. And you've handled a full caseload with skill."

Barmilli hadn't summoned him to the nineteenth floor to pat him on the back. Brian waited for the blow.

"But I'm afraid that, barring some extensive changes, we're going to have to reevaluate your position at this agency."

What? Brian realized his mouth was limp. "Mr. Barmilli—sir—" He'd been prepared for a reprimand, a chastisement, but never—"Is my performance not—satisfactory?"

Barmilli sighed and contemplated an abstract art painting on the wall. "Your performance is very satisfactory, yes. Unfortunately, it's clouded by your—indiscretions."

Indiscretions? Heat snaked up the back of his neck. What had Barmilli heard? He clenched his jaw. Time for damage control. "If this is about the situation with the janitor—"

Barmilli's eyebrow lifted a fraction of an inch. "What janitor?"

"Uh—" *Course-correct.* "Perhaps you should tell me the, um, allegations. Sir."

Barmilli narrowed his eyes but sighed. "Very well. This is not an isolated incident, Felding. The red flags keep accumulating. In the last six months, we've received four complaints from your clients." He paused for effect. "All seem to indicate that your treatment is unnecessarily—harsh."

Four complaints? Seriously? Brian gritted his teeth. "Who were the complaints from?"

"The women asked that anonymity be preserved."

Of course they did. Cowards. Brian shrugged. "Sir, I'm a coach. Naturally, I endeavor to—uh—motivate my athletes and help them reach their goals. Sometimes I have to use tough love to—"

"Yes, well." Barmilli's tone sidestepped Brian's excuses. "There's also that issue with the Pennington girl."

"Mr. Barmilli, I thought we had handled that." Brian forced his voice to remain calm. "I have assured you I did not mean anything—inappropriate. I was simply engaged in conversation with her when her mother got all—when her mother objected."

Barmilli pursed his lips thoughtfully. "The mother has a different story, as you well know."

"So you would believe a hysterical parent over your trusted employee?"

An odd little smile curled on Barmilli's lip. "Not over a *trusted* employee, no." Before Brian could react to the jab, the man continued. "Really, though, the clincher was this whole sordid mess with Addisyn Miles."

Addisyn Miles?

The anger began throbbing in his temples. The same anger that ripped through him every time he thought about Addisyn. "What are you saying, sir?"

Barmilli leaned back in his chair and steepled his hands. "Felding, you coached Miss Miles for three years. And during those three years, she became one of the most lucrative and promising clients for this agency. Talent, personality, determination—the complete deal."

"Yes, sir." The anger mounted with the enumeration of Addisyn's charms.

"And then—in February she falls off the radar, and you spend your summer negotiating some—" Barmilli waved his hand vaguely—"alternative plans for her. And then in August, her case file is closed, and suddenly she's not on the roster anymore."

"She left because she made the decision to retire." Let Barmilli play the big man. He'd find that Brian Felding would not back down. "As I've stated." Okay, so maybe some other factors had played into her departure. But she really had retired. He'd been reviewing the athlete lists for Regionals, and her name was nowhere.

"Right. As you've stated." Barmilli tilted his head. "But I wonder if she left to pursue something…or to escape something." He leaned across the desk, into the tension between them. "Let me be blunt. I hold you responsible for driving away our top client."

Well, there it was. Sweat prickled across his shoulders, but Brian maintained his poker face. "Me?" He forced a laugh and pointed at himself. "How would I—"

"I have heard some—talk—about your relationship with Miss Miles." Barmilli rubbed his eyes. Disapproval was draped across his expression. "You know it is entirely improper for a coach to have, uh, romantic relations with a skater."

Keep it cool. "Romantic relations? Who said that?" Brian worked his face into a shocked expression. "I can assure you that—"

"And not only am I faced with the possibility that you have violated our code of conduct in an egregious way, but I'm also realizing that this agency may have lost its top-performing client because of a lovers' quarrel."

This conversation was escaping his grip, and quickly. "Mr. Barmilli, sir." Brian fought to keep the desperation from leaking into his words. "Miss Miles was an exceptional skater, as you've said." Even that admission brought a bitter taste to his mouth, but he kept going. "However, she simply made the decision to retire. Not a wise one, perhaps, given her potential, but still, her personal choice. To assume anything else would be ridicu—er, misguided."

Barmilli shook his head. "I'm sorry, Felding. Too many things are not adding up here."

Surely this wasn't—was he getting *fired?* Brian searched Barmilli's face. "I have a long history of loyalty to this agency. I've—"

"Spare me the rhetoric." Barmilli's tone had dropped fifteen degrees since the beginning of the conversation. "No, I'm not terminating you. Yet.

Although I probably should." He sighed and rubbed his forehead. "I'm giving you the opportunity to correct your mistake." He gave a sarcastic half smile. "Offering you a second chance, as it were."

Acting grateful would be tacitly admitting that a mistake had occurred. "What do you want me to do?"

"I want you to be wise." Barmilli's words were clipped. "Stop tarnishing the name of this agency, and stop driving away our high-performing clients. And please keep your personal and professional lives separated. If I find further evidence that a violation of any sort has occurred, there will not be another opportunity. Do you understand me?"

"Yes, sir."

"Good. Then we have an agreement." Barmilli stood, and Brian nearly sagged with the relief. He was halfway to the door when Barmilli spoke again. "Felding?"

"Sir?"

Barmilli crossed his arms. "Your story about Miss Miles had better be accurate. I do not want to turn on my television one day and see her skating for another agency. And if I have evidence that you have misled me in that regard, then you will face immediate dismissal. Is that clear?"

"Yes, sir." Humiliation squirmed over Brian's spine.

Brittany's desk was vacant as he reentered his office. Just as well. He had enough on his mind without her incompetence.

He kicked his desk chair aside. The frustration wouldn't allow him to sit right now. Instead, he paced in front of his fourteenth-floor window. The rectangular labyrinth of New York sprawled to the horizon with a restless energy and power that had always swept him along like a wave.

A wave he would still be riding, if not for Addisyn Miles.

He gritted his teeth as his anger doubled. Was it not enough that she'd dumped him? Not enough that she'd practically spit in his face and waltzed out of his life, touting some made-up accusations? Now he was going to be fired because of her?

Rage was pounding in his chest, the kind that steered him toward conduct that Barmilli wouldn't consider wise. *Get a handle, man!* Brian forced a deep breath. He'd learned the technique in an anger-management class the agency had required him to take a few years back, when he'd had another little, uh, hiccup in his career. The breathing had seemed stupid at the time, but since then he'd noticed that sometimes it really did help.

And he couldn't afford to blow up or lose his cool. No, he needed to make a battle plan. He leaned on the window. He wasn't about to give up this view.

Certainly not because of some stupid female who'd thwarted all his plans.

He returned to his desk and slumped into his chair. The walls were squeezing him in, claustrophobia wrapping around his lungs. Space, that's what he needed. Space and distance. He glanced down at his task list and blinked when he noticed the item he'd penciled in on Monday: *Schedule out-of-state client auditions.*

Now there was an idea. Why couldn't he leave now and spend the weekend on the auditions? Approved agency business, after all. He could fly out tomorrow morning, stay there over the weekend or even into the first part of next week. By the time he came back, Barmilli would have moved on to other topics.

Perfect. The fire inside began to fade. Brian glanced out his window again and nodded at the panorama. This kingdom was still his. Addisyn was retired—not even a blip on the radar. He'd spend the weekend on the interviews, and then he'd come back and pick up where he left off.

Booking plane tickets should have been Bethany's job, but this time, he'd handle it himself. Within five minutes, he had the flight reserved—the one that would take him away from Barmilli's scrutiny and to one of his favorite cities. A city where he'd found many successful skating prospects.

Denver.

◬ ◬ ◬

"THAT'S IT!" LENNY slapped his hands together exuberantly. "It's like you never left this center, buddy."

Yeah, right. Darius clanged the weights back into their holders, grimacing as fire rushed up and down his arms. These exercises demanded every ounce of strength he had. "Well, believe me, it feels like I did."

Lenny laughed and flicked Darius's complaints away. "Take thirty seconds."

"Gladly." Darius glanced at the silver stopwatch in Lenny's hand. He'd been meeting Lenny every evening after work—right here in the therapy room at the Whistler Athletes' Centre. They'd work for a couple of hours, teasing apart weakness and strength. And praying. Like Darius, Lenny was a firm believer in the power of prayer to heal broken bodies and wounded spirits.

"Time's up." Lenny brandished the stopwatch.

"Already?"

"Yep. Come on now! Last exercise of the night." Lenny tapped his toe against a padded mat on the floor. "Let's give your TVA one more round."

"Ugh." Darius wiped the sweat out of his eyes and lowered himself to the mat. TVA—transverse abdominis. Lenny was convinced that strengthening the deep core muscles would provide better stability and protection for Darius's back. The routine had started off as simple supine braces with leg movements, but Lenny upped the intensity every few days. "You would have done great as a drill sergeant, you know?"

"You got this, man! How 'bout some three-legged planks?"

"Oh, just wonderful." Darius shook his head and pushed himself into a plank position. Then he extended his left leg behind him, grimacing at the burn in his pecs and abs.

"Atta boy. Give me some leg pulses with that extended leg, okay?"

Darius gritted his teeth and focused on moving his leg up and down in the smooth rhythm Lenny had demonstrated. Instead, it jerked spasmodically. "Lenny!" It was more gasp than groan.

"Hey, it's going well." Lenny's hands were on his calf, helping his leg find the rhythm. "Tighten those abs! Dig deep now. That's the secret. Yeah, you got it!"

Darius could feel the difference, and once he settled into the groove, the fire in his muscles carried a strange kind of elation. Even six sets later, when he flopped on the mat, the glow didn't leave him. "Whew! Dude, you're killing me."

"No, man. Just making you strong." Lenny tossed him a towel.

The sweat was stinging his eyes. "Is there a difference?"

Lenny laughed. "Not really."

Darius chuckled softly and scrubbed the towel over his face. The good-natured teasing was part of every workout, but in all seriousness, he knew the sequence Lenny followed with him was carefully choreographed. First had come exercises designed to increase the strength of his core muscles, making him less susceptible to future back injuries. Then stretches and exercises that targeted his flexibility—something he discovered had deteriorated since his injury. He'd also scheduled chiropractic visits with a doctor Lenny recommended, and his first follow-up with Dr. Patel was in two weeks.

"Good work." Lenny scribbled something on a clipboard and nodded at Darius. "You're gonna get back on that ice and get a medal, man!"

"A medal?" The burn in Darius's muscles was gradually fading. He lay back on the mat and shook his head. "It's a benefit program, Lenny. There are no medals involved."

Lenny rolled his eyes. "You don't watch enough sports movies, buddy. The big comebacks always start this way. You know—'Retired athlete returns to greatness while heroic coach propels him onward!'" He winked and gave a mock bow, the fluorescent lights glinting off his bald head like a halo. "'Heroic coach' being me, of course."

Darius laughed in spite of himself. It was impossible to not like Lenny. Now around forty, he'd been working at the center since his internship there as a college senior. He was nearly a head shorter than Darius, with a wiry frame and a disarming gap-toothed grin. But he was also tough, with the bludgeoning courage of an athlete, and it was not for nothing that he'd received all Dr. Patel's referrals for over a decade.

"Tell me seriously, Len." Darius looked around the therapy room— the familiar place where bodies were broken down and built back up. "Is it really going okay?"

"Absolutely." The confidence in Lenny's voice was as solid as the weights themselves. "It's better than okay. It's fantastic. You're making good progress." He tipped his head to the side. "Heard any more from the girl who's supposed to perform with you?"

"Not yet." Addisyn's face floated into Darius's mind like a note of music. "But I'm sure she's going to come. She seemed really excited, just had to sort some stuff out."

"Good." Lenny dropped to the floor beside Darius. "Remind me how you know her."

Darius pulled himself to a sitting position on the mat. "She came to Whistler last February to cope with some—stuff that had happened to her. We got to know each other while she was here."

"That's nice." Lenny slid Darius a smirk.

Darius laughed. "What's with the look?"

"This girl pretty?"

His face flushed beneath his beard. "Well—yes." He cleared his throat. "She's pretty."

"Mmhmm." Lenny's smirk stretched wider.

"Stop it!" Darius swatted his friend on the arm. "We're just friends."

"Sure. Right." Lenny chuckled. "I guess that's why you look like a fool when I mention her."

Darius groaned and dropped his face into his hands. Lenny had known him too long. "Is it that obvious?"

"It's slapping me across the face." Lenny cocked his head. "How 'bout her? Does she feel the same way?"

The humor faded from the moment. Darius raised his head and sighed. "I haven't asked her." He spread his hands helplessly. "I don't know how."

"Gotcha." Lenny scratched his chin thoughtfully. "When are you planning to do that?"

"I—I don't know." The blasting air conditioner was making his sweaty clothes cold against his skin. "I mean—I can't think how to do it."

"You want my advice?"

"Yeah."

"I went through the same thing with Keisha." Lenny smiled slightly, staring at the wall opposite them as if watching the moment play out. "I was so intimidated by her. Here I was, some little punk kid right out of college, and she was this gorgeous chick. I just knew she was way above my level."

Addisyn's face, her voice, wrapped around Darius's thoughts. "I get that."

"But you know what? When I finally got up the guts, she'd been waiting for me to ask. Said she was in love with me." He shrugged and grinned. "And I'll never know why. But I'll always be thankful."

Darius considered that for a moment. "So you think—I should just ask."

"I do." Lenny raised his eyebrows. "Love requires risk."

"I don't want to hear that."

"Nobody does. But it's true." Lenny clapped his shoulder and stood. "I better be getting home. I think next week you can try the exercises without the brace. You're getting there now."

The distraction was welcome. Darius scrambled to his feet and reached for his bag. "Perfect. Whatever you say, boss."

"I say you're gonna get back on that ice." Lenny flashed his trademark grin. "Enough for tonight. Get on home and get some rest!"

"Thanks, Lenny." Darius shrugged his jacket on over his workout clothes. Funny—even though the exercises felt as if they were ripping him apart at times, he could slowly feel the tightness easing, the inflammation lessening, his body returning to health.

"Should've done this sooner, man." Lenny shook his head as they walked to the exit. "I would've helped you whenever you said the word. Especially since you're the greatest figure skater ever."

Darius smiled and shook his head. "Now I bet you tell all your clients that.

"Not all of them. Just the ones who are skaters." Lenny winked and Darius laughed out loud. "Seriously, though. Ninety percent of it is up here." He tapped his forehead knowingly. "Have faith, and you're well on your way."

They were through the gates now. The evening was surprisingly cold, but a million stars pierced the darkness, the seemingly random lights still forming an intricate pattern above the mountains. *Have faith.*

"Yeah...for sure." Darius's words were a cloud around his mouth. He was starting to shiver, the cold soaking through his nylon jacket. "Well...tomorrow."

"Sure, see you then!" Lenny waved and pulled up the hood of his coat as he turned away.

Darius jogged to the car and climbed in. He turned the key and rubbed his hands together, waiting for the welcome warmth to puff from the heat vents. Taking a moment to fasten his seatbelt, he watched in the rearview mirror as Lenny's little sedan zoomed away.

Have faith. He hadn't. He'd believed that everything good about him, everything that made him Darius Payne, had bled away on that ice. He'd spent years blaming himself for his mistakes, burying himself in regret. Until God reached out—and faith brought him back to life. In large measure due to Addisyn.

This girl pretty?

Again, his eyes found the photo on the dash. Addisyn gazed back at him—perfect features, flowing brown hair, eyes bright with an incandescent joy. But no photo could truly capture her kind of beauty— the ethereal magic that hovered around her, as if she danced through life to a song only she could hear.

Maybe Lenny was right. Maybe Addisyn felt about him the way he felt about her. And then when the moment came…

He turned up the heater and drove off into the dusk of the mountain night, the photo fluttering in the warmth.

△△　△△　△△

JUST AFTER TEN o'clock on Sunday morning, and she was well on her way.

Addisyn flexed her fingers on the steering wheel and glanced at her phone, propped against the dashboard. The little blue triangle on the GPS map was still slicing forward. She'd followed its guidance all the way—Highway 36 to Lyons, then Highway 66 east toward I-25. She'd just come through Longmont, already thirty miles from Estes Park.

In no time, she'd be in Denver—and on the ice.

This was the complicated part, though—the junction with the interstate. The extra lanes and cloverleaves ahead made the junction resemble a tangled knot of asphalt. Addisyn bit her lip and concentrated on the merging traffic. It had been a long time since she'd driven on any roads this hectic.

She checked the side mirror and pulled into the artery of cars. There. She'd done it. Not that hard after all. Now she could flip on cruise control for the straight shot to Denver.

Had Avery driven this way to La Junta? If so, had the traffic made her nervous too?

So far, her guilt over this trip had ridden in the backseat. But at the thought of Avery, it reached forward and tapped her on the shoulder. She sighed. All day Friday, after saying goodbye to Avery in the morning, she'd played tug-of-war with her conscience. What if Avery got lost? Or needed Addisyn's help at the expo? Or what if her clunky old truck broke down? It wasn't safe for her sister to travel such a distance by herself. Especially when she would undoubtedly let her phone go dead.

The empty evening in the house hadn't helped. Addisyn had switched on all the lights, double-checked the locks, and turned up the radio. But the house that welcomed Avery didn't extend her the same courtesy. Underneath the music, an ominous silence had buzzed through the rooms. Even Mercy had seemed restless.

By the time Addisyn had finished off a frozen dinner while watching the shadows pooling beneath the trees, she'd been toying with the idea of just loading her car, dropping Mercy with Chayton and Skyla, and following Avery to La Junta—wherever that was. She'd grabbed her phone. It had taken four rings for Avery to answer. "Addisyn?"

"Hey, A." Addisyn had absently rubbed Mercy's ears. "I was just calling to see how everything was."

There had been a lot of background noise. "Fine. Just fine." Avery's voice had sounded rushed. "Look, Addisyn, can I call you back? I've got to get this stuff packed up."

That was it? Addisyn had bitten her lip. "Sure. Okay." She had started to ask if she could drive down, but a dead silence filled the line. Her sister had already hung up.

An eighteen-wheeler barreled past in the fast lane, and Addisyn gripped the wheel. The traffic was making her uncomfortable. Or maybe the memories.

That conversation on Friday had been echoed on Saturday. Again,

Avery had been rushed, distracted, but insistently fine. She had everything under control. As usual. And obviously she was busy. Far too busy to talk to Addisyn.

So there. Addisyn dared her guilt to defy her logic. *See? I tried. She's fine without me.*

And her guilt must have conceded. Because a Tetris game of skyscrapers was rising before her, and a far more pleasant emotion was now riding shotgun. Excitement.

An endless cycle of planes wheeled overhead like a carousel in the clouds, going and coming from DIA—the same airport she and Avery had flown into when she'd first come to Estes Park. But then it had been around midnight. The night had been too dark and Addisyn had been too tired for her to see much.

Now she looked around with wide eyes. The land here was much flatter than Estes Park, the mountains reduced to a hazy border on the horizon. And the city itself was far bigger than she'd anticipated. Sleek skyscrapers stacked themselves like sentinels on either side of broad four-lane streets.

It took half an hour, an unexpected detour around construction, and more than a few wrong turns, but finally Addisyn saw the rink—an impressive bowl-shaped structure of glass and metal. The sun glinted off the glass dome as she pulled into an adjacent parking lot and stepped out of the car.

A brisk wind whipped at the U.S. and Colorado flags in front of the door. A breezeway arched from the rink to a slender skyscraper—the Denver agency, where Brian had sometimes come.

For a moment, déjà vu tilted the asphalt under her feet. She was standing in her own shadow steps. She'd been here with Brian, and she'd trained on that ice, and she'd walked out of that building by his side. Talking about her next competition or heading to the rink to train or dreaming of a romantic evening with the man she'd mistaken for the love of her life.

Maybe Avery was right about skating. After all, the fact was that without the ice, she never would have met Brian. She never would have been drawn into his whirlpool. And she never would have been cut off from her sister for three years.

The flags popped in a fresh gust of wind, and she shook her head. This was ridiculous. She was just on edge—nerves jittery from the trip and the excitement and the guilt and the secret. She had nothing to worry about. Brian was in New York—along with the rest of her past. There was no need to let her memories tug her back to that dark place.

She squared her shoulders and marched purposefully across the parking lot to the door. A security guard stopped her just inside. "Credentials, miss?"

"Yes, sir." She handed him her U.S. Figure Skating card and kept her chin up. She was still technically a member, after all. She had a right to be here.

He glanced at the card and handed it back. "Have a good day."

That was it? "You too." She hoisted the bag she carried and marched down the hallway. Odd, how even now she remembered the layout of the rink. She'd worn her exercise clothes during the drive, so she bypassed the changing rooms and headed straight for the ice.

When she opened the door, a wave of memories billowed out. The fluorescent lighting, the squeak of skate blades from the other athletes, even the gentle swoosh of the air conditioner—yes, this was her world.

A ghost sat in every empty seat. She crossed to the ice and gripped the railing. It was on ice just like this that she'd taken all the pain from her terrifying childhood and transmuted it into passion. It was on ice just like this that she'd smiled and bowed at the end of each successful competition while applause rose to the ceiling and flowers showered the rink. It was on ice just like this that she'd lived out what had always been her greatest dream.

But it was also on ice just like this that she'd watched that dream dissolve. That she'd traded her convictions for convenience. That she'd met Brian, tumbled into the heady infatuation she'd thought was love, listened to him tell her—

Her breathing was loud, almost frantic, in the quiet space. What was wrong with her? "Come on." She hissed the words at herself. "You drove an hour and a half to be here. Get on with it."

Lacing up her skates was still automatic. Addisyn snapped the guards off the blades, and then with a final deep breath, she was on the ice.

Her first glide, and an instantaneous release—as if she'd relaxed fists she hadn't known were clenched. After six weeks of struggling desperately to reinvent herself, of cramming herself into her sister's world—here she was, effortlessly at home on the ice. As if she'd found just the key to unlock every door. She skimmed over the smooth surface.

Finally, a place that was frictionless.

She did simple crossovers for a few minutes, just to settle her nerves. Then she turned to more advanced moves—Lutz, Axel, combination spin. Every step still felt as familiar as her own name. Her movements were as smooth, her confidence as strong, as the last time she was on the ice. Except this was far better, because then she'd been a pawn in Brian's power game. Now she was on her own—and free.

It wasn't until she felt the wind on her cheeks that she realized she was crying. She swiped her sleeve across her face with a laugh that was half sob. Never mind the reservations she'd had. Never mind the odd hesitancy that had pulled her back. Never mind the lingering voices of her past. This was, without a doubt, where she was meant to be.

She'd been right to come to Denver. The decision was easy now. She'd wait until Avery got home, and then she'd tell her everything.

And next, she'd call Darius. Because now she knew what to say to him. Only one word.

Yes.

CHAPTER 6

"Thank you for this opportunity, Mr. Felding." The dark-haired skater smiled hopefully at Brian as she stuffed her skates into her bag and zipped up her jacket. "I'm glad I was able to audition for you."

"Absolutely. My pleasure." Her audition had been the weakest one of the bunch. Brian tipped his clipboard up so she couldn't see him scratching off her name.

"So, uh—will I get a call, or—"

"If the agency approves your audition, you'll receive a phone call from our HR department." His standard response. No way would this girl be getting that call, but he wasn't about to tell her that and then have her get all weepy on him. He opened the rink door and nodded to her. "Hope things go well for you."

Her shoulders sagged slightly. Maybe she'd read the message in his face after all. "Thank you." She shouldered her bag and walked out without looking back.

Brian let the door fall shut behind her and flopped into his chair. What a joke she'd been. Every turn was under-rotated, and the height on her jumps was absolutely pitiful.

He glanced at his clipboard. Fifteen names. Eleven scratched off. Four still to go.

Well, maybe the next one would be the ticket. He fumbled through his files until he found the paperwork on his next prospect. Anna Zinkas. Eighteen—pretty—placed high in Regional Championships last year, Southwestern division. Free skate score of—he ran his finger down the page—89.70. Hmm. Not that great. Even at the beginning of her career, Addisyn had never scored below 94-something.

Frustration boiled over, and he slammed the file down. That was the problem, wasn't it? None of these girls could begin to compare to Addisyn. They were still wobbling through simple Salchows, but from the moment she'd started working with him, Addisyn had possessed an innate grace that guided her through even the most challenging moves. And she'd been fiercely, furiously competitive—driven by a laser-like focus to turn farther, jump higher, be brighter than every opponent. But most of all, she'd skated with a passion larger than life. She held out her heart in each performance until everyone in the audience believed in her.

Fury sizzled all over him. This trip had been a waste of time. He could comb through the ranks of girls like Anna Zinkas. He could hand-select the best. He could train them in New York and take them to championships. But he would never be able to find a replica for Addisyn's one-in-a-million combination of talent and passion. And where did that leave him? A liability to Barmilli? A laughingstock among his colleagues?

No. He wouldn't accept that. He set his jaw and crammed the files into his briefcase. There were plenty of pretty faces out there. Plenty of starry-eyed hopefuls. He might not be able to duplicate Addisyn, but that didn't mean he wouldn't find another golden girl.

He glanced at his watch. He still had an hour before Anna Zinkas's audition. Maybe he should stop in and check the practice rinks. You never knew when an unknown was waiting to be discovered. After all, he'd found Addisyn that way—she'd been skating for fun on a public rink, completely unconscious of her own talent.

He forced the memory aside and headed for the first of the three practice rinks. Cracking the door open, he peeked inside. Nothing here except some pairs skaters practicing crossovers while a coach watched.

The second rink was full of skaters, but no one remarkable. The third rink was empty, ice gleaming under the overhead lights. Brian glanced around and shook his head. Why would nothing go right for him lately?

Well, he might as well grab some lunch. He was just reaching for the door handle when a movement caught his eye. The rink wasn't deserted after all. A girl was sitting on the front row of bleachers, unlacing a pair of skates.

Brian's fingers tightened over the door handle. It looked like—

No. It wouldn't be. It couldn't be. It was just a weird mind trick because he'd been thinking about her so much. But still—

He took a step closer, but the girl didn't look his way. Probably she hadn't even heard him come in. She sat up and reached for a bag next to her.

Her face clanged in his mind like a warning bell. Addisyn Miles was not in retirement. Instead, she was in an ice rink.

Sitting right in front of him.

ADDISYN TUGGED HER boot on, stomping her heel lightly on the floor. Her skates were already in her bag. Now that she'd made her decision, it all seemed possible. Avery would be home tomorrow, and she'd tell her everything immediately. Then she'd call Darius and—

A shadow flicked over her just as a voice cut through her thoughts.

"Well, imagine seeing you here."

No. Her heart tumbled into a free fall, and she jerked her head up.

There he was. Brian Felding, straight from her nightmares.

"Come on, Addisyn." Every detail was still just as she remembered. The expensive haircut, the gold Rolex, and the signature sneer. "You could at least say hi."

"Brian." She hissed his name and scrambled to her feet, but her back was to the bleachers, and he stood between her and the door. "What are you doing here?"

"Well, I should ask you the same thing." He raised his eyebrows. "I figured you were back in Whistler, actually."

A wave of nausea rocked her, but she lifted her chin and forced herself to meet his gaze. "So what, are you stalking me or something?"

"Of course not." He rolled his eyes, even though the possibility was far from ridiculous. "I'm here this weekend for client auditions."

He was only here for a weekend, and still their paths had coincided. Of course. She glanced around the rink, but the other athletes who'd been practicing were gone. The place was deserted.

"Funny thing about the auditions." Brian casually crossed his arms. "I've gone through eleven prospects so far. Eleven, Addisyn. The top stars from all over the Southwestern Region. And you know something?"

Her reply was unwilling. "What?"

"Not one of them has your talent." His jaw tightened ominously. "You had the world by the tail, Addisyn Miles. I'll never understand why you threw it all away."

She bit her lip, sealing in all she wanted to say. She wouldn't allow him to drag her to his level. Not this time.

"What are you doing these days, anyway?" He adjusted his watch. "Still living out of a hotel?"

"Not on your life. I'm staying with Avery." The instant the words escaped, she wanted to yank them out of the air. He'd transform any information to ammunition. She couldn't allow anger to make her careless.

Shock slipped past his facade. "With—no way." His laugh wasn't the slightest bit funny. "So Avery took a risk on you again, huh?"

"She did." Her sister had shown her grace and love. Neither of which Brian knew anything about.

"Crazy." He raised his eyebrows. "And you two get along? Even with the whole—" he waved his hand vaguely—"personality clash?"

"We get along great." The tension between them was only surface. And anyway, he didn't deserve to know about it.

"Interesting." He looked around the rink. "So—then you're living in that little hick town? Park something, right?"

Whatever cat-and-mouse game he was playing, she was getting tired of it. "Brian, I need to leave."

"Not yet." His smile didn't remotely reach his eyes. "See, I have a problem."

"What's the problem?" Addisyn's voice sounded strange to her. She tightened her grip on the strap of her bag.

"You." His eyes narrowed slightly. "You're the problem, Addisyn Miles."

Her heart was hammering double-time, but she worked to keep her face straight. "I don't see how. What I do doesn't concern you anymore."

"Well, and that's where the problem comes in. Because unfortunately, what you do still concerns me very much. You see, Barmilli isn't happy you left the agency."

Brian's boss? What did that have to do with her? "So?"

"So he's going to be very unhappy when he finds out you are skating for another agency."

Another agency? The conversation was crazy. None of this added up. "Brian. You're not making sense."

"Well, I'll make it plain for you." He took a step toward her. She couldn't back up with the bleachers behind her. "You see, I told him that you were in retirement. But now—I find you here. Which means you're obviously training again. For some other agency."

Realization crashed over her like a looming tidal wave. "Brian, I'm not training. I'm in retirement." Part of her wanted to keep him sweating, but escape was more urgent than revenge. "I just came here to—to practice."

"Practice?" His voice was dangerously low. "For what?"

"Just to practice, Brian!" No way was she telling him about Whistler. It wasn't a competitive event anyway. "I was just here to have fun."

"Like heck you were." The words ground between his teeth, and he took another step forward. He was too close now, way too close. "I know you, Addisyn. You can't stay away from the ice." His tone made it sound like an addiction.

"Brian, it's the truth. I just came down here to have fun practicing. I don't have a coach or an agency or anything."

"I don't believe you." His face flushed, the anger rising from his collar. The vein in his neck was beginning to throb.

"And I don't care!" Her own rage was swimming in her soul. Why did she even have to explain herself to this jerk? "You made my life a nightmare, Brian! Isn't that enough for you? Why are you on my case?"

"Because you're lying to me. If you weren't training, you wouldn't be here. Don't think I'm stupid, Addisyn."

He reached toward her, but she sidestepped. "Don't touch me!"

He took a step back and rubbed his hand over his face, a gesture she recognized. It meant he was fighting for control. When he spoke again, his tone was more normal. "Okay. Think about this, Addisyn. You skipped out on the agency, you're undermining my career, and now you're lying to me and making me look stupid in front of my boss." The anger was overpowering him again. She could see it. "Tell me. Who are you with?"

"Nobody! I don't know what it would take to convince you!" Her fists were clenched, fingernails digging into her sweaty palms. "I swear, I only came to practice!"

He studied her for a moment, then sighed. "Fine. Don't tell me, then." His breathing was still ragged. He yanked his sleeves down and glared at her. "But I *will* find out what agency you're with. And then you'll regret it."

"Brian." Addisyn could hardly see through her hatred. "Are you threatening me?"

"Just reminding you." His voice was as cold and sharp as the ice itself. "I have friends, Addisyn. Lots of friends at lots of agencies. And they'd all be very interested to hear about your—mistakes."

"*My* mistakes?" Her stomach wrenched. "My mistake was trusting you!"

"Not from my point of view." Brian's smirk was like salt in a paper cut. "I mean, you caved under pressure at Regionals. Walked out of your Team Unlimited audition. And, of course, even tried to seduce me. Your coach." He clicked his tongue mockingly. "A clear ethical violation."

She would throw up now. She was sure of it. Humiliation and regret were strangling her. "You're joking."

"Of course not." He folded his arms. "Simple, Addisyn. If you won't skate for me, you won't skate for anyone. So if I were you, I'd keep hiding under my sister's shadow and living in Hicksville. But I would not come back to the ice. Got it?"

A longing to make him hurt wrenched at her. If only she could wound him the way he'd wounded her. But as always, he held all the power. Even now, a thousand miles away from who she'd been, he could still inject his venom into her life.

"Go on." He flicked his hand at her, as if shooing away a gnat. "Get out, Addisyn."

She shouldered her bag and brushed past him. But she didn't start running until she was out of his sight.

△△　△△　△△

THE PAIN HAD been there ever since she left the mountains.

Avery pressed her fingertips into her temples. She'd expected to enjoy an expo celebrating the outdoors, but she'd spent every moment so far with a throbbing headache. The whole convention center was one buzzing beehive—crushing crowds and unceasing noise. Like a hailstorm on her heart.

At one time, she'd kept a bottle of Tylenol in her bag. She pulled the brown crossbody onto her lap and stirred the contents. A dog-eared hiking map…a camo flashlight…her pocket New Testament…a squashed package of that loathsomely artificial berry blast gum that Addisyn loved for some reason. But nothing that might help her headache.

She rotated her neck slightly, trying to dislodge the knot of tension between her shoulders, and propped her elbows on one of the few empty spaces on the table. She'd just have to push through. She still had four hours until the expo closed for the day. And then it would take at least another hour to pack up all the merchandise and drag everything back to the hotel.

A child shrieked at the next table over, and Avery flinched. The people and noise were increasing moment by moment, the walls of the convention center beginning to tilt toward her. Avery gripped the edge of the table and closed her eyes, blocking the barrage. *Relax. Deep breathing.* She hadn't known the place would be so crowded when she agreed to this. Of course, even if she'd realized, she would have been far too embarrassed to confess to Laz that big, busy places always rubbed her soul raw. Probably because of all the years she'd spent in the whirlwind of New York City.

This would have been much easier if Addisyn had come along. Avery fought again to quell her irritation. It was unjustified, after all—Addisyn did have to work. And anyway, things were different now. She couldn't expect her sister to shadow her everywhere as she'd done when they were younger. They were both adults. Feeling abandoned was simply ridiculous.

91

A weary-looking man and woman wandered up to the table. Avery donned the shield of her professional smile. "Hi there."

The man nodded. "Hi." The woman only held up her hand in a limp greeting and leaned on the stroller she was pushing. A little boy in an orange T-shirt was sleeping soundly in the stroller. Avery knew exactly how he felt.

"How much are these hats?" The man examined one of the ball caps with the embroidered Live Bigger logo.

"Nineteen ninety-nine plus tax." After two days, Avery didn't even have to consult the price list anymore.

The man frowned and set the hat down, then turned toward his wife. "Everything is so expensive here." His mumble was loud enough that she suspected he wanted her to overhear. Without saying goodbye, the couple trudged away.

Avery sighed and slumped deeper into the chair. Laz's prices were competitive, but still, the reaction was a common one. So far, she wasn't sure she'd even sold enough merchandise to justify the trip. Didn't people understand that small businesses had bigger overhead? Especially when they were selling quality products?

Her head throbbed even worse at the thought of having to give Laz a gloomy report. He'd said the booth normally did well. What was she doing wrong? Could she offer discounts? Arrange the merchandise differently? Maybe she could—

Danger.

The knowing hit hard, an urgency that twisted her soul. She lurched upright in her chair, frantically scanning the crowds.

Danger.

No. Not here. Not today. Her heart skipped staccato, and she pressed her palms against the table. *El Shaddai…what's going on?*

No answer came, but the crackling insistence of the knowing gripped her harder.

El Shaddai…show me…

One heartbeat, two, and then there was Addisyn's voice. Not in the swirling crowds of the expo, but in the hallways of her spirit. Calling to her…frantic…frightened…

"El Shaddai. Not Addisyn."

The knowings were baffling, but they were uncannily accurate. Without another thought, Avery grabbed her cell phone and caught the eye of the woman at the next booth. "Can you watch my table for me, please? I need a moment." She barely waited for the woman to nod before she hurried to the hallway just outside the big doors. The noise was less here. She leaned against the wall and jabbed Addisyn's number.

One ring. Two rings. Three rings. *Come on…come on!* Four rings, and a smug metallic voice informed her that Addisyn hadn't set up her voicemail.

Typical. Avery tightened her jaw and pulled up a blank text, her thumbs racing over the keyboard. *Addisyn, are you okay? Need to talk to you. Call me.*

She waited until the count of twenty, then tried to call again. And then one more time. Nothing.

The fear was making her head pound more insistently, her breath coming hard. She tucked her phone into her pocket and scraped her sweaty palms against her pants. She had to calm down, had to wait and listen for El Shaddai. Praying under her breath, she went into the restroom and splashed some cool water on her face, trying to pull herself from the panic.

As she came out of the restroom and tossed her wad of paper towels into a trashcan, her phone rang. She ripped it out of her pocket to see her sister's face on the screen. She couldn't swipe to answer fast enough. "Addisyn, what in the world? I called you three times."

"I'm sorry. I wasn't looking at my phone." Addisyn's tone was strange, tightened somehow. But maybe it was just the cell connection. "Is something wrong?"

"You tell me." The fear was still fraying the edge of her heart. "What are you doing?"

"I—what?" Now Addisyn sounded caught off guard. "Avery, what do you mean? What's going on?"

She was scaring Addisyn. "Okay. I'm sorry." Avery leaned against the wall, reaching for relief. "It was—it was a knowing, Ads. I was at the expo—and I just—I just felt it. This—urgency about you. And so I tried to call, and then when you didn't answer, I was worried."

"Oh." The flat syllable told Avery exactly how Addisyn still felt about the knowings. A few awkward moments stretched before Addisyn spoke again. "Well—I'm okay."

She sounded far from okay. Avery narrowed her eyes. "Addisyn, are you upset? What's going on?"

"Nothing."

Nothing? Did her sister expect she would believe that? The fear was sharpening to frustration. "Addisyn, I can tell something is wrong, okay? So why don't you just tell me—"

"Avery, I told you. I'm fine." Addisyn's words were still level, but a hardness was creeping into her tone.

She couldn't be fine. Not according to the knowing. "So where are you right now?"

"I'm, um—I'm in town."

In town? "Why? You don't have work today."

"I just am, okay?" Irritation yanked at Addisyn's words.

What? Avery blinked. Addisyn hadn't been that sharp with her since—well, since before. "Hey. What kind of answer is that?"

"What I said. I'm just in town." Every syllable dripped with defensiveness.

"But *why* are you in town?" What was Addisyn doing, just joyriding around Estes on her day off? "Look, Addisyn, I thought you would be at home today. Now if you're going to be somewhere unexpected, I need to know."

"Why?" Addisyn hurled the word with all the drama of her teenage rebellion. "So I can get a hall pass from you first?"

"Of course not! I just need to make sure you're okay."

"I *am* okay."

Avery's patience had already been frayed, and this conversation was unraveling the loose ends. "Well, since you wouldn't answer your phone, I had no way of knowing that, did I?"

"I had my phone with me. I just—" Addisyn's voice broke for a moment. Cell service again? "I was in the middle of something. I checked it after—when I got back in the car. And then I called you right away."

"Yes, but we've talked about this, Addisyn. I've told you: I have to be able to get in touch with you." Had they stumbled into a replay of their teenage years?

"So what, you just keep tabs on me all the time?" Addisyn's words were tumbling over each other the way they always did when she was mad. "Because I can't take care of myself without my big sister hovering?"

Look at your track record. "Just answer your phone, okay?"

"Right! Like you always do?"

"Addisyn! That's not fair." Frustration grabbed at her voice, but she fought it back. "Look, try to calm down and—"

"You're telling *me* to calm down?" Addisyn made a sound of disbelief. "*You* started this. Calling out of the blue to—to interrogate me."

The headache might split her skull any second. "Addisyn, I need to know if—"

"Avery, stop." Now the anger was mixed with desperation. "You're doing your bossy-big-sister thing again."

How had this conversation gotten so out of control? Avery put one hand over her forehead and squeezed her eyes shut. This was getting them nowhere. But apparently Addisyn was all right. And that was the main thing, anyway.

"All right." She took a steadying breath. "Listen, I have to get back to the expo. Just go on home now."

"Fine." The word was chopped short. "I was getting ready to head that way anyway."

"And text me when you—"

The line clicked, then buzzed. They'd lost their connection.

Avery's hands were shaking. She slid her phone back into her pocket and blindly threaded her way through the crowds, back to the booth.

She'd only wanted to make sure Addisyn was okay. Instead, she'd somehow sparked a fuse. Frustration fought to the top of her emotions. Didn't Addisyn understand that it was important for Avery to be able to keep up with her whereabouts? What if something happened? But no, in Addisyn's mind, she was bulletproof. That inflated confidence had always been her undoing. And she would forever interpret Avery's concern as control.

The woman at the next table seemed absorbed in her own customers, but thankfully the Live Bigger table appeared undisturbed. Avery huddled on the uncomfortable metal folding chair and closed her eyes, trying to decode the last few minutes. If Addisyn was fine, why had there been something wrong in her voice? And what about the knowing? But it wasn't possible that Addisyn was lying to her, was it?

Was it?

Avery, stop. You're doing your bossy-big-sister thing...

Her phone rang again. Of course it wouldn't be Addisyn, calling back to apologize, but still her irrational hopes crumpled when she saw Laz's name. "Hello?"

"Hey there, Miz Avery. How's the expo goin'?"

"Um...not great. There's not been a lot of interest, actually." She braced for his blame. He'd only been gone four days, and she was already failing.

"That happens sometimes." His voice was still unconcerned. "Some years folks are tighter with their wallets. I wouldn't worry."

"But—I want this to go well—"

"Avery, girl." His chuckle filled the line. "The world don't rest on yer shoulders. Jes' quit frettin'."

"Okay." If only it were that easy.

"So is worryin' over our profits why you sound like you've been wrung out and left to dry?"

Laz's colorful description was in fact exactly how Avery felt. "Well— Addisyn and I just had a—an argument over the phone. I—I was worried about her, and I was asking her where she was, and she got mad that I was asking, and I got mad that she was mad, and..." She wouldn't mention the knowing. "I just wanted to check on her. Why would she get mad?"

"Mebbe she thinks you don't trust her." Laz cleared his throat. "Do you?"

"I—well—" Honesty won over wishfulness. "I don't know."

"You don't know?"

"I believe that she wants to do the right thing." Each word was slow, rising from a reality she hadn't examined until now. "But—I trusted her before. And while I was busy trusting her, she was out with Brian." She almost choked on the bitterness of the memory. "Lying through her teeth when I questioned her. Turning her back on me and everything I'd tried to teach her."

"That's history, girl."

"History repeats itself."

"That what you believe?" Laz's tone was still kind, but undeniably firm. "Then mebbe it's the Good Lord you don't trust, 'stead of yer sister. Seems to me we already talked 'bout not holdin' wild things too tight."

So even Laz wasn't going to take her side? "There's a difference." Defensiveness peered through her words.

"Not much of one. But all right." He sighed. "Jes' hear this one thing. Sometimes history repeats itself 'cause yer sittin' 'round waitin' on it to do jes' that."

The words hit heavy, sinking deep into the soil of her heart. Suddenly Avery was so tired, so weary of the worry and the uncertainty and the uneven ground between her and her sister. She swallowed hard and stared at the ridge of mountains on Laz's logo. If only she were there now, in the clarity of the High Peaks, where all the fog in her mind would fade.

"You hear me, Avery girl?"

"Yes." She traced the mountains' outline with one finger. "I'm listening."

"All right. Be sure you do." He cleared his throat. "Now, let's talk 'bout this expo."

Avery tried to focus through the rest of the conversation, but when Laz finally said goodbye, she hung her head. He was right. She had done wrong. Her words had been sharp, her own heart clouded by an unfounded distrust.

El Shaddai…forgive me. The prayer released the clenching tension in her spirit, and she took her first deep breath. *Help Ads forgive me too. I did not do well.*

She reached for her phone but paused. She'd give Addisyn some space. She didn't want her sister interpreting an apology as a pretext to check on her again. But she'd be back home tomorrow afternoon, and then she'd make things right in person.

She glanced at the mountain logo once more, and a peace settled into her soul. She'd had a bad moment, that was all. She'd been wrestling with too much—the stress of the expo and the exhaustion from traveling and the lingering hurt that Addisyn hadn't come with her.

But tomorrow she'd be back in Estes Park with her sister. And nothing like this would ever happen again.

CHAPTER 7

The day was fading, the sun just sliding off the edge of the mountains. Every peak poured a pool of shadow toward the cabin. Leaning against the window, Addisyn glanced at the clock again. 6:13. Her sister should be home any minute now.

And then maybe the lengthening shadows would stop reaching for her.

Her first step was to make things right with Avery. Her sister had called her only twice since the Denver incident yesterday—once last night and once this afternoon to report that she was leaving for Estes. Both calls had been perfunctory; together they hadn't taken five minutes. No doubt Avery was still mad.

Addisyn's annoyance, on the other hand, had cooled before she'd even exited the interstate. Sure, Avery had been bossy, but Addisyn should have never lashed out the way she had. All she'd accomplished was to make herself look irresponsible and immature—just the way Avery already perceived her.

She ran her finger over the slick glass. When Avery arrived home, she'd be able to apologize. But she wouldn't be able to divulge the reason behind her reaction. It had been Brian, of course. Her emotions had been completely unbalanced, and the whiplash of the encounter had directed itself at Avery. She simply hadn't known how to process all the pain that seeing Brian had awakened.

A day later, she still didn't.

Headlights sliced around the curve, and there was the green truck at the gate. Addisyn darted for her jacket, Mercy underfoot as she rushed out the door. She winced at the way the truck protested when her sister put it in park. With her own vehicle making noises like that, why was Avery so fixated on the supposed clicking in Addisyn's car?

"Hey." Avery stepped out of the truck with a smile shadowed by uncertainty.

"You're back." Addisyn scuffed a foot across the gravel. Inside her pockets, her fingers fisted, then relaxed.

"Yeah." Avery glanced down and laughed softly as Mercy's wagging tail swished against her legs. "Hey, Mercy."

"She missed you." Addisyn shrugged awkwardly. "So did I."

The tightness eased from Avery's expression. "I know. I missed you too." She crossed the space between them and pulled Addisyn into a hug.

Who but Avery would be gracious enough to make the first move back toward together? Addisyn squeezed her sister gratefully and gestured at the cabin, where her peace offering waited. "I got dinner ready. I figured you would be hungry."

Avery stepped back, her eyebrows rising. "I am. To the point of hallucination, apparently, since I just heard you say that you prepared food."

Relief lifted the tension. "Oh, very funny. I didn't say I cooked it." If Avery was willing to joke, maybe she wasn't as mad as Addisyn had feared. "I ordered takeout. I figured you might want food you could actually eat."

Avery laughed. "Great. I'm starved." She glanced around. "Hey, let's do something fun. Let's eat out here."

"Out here?"

"Yeah. I'll start a fire in the fire pit. We haven't used it since you've been here." Avery grinned. "We might hear the elk bugling too."

"Okay." Eating outside wasn't normally Addisyn's idea of fun, but this did sound sort of neat. "I'll grab the food while you start the fire."

Ten minutes later, flames were snapping in the stone pit on Avery's deck. Relaxed in a lawn chair, Addisyn opened the Styrofoam takeout containers and listened to Avery's account of the expo.

"There were vendors from all over the Four Corners area. Colorado, New Mexico, Arizona, Utah. There was even one business from Nevada."

Avery scooted her chair closer to the fire. "There were so many people."

Addisyn winced at the image of her shy, sensitive sister in the middle of all the chaos. "I know you hate crowds."

"I do. It wasn't fun. And I got really tired after the first day."

It had been a hard weekend for them both, in totally different ways. Addisyn glanced toward the west. The sun was a faint stain by now, the dusk beginning to spin cobwebs under the trees. An elk bugled somewhere down the hillside.

"I'm so glad to be back home." Avery's smile curved around her words.

"I'm sure you are." All Avery had ever wanted was what she had now—the mountains, the trees, the sky. The cabin and the hiking and the sunsets.

And Addisyn. Always Addisyn. Even when she was at her worst.

"See the stars?" Avery pointed over their heads. "There's the Big Dipper. And Draco. He's the dragon, you know."

"The dragon." Addisyn blinked away Brian's face.

"Yeah. Oh, and there's Aquila. The eagle." The fire splashed light over Avery's face. "In mythology, he was the bird of the gods. He held thunder in his feet."

"Really?" Addisyn tipped her neck back. Avery had always loved the stories scribbled across the sky. "Where is he?"

"Right where those two bare branches are, see? Above that mountain with the crooked top. Those three really bright stars, and then that triangle below them."

The stars swirled randomly to her. Why could Avery always read them with ease?

"So…about yesterday." Avery's expression was unreadable in the flickering light.

The words punched a hole in the fragile peace of the night. Addisyn's stomach tightened. "Yesterday."

"Yeah." Avery leaned forward, her eyes serious. "I want to apologize, Addisyn. The way I jumped on you over the phone—that wasn't okay."

Avery was apologizing to her? "Oh, Avery—it was really my fault— I was in a mood."

"And I was tired and worried and stressed. But that's no excuse." Avery shook her head. "I didn't mean to react that way, and I won't do it again."

"It's—it's okay."

"And—" Avery cleared her throat. "I feel really bad that I acted as if I didn't trust you. Asking where you were, and everything."

"Oh…" Sweat prickled across her shoulders. She scraped her chair a few inches away from the fire.

"It was—well, I realize you don't want to hear this, but it was the knowing." Avery's brow creased slightly. "I just don't understand. It was a strong feeling—I was sure you were in danger. And the knowings have never been wrong." She shrugged. "But I was awfully frazzled at the expo. Maybe I misinterpreted."

"Yeah. Maybe."

"I just—I just worry about you. I don't ever want to lose you again." Now Addisyn was sure she saw the shimmer of tears in Avery's eyes. "But…I do trust you. I want you to know that."

Guilt was back, watching her from the shadows. "Well—thank you."

"I'm glad that's settled." Avery stood and squeezed Addisyn's shoulder. "Now, do you want to roast some marshmallows? Make s'mores?"

Things were far from settled, but Addisyn forced a smile. "Sure."

"Great." Avery headed for the door. "Let me get the stuff. I'll be right back."

A quiet, empty and listening, wrapped itself around the deck. The last bit of light softened over the profile of the mountains—light battling uselessly against the encroaching night.

It was a strong feeling—I was sure you were in danger.

She didn't understand her sister's feelings or knowings or whatever she called them. But there was no doubt that whatever Avery had sensed yesterday had been spot-on.

The fire snapped, and a burst of sparks whirled upward. Addisyn watched them disappear into the unreadable stars. When she'd first met Brian, he had held all the scorching strength of that blaze. He'd ripped through her world like a wildfire, and she'd been stupid enough to dance in the flames. Until she saw the blackened wasteland he left behind.

If you won't skate for me, you won't skate for anyone.

The threat still made her shudder. She'd shivered the whole time she'd driven home from Denver yesterday, pushing the speed limit with memories clinging to her car. She'd gone straight to the cabin, locked all the doors, and sobbed in the shower until the hot water ran out. But no running could keep Brian's face from throbbing in her mind. No washing could scrub away the dirt of the past.

"I'm back!" Avery flopped into her lawn chair. She skewered two marshmallows on a metal rod and handed it to Addisyn. "Ready to cook?"

"I am." Addisyn twirled the rod. The flames licked higher, ribbons shredding into the darkness.

"The fire is mesmerizing, isn't it?" Avery's voice was soft, her eyes focused on the gleaming bed of coals.

"Yeah." Fire always was.

Fire and ice. The two extremes of her life. If she wasn't burning hot, she was freezing cold. Would she ever find the balanced path her sister walked?

She should have never gone to Denver. Never set foot back in that world.

I know you, Addisyn. You can't stay away from the ice.

The darkness around her was intensifying, the fire narrowing to a single bright point. Addisyn took a deep breath, fighting down the fear. She was scared of Brian, yes. But mostly she was scared of who he had made her to be. And the only solution was to slam shut the door between her past and present. To be done with fire…and with ice.

"I think they're ready." Avery pointed at the marshmallows. They were blistered from the heat, skins cracked brown.

"Great." Addisyn held the rod toward Avery. A wisp of smoke spiraled upward from the marshmallows.

"They're hot." Avery captured the first marshmallow between two graham crackers with chocolate and handed the s'more to Addisyn. "Be careful. Don't get burned."

Addisyn swallowed. "I won't." Not this time.

Avery took a bite of her s'more. "Delicious. True campfire food." She grinned. "I'd tell you a ghost story, but then I think we'd both be up all night."

"Yeah." Addisyn's heart twisted. She definitely didn't need a ghost story.

Not when her own ghosts were never more than a heartbeat away.

△△ △△ △△

THE BIGGEST GAME of the preseason yet, and Darius couldn't wait.

"Ready?" He plopped onto his threadbare couch and grinned at the guys gathered in his living room.

Dexter high-fived him. "So ready, man. This is our year!"

"Vancouver Canucks take the Stanley Cup!" On the other side of the room, Lenny pumped his fist. "The Oilers will never know what hit 'em." He nodded at Josh, who was already ripping into a package of Oreos. "Kind of like our snacks if we don't hide some of them from the Cookie Monster over there."

Darius nudged Josh's leg with his toe. "He's getting his comfort food, Lenny. Bracing himself to watch the Canucks take his Oilers apart like a cheap watch."

"Are you kidding?" Josh rolled his eyes. A skinny farm kid who'd grown up near Calgary, he was the only Oilers fan in the group and unfazed by the other guys' ridicule. "Let me remind you *gentlemen* that the Oilers were first in the Pacific last year. And they've won both their preseason games so far."

"That's because they haven't played us yet." Dexter laughed. "That record is about to get dirtied a little."

Josh shook his head and popped another Oreo in his mouth. As soon as he could speak, he gestured at the TV. "That's okay. You guys can eat crow later."

The pregame commentary was in progress, but the banter in the room overpowered the analysis of the TV guys. Dexter reminded Josh that the Oilers' top forward was coming back from an injury, and Lenny commented unfavorably on the goalie's reflexes. Finally Josh shrugged. "Fine. Have it your way." He pulled a bill from his pocket and flipped it onto the coffee table. "Fifty bucks says the Oilers take home the win."

"You're crazy. But I'll take that bet." Dexter slapped his own fifty on the coffee table next to Josh's.

"Count me in too, but my wallet's in the car." Lenny raised his eyebrows. "Of course, that won't matter, since you'll be paying me."

"Darius?" Josh grinned in his direction.

Darius shook his head and laughed. "You guys play too high for me."

"Well, then." Josh tore into the second package of Oreos and glanced at the TV just as the NHL logo flashed forward amid cinematic music. "I'm looking forward to making a hundred bucks tonight. Let's watch some puck."

Late in the first period, Darius had to admit that Josh's prediction might not have been so far-fetched. The Oilers were playing surprisingly well, their forwards moving like a freight train, and holding a two-goal lead. Just as the Canucks finally set up a decent offensive drive, Darius felt his phone vibrating in his pocket. He pulled it out just far enough to see the name.

Addisyn Miles.

His heart leaped into his throat. *C'mon, Payne. Play it cool.* "Hey, I gotta take this." He waved his phone at the guys and scrambled off the couch before they could ask too many questions.

"Right now, man?" Dexter gestured at the TV. "Canucks are going into a power play."

Darius was momentarily uninterested in hockey and already halfway out his back door. "This call can't wait."

"Must be a girl." Josh smirked.

Darius let the door slam on Josh's words, pretending he hadn't heard. The night air was cold enough to suck his breath away, but it was far better to be a little chilly than to talk to Addisyn over the commotion of a hockey game while his buddies eavesdropped. He leaned on the porch railing and punched her number.

She answered on the first ring. "Darius?"

How was it that her voice always carried its own music? "Hey, girl." He watched his breath float away in the dim glow of the porch light. A bird gave a sleepy chirp from the pine tree next to his house. "Sorry I missed your call."

"No, it's okay." She hesitated. "Are you busy?"

"No." The answer came quickly. "Just watching a hockey game with my buddies." A sudden cheer vibrated through the walls. Vancouver must have scored.

"I can call back later—"

"No, no, it's fine." He'd rather talk to her than do anything else. But before he could scrape up the courage to tell her so, she spoke again.

"Well, I—" Her voice dipped with uncertainty. "I made a decision."

"You did?" His heart rate doubled. She'd be here soon. He could almost feel her in his arms. They would explore Whistler, and he would tell her—

"I'm not coming."

What? Darius pressed the phone tighter to his ear. "I'm sorry—what did you say?"

"I'm not coming." Her voice held an undertone of something like despair. "I can't do it."

No. No, no, no. She wasn't coming? Even after how excited she'd seemed? "But, Addisyn—"

"Darius, I'm sorry." Her voice sounded remote, detached, as if she were already backing away from the issue. "I just—I just can't."

Was this happening? Addisyn really wasn't coming after all? Darius rubbed a hand over his face and tried to hear his thoughts over the crash of his falling hopes. "What—what changed your mind? You seemed so sure the other day."

"I know. I just thought about it some more, and—well—my life is here now—and—"

"But I thought you missed skating." Darius fought to keep from sounding like a whiny child.

"I do." Addisyn's voice turned thick with longing.

Then why was she telling him no? Especially when she sounded as if the decision upset her as much as it did him?

"I'm sorry." Her sigh filled the phone. "Are you—are you mad at me?"

"Of course not." Confused, yes, but not mad. "Addisyn, I want to—"

"Darius, please." Her voice was trembling now. "Don't."

He was being a heel. This was her decision. He had no right to badger her. "I'm sorry." He waited for the confusion to clear from his voice. "I was—well, I was looking forward to skating with you."

"Me too." Soft sniffles told him she was crying. "Skating isn't my life anymore. I—I have to accept that."

Nothing about this made sense. "Addisyn, please talk to me. Is everything—"

"I have to go." She was pulling away, already turning the key in her own personal lock. "I've got, uh, some things to do."

"Addisyn—"

"I'm sorry, Darius." She sighed. "Bye."

The line clicked dead. Darius stared at his phone, then tucked it into his pocket and scrubbed his hands over his face. What on earth had happened?

Addisyn wasn't coming. All the hopes he'd held, all the plans he'd made—and she wasn't coming. Which could only mean one thing: his fears had been terribly true. She didn't feel for him the way he felt for her. He was her friend, nothing more. This refusal must be her way of letting him know that.

Another cheer rose from inside. He didn't feel like going back in, but he didn't want the guys to come looking for him either. As he shuffled through the doorway, Dexter jabbed his finger at the TV. "You missed it, man! We made the goal!" He pumped his fist and whooped. "Yes! Way to light the lamp!"

"Wow. Awesome." Darius forced the closest expression to a smile that he could muster.

Lenny must have seen the look on his face. As Josh and Dexter began ribbing each other, he slid next to Darius on the sofa. "Man, what's wrong? Was that Addisyn?"

"Shh." Darius gestured to the other guys. The only thing that could make this night worse was to be harassed by those two jokers. "Yes, that was her. She's not coming."

Lenny kept his voice low, but his shock was unmistakable. "Not coming?"

"Right." Darius stared past Lenny at the dark night outside the window and worked the muscles in his jaw. "She says her life is in Estes Park now."

Lenny bumped Darius's shoulder. "Man, I'm sorry. I know you wanted her here."

That was an understatement. "Yeah." He blinked to force the threatening tears away.

"That's too bad." Lenny shook his head. "I actually got online and watched some of her video, by the way."

"You did? What did you think?"

"I was impressed. Beyond impressed, actually. Her technique is stellar. And her style is very similar to yours. I could envision the two of you fitting really nicely together. Especially considering your existing—friendship."

Even Lenny realized what a perfect match this could have been. Darius shook his head. "I just don't understand why she won't come."

"Well—" Lenny glanced at the other guys, but they were engrossed in the game. "It's her decision."

"Yeah, but—I mean, it doesn't make sense." Darius spread his hands, willing Lenny to understand his point. "She was really excited when I first called her, you know?"

The scoreboard shifted again, and Dexter cheered while Josh groaned. Lenny leaned closer to be heard. "Did you hear from her after that?"

"Yeah. She texted and said she was going down to Denver to practice on the rink there before she gave me a final answer."

"Do you know if she went?"

"No." He should have asked. "She didn't mention it."

"So maybe she didn't go. Or maybe she went, and something happened to change her mind."

"But what could have happened?"

Lenny shrugged. "I don't know, man."

Darius exhaled and slumped into the couch. "It's just weird. It's like she had this whole attitude flip all of a sudden."

Lenny raised his eyebrows. "Sounds to me like she's mad."

Oh, great. He stared at his friend. "Seriously? Why would she be mad?"

Lenny held out his hands. "All I know is that's the kind of thing Keisha does when she's ticked."

"What could I have done to make her mad?"

"Same question I'm always asking myself about Keisha." Lenny laughed and tapped Darius's arm. "Listen, if there's one thing you learn from eighteen years of marriage, it's this: women are mysterious creatures."

Darius couldn't help but agree. Clearly he didn't have enough experience with girls.

"Hey, man." Lenny bumped his arm. "Chill about it. We'll talk more later." He grinned and pointed at the TV. "For now let's watch the Canucks destroy Josh's sorry Oilers."

Darius forced a feeble smile. He couldn't focus on hockey tonight. As the game continued, he tuned out the action and instead rolled the situation around in his mind.

Was Lenny right? Was Addisyn mad at him for some unknown offense? The idea just didn't fit. She'd seemed fine the last time they'd texted.

So then, had something happened in Denver? That didn't seem likely either. What could have changed her mind so abruptly?

None of the possibilities made much sense, but the more he replayed their conversation, the more concerned he became. Something wasn't right. Addisyn had seemed guarded, even frightened. It was a long shot, but was she maybe in some kind of trouble?

He clenched his jaw. If she truly didn't want to skate with him, that was one thing. But this seemed like something else entirely. And no matter what was going on, he didn't want these unspoken words between them. If she was mad, then he needed to make it right. And if she was in trouble…then she might need his help.

Slowly an idea tapped on his shoulder, growing in power and possibility throughout the rest of the game. Yes, it was radical. Maybe a bit crazy. But by the time the Canucks buried a goal in overtime and Josh began dispensing fifties with a groan, Darius knew exactly how he was spending his weekend.

△△　△△　△△

"THESE ARE REALLY cool, Mrs. Jameson." Addisyn peeked inside the cardboard box at the orderly rows of handmade bookmarks. "Thanks for bringing them in."

"It's my pleasure. I love making them. Helps pass the evenings, you know." Mrs. Jameson was a mountain woman through and through, with sun-crinkled skin and silver-threaded hair and a peace that hovered over her expression like the alpine mists. No doubt the way Avery would look in a few more decades. "Please thank Skyla for me."

"I will. We'll put these on display today, and you can pick up your commission whenever you're next in town."

As Mrs. Jameson drove away in her dusty Jeep, Addisyn set about unpacking the bookmarks, fanning them over an end table. She paused to appreciate a particularly lovely one—a warm beige background decorated with pressed aspen leaves and a verse from the Book of Psalms. Something about a tree by the rivers of water.

Avery would like these. Addisyn rubbed her thumb thoughtfully over the verse before laying the bookmark with the others. Come to think of it, her sister's birthday was in a little over a month, and she hadn't chosen a gift yet. She'd always been a horrifically last-minute shopper. Maybe she could buy Avery one of these bookmarks and then a book to go with it.

But what kind of book? Addisyn twisted her lips in concentration, trying to remember what she'd seen Avery reading during evenings in the cabin. Trail guides, books on hawk rehab, and of course, her dilapidated Bible. During their childhood, Avery had devoured the classics—*A Tale of Two Cities*, *The Secret Garden*, *A Wrinkle in Time*.

And her favorite—*A Girl of the Limberlost*. In the summer of Addisyn's fourth-grade year, Avery had perched next to her on the bed each evening and read that story to her, a chapter at a time. If she closed her eyes, she was back there—in those safe and peaceful summer evenings, Avery's soothing voice mingling with the chirp of crickets from the open window, the story carrying them both between its wings. Addisyn had always sat perfectly still while Avery read, unwilling for the slightest noise or movement to puncture the rare moment of peace and send the nightmare of their home lives rushing back in.

But that was a lifetime ago. Addisyn blinked and turned back to the bookmarks. Who knew what kinds of books Avery liked these days. Now that she lived in a story Addisyn could no longer read.

Addisyn shrugged off the uncomfortable thought. There were other options, of course. Decor for the cabin, perhaps, or even hiking equipment—although she knew nothing about either of those categories. Skyla might have a suggestion, but there was no asking her now. For two hours most afternoons, when the traffic in the store was usually lightest, Skyla would disappear into her art studio. She'd explained as much to Addisyn during her first week of work. *"When I am in my studio, I would prefer not to be disturbed, but if you need me, I will be available."*

It had only taken one incident of interrupting Skyla with a question about a consignment article for Addisyn to realize that *needing* Skyla should be reserved for notifying her that the store was on fire. Anything less, she'd have to handle herself.

The copper bell above the door jingled. Addisyn glanced up in time to see a woman hesitating on the threshold. Her clothes were tourist-trendy, a sunny yellow scarf wrapping her curly hair, but her eyes held an ache. Addisyn donned her customer-service smile. "Can I help you?"

"Um…yes…maybe…" The woman cast a confused glance around the shop. As if she'd surprised herself by walking inside. "I—I think—well, a friend told me that there are paintings in here with—with Bible words on them. Paintings of birds, perhaps?"

"Yes, right this way." Addisyn set the box of bookmarks down and crossed to the display wall. "Here they are." She swept her hand in a gesture that would have made Vanna White proud. "All painted by the lady who owns this store."

The woman took a breath tinged with awe. "Oh…they're beautiful." She glanced around. "Is she here now? The artist?"

"She's in her studio right now, so she's not available." Addisyn straightened her shoulders. "But I can answer any questions you might have." Wouldn't Skyla be pleased if she emerged from her art session to find that Addisyn had sold a piece for her?

The woman wandered from painting to painting, pausing in front of the chick emerging from the egg—the same creation that had caught Addisyn's attention on her first day of work. "2 Corinthians 5:17." She peered at Addisyn with a question mark in her gaze. "What—what does that say?"

"It's, um—" New life, right? But she couldn't remember the exact words. Addisyn slid her phone from her pocket. "I'll find it for you." She Googled the reference and read the first search result. "'Therefore, if anyone is in Christ, the new creation has come: The old is gone, the new is here!'"

The woman's brows drew together. "A—a new creation?" She frowned. "Like—rebirth?"

"Um—sort of." She'd offered to answer questions about the paintings, not deliver a sermon. What had Skyla said that day? "It's—uh—it's talking about how God makes people different." There. Simple and safe.

"How does He do that?" The woman's voice reached with a desperate kind of searching.

"Well—uh—" She was at the end of her religious rope. "He—gives people new hearts. When you trust Him, then He makes you different." If only Avery were here! What would her sister say in this situation? Addisyn cleared her throat, scouring her memories for the footprints of Avery's religious ramblings. "In fact, my sister—she told me once that it's kind of like—like people have cracks in them. They break apart, and then God puts them back together. Better. Stronger."

Was that right? Had she stepped on any theological toes? Awkwardness writhed through her, and she kept her eyes on the painting instead of the woman—until she heard sniffling. "Thank you." The woman brushed tears from her cheeks and nodded at the painting. "I—I want to buy this."

"Okay. I'll ring it up for you."

She carried the painting to the register and began wrapping it in the heavy brown paper Skyla used, trying to decode the crazy conversation. Something she'd said had resonated with the woman, obviously. But how, when she didn't really believe it herself?

"I—could you do me one more favor?" The woman leaned over the counter.

"Sure." Probably she wanted the painting carried to her car.

"Would you pray for me?" The woman's voice broke. She sniffed and dabbed at her eyes. "That—this—" she placed her hand over the painting—"would be true in my life?"

No. She couldn't keep up this ridiculous pretense, not without feeling like a total fraud. But the woman seemed truly broken, and the words to deny her request wouldn't come. "Uh—yes. I'll pray." She didn't have to be a saint to write the woman on Avery's little prayer list on the refrigerator.

"Thank you." And the woman bowed her head and closed her eyes obediently.

What? Like, now? The woman expected her to pray right here on the spot? She didn't even know how!

Addisyn threw a frantic glance over her shoulder, but Skyla's door remained inexorably closed. Okay. She could get through this. She'd just have to remember how Avery normally prayed. Hopefully God would still help this woman. Or would He consider Addisyn's inexperience as disqualifying the whole prayer? Did that happen?

"Um—God." Avery usually started with *El Shaddai*, but no way was Addisyn trying for some name she couldn't even spell. "Uh—" Where to go from here? "You see this woman's heart. You know how much she wants this, uh, new life."

Addisyn cracked one eye open to see the woman nodding soulfully. So far, so good, apparently. She took a deep breath and plowed forward. "We just read that You promise this to people who, uh, trust You. So, please help this lady have faith and—" She'd never been so uncomfortable. "And—and feel You inside her heart."

And then, suddenly, the moment shifted, something stirring in the deep places of her soul. Like a wind rushing over the landscape of her heart. She'd only felt this one other time—when she'd first tried to pray back in Whistler, before she found Avery. What was going on?

"Please do what You do." Tears pricked behind her eyelids. Was the prayer still for the woman? Or was it now for her? "Please—um—hear her heart. Our hearts." She had to end this, had to escape this disorienting moment. "Thank You. Amen."

She opened her eyes, but she couldn't shake the awe, the certainty that holiness had just walked by. El Shaddai—the Spirit—whatever His Name, He'd been in the store with her. Cold chills tingled on her arms.

"Thank you. That was beautiful."

The woman. In the intensity of the encounter, Addisyn had nearly forgotten her.

The woman was still wiping tears, but now there was a peace to her expression. "And please—thank the artist for me."

"I will."

As soon as the woman left, Addisyn sank onto the stool behind the counter. Disbelief wedged itself between her thoughts. She'd prayed. And God had heard her. What in the world?

Oh, it wasn't that she didn't believe in God. She knew He was there, somewhere, in Heaven or wherever. She'd seen Him working before—when Avery found her. And of course there were the knowings—no matter how unsettling her sister's ability was, there was no question the words and pictures and feelings were whispered from another world.

But still, she'd always thought of Him as—you know, as Avery's God. He loved Avery, of course, because she was a good person and did all the right things. But Addisyn—well, the best she could hope for was to be tolerated for her sister's sake. Like, God poured all this grace on Avery, and then maybe some of it kind of spilled over onto Addisyn.

Now, though, she couldn't help wondering. Maybe—maybe she didn't have to hide in Avery's spiritual shadow. Was it possible that God might actually listen to her? With all her mistakes and failures? The same way He listened to Avery?

The idea was outlandish, but the longer she considered it, the stronger the voice of hope became. After all, she had been given a new chance, hadn't she? Maybe God was watching her to see how she handled it. To see if she could turn herself around. And maybe if she did well this time, then He'd give her exactly what the verse promised.

A new heart.

CHAPTER 8

Doing laundry at nine o'clock on a Wednesday night while Addisyn was once again at the gym was not Avery's idea of a relaxing evening, especially after all the stress of the last few days.

She frowned at the stack of towels she'd just folded. She tried to take care of household chores—cleaning and vacuuming and such—on Saturdays, while Addisyn was working. But the routine had been disturbed this past weekend, when she'd been at the expo. There were simply too many tasks to juggle.

She'd heard from Laz often, including a phone call this afternoon as she'd been closing the store. He was coming back just for the weekend to be present for the Mountain Man Festival in Bond Park, but after that he'd need a little more time in North Dakota.

"How are you doin', Miz Avery? Everythin' okay there?"

What was she supposed to say? *No! Please come back. I can't handle everything.* "Yes. Everything's fine."

"You sure?" His voice was gentle but firm. "'Cause I can be comin' back there any time it gets to be too much for you, understand?"

There was nothing she could say that wouldn't sound like whining. "No. I mean it. Everything is good."

As if.

In reality, she was overwhelmed. He hadn't even been gone two weeks, and already the responsibility bore down on her with the groaning weight of Tyndall Glacier. There had been an unbelievable number of customers the last few days—most of them out-of-towners who'd expected not only gear but also driving directions, trail recommendations, and weather forecasts. She was behind on taking inventory, and she'd received an email that afternoon from a supplier who wouldn't be able to ship the next order of hiking boots when promised.

Isaiah wasn't cooperating either. Chay had fed him during the expo, but when Avery had tried to take over the responsibility yesterday, Isaiah had refused to eat. She'd called Laz in a panic, but he'd seemed unconcerned. "Eh, hawks can be mighty skittish if somebody new is takin' care of 'em. Lotsa times they won't eat if they get a new caregiver."

Avery had blinked as Laz's words sank in. "He won't eat because of *me?*"

"Now, now." Laz had used the tone he usually reserved for injured animals. "Ain't nothin' you've done wrong. Jes' how he's wired. I'll call Chay and tell him he'll need to feed Isaiah every day 'til I get back. Jes' do the weigh-in like normal, and Chay'll do the rest."

Avery set the towels to the side and began folding the next load of laundry. Well, how come Isaiah seamlessly made the transitions between Chayton and Laz? Maybe it was because they were both men. Or maybe, more likely, it was because he could sense the obvious. Regardless of the assurance she tried to project for Laz or the confident strength she modeled for Addisyn, she didn't know what she was doing. Plain and simple.

Avery shook her head. It would be okay. She could handle it all. And tomorrow, she'd have Addisyn's help at Live Bigger. Skyla was closing her store for a couple of days—taking a trip, or something like that—and Ads had volunteered to give Avery a hand. And then on Friday, Laz would be back, even though only for the weekend, and it would all get better.

Right?

Avery sighed and grabbed the stack of laundry—the only thing orderly and tidy in her life right now. At least she'd have this chore done within the hour. One more thing off her burgeoning to-do list.

Balancing Addisyn's share of the clothes, Avery climbed the stairs and cracked open the door to her sister's room. She grimaced at the mess that met her eyes. The quilt was flung haphazardly over the bed, clothes were draped over the footboard, and her sister's purse was spilled in the corner. Typical.

The clutter was the tipping point. Avery wouldn't intrude on her sister's privacy, but she couldn't just walk away from a mess like this. She plopped the stack of clothing on the bed and began trying to tidy what she could—straightening the quilt, lining up Addisyn's shoes, consolidating the clothing.

The desk in the corner was covered in a snowfall of papers. Avery capped a few open ink pens—seriously, what if they'd fallen on the rug?—and glanced over the contents. Nothing else, except—

She blinked at a familiar pink book on the corner. A photo album. She brushed her hand over the cover and remembered Addisyn's serious face as her sister sat for hours, painstakingly gluing in the photos. Photos from skating.

Avery pulled the album off the desk and settled onto the floor. She flipped the first page—stiff with glue, heavy with snapshots of her sister's life.

Memories trapped between the pages leaped up. Avery couldn't keep from smiling at the sight of Addisyn's seven-year-old face peering into the camera. She was wearing a shiny blue outfit and skates that looked as if they were waiting for her feet to catch up. And she was already clutching a medal.

What had Addisyn won that year? Avery tapped the page, struggling to remember. Some junior program or another, wasn't it?

The next page held more pictures from the same event. Avery's stomach knotted when she saw Addisyn standing between their parents. Their mother's face was the same mask of artificial happiness she'd always worn, her eyes squinting as though she couldn't look directly at the truth.

And their father had a heavy hand on Addisyn's shoulder, smiling tightly in a way that didn't begin to erase the darkness in his steel-colored eyes.

Avery stared at the grip of his fingers on Addisyn. She'd often wondered why he'd even allowed Addisyn's skating. His daughters weren't expected to cause extra expense or familial inconvenience. Not if they wanted to dodge terrifying tirades or brutal blows. But Addisyn's skating had been the one exception to the unspoken rule. Their father had paid for Addisyn's lessons, driven her to practices, and attended her performances without complaint.

It wasn't because of a desire to promote her happiness—that much Avery knew. Maybe he'd seen her talent as a reflection on him. Or maybe he'd just wanted to add another layer to their elaborate happy-family myth. Smiling beside an ice rink with his prize-winning daughter sure looked good on a Christmas card.

Seeing his hand on Addisyn, even in a fifteen-year-old photo, clenched Avery's heart. Had Addisyn ever truly escaped his grip? Sometimes Avery wondered if part of Addisyn's dedication to skating came from a place that longed to please. A place that still remembered skating as the one accomplishment that had ever brought even a smidgen of approval from their parents.

Tears stung Avery's eyes at the thought. She breathed out and flipped through some more pages. Addisyn was eleven or twelve in these photos, and the innocent joy in her eyes was starting to transform to something more desperate. Avery stopped on a photo of Addisyn in workout clothes, stretching with a serious expression. The U.S. Figure Skating logo was on the wall behind her.

The next page was blank. Across it, in purple ink, Addisyn had scribbled simply, *Part 2.*

Avery knew exactly what her sister meant. After they'd gone to New York City, Avery had assumed Addisyn's skating was over. She'd viewed it like any other extracurricular activity—no doubt an enjoyable hobby, but well worth sacrificing to escape their father.

But Addisyn's commitment to skating had run far deeper than Avery had realized. Her sister had remained determined to find a way to compete again. And that's when skating had opened a dark and dangerous door.

Avery flipped to the new batch of photos. Now Addisyn was sixteen, and the turmoil in her eyes had flared into restless rebellion.

These pages were crammed with snapshots, but there were also empty gaps where pictures had once been. Avery stared at the blank rectangles for a few moments before realization sank in. Those must have been shots of Brian.

Avery still remembered the first time Addisyn had told her about Brian. Her sister had been waiting in the kitchen of their tiny apartment when Avery came home at ten o'clock at night from her second job. "Avery!" Her face had practically glowed. "I'm going to get to skate again!"

The announcement had come so completely out of left field. "Wait, what? How?"

"Well, I was skating today downtown." Addisyn had often gone after school to skate on the public rink. "And I met this guy, and he said—"

Even now, Avery could remember how quickly she'd switched to defense. "Hold up. A guy?"

"Oh, Avery." Addisyn had slid her a disgusted glance. "Not like that. His name is Brian. He's a coach, and he liked my skating. He offered that I could come practice at the private rink." Her eyes were bright again. "A real USFS rink, Avery, can you believe it?"

"How much will it cost?" Life in New York had trained Avery to look at every price tag first.

"Free! He said he wouldn't charge." When Avery didn't respond, Addisyn had scowled. "Well, don't be too excited."

"I'm sorry, Ads. But—" She'd struggled to find words that wouldn't shatter her sister's innocence. "Sometimes when people—especially men—do things for free, then they expect—"

"Avery, he's a nice guy." Addisyn's eyes had narrowed with hurt. "Why is it that you never want me to skate?"

"Oh, honey, no." Avery had crossed the room and gathered Addisyn into a hug—the kind her younger sister had already been allowing less often. "That's not it at all. I'm happy you'll get to skate. I just want to make sure everything is okay."

Addisyn's typical teenage attitude had flared to life with her sigh. "I'm not a little kid anymore, Avery." She'd shrugged away from the hug. "Everything is fine."

But it hadn't been. And Avery's every fear had come terrifyingly true.

Avery refocused on the album and flipped past the gap-toothed pages until she reached one with only a single photo. An 8x10 shot of Addisyn at seventeen, holding a bouquet and brandishing a gold medal over her head.

Guilt prickled in her heart. She knew the picture, of course. It was the same one that sports news outlets had used for three years after that moment. With Brian coaching her, Addisyn had won—what was it?

Regionals? Or Sectionals? Something big.

But to Avery, the photo would always represent the beginning of the end. An end that she could have prevented.

Enough. She didn't want to see any more pictures. Didn't want to remember the disastrous past. She returned the album to Addisyn's desk and hurried downstairs, the memories nipping at her heels.

She was folding the next load of laundry when the realization hit her. The simple reason she had always been so uncomfortable with Addisyn's skating. The reason she prayed her sister would never go back.

In the whole album, there wasn't one shot of Avery.

No pictures of her and Addisyn. No snaps of her standing beside the rink. Not even a place for her in the family portrait.

Which was fitting, really. Because skating had always taken Addisyn away.

To a world where Avery didn't exist.

△△   △△   △△

"I'M READY FOR work." Addisyn laughed nervously as she headed into the store alongside Avery.

"Awesome." Her sister shot her a grateful glance. "Thanks so much for helping me out here, Ads."

"Sure." Working in an outdoors store was definitely not Addisyn's element. But with Avery running herself ragged, it was the least she could do to help out. Especially since Skyla would be gone today and tomorrow—on a trip to release a bird, she'd told Addisyn. *"A Barn Owl. We are taking her to the national forest land up north. It is often easier for the wings to be found when the trees are close."*

Addisyn had just nodded vaguely. Was she supposed to understand that? Half the time Skyla seemed to be talking in her own personal code. At least Avery would do a better job of communicating what she needed today.

"Okay." Avery tossed her coat over the stool behind the counter and darted around the store, flicking on lights and bringing the neon OPEN sign to life. "So, the first thing we do each day is start up the POS."

POS. Point of sale. That much Addisyn knew from the coffee shop. "I can get that ready." She glanced at the white console. "We used that same system at my last job."

"Perfect." Avery ducked into the back room. "While you're doing that, I need to grab these boxes."

The reassuring familiarity of powering up the system and checking the cash drawer boosted her confidence. At least she could handle this part.

"Okay." Avery emerged from the back room with a huge box, Mercy on her heels. "So can you unpack these gloves for me? I need to run and take care of Isaiah."

"Sure." Addisyn hefted the box as Avery disappeared out the door. Why hadn't she asked where they belonged? Well, with the winter stuff, right?

She went to work on an empty endcap, sorting the gloves by size and color. John Denver crooned "Annie's Song" in the background. The store smelled faintly of pine, and a peace she hadn't expected worked its way through her. She could see why Avery loved this job so much. Working at a store that brought the outdoors in was a perfect fit for her sister.

A smile tugged at her as she remembered the day when she was six years old and found Avery lying on the ground in their suburban backyard. "What are you doing?"

"Smelling the grass." Avery had closed her eyes and taken another deep breath. "Doesn't it smell good?"

Addisyn had flopped down beside her and wrinkled her nose. "Smells like grass."

"No." Avery had rolled onto her side and looked at Addisyn seriously. "It smells like the place I'm gonna live someday."

"Outside?" Addisyn had giggled, and Avery had joined her.

"As close to outside as I can get."

The ringing of the phone shattered the memory. Addisyn rushed to the counter and sprang on the receiver, out of breath. "Hello?"

"Hi." The voice sounded uncertain. "Is this Live Bigger Outdoor Supply?"

Her greeting had been totally unprofessional. Addisyn cringed. "Yes. Sorry. This is Live Bigger."

"Um, I was wondering if you had a particular item."

"Okay." There was a computer behind the counter. That must be how Avery looked up inventory. "Do you have the name of the item?"

"Yes, it's the Liv-Tech hiking socks. I need three pairs, size 8, 13, and 9, all in the sage gray."

"Yes. Okay." Addisyn jiggled the mouse, but the screen stayed black. *Wake up!* "I, uh, I need to check on that for you. Let me put you on hold."

There was probably a way to turn on music or something, but Addisyn just laid the phone down on the counter and sprinted to the back window. Isaiah's enclosure was open, and Avery was nowhere to be seen. She had to be up at Laz's house in the garage.

Okay. Addisyn didn't have time to run all the way up there and back. She'd just try to find them herself.

She dashed toward the wall of hiking boots and peered through the displays until she found socks. And there were the ones the customer had asked for. What color had she said? Gray something. There! *Sage gray.*

Victorious, Addisyn scurried back to the phone. "Ma'am?" She tried to swallow her breathlessness. "We have those socks in the color you requested."

"Okay." The woman didn't sound impressed. "And do you have them in those sizes?"

The sizes! Addisyn writhed. "Oh—uh—I'm sorry. What were those sizes again?"

"Eight, nine, and thirteen." There was a definite edge to the woman's voice now. Addisyn didn't blame her.

"One moment." She put the phone down and again raced to the display. There was an eight—a nine—come on, come on—a thirteen. Perfect!

The woman's chilly attitude didn't thaw when Addisyn informed her they had the sizes in stock, but she did say she would come by to pick them up. "What time do you close today?"

"Five o'clock." The first question she could answer with assurance.

Just as the stressful call ended, Avery breezed back through the door. "Isaiah has gained another half a pound."

Addisyn just nodded. She'd needed Avery a lot more in the last few minutes than that hawk had. "Avery, how do you look up inventory?"

"Look up inventory?" Avery blinked at her.

"Yeah. This lady called and wanted to know about socks, and I didn't know how to find out if we had them." She gestured to the computer. "That thing wouldn't work."

"No wonder." Avery laughed, reached under the counter, and held up the plug end of a cord. "It hasn't had power in years."

No computer? "Then what do you do?"

"Well, by this point, I know all the brands we have." Avery shrugged. "But also, it's in the books." She tapped a spiral-bound notebook on the counter.

Addisyn flipped it open and saw page after page of products, dates, prices, and sizes, all in Laz's unruly scrawl. She stared at her sister. "You run the store out of a notebook?"

Avery sighed. "I do wish Laz would adopt a more modern approach, but I have to say, it works."

Surely Avery couldn't be serious. Then again, since she apparently carried the whole inventory around in her head, it probably didn't cause her too much stress.

"So did you get the caller straightened out?" Avery pulled a to-do list from her pocket and examined it.

"Yes. We had the socks she wanted." Addisyn stood a little taller. "She'll be in this afternoon."

"Awesome. And what about the gloves?"

"Right here." Addisyn led Avery to the display. "Good?"

"Oh—" Avery bit her lip. "I didn't tell you. These are climbing gloves."

"So?"

"You put them with winter gloves. But these are tactical gloves." Avery said it as if the statement should make sense. "They would be on that wall with the carabiners and paracord."

Addisyn didn't know what either of those two things were, but one thing she did know: the display she'd spent twenty minutes on had to be redone. "Oh. Okay."

"Don't worry." Avery patted her on the shoulder and began

dismantling Addisyn's careful arrangement. "You'll figure it out."

By that afternoon, Addisyn wasn't so sure. Avery apparently knew every note in the song of running the store, from placing orders to unloading inventory to answering customers' questions. But Addisyn couldn't find her place in the harmony. By three o'clock, Avery had relegated her to ringing up purchases—the only task she could handle without causing extra work for both of them.

"Did you find everything today?" She smiled at the older man as he laid his purchases on the counter.

"Yep." He nodded. "Where's Avery? The girl who normally works here?"

"She's—" Addisyn glanced over her shoulder just as Avery emerged from the back room.

"I'm here, Mr. Pike." Avery waved as she carried two new boxes of hiking boots toward the wall.

"Hi there, Miss Avery!" He glanced back at Addisyn. "Are you a new employee?"

"I'm Avery's sister." She couldn't keep the weariness from her voice.

"Really?" He glanced at her bright pink shirt and raised his eyebrows. "Hmm."

Addisyn didn't want to decipher that remark.

"That one's on sale." He pointed to the water bottle. "Ten percent off."

"Okay." Addisyn gave him the markdown without checking to confirm. If he was wrong, she'd make up the difference later to Avery.

"My nephew's coming out next weekend. He's into hiking and wants to go out to Glacier Gorge. What are some good options for him?"

Addisyn blinked. "Glacier Gorge?"

"In the park." He tipped his head. "You know, on the way to Bear Lake."

If Avery had mentioned either of those places, she didn't remember. "I'm sorry, I can't help you." She shrugged. "Have you tried asking at the ranger—"

"What's the problem?" Avery stepped up beside her.

Mr. Pike looked just as grateful to see her as Addisyn felt. "Looking for some good Glacier Gorge trails for my nephew."

"Pete? He's finally coming up from Boulder?" Avery smiled. "I know you'll be happy to see him."

"Absolutely." He grinned. "Been a long time coming."

"So he's wanting to go up by Bear Lake." Avery tapped her chin thoughtfully. "Well, I'd start hiking toward Alberta Falls and continue to The Loch. That's a steep distance, though."

"Shouldn't be a problem for him."

"Okay, then." Avery reached under the counter and pulled out a map, tracing a skinny black line. "Tell him to go here—and here. If he goes past The Loch, he can see Timberline Falls and Sky Pond."

"Have you been up there?" Mr. Pike was studying the squiggly lines.

"I've been as far as Timberline Falls. It's terrific." Avery tapped another spot on the map. "And then he could add either of these spur trails. There's Mills Lake—it's incredible, and there's a connection to Black Lake farther up, but that would be quite a distance for a day hike. Or there's a trail to Andrews Glacier too." She folded the map and slid it across the counter to Mr. Pike. "That should be enough to get him started."

"Wonderful. I'll give him this. And I'll let him know to ask here if he has any questions." Mr. Pike's eyes flicked to Addisyn and back to Avery. "I'll tell him to ask *you*, Miss Avery."

Just as Mr. Pike turned away, a woman with a severe ponytail and a black nylon jacket shouldered up to the counter. "Excuse me." Exasperation huffed through her voice. "I spoke with someone at your store earlier today who told me you had the Liv-Tech hiking socks, but I can't find them anywhere."

"Liv-Tech?" Avery's brow furrowed. "I'm sorry, ma'am. We haven't carried those in several months." She slid a look at Addisyn.

"I—I was the one who talked to you." The words felt like an admission of guilt. "But I know we have the Liv-Tech socks. I checked personally for them."

"Addisyn, we don't carry them." Avery's voice was barely above a whisper.

"A, I saw them, I swear." Addisyn smiled weakly at the woman. "Here. I'll take you to them."

Avery trailed behind as Addisyn led the way to the display. To her relief, she hadn't imagined the black packages of socks. "Right here." She tapped the logo. "Sage green, like you said."

The woman's lips tightened. "These are Lok-Tech, not Liv-Tech."

No way.

Addisyn looked at the packaging again. Sure enough. If only she could slide through the cracks in the floorboards. "I—wow. I am so sorry. I saw the 'Tech,' and I guess I—"

"I drove all the way from Fort Collins." Irritation increased with every syllable. "I needed those specific socks for an upcoming trip."

Avery cleared her throat and stepped to Addisyn's side. "I'm so sorry, ma'am. Especially for the—misinformation. Actually, we haven't been able to get the Liv-Tech socks for several months. I think they've been discontinued. However, we've received some great feedback on the Lok-Tech socks. They're made by the same company, and they're the closest replacement."

The woman perched her hands on her hips, elbows jutting at sharp angles. "If you don't carry Liv-Tech, why wasn't I told that before I drove an hour and a half?"

Because I am not my sister! And because her boss is a kooky old man who handwrites everything! Addisyn swallowed. "I—I apologize." She threw a desperate glance at Avery.

"Ma'am, I am so sorry for the inconvenience." Avery was handling this like a pro, but tension was building in her expression. "I'd be happy to offer you fifty percent off the price of these socks if that would help."

"It would not." The words were so sharp that Addisyn took a step back. "I needed the Liv-Tech, not the Lok-Tech. I think it's very irresponsible of your employees to give customers false information."

Addisyn lifted her chin, remorse drowning in a rising tide of anger. All this over a stupid pair of socks? "Look, it was just a mistake, and anyway, I think—"

"Addisyn!" Avery's tone held a warning.

"Never mind." The woman spun and headed for the door, ponytail switching back and forth. On the threshold, she glared over her shoulder. "All this way for nothing. I will *never* come back to this store!"

The door slammed shut, indignation echoing. Avery sagged against a display, and Addisyn winced. "A...I'm so sorry."

Avery rubbed her forehead, then looked at Addisyn with a sigh. "Ads, you can't do that, okay? You can't tell people we have stuff we don't have."

"I thought we had them!" Addisyn threw her hands up in exasperation. "Aren't they basically the same, anyway?"

"No. Liv-Tech used more polyester. Lok-Tech has more cotton, so it's a heavier sock."

Did Avery know every detail about every product in the whole store?

"It's all right." Avery summoned a lukewarm smile. "You were trying to help."

Trying to help was not the same as helping. Addisyn stared at Avery, and for a single disorienting moment, she didn't see her sister. She saw instead the mountain girl, the one who knew which trails to combine and how hiking socks compared and what a carabiner was. She blinked, and it was Avery again. But there was more space between them than six feet of hardwood flooring.

"I'm sorry." Why was she going to cry?

The bell over the door jingled again, and her sister hurried off. "Can I help you?"

Addisyn slumped against the display and watched her go. *Yes. You can help me climb the mountains that are so easy for you.*

CHAPTER 9

When they'd returned from work yesterday, Addisyn had offered to help her sister again, but Avery had just given a smile stiff with discomfort. "That's sweet, Ads. But Laz will be back tomorrow, and—I think we'll be good."

Of course she could hear the words her sister was too kind to say.

So this morning, Laz had returned, and he and Avery had used the day to get ready for that festival that started tomorrow in Bond Park—Mountain Man, Avery had called it. And Addisyn had spent her rare day off alone—roaming Estes aimlessly, hitting the gym. And thinking—too much, no doubt.

Now, though, things were about to get better. She was waiting at Live Bigger for the store to close, and then Laz was taking both her and Avery to dinner at the Alpenglow Restaurant—his treat, he claimed, to thank Avery for all she was doing in his absence.

It would be cool to finally see inside the Alpenglow. Addisyn had passed the restaurant every day on her commute and always thought how welcoming it looked—like the perfect place for a date, although she wouldn't have shared that impression with Avery. Now she finally had an invitation to go there. Okay, so she'd be with her sister and her sister's boss, but still.

And tomorrow would be exciting as well. The festival would surely be fun. She'd be back at work during the day, but she'd be off in time for the country concert that night.

Yes, it would be a great weekend, and as soon as Laz and Avery wrapped things up here, it could begin. Right now, though, they were both out back, looking at that hawk Avery was always talking about. They'd invited Addisyn to come with them, but the blast of cold air that rushed in when Laz opened the door was less than inviting. Plus, what did she know about hawks?

Or anything else in Avery's world, for that matter.

No, better to just stay inside. Where she couldn't scare the hawk or ask a dumb question or further accentuate the differences between herself and Avery.

The creak of the front door jerked her from her thoughts. Her view was screened by a rack of hiking shirts, but she heard footsteps and the scrape of a man clearing his throat. Oh no. A customer, seriously? Five minutes from closing? At this rate, they would never get out of here.

Well, yesterday had proven that she knew nothing about the outdoors equipment sold in this store, but maybe she could at least point him to whatever he was looking for. It might save time. She stepped around the counter just as the man looked up—

Darius Payne.

"Darius!" Her heart gave a single bound and galloped away. Was she imagining things? "What on earth—"

"Addisyn!" His smile still had that adorable twist. "I found you."

"Why are you here?" Oh, that had come out totally wrong. She cringed at the way his expression sank. "I mean—I just never expected—"

Darius jammed his hands into the pockets of his blue windbreaker. "I, uh, I had a couple days free, and I wanted to come see you." Unease pulled his features tight. "Unless, you know, you don't want me to."

"No. I mean, yes. I mean, yes, it's okay. It's great." The words had no air behind them, her thoughts spinning away in every direction.

His shoulders relaxed, and he ducked his head slightly. "It's good to see you."

Her dry throat pinched when she tried to swallow. "It's good to see you too." She'd known he was handsome, of course, but—wow, he was even more gorgeous than she'd remembered. Why did he have to show up on her day off, when she was wearing one of Avery's sweatshirts and had yanked her hair into a messy ponytail?

"So, um—" What could she say next? The air between them had

never felt this stifling in Whistler, the awkward silence like a force field.

Voices and footsteps pressed against the door, and the next moment Laz and Avery stepped into the shop. Avery was cradling a pinecone-laden branch in one arm. "Hey, Addisyn, look what I found by the—" Her eyes caught Darius, and she froze. "Oh." A question mark hung from the syllable.

There was some rule about how to word a proper introduction. But it had left town along with the rest of Addisyn's logical mind. "Avery, Darius—you know, Darius Payne, from Whistler. He, uh—and Darius, this is Avery, my sister Avery, you know, she lives here, I mean, not *here* at the store, but here in—" Heat throbbed in her cheeks. She bit her lip and threw Avery a silent plea.

With a definite air of duty, Avery shifted her branch to her other arm and swiped her palm across her hiking pants. Then she stepped to Addisyn's side and held out her hand. "Darius." Her tone stood on middle ground. Not enthusiastic, but not unfriendly either. "I've heard a lot about you from Addisyn."

"Likewise." Addisyn hadn't thought it possible, but Darius seemed even more tense now. "It sure is great to meet you. Those are some nice pinecones you have."

"Thank you." Avery was hiding behind her polite face, the one she used when speaking with customers she didn't necessarily approve of. "Addisyn didn't mention you were coming."

"I didn't know." Again, the words sounded all wrong. Addisyn winced.

Avery motioned to Laz, still waiting patiently behind her. "This is my boss, Laz Jobe. He owns the store."

A grin that could only mean trouble spilled over Laz's face as he examined the group. Obviously the dots were connecting. "Good to meet you, son." His hand shot out and swallowed Darius's. "So, you the boyfriend, huh?"

"Well, I—"

"No, not—"

Addisyn's words collided with Darius's as heat flashed into her face. Busy avoiding eye contact with Darius, she noticed Avery jabbing Laz with her elbow.

"I'm, uh, I'm a friend." Darius cleared his throat. "I just came down to see Addisyn, say hi."

Why couldn't she rewind this whole encounter and try again?

"Is this your first visit to Colorado, Darius?" Avery was still talking, still leading them all out of this incredibly awkward moment. Or maybe she was just seizing the opportunity to interrogate Darius.

"Pretty much. I did go to a skating center in Boulder once as a kid."

Skating. A fresh wave of apprehension rose. He had to be here because of skating. Oh, what if he said something in front of—

"Well, Boulder's nice, but Estes Park is much prettier." Avery's tone didn't allow for disagreement. "Maybe you'll have the chance to see some of the national park while you're here."

"That'd be great."

She'd hidden in Avery's shadow long enough. Addisyn took a deep breath. "How long are you here?"

Why had she said that? Like she couldn't wait for him to go? Judging by the expression on his face, he'd had the same thought.

"Just for two nights." He studied a crack on the wood floor and rubbed the back of his neck. "I have to leave on Sunday."

Two nights? He'd flown fifteen hundred miles to be in Colorado for two nights? Something was going on. Addisyn's heart rate tripled. "Where are you staying?"

"Denver. I rented a car. I couldn't remember the name of the place you worked, but I did remember this name, for some reason. So I came here."

"And we're glad you did." Laz slapped Darius on the back with a gusto that must have nearly knocked him off his balance. "As it happens, we were all about to close the shop an' go out to eat this evening. Why don'tcha tag along?" The grin he slid Addisyn was nothing short of evil. "That'd be...fun."

Oh, no. No way. She was not about to have dinner with Darius with Laz and Avery sitting there thinking that—

"I'd love to go with you all." Darius's eyes crinkled hopefully. "I mean, if it's okay with everyone."

What could she say? All three of them were staring at her. There was nothing left to do except resign herself to the most uncomfortable evening of her life. "Okay."

"All right, then." Avery frowned at Laz's smirk and tugged on his sleeve. "Laz, let's lock up here and be on our way."

△△ · △△ · △△

ADDISYN HAD BEEN sure the situation couldn't be more awkward, but that was before Avery offered to drive them all to the restaurant in her truck. Avery and Laz were up front, while she and Darius were squished together in the sliver of space that was supposed to be a backseat. She'd pressed herself against the door, but even still, his knee kept brushing hers.

Since the truck made far too much noise for anyone to consider a conversation, Addisyn's mind had plenty of time to spin circles. Her concerns ricocheted around the situation, darting into every corner and rebounding from every angle. She had to focus, had to gather herself, had to quit being distracted by Darius's presence beside her.

Why on earth was he here—especially when she'd already told him no? Was there a problem he needed to discuss with her? Or had he come to ask her again? The thought of having to tell him no in person ripped at her heart. Oh, why had he come? And why hadn't he called her first? And why was this whole situation so—so—*weird?* They'd had an easy camaraderie in Whistler, not this tense uncertainty.

Maybe it was because everything was playing out under Avery's watchful eyes. Addisyn hadn't missed the number of times her sister's gaze had flicked to the rearview mirror during this drive. No question, her watchdog mentality was fully engaged.

Which meant there would be no chance now to talk to Darius alone. And what if he said something about skating in front of Avery? He would naturally assume she'd talked to Avery about his offer. The way he'd asked her to.

Laz glanced over his shoulder and smirked at them knowingly. Addisyn shot back her best glare. She didn't want to imagine the jokes he'd crack later. Would Avery be able to keep him in line at the restaurant?

They were making the final turn. The momentum pushed her toward Darius, but she braced her feet on the floor instead. She glanced at him only to see his sky-colored eyes fixed on her face. He flushed slightly and gave her a sheepish smile that tugged at her heart. She glanced down to where his hands rested on his knees. For a moment she had the urge to slip her fingers into his.

Ridiculous. She tucked her hands under her thighs and tried to scoot farther away.

The tires crunched across the gravel parking lot, the restaurant spilling a warm glow in front of them. The instant the wheels stopped turning, Addisyn scrambled out of the truck so quickly she caught her heel on the running board and nearly fell.

"Okay?" Right behind her, Darius grabbed her elbow.

His touch carried a strange current, and she jerked her arm away. "Yes. I'm fine." She glanced ahead to Avery and Laz, already walking toward the restaurant. "Darius, listen. Don't say anything about skating."

"What?" Complete bewilderment hijacked his expression.

Addisyn swallowed down her impatience and started walking. Any second, Avery would realize they weren't right behind her. "Avery doesn't know about the skating thing. Not the invitation, not anything. Please, please, don't mention it."

The soft light of sunset wasn't dim enough to hide the hurt on his face. "Wait—you didn't even talk to her about it?"

Of course he would be upset. "No, I—" Avery was looking over her shoulder. Addisyn bit her lip as they stepped up to the entrance. "Please, Darius. I'll explain later."

The Alpenglow was a rustic family-style restaurant with solid wood tables, floor-to-ceiling windows on the western wall, and an enormous moose head mounted behind the counter. A waitress—a girl named Lily who had been in Skyla's store a few times—showed them all to a corner table and left them with the menus and an appetizer. As if she'd spent the entire drive spooling up conversation starters, Avery immediately launched into a discourse about, of all things, the hawk. "He's doing really well. Getting stronger every day."

Although Darius probably wasn't that interested in hawk rehab, at least somebody was talking. Addisyn tried to study the menu, but the options floated disconnectedly in her mind.

"Yep. Miz Avery's done right well with our hawk." Laz leaned forward, a piece of breadstick in his hand. "She feeds him his frozen mice ever' day."

Frozen mice? Addisyn jerked her gaze up, but Laz kept going, apparently not noticing that Darius had paused with his water glass halfway to his mouth. "Lotsa gals wouldn't touch a frozen mouse, but Miz Avery grabs 'em up like nobody's business. Hawks gotta have mice, you know. And sometimes rabbits, or we get roadkill and—"

There was a slight movement under the table, and Laz winced. He cut his eyes to Avery, who seared him with a warning glare.

"That's, uh, interesting." Darius's gaze shifted toward Addisyn, but she stared at her menu again. She was at a restaurant with Darius, and Avery and Laz were going to talk about hawks and roadkill. Should she laugh, scream, or just crawl under the table?

"Ready to order?" The waitress was back, and the process of ordering helped to move them past the uncomfortable moment. Avery once again took charge of the conversation, keeping talk fairly harmless until their food arrived. "So, Darius, do you enjoy living in Whistler?"

"It's—it's nice." He examined his salmon filet as if it were a riddle to solve.

Nice? What was the matter with him? He was stiffer and more aloof than he'd ever been in Whistler. What if Avery thought he was standoffish?

Of course, did Avery's impression of him matter? He was a friend. A friend. He'd said that himself. Which was fine.

"Is Whistler anything like here?" Avery stirred her soup.

"Quite a bit, actually. It's very mountainous." A bit of the tension left Darius's face. "There's a lot of outdoor stuff too. But we have the ocean pretty close." He gave that endearingly crooked grin, and Addisyn couldn't stop her heart from squeezing. "Not something you folks have here."

"That's true. It sounds lovely."

Was she imagining things, or was there a slightly warmer undertone to Avery's words?

"Whaddya do up there?" Laz wrapped both hands around his buffalo burger.

Don't say anything about skating. Please no.

"I'm a climbing guide."

"He leads groups up Whistler Mountain." Addisyn caught Avery's eye. This was bound to score some points with her outdoorsy sister.

Laz gave a low whistle. "Impressive." He grinned. "Miz Avery, I like this dude."

Avery ignored Laz and steered the conversation to Darius's hobbies. By the time dessert arrived, Avery had asked about everything from Darius's job to his family to his interests, with Addisyn inserting a comment where she could. Laz just dug into his cake with such oblivious satisfaction that Addisyn wanted to shake him. Although maybe it was good that at least someone was enjoying this meal.

All she wanted now was to get out of the too-warm restaurant and back home. Away from Laz's smirks and Avery's probing and that ridiculous moose head. Away from her own awkwardness and Darius's stiffness. And most of all, away from the truth that was staring her in the face.

Turning him down once had been hard enough. Now she was going to have to tell him no…again.

△△　△△　△△

THIS WAS, HANDS down, the most uncomfortable evening Darius had ever suffered through. Folded into Avery's cramped backseat, he glanced over at Addisyn, but she was staring out the window.

The whole experience had been the reverse of his hopes. The minute he'd seen Addisyn in the outdoors store, every shred of sanity had whipped right out of his mind. She was beautiful in a way that shone straight from her heart, her every move part of a delicate dance. His feelings for her had swept him downstream in a relentless tide, and he'd barely been able to keep his head above water.

But in Whistler, Addisyn had been open and friendly, a girl who wore her sparkling heart on her sleeve. Tonight, she was inaccessible, her soul closed off behind barred gates. She'd made it clear from the beginning that she wasn't happy he'd come.

Maybe Lenny was right. Maybe she really was mad. And had she really given his invitation so little consideration that she hadn't even thought it worth mentioning to Avery?

Avery. Another way the evening had slid sideways. Apparently he'd done something to make an unfavorable impression on her. She hadn't been unfriendly, exactly, but he'd had the distinct conviction that she was probing his soul—and not entirely satisfied with what she found. Was Avery's response due to something Addisyn had said about him? Or had he just made a bad impression all the way around?

Regardless, the visit was a disaster—a toxic cocktail of hurt over Addisyn's behavior, exhaustion with Avery's barrage of questions, and embarrassment from Laz's constant insinuations. He'd been so preoccupied during dinner he could barely remember what he'd eaten, much less anything that was said. Except Avery giving the hawk frozen mice. He could distinctly remember that. Not that it mattered now, but had Avery been feeding the hawk right before she shook his hand?

The smart thing would be to leave. Cut his losses, head back to Whistler, and quit trying to force the issue. But...

He glanced at Addisyn again. She was looking straight ahead now, and even in the fitful glow from the passing headlights, the shadow of sadness across her face was obvious.

He clenched his jaw. No. He wasn't going to run away. Addisyn was in some kind of trouble—he could feel it, the way he could feel storms approaching Whistler Mountain. The refusal she'd given him was rooted in something other than her true feelings. And he wasn't leaving until he knew what was going on.

His renewed determination held as they all climbed out of the truck in the parking lot of the outdoors store, where his rental car was still parked. "So—" He scuffed his boot along the gravel. "Could I come back tomorrow?"

Addisyn looked at Avery as if seeking permission. "Uh, yes. Sure."

"Okay." *Don't back down.* "How about tomorrow morning?"

Again Addisyn glanced at Avery. "I have to work."

She wasn't going to make this easy for him. "Well, what time do you get off?"

"Five thirty."

Avery's eyebrows rose slightly. "You have to help Skyla close up afterwards."

"It'll be fine, Avery." Addisyn's face tightened.

Laz coughed and stepped up. "I have an idea. Miz Avery and I could use a strong young dude like you tomorrow to help us at the booth. Then Addisyn can join us when she gets off work."

"The booth?" He had no idea what they were talking about. Not that it mattered, if it was a way to see Addisyn again.

"The Mountain Man Festival is tomorrow in Bond Park." Laz rubbed his chin. "Music, food, crafts, stuff like that. We're havin' a booth for the outdoor store all day until the country music concert tomorrow night."

"Now, Laz." Uncertainty pulled at Avery's words. "Darius probably doesn't want to——"

"I do." The invitation brought a wave of relief. At least he'd won someone over tonight. "That's perfect. I'd be happy to help."

"Okay." Avery didn't sound enthusiastic, but the smile she gave him still looked genuine. "We really could use another hand."

"Meet us at Bond Park tomorrow mornin'." Laz dug his hands into his pockets. "Is eight o'clock too early?"

"Not a bit." It would mean leaving Denver at six thirty, but for the chance to see Addisyn, he would've slept in Bond Park overnight.

Avery pulled out her phone. "Let me give you my number in case you need directions."

After he traded numbers with Avery, Darius shook hands with her and Laz. "I had a good time tonight." Well, that might be a stretch. "Thanks for letting me join you." He reached Addisyn and hesitated for an awkward moment. "Addisyn, I—it was good to see you again."

Even in the dim lights of the parking lot, he could see something stir in her eyes. "Yes." This time she didn't glance at Avery.

He started to hold out his hand, but she suddenly wrapped her arms around him. "Thank you. We'll talk tomorrow." Her words were the softest breath against his ear before she stepped back.

His hopes rebounded as he found her eyes again. She was smiling now, her expression once again glowing with the light he'd always seen there.

He couldn't contain his grin. "Tomorrow."

As he pulled out of the parking lot, he glanced in his rearview mirror. She was still standing by Avery's truck, arms wrapped around her torso. Watching him drive away. He lifted his hand in a wave.

That one hug had redeemed his whole night. It was all going to be okay. She wasn't mad. He was sure of it. Whatever the problem was, they'd work through it together.

As he drove back toward Denver, he realized there were a lot of good things that had come from the night, after all. He'd made a good impression on Laz. He'd gotten to meet Avery, and maybe she was just protective of Addisyn, which he could respect. He'd seen the hope in Addisyn's eyes when she hugged him.

And best of all, he'd be seeing her again tomorrow.

CHAPTER 10

Avery had fully intended to dislike Darius Payne.

Until now, she'd put no stock in Addisyn's vouching for his character. After all, her sister had once been infatuated by Brian too. But judging from Darius's behavior last night and today, Avery had to admit that so far, he actually seemed quite decent.

He had arrived this morning right on the dot of eight, and he'd been working hard ever since—loading towers of merchandise boxes into the bed of Avery's truck, setting up the open tent that covered their table, and now, helping customers with a warmth and charm that didn't seem contrived.

"Here you go, ma'am." Darius finished wrapping two of Laz's carved wooden spoons in paper and handed them to the waiting customer. "We hope you enjoy these."

"I'm sure I will." The woman gave him a lingering smile. As had every other female who'd come by that day. With his dark hair, lean frame, and strong features, it wasn't hard to see how he'd caught her sister's eye. And his down-to-earth manner was a refreshing change from Brian's posturing GQ facade.

Darius turned to Avery. "We'll need to open the next box soon."

"That's good. Laz will be excited." Avery glanced toward the neighboring booth, where Laz was catching up with a buddy. She reached for another box and nearly tripped over Mercy, who was panting contentedly under the edge of the table.

"Here, let me." Darius hefted the box and sliced the tape with a pocketknife. "So, Avery, how long have you lived in Estes?"

"A little over a year." She'd never stop being thankful for her home here. "I love it."

"I can see why." Darius glanced across Bond Park. The stony cliffs of Lumpy Ridge reflected in his iridescent sunglasses. "Nothing like the mountains. You can hear God's heartbeat."

"That's what I always think." It was hard not to approve of a guy who appreciated the High Country. But of course, that didn't necessarily give him the right to be interested in Addisyn.

"I've always felt close to God in the mountains." Darius looked toward the west, where the High Peaks were framed by the businesses along Elkhorn Avenue. "I had a—a hard few years with Him. But even then, I could go into the mountains and feel His love."

She couldn't let her guard completely down. Not yet. "This is His country."

"Amen." He bent to pet Mercy, who gazed at him with pure adoration. Avery swallowed a sigh. Even the dog was charmed by Darius Payne.

"So, Darius." She busied herself arranging the spoons in orderly rows. "Addisyn never told me how you two met."

He gave a soft laugh. "It was just a crazy run-in, you know? I was in the coffee shop, and she was in line behind me. I was turning to leave and heard her hesitating about what to order. So I started talking to her about coffee."

The scene was easy to picture. Her sister had been lost, alone, in a strange place, and suddenly Darius had been there. But something didn't make sense. "Why was she at a coffee shop? She doesn't even drink coffee."

Confusion hollowed his laugh. "Are you kidding? She loves coffee. She even worked at the shop, after a while. She always had a latte in her hand."

Addisyn had worked at the coffee shop? She'd mentioned a job, but not where it had been. Avery narrowed her eyes. She knew Addisyn far better than Darius Payne possibly could. And she knew for a fact that an aversion to coffee was one of the traits she'd always shared with her sister. They didn't even have a coffeemaker at the house.

But before she could argue with him, Darius pulled his sunglasses off, revealing his blue-green eyes. Eyes the color of Dream Lake on a sunny day. Eyes that could easily sway a girl like Addisyn. "She talked about you all the time, you know."

Avery blinked. "I—no. She was—she was mad at me then."

"That's what she said." He shrugged. "But then in the next breath she'd be telling me about memories she had with you. Things you two had done. Advice you'd given her."

So even when there'd been a continent-wide rift between them, Addisyn hadn't let go. Not entirely. Avery blinked the tears back. "That—means a lot." *Stop.* She would not cry in front of Darius. She cleared her throat and gave a little more weight to her next words. "She's everything to me."

"I can tell. The bond you two have—it's special." He squinted at her in the sunshine, tapping his sunglasses against his palm. "I'm really glad she's back with you now."

"So am I." Avery glanced to the next booth, where Laz was wrapping up his conversation. Now was the time to drive home her final point. "I'd fight wildcats to stop anybody who tried to come between us."

Darius's expression tightened slightly. "I'm sure you would."

Laz was shouldering up to the table. "Miz Avery, how's our recruit?"

Avery sent Darius a *hold-that-thought* glance and then smiled at Laz. "Doing just fine."

Laz bumped the younger man on the arm. "Yep. He's one of the good ones!"

One of the good ones. Avery chewed her lip. She would have probably agreed...if the so-called good man weren't one of the many forces trying to tug Addisyn away again.

Darius began describing trout fishing in British Columbia to an enraptured Laz, and Avery gazed at the place where the boulders of Lumpy Ridge jumbled against the sky. Maybe she was being too hard on Darius, but she couldn't shake the memory of Brian.

She'd known from the beginning that he'd been up to no good—the darkness had wrapped around his face like smoky death. Every time she looked into his soul, past the plastic image he tried to project, she saw churning shadows.

She'd taken a few reads on Darius today, and so far, she'd seen nothing like that. Sure, she'd noticed some scarring on his soul, but most of the stronger hearts bore that. And the light was bright behind his eyes.

She should trust the read, trust the knowings, but she couldn't relax completely into her intuition. She would never let Addisyn be pulled away into something unhealthy again.

Actually, she would never let Addisyn be pulled away, period.

Of course, Addisyn wouldn't even admit there was an attraction between the two of them. Even last night at home, Addisyn had stuck to her ridiculous *we're-just-friends* story.

"Are you sure?" Avery had pinned Addisyn with the most intimidating big-sister look in her arsenal.

Addisyn had squirmed but shrugged. "Of course I'm sure."

"I don't want you getting mixed up with another guy who's going to—"

"Avery, I'm not *mixed up* with him!" Addisyn must have realized she was turning pink. She swallowed painfully and brushed her cheeks self-consciously. "But even still—he's a good guy." The pleading in her eyes had made her look much younger. "You've got to believe that, A."

"But you two are just friends."

"Right." A door had closed in Addisyn's expression. "You heard him yourself, didn't you?"

A woman in a Colorado T-shirt stepped to the other end of the booth, pointing to the spoons with a question Avery couldn't hear. Darius leaned forward and nodded, the sun glinting off his thick dark hair.

Just friends. As if.

Avery had seen Addisyn as a teenager, giggling over cute boys at school. She'd watched her swoon over TV actors and singers in popular boy bands. She'd once witnessed her flirting with a random boy in a convenience store—a moment that still made Addisyn flush sunburn-red every time Avery brought it up. And of course, she'd been there through the whole rollercoaster of Addisyn's infatuation with Brian.

But through all the chapters of their lives, she'd never seen Addisyn look at any guy the way she had looked at Darius Payne when she had hugged him last night.

"Hey, what time does Addisyn get off?" Darius studied his watch. "Five thirty, right?"

"Yes." Avery glanced down the street. She could almost see Skyla's store from here. "I'd expect her here by five forty-five or so."

"Awesome." His grin flashed before he turned back toward Laz.

Avery ran a finger down the grain of one of the spoons. Yes, Addisyn could say they were just friends. She could concoct whatever narrative she chose to try to fool Avery—or herself. But Avery knew as surely as autumn followed summer that what Addisyn felt for Darius Payne was far more than a crush.

And from the looks of things, the feeling was mutual.

△△　△△　△△

MUSIC WAS THUMPING from the park as Addisyn walked down Elkhorn from Skyla's store. The country concert was obviously in progress, and her heart was thudding harder than the drumbeats. She peered down the road, where the pointy white peaks of tents lined Bond Park's brick sidewalks.

Her emotions tipped her at one moment toward excitement and at the next toward dread. She'd worn nicer clothes than usual to work today—her pink cardigan, black jeans, and the suede boots Avery had given her for Christmas years ago. *"Boots for confidence,"* her sister had told her.

Which she needed plenty of.

Addisyn followed the sidewalk until she saw the Live Bigger booth. And Darius was leaning against the table. She shoved away the fear that she might choke on her heartbeat. "Hey."

"Hey yourself." Darius smiled. "Off work?"

"Yeah." She couldn't let him know how the sight of him affected her. The band ended a song with a drum crash, and she raised her voice. "Where are Avery and Laz?"

"Down front." He gestured toward the crowd clustered by the stage as the next song began. "I told them I'd wait here for you."

A heartbeat passed, then he stepped forward and wrapped his arms around her in an embrace deeper and longer than the one last night. The feeling warmed places in her soul that she hadn't even known were cold, melting away the uncertainty between them.

"I've missed you so much." Darius's words were soft against her ear.

"I've missed you too." For the briefest moment, she rested her head on his shoulder. But she couldn't stay in his arms. Not if she wanted to keep from spilling her whole heart to him. Not if she wanted to still be able to tell him no at the end of the night. She pulled away, back into the chilly evening air.

"So—" Darius looked confused, but determined. "I was wondering—would you maybe just want to walk for a few minutes? Before we go over to the concert?"

Addisyn glanced again toward the crowd, but she didn't see Avery anywhere. This was their chance. "Yes."

The band's rendition of Luke Combs's "Beautiful Crazy" faded behind them as Darius led the way down the sidewalk. Shop windows glowed in the gathering evening, and the cozy Dickens-style streetlamps were flicking on. The silence stretched between them again, but this time it felt softer, safer. Unhurried.

They'd strolled the length of the block before Darius cleared his throat. "Well, first of all, I'm sorry for barging in on you. You know, showing up at the store and—and everything." Hesitation hung from his grin. "I thought I'd surprise you—but I should have called or asked you if—"

"No." She stopped and brushed her fingertips against his arm. "I'm glad you came, Darius. Really."

"Good." His smile crinkled the corners of his eyes. "I wasn't for sure last night. You seemed sort of—I don't know, distant."

She couldn't let him know that she'd been spinning from the way his presence had collided with her heart. "I know. I'm sorry."

"It's okay." The streetlamps caught a glimmer of fun in his eyes. "I was just relieved you remembered me. At first I wasn't sure."

"Oh, very funny." Addisyn tapped her chin and pretended to concentrate. "Of course I remember you. Aren't you the guy addicted to Cuban lattes?"

His laugh whirled warmth through her. "Sure. That's me. Is that why you were so quiet last night? Trying to think who I was?"

"You know, it wasn't the best situation." She raised her eyebrows at him. "I mean, I couldn't really get a word in with my sister explaining how to handle hawks."

"C'mon, girl, that's useful information." He bumped her shoulder with his. "You never know when I might find me a hawk to take care of."

"So you learned something last night, is that what you're saying?" The jokes carbonated the air between them, the fun that had always marked their relationship sparkling again.

"Oh, definitely. How to check a hawk's wing, what cage size is best, how long a broken wing takes to heal." Darius ticked off each item on his fingers. "Oh, and what to do with leftover roadkill too."

"Darius!"

"I'm just saying. Next time Terry sets mousetraps at the center, I'm gonna tell him to freeze all the little guys and mail them down to you."

"Stop!" She shoved him but not before her giggle escaped.

He worked his face into a more serious expression, though the spark in his eyes remained. "So under the circumstances, I guess I can understand why you were a little quiet."

"Yes." She gave a soft laugh.

Dusk was draping over downtown, turning the air grainy like an old movie. The blurring of the edges brought its own kind of courage, as if the evening could hold their secrets. She could reach out now, be drawn into his arms, whisper how she felt about him and how much she—

A car whooshed by, its headlights spraying across their faces. Addisyn jerked away from the possibility. What was she doing? Thinking about how fun it was to tease him and how safe she felt with him beside her? She'd already fallen too far to escape without wounds.

"What's wrong?" He must have seen the change on her face.

"Oh—" She turned away and began walking again. She'd stood in one place long enough. "I was wondering."

"Wondering?" He jogged a couple steps to be by her side again.

"Yeah." She injected her tone with a lightness she didn't feel. "Wondering why you came over a thousand miles to learn about hawk rehab."

"Well, actually—" She could feel his eyes on her, but she wouldn't look his way. "I came here to talk to you about skating."

There it was, and the remains of the magic evaporated. "Darius." She gazed above the town lights, where the stars should be, but the night was darker than she'd realized. "I'm so sorry, but I already told you, I can't—"

"Hey, now." The kindness in his voice was its own kind of light. "I just—I just want to know why."

"Why—"

"Why you were really excited, and then all of a sudden you weren't."

She didn't have an answer. At least, not one she could share.

"Talk to me, Addisyn. Please." He stopped and touched her shoulder, waiting until she turned to face him. "I sort of feel like—like maybe I did something wrong. Made you upset or made you feel uncomfortable. If I did something—if I stepped out of line—I want to make it right."

He thought it was his fault? "Oh no, Darius!" Addisyn shook her head, begging him to see her sincerity. "It wasn't you at all. I promise."

"Then can you tell me what it was?" A soothing gentleness underscored his words.

Brian's face throbbed in her mind. Addisyn shivered in the darkness. "It's—it's complicated."

"Addisyn." His eyes locked on hers. "Are you in some kind of trouble? Is something wrong?"

If you won't skate for me, you won't skate for anyone.

"Addisyn, talk to me."

No, she could never tell him about the terror and humiliation of Brian's threat. "I'm fine." The answer was pure instinct.

Concern lingered in his eyes, but he nodded. "Okay."

She had to say something else, had to try to paint with broad strokes. "I went to Denver." She paused, watching the words waft away in the cloud of her breath. "I wanted to see how it would feel to skate again."

"And it felt bad?"

"No. No, it felt—great." She sighed. This couldn't be making sense to him. "But then—then I remembered some things I wanted to forget."

Just glancing toward her past tightened her throat. "Things that were—connected with skating. Before."

Understanding washed over Darius's face. "Addisyn, that's in the past. It's behind you now."

"Sometimes, Darius—" She fought for control, but tears were lapping at the edges of her words. "I don't know if it ever will be."

"Come here." He reached toward her with a warm and rich compassion. She clung to the distance for only a moment before letting him gather her in his arms.

"You're past all that." He drew her closer, as if trying to shield her from the darkness of the night. "That's behind you."

He didn't understand that her past was far from a distant reality. Didn't know that the person she'd been was still as close as her own shadow. She tried to muffle her tears, but she couldn't keep her shoulders from shaking.

"Hey, now. This is a new start." His hand circled soothingly on her back. "It's nothing like it was."

"I want to believe that, Darius." Brian's voice echoed in the canyons of her heart. "But I can't. It feels like—like my past is always one step behind." A desperate despair fogged over her. There were so many threats that even the security of his embrace couldn't guard against. "If I stop running for just one second, it will catch up."

"No." She could feel him shaking his head. "This isn't yesterday. This is today." He pulled back just far enough to meet her eyes. "Skating now—it would be all different. You wouldn't be competing. It's just a charity event, so no pressure or anything. And of course—" his tone lightened—"you'd have me right there to keep you out of trouble."

A shaky laugh came in spite of herself. She wiped her face and stepped back. "Is that so?"

"Definitely." He grinned, but there was still a serious light in his eyes. "Don't you see? Skating this time would be—" he glanced up, as if the right word would be written in the stars—"redemptive. For both of us."

Redemptive. The concept worked its way into Addisyn's soul. Darius was right, wasn't he? Skating with him would be a chance to rewrite the story. A way to go back to the place she'd fallen down and this time find a way to stand tall.

"So? What do you think?" His eyes held the question.

"I still don't know, Darius." The practical angles poked at her from all directions. "I doubt Avery would be happy about it. And she's put up with so much from me. I can't hurt her again."

"I don't want you to." Darius leaned against the light post. "She loves you to the moon and back. That's obvious. But what makes you so sure she wouldn't want you to do this?"

"Because—because skating came between us. Before."

"But again…that was before." Darius's tone was still calm. "Just talk to her about it. See what she actually thinks."

Addisyn bit her lip. She already knew what Avery thought—about skating and about Darius. But she could deal with that later.

"Come on, girl." Darius must have seen her wavering. "Come to Whistler."

"Just like that?"

He laughed softly. "Sure. I've thought this through." He started walking again, back toward Bond Park, and she fell into step beside him. "The performance is in January. So you can come up now and learn the routine, memorize the steps. Then after Christmas, you can come back a week or two before the actual event. We'll practice on our own in between. I've even got a choreography video."

When he put it like that, the idea sounded almost plausible. "Well…"

"The organization covers your travel expenses too. I already asked about that."

"Really?" Another barrier crumbling.

"Yeah. You'd get a nice performance fee too, you know."

She hadn't considered that. And she'd been hoping for a way to pay Avery back, hadn't she?

"And it's just one event. Nothing long-term. No commitment."

There were no objections left, but Addisyn could still feel herself stalling. "What about my job?"

"Didn't you say it was temporary? When will it be over?"

"The third weekend in October." She tried to picture her wall calendar. "I think it's the nineteenth or twentieth."

"Fine. So you come to Whistler the next week."

"I don't know much about pairs skating."

"You can learn it. The routine is really simple."

"It might be hard to get a flight that close to the holidays."

"A month before Thanksgiving?" Darius shook his head and grinned. "C'mon, girl. I'm not taking any more excuses."

He smiled into her eyes, and her heart swooped all over again. He was so wonderful—a guy like no other. And he was offering her a chance to rewrite the story of her dreams.

If you won't skate for me, you won't skate for anyone.

Anger flared within her. Why should she let Brian intimidate her? Why give him the power to call her shots? Her past couldn't intrude on the sacredness of her now. And really, knowing Brian, his threats were probably nothing but bluff.

The answer was rising to the surface of her heart, pushing past all the memories of Brian. The decision was crazy, but it was also the only one that made sense.

"Okay, Darius." They were back to Bond Park, the air swirling with music and laughter and celebration. "I'll come."

△△　△△　△△

AVERY WAS HELPING Laz load up the leftover inventory from the festival when Addisyn strolled up, Darius in tow. "Hey." She gave Avery a quick hug and gestured to the boxes. "Do you two need help getting those back to the store?"

"Uh—maybe." The streetlamps weren't giving out as much light as Avery would have liked. She aimed her pocket flashlight at the stacks of boxes, mentally compiling a to-do list. "But are you busy, or—"

"Well—" Addisyn glanced over her shoulder at Darius. "Darius mentioned we could talk for a few minutes before he left, but if you need me, then I can—"

"No, stay with him." Avery rubbed her eyes and stared at the boxes. It was going to be a long night.

"Are you sure? I mean—"

"Addisyn, I'm sure." She didn't have any more time or energy to continue the dance of pretend reluctance. "Hang out with Darius, then go on home. Okay? I'll be there soon."

Of course, *soon* was a relative term. It took a solid two hours for her and Laz to pack up, transport, and unload the remaining items—plus all the booth equipment. By the time Avery finally left the store, the moon was a half-closed eye over the mountains. But the turn onto her gravel driveway revealed lights gleaming from the downstairs windows. Addisyn must be home—and still awake.

She shuffled through the door and almost tripped over Addisyn's coat, sprawled haphazardly in the hall. She closed her eyes and bit back the annoyance. Oh, Addisyn was home, all right.

"Addisyn?" She snagged the coat on the hook—how hard was it to just hang up clothes when you took them off?—then peered into the kitchen. "There you are."

Addisyn was perched at the kitchen table. "I waited up for you."

"That was nice." Avery pulled out the chair across from Addisyn and studied her sister. In the old days, Addisyn had never waited up—unless she needed something. She chided herself for being so suspicious. "Guess what? It's snowing just a little."

"Wow!" Addisyn wrapped her fingers around the Styrofoam cup in front of her. "Isn't this early?"

"Nope, not at all. I doubt we'll get much here, but the High Peaks will be pounded."

"Will the store be closed tomorrow if it snows?"

"Around here?" Avery smiled. Addisyn still had so much to learn about the mountains. "It takes a couple feet of snow before businesses start shutting down. I should probably get my snow chains on soon, though." She blinked as a thought hit her. "By the way, have you gotten that clicking sound in your car checked out yet?"

Addisyn folded her arms. "No. I don't hear anything."

One easy chore, and Addisyn kept putting it off. Avery worked to keep her tone neutral. "Addisyn, I promise you, there's some kind of problem. You really need to get it checked out."

"Okay, okay." Addisyn held her hands up. "I'll take it to the mechanic soon." She took a sip from her cup.

Avery sniffed. Why did she smell—"Is that coffee?"

Addisyn glanced down at her drink, then back at Avery. "Yeah. Cuban latte."

So Darius had known her sister better than she thought. Better even than she did, apparently. "I didn't know you drank coffee."

"I started when I was in Whistler." Addisyn shrugged one shoulder casually and took another sip.

"You never mentioned it." The ache inside was silly. It was just coffee, for goodness' sakes.

Addisyn's expression was a mix of caught and confused. "I—well, I didn't know it was a big deal."

"It's not." Avery laced her fingers together under the table. *Back off.* It was ridiculous to see this as a reminder of how far apart they seemed to be, or of how little Avery really knew about her sister anymore. "Just—I would have gotten a coffeemaker here at the house. If I'd known."

"Oh, it's okay. I don't drink it every day. When I do, I just get it at the little shop downtown." She nudged the cup toward Avery. "Want to try a sip? You might like it."

"No." Why was she about to cry over coffee? She must be even more tired than she realized. She stood up. "I'm going to bed."

"Oh—" Addisyn pulled a sheepish expression. "Actually, I, uh, I had something I wanted to talk to you about real quick."

There it was. Avery ignored the sour taste in her soul as she sat back down. "Okay. What's up?"

"Well—" Addisyn took a long drink of coffee. Then she set the cup down and leaned back. "Darius asked me to come to Whistler for a couple weeks to—uh—"

"Go to Whistler?" Her voice was loud in the quiet house. Avery paused and took a breath. "By yourself?"

Addisyn tilted her head. "I wouldn't be by myself, A. Darius would be there."

Small help that was.

"Anyway—" Addisyn narrowed her eyes slightly. "I did it before."

"Yes, I know." The words were curt, shoving against the reality of

Addisyn's independence. So Darius *was* trying to lure Addisyn away. As she'd suspected. Addisyn didn't have money for a trip like that, so he was apparently paying her way, even. "Why does Darius want you to go up there?"

Addisyn took a deep breath, then let it out. "Just to visit."

"Where would you stay?"

"In a hotel. Of course." Addisyn's expression frosted slightly. "What are you implying?"

She shouldn't have gone there. "Nothing at all." Avery held up her hands. "I was just—checking."

Addisyn didn't look convinced. She took another drink. "I love Whistler. It's a fun place. And—actually—"

Avery waited, but Addisyn's sentence had stalled. "And actually what?"

"And actually—I really want to go. I told him I could leave right after my job was over, stay the next couple of weeks."

"You already told him you would go?"

Addisyn twirled her coffee cup on the table. "If it's okay with you, of course."

Was she really having this conversation? Really sitting here while Addisyn drank coffee and announced her intentions to jaunt off to a foreign country to visit a man Avery barely knew?

Well, not on her watch would this happen. The whole idea sounded risky, and anyway—

"Come on, A." Addisyn drank the last of her coffee, then folded her hands under her chin and tilted her head in the same adorable expression she'd worn when she'd begged Avery for a visit to the mall or help with homework. "Please? I really want to go." Her expression turned more serious. "Whistler has always helped me. Being there—it makes me happy. It helps me remember what's important."

Avery rubbed her eyes. The situation had her caged in a corner. She wanted to protest, wanted to launch into the litany of reasons this was a crazy idea. But if she pushed back now, she'd spark another argument like the one they'd had during the expo. And she couldn't risk giving Addisyn any more reasons to pull away.

Her sister was watching her with an expression ready to challenge. Avery sighed. "Just a visit, right?"

Something flickered over Addisyn's face, but in the next instant it was gone. "Right."

She was checkmated. "Well. Okay."

"Thanks, A!" Addisyn's chair toppled as she sprang up and flung her arms around Avery's shoulders. "You're the best."

Despite her misgivings, Avery gave in to her reluctant smile. She pulled Addisyn closer. "You know I'll want pictures."

"You'll have them." Addisyn grinned, the aroma of the coffee hanging on her breath. "I'll send you so much stuff, it will be like you're living the trip with me."

"That's what I want." Photos would keep them connected. Avery reached for Addisyn's empty Styrofoam cup and tossed it in the trash. "Now we'd better get to bed."

Despite the exhaustion and stress of the last few days, Avery couldn't sink into sleep. She stared into the darkness long after Addisyn's even breathing rose from the room down the hall. She still didn't like this idea, but surely she didn't need to worry. Addisyn wasn't going to Whistler to get into trouble. She just wanted to see a friend and explore a beautiful place.

There was nothing more to it than that.

Anyway, maybe it would be good for her. A little time away might help her be more settled when she came back. And by her own admission, Whistler was a place of peace for Addisyn. So maybe—if she truly was wrestling with something—being there would help her figure it out.

Avery burrowed further under her heavy quilt as the wind shuddered against the house. She swallowed the lump in her throat. She would miss Addisyn, but she wouldn't stand in her way. Especially not when the trip might offer Addisyn the one gift that so far, Avery hadn't been able to give her.

Happiness.

By Sunday evening, Laz was gone, and Avery was once again wearing her scrunched-up face. It seemed to Addisyn that he hadn't helped Avery all that much by simply blowing in and out for a single weekend. However, he claimed that he'd be back for good in about three weeks.

Right around when Addisyn would be leaving for Whistler.

Now it was Monday morning, and Addisyn was using her day off to help Avery at the store. After the epic hiking sock disaster, she had rather expected that Avery might banish her from Live Bigger entirely. But her sister was kind enough to find simple tasks for her to complete—although Addisyn still suspected that Avery would have probably managed better on her own.

Addisyn was sweeping the floor when the chime over the entrance rang. She peered around a display to see Skyla walk in. "Skyla!" Addisyn leaned on the broom. "Hi."

"Good morning." Skyla nodded with the faint warmth that passed for her smile. "It is a beautiful day. Many elk in the meadow."

"Yes, there's been a herd hanging around. Two or three bulls with them." Avery came from behind the counter. "Welcome, Skyla. Have you come to see Isaiah?"

"In a way." Skyla twirled her turquoise bracelet. "I am beginning a new painting with Isaiah in it. I need to sketch by his enclosure."

"Absolutely." Avery gestured to the back door. "Do you have anything you need us to help you carry?"

"My easel and supplies are in my car."

Avery glanced at Addisyn. "Ads, can you go help Skyla set up?"

Obviously, she could be spared. "Sure." Addisyn parked the broom in the corner and jogged into the gravel lot after Skyla. "Skyla, do you always paint in real life?"

"Paint in real life?" Skyla opened the trunk of her Bronco and glanced at Addisyn.

"Well, I mean, like, with real subjects. Instead of photos or something. Not that photos aren't real. Just—"

Surprisingly, Skyla's face relaxed into a true smile. "I understand. And sometimes I paint from photographs." She maneuvered a black portfolio from the trunk and handed it to Addisyn. "But it is always better, if possible, to paint with all the senses. And so when I paint in real life, as you say, I am not limited only to sight."

That was pretty vague, but Addisyn kind of understood. Maybe it was the same way Avery talked about getting a *"feel"* for certain things or places. "That's neat."

Skyla tucked a folding easel under her arm and closed the trunk. "We need to go. The lighting will change soon."

Lighting. Another aspect of painting that Addisyn had never considered. She squinted at the sky as she followed Skyla around Live Bigger toward Isaiah's cage. The sun was still soft this time of day, the shadows of the mountains blurring over the valleys.

Skyla was striding with purpose, skirt swishing through the dry grass. She had already propped the easel open by the time Addisyn hurried up with the portfolio and deposited it gingerly on the ground. "Here."

"Thank you." Skyla retrieved a large pad of drawing paper from the case and leaned it on the easel, adjusting it by a fraction of an inch.

"That's not a canvas."

"No. I am only doing sketches today." Skyla glanced toward Isaiah's enclosure. "He will need to be placed a certain way for the story of the painting."

"Oh. Okay."

Skyla lifted her face to the sky and closed her eyes, silent for enough time that Addisyn itched with restlessness. Just as she had almost decided to tiptoe back to the store, Skyla opened her eyes. "I was asking the Spirit to guide and guard." She pulled a handful of pencils from her bag and examined the tips. "It is always the first step."

"I see." The words would have felt awkward if Addisyn hadn't witnessed for herself the spiritual impact Skyla's paintings held. Who was to say that the God her sister called El Shaddai didn't pour His power through Skyla's brush?

"And the hawk!" Skyla swept a graceful bow in the direction of the cage, palms pressed like a prayer. "I always thank the birds."

"That's nice."

She should head back to the store, but there was something soothing in this moment, watching Skyla's restless pencil dance over the paper, listening to the dry grass murmuring with the wind.

"Skyla?"

"Hm?" Skyla took the extra pencil from between her teeth. "Yes?"

"May I stay and watch for a moment?"

"If you would like. But you may not look at the paper." Skyla gave the first laugh Addisyn had ever heard from her, a warm sound that pierced her reserve. "It would make me too nervous."

They were suddenly in the same sphere for the first time, and Addisyn laughed with her. "I understand." She plopped down in the grass and folded her legs under her. "I'll stay over here to the side."

The ground was warm and not as hard as she had expected. Addisyn breathed in the stillness and relaxed into the splash of sun over her head and shoulders. Skyla was wrapped fully in the holy hush, eyes probing from the bird to the paper, as if following invisible lines of power stretching between her and the hawk.

The hawk. Addisyn glanced at the cage. Why had Skyla chosen Isaiah? He was certainly more alert than he'd been the day Chayton had brought him to the store, with glossier feathers and more fluid movements. But he still couldn't fly, and he was still hunched in a narrow cage with his wing weighed by a bulky bandage. Maybe Skyla, with her artist's eye, had a different perspective.

"Hmm." Skyla glanced up at the sun, then back at the paper. "It does not come easily today."

"Why?"

"Something in the spirit, I suppose." Skyla tapped her pencil, then leaned toward the paper again. "The story of this painting is a challenging one to capture."

"The story? Like, the theme?"

"Yes. All my paintings have had a story. Ever since I began."

"How long ago was that?"

"Oh—" Skyla brushed her hair over her shoulder. "Long enough to have been taught by what I have painted. I suppose I truly began painting seriously in college. Fifteen years ago. I was an art major."

"Really? That's cool." Addisyn picked at the dry grass, the seeds crumbling between her fingers. "What college?"

"University of Colorado. Next to Manitou Springs."

A wall had risen in Skyla's tone. Addisyn angled her head. "Did you paint birds in college?"

Skyla's pencil froze. "No." She cleared her throat and erased the last line she had made. "Not yet."

Addisyn waited, but apparently no more of that history was coming. She glanced toward Isaiah again. "So…why did you want to paint Isaiah?"

"Because the story of this painting is healing." Skyla shaded her eyes and glanced at Addisyn. "He is the perfect bird for a painting on healing, do you not think?"

Actually, he seemed like the opposite. "He's not healed yet."

"Yes, but that is what makes him so perfect. He is in process. As are we all." The pencil was flicking over the paper once more. "Are you not?"

Once again, Skyla was ignoring the No Trespassing signs in her soul. "I—I don't know what you mean."

"You do. If you are still, you feel it inside yourself."

Addisyn shut her heart against the idea. "I don't understand."

"We all are wounded, yes? Wounded in so many ways." Skyla glanced upward. "Like the birds who come to the center. Some were hurt in ways for which they could not have been blamed. Gunshot wounds or poisoning or predators. But others—others were wounded by their own choosing."

The sun had transitioned from warm to hot. Addisyn shifted on the ground.

"And all our lives, we seek to be healed." Skyla's pencil dashed unerringly across the paper. "But the journey of seeking healing—of falling down and getting up and being broken and then made new—it is in that journey that wholeness is found."

Addisyn's legs were prickling from being tucked underneath her. She stood, stretching away the discomfort. "Isaiah is healing, and he's still in pain."

"Yes, but healing hurts." Skyla spoke with a quiet conviction. "There is much pain in that process, more than some can bear. Which is why they never learn to fly again." She tipped the pencil toward Addisyn. "Stay. Watch some more."

Addisyn was already backing away. "Thank you, but I have to go. Avery needs my help." Well, not entirely true, but true enough to escape from this conversation. "See you later, Skyla."

◬　◬　◬

THE HAWK TOOK Avery's breath away.

He'd always been striking, even at first, when his innate majesty had been veiled by injury. But now, after almost six weeks of care, he was nothing less than resplendent.

And today was another milestone. After examining the hawk, Chay had declared him healed enough to attempt flying again. And so he and Skyla had come to help Avery transfer Isaiah to the flight cage.

"So, this is it, right?" Avery felt the buoyant hope in her own words. "I mean, now that he can fly, isn't he healed?"

"Not yet." Chay scratched his chin. "His wing muscles have atrophied quite a bit. He needs to rebuild his stamina now. And he has to be able to master the more intricate elements of flight. Turning and landing and diving and so forth."

"Oh." Avery sighed. "So this isn't the finish line."

"More like the halfway point." Skyla glanced toward the woods, adjusting her autumn-colored knit poncho. "That is the purpose of the flight cage. He will remember how to fly, and he will grow strong again."

"Avery, you'll have to exercise him." Chay smiled at her. "But today, just watch me and see how it's done."

"I can do that." Avery brushed her palm against the top of Isaiah's box. He was quiet inside, settled except for the occasional rustle of a wing. Was he nervous? Did he somehow sense the weight that hung on the next moments?

Chay hefted the box and led the way along a short, narrow trail that tunneled into the woods. Avery blinked in astonishment when the path presented a clearing with something that looked like a cross between a cage and a greenhouse—a long lattice structure with walls of narrow boards spaced like fence palings. "Is that the flight cage?"

"Yes." Chay laughed. "It took me and Laz a darn long time to get this thing up. But it's been well worth it. Many birds have healed here."

Avery stepped inside the enclosure, her boots crunching over sawdust and dry leaves. The interior held its own mysterious kind of light, striped sun fitting through the boards. Strategically placed dead limbs, clearly meant to be perches, swung from the ceiling or rose from the floor.

"Like I said, I couldn't be happier with the bird." Chay's grin, as always, was contagious. "You've done a tremendous job, Avery."

She'd only done her best—far too little, no doubt. Avery ducked her head. "I just like helping him, is all."

"Well, you're very good at this kind of work." Chay latched the enclosure door behind them, then lifted Isaiah from the carrier. With his legs pinned in Chay's hands, the bird stretched skyward and thrashed his wings against the air.

His restlessness wrenched at Avery's heart. "He wants to fly."

"And we want that for him. That's what we're here for." Chay crooned soothingly to the bird. "Yeah, you've had a rough time? That's okay. We'll have you back out there real soon now. You ready?" With a sudden release, he tossed Isaiah upward.

A flurry of awkward flapping, wings tilting sideways, frantic grapple with gravity. Then Isaiah fluttered, none too gracefully, to the floor of the enclosure. He lurched to a standing position among the sawdust shavings, swiveling his head to inspect every corner of his new surroundings.

"Is he okay?" Avery crossed her arms over her chest to stop herself from dashing forward. "Did he hurt himself again?"

"Nope. This is normal." Chay clapped his hands behind Isaiah, and the hawk flapped forward a few feet. "He just needs more practice. He'll get it."

As Chay and Isaiah continued haltingly down the enclosure, Skyla stepped up beside Avery. "It is miraculous." Reverence shone from her words. "Seeing a bird take to wing again."

"Like holy ground, isn't it?"

"Yes." A rare smile flitted over Skyla's expression. "A reminder to hope again."

"Exactly." An understanding that Avery hadn't expected stretched itself between them. Maybe Skyla wasn't as formidable as she appeared. "By the way, my sister has enjoyed working for you this fall."

"Your sister! Yes!" Skyla's eyes widened. "I had forgotten you two are sisters." She peered at Avery with a gaze like a shaft of sun over the mountains. "Yes, I can see it. You are both much like each other."

Wistfulness weakened Avery's laugh. "Everybody says that. I think we looked more alike when we were younger, though."

Skyla shook her head. "Your sister does favor you. The lines of your faces are the same. But I was referring to essence, not appearance."

Essence? Avery blinked. What did Skyla see, especially now, when the cobweb threads that laced her and Addisyn together frayed more every day?

"Addisyn is a gifted soul." Skyla fingered the fringe on her poncho. "I'm sure you're proud of her."

"I am." Nothing could change that.

"She is on a journey to healing. I would be honored to have her work in the store once more next season. I always need help in the summer months and the early fall."

"Yes—I'll mention that to her." Addisyn would be around next year. Avery wouldn't consider the alternative. She turned away from the uncomfortable subject. "How long have you worked with the birds?"

"Since I met Chay." Skyla's face softened. "He taught me to watch for the wings. And to listen." A light breeze ruffled the air between them, Skyla's poncho fluttering slightly. "There is much to hear when one is truly aware."

"Yes." That much was true.

Stillness draped over the moment. Avery glanced up to where the clouds tumbled end over end across the swinging sky. She hadn't forgotten about the knowing she'd received when Chayton had brought Isaiah to the store—all those spinning wings, and the weightless wonder, and the cryptic words. *The wings will rise.* She'd prayed and pondered, but there had still been no answer. She was considering sharing the knowing with Skyla when the other woman spoke again, pointing down the enclosure. "They have reached the end."

Avery followed her gaze to see Chay at the far end of the flight cage, Isaiah flapping to an awkward halt on one of the suspended perches. She glanced at Skyla. "How does he look to you?"

"Most excellent." Skyla twisted her copper bracelet. "Weak, still, but moving skyward." Her gaze angled curious. "So you have been caring for him?"

"In a way." Avery shrugged. "I'm not a rehabber, of course. But since Laz was gone, your husband graciously agreed that I could help. With his oversight, of course."

Skyla turned her gaze to the hawk again. A few moments passed before she spoke. "You have done well."

Simple words, but coming from Skyla, they were heavy with honor. Avery smiled. "Thank you."

Another flurry of flapping, and Isaiah was airborne again. His movements were still jerky, but already, he could remain aloft for longer spurts. He flapped past Avery and Skyla, then once more gathered himself onto one of the perches.

"So you see how it's done? Just like this." Chay jogged up, his boots crunching over the sawdust. "You just run him back and forth, see? He'll fly a little bit, and you keep moving him down to the end. Then you start back the other way. Back and forth enough for him to practice."

"Okay." Avery still wasn't sure. "Won't that tire him out?"

"Not if you're careful. We'll start with just three laps." He pointed to her. "Your turn."

Avery took a bracing breath of the chilly October air. "All right."

She ran down the enclosure and jumped at the perch, waving her arms as Chay had done. "Come on, boy!"

His wings flashed free, and he swooped into air, so low over her head that she could hear the whip of his wingbeats. This time he glided nearly halfway down the enclosure before he sank to the floor in an awkward, but definitely improved, landing.

"Yes! That's it!" Chay's excitement was electrical. He slapped Avery's palm in a high-five as she jogged by. "Keep going!"

There was a certain magic to the process that Avery hadn't expected. The whirl of the world beyond the flight cage faded away. There was only the running back and forth in the flickering lattice light, the deep green scent of the pines, the wind tumbling her hair and the wild wings overhead. Far too soon, Chay held up his hand. "That's enough for today."

"Already?" Avery unzipped her jacket, warmed all through.

"Yeah. We don't want to tire him out here at first. Later he'll work up to more laps. And then every two weeks—" Chay tapped the clipboard he held—"I'll be evaluating his flight."

"To know when he's ready to go free." Avery was still breathless from the wings and the wonder.

"Exactly."

"Until then—" Skyla touched Avery's shoulder in an unmistakable blessing. "You will help him remember how to fly."

◬ ◬ ◬

HER FINAL DAY of working at the Bluefeather Boutique. Unexpected reluctance dragged at Addisyn as she prepared to leave for the last time. The little shop that had seemed so foreign when she'd first arrived was now a familiar friend.

"Addisyn, I thank you for helping me this autumn." Today Skyla was wearing a crinkled golden peasant dress with a deep orange scarf over her hair.

"It was fun." Addisyn was surprised by the truth of the words. "Thanks for letting me work here."

"It was the Spirit Who sent you." Skyla glanced upward. "Thank Him instead."

Addisyn cleared her throat. "Yes. Of course."

A movement out the front window caught her eye. Avery's truck was nosing into the parking lot. Her sister had insisted on driving her to her last day of work and picking her up, the way she used to do on Addisyn's first and last days of school.

"I believe that the patterns of our lives intersected for a reason." Skyla tilted her head. "To work with you has been a blessing. I wish you joy in your journey."

A blessing. And to think she'd once considered this woman aloof and unfriendly. "Thank you, Skyla. That means a lot."

There was searching in Skyla's gaze. "I hope you do find the healing you seek. Always remember how close the light is."

"I—I will."

The bell over the door sang out, and a blast of cool air swirled in around Avery. "Hi there, Skyla!"

"Greetings to you, Avery." Skyla nodded. "Your sister has done well. You should be proud."

"Oh, I am." Avery's smile was the kind that had always made Addisyn feel special. "Ready to go, Ads?"

As soon as they stepped onto the sidewalk, Avery swept her into a victory hug. "You did it!" She drew back and grinned. "Skyla is right. I'm very proud of you."

"Really?" Her sister's praise washed warm inside her soul.

"Of course." Avery started walking toward her truck. "Now, time to have some fun."

"What do you mean?" Excitement sparked in the air. What with the overwhelm at work and the tense moments between them, it had been a while since she'd seen Avery in this buoyant of a mood.

"Well, it occurred to me today that even after all these weeks, I've never taken you on the River Walk." Avery opened the truck door. "Toss your stuff. I'm going to show you the town."

"The River Walk?" Addisyn dropped her purse in the seat, slammed the truck door, and trotted after Avery, reaching her where the sidewalk wound behind Skyla's store. "Wow. This is so neat."

"You think?" Avery spread her arms with a grin. "Welcome to the

River Walk."

The concrete walkway meandered before them—the back doors of the shops on their right, the river tumbling past the base of a wooded slope to their left. Cottonwoods arched protectively over wrought-iron benches, and pansies lifted expectant faces from landscaped flower beds.

"What do you think?" Avery watched her like a parent presenting a child with a new toy.

"I love it!" Now she understood why so many customers had come into Skyla's shop through the back door. The welcoming aroma of Italian food puffed toward them as they passed an outdoor cafe, artsy tables circling under rafters strung with lights. "I mean, I knew there was something behind the store, but I never really saw it. I always parked out front and came in through that little plaza area."

"It's a neat world back here." Avery sidestepped a couple with a wide stroller.

"For sure." Water bubbled from a polished stone fountain to their right. "How far does this go?"

"All the way across town and over to Performance Park. But there's a courtyard where we can turn around in about a quarter mile." Avery gestured to a building behind the fountain. "This is a cute shop. Wanna go in for a minute?"

"Absolutely." How had she lived all these weeks on the verge of this special place and never found it? What else had she missed?

They wandered in and out of a few of the trendy little boutiques, which offered everything from souvenirs to clothing to home decor. Several had a selection of handmade goods, but none featured articles quite as unique as those in Skyla's store. In one shop, Avery pointed at a rack of T-shirts with a smirk. "Hey, Ads, you should get one of those."

Addisyn tapped the block lettering across the front of the camo material. "'Mountain Girl.' Yeah, I think not." She raised her eyebrow at Avery. "That'd be more your shirt, A."

"Nah, true mountain girls don't have to proclaim it across their shirts. I think I'll find something else." Avery glanced around at the displays, then pulled a floppy pink sunhat from a shelf and plopped it on her head with a silly face. "How 'bout this? Should I wear it to work once Laz gets back?"

The clash between the frilly hat and her sister's no-nonsense mountain clothes was the funniest thing Addisyn had seen in a while. She sagged in a fit of giggles. "Sure. As long as I'm there to see the look on his face."

Avery faked a hurt expression. "What? You don't think it would be perfect for my high-society life?" She drew herself into a pose straight from the pages of *Pride and Prejudice* and adopted a posh accent to match. "A truly accomplished lady should always attire herself in a hat such as this. Clearly your fashion sense is lacking, sister dear."

After the tense days they'd had, the laughter was a wonderful release. Addisyn shook her head, her words barely able to squeeze past the mirth. "Hold on." She fished her phone from her pocket. "Let me take your picture."

Just as Addisyn snapped the shot, the hat drooped forward over her sister's eyes. "I do believe it's big enough for Isaiah to nest in." She laughed and tossed the pink concoction back onto the shelf, smoothing one hand over her hair.

"Come on, Mountain Girl." Addisyn linked her arm through Avery's, the giggles still skating across the surface of the moment. "Let's get going before somebody throws us out of here."

They passed a playground overrun with squealing children and crossed Riverside Drive, then wandered through a flagstone courtyard. As they stepped off the wooden footbridge across Fall River, Avery grabbed Addisyn's arm. "Hey, check out the statue."

Boulders were stacked high amid a copse of gold-tipped aspens at the edge of the stream. And on the uppermost stone was a life-size bronze eagle in flight, one wing pointing skyward, the other seeming to barely balance on the rock. Addisyn gasped. "Whoa. That's gorgeous."

Avery squinted at the words on the plaque below the statue. "'Winged Rapture.' Reminds me of Isaiah."

"Yeah—me too." The raptor seemed to tremble with life, its placement atop the rocks making it look ready to soar into the scudding autumn clouds above. "Isaiah will fly like that one day soon."

"I hope so." Avery was watching the wings. "He's doing well in the flight cage, but it's a slow process."

Addisyn didn't know what the flight cage was, but she just nodded. "When can he be released?"

"I don't know." Avery shrugged and turned back the way they'd come. "Whenever Chayton thinks he's ready. After he passes his flight exams."

"Yeah." The roll and rush of the river flicked a fine spray at them. "You've done great with him."

Avery always held praise awkwardly, as though looking for someone else to pass it to. "I don't know about that. I've just done what I could. I love it, though."

The River Walk was more crowded now—couples chatting confidentially, teenage girls crowding around each other for selfies, mothers tugging on toddlers' hands. Addisyn smiled at an eager Jack Russell terrier trotting alongside a woman in a green sweater. "This is so neat, Avery. It kind of reminds me of Whistler."

The moment the comparison slipped out, she cringed, but Avery's expression didn't change. "So, this time tomorrow you'll be there."

"Yeah." Addisyn zipped her jacket higher. The temperatures were dropping with the sun, and the breeze off the river was brisk.

"You have your plane tickets, right? And is everything packed?"

"Yes. Tickets are good. And I've packed everything except a few things I needed today." She'd been ready for a week, actually. She'd already booked a room in the Gold Aspen Lodge—the same place she'd stayed during her last visit—and let Darius know her arrival time. And of course, she'd watched the choreography video over and over, analyzing the routine and thinking through the movements. But she didn't intend to share those last preparations with Avery.

"And you'll be back in two weeks, right?"

"Yes. That second Sunday. The eleventh, I think."

"Okay." Avery wandered to the railing next to the river, trailing one finger along the damp metal. "So what will you do there?"

"Uh—" Addisyn sorted through her words. "Well. There's lots of outdoor things. You know, festivals and farmer's markets and stuff. Cool shopping downtown. And mountain biking."

"That all sounds fun." Avery gripped the railing. "You'll have a great time."

"Yeah." All of those activities together weren't bigger than the blank of what she'd left out. Guilt sidled in next to Addisyn, its prickly shadow crawling over her soul.

Maybe—maybe she should tell Avery everything. Her sister couldn't force her to cancel her trip, could she? Not with the plane tickets already booked. Anyway, maybe she would understand. Even be supportive.

Or maybe everything would run the other way. Maybe they'd be dragged back into the irresistible current of conflict. Maybe the links would grow longer on the chains of worry her sister was forced to wear. Maybe moments like these—exploring the River Walk and giggling over hats and watching Isaiah grow strong—would wash downstream like the relentless waters of the river.

No. She'd simply go to Whistler and come back in two weeks, and there'd be no need to test the fragile cords that tied them to each other. Addisyn turned away from the guilt. *Not now. Not here. Not between us.* "When does Laz come back? Day after tomorrow, right?"

"Yes, and I'm so ready." Avery pushed away from the railing and started walking again. "I think things might finally settle down."

"Tourist season is almost over, isn't it?" Addisyn sidestepped an eager mom and dad photographing their three towheaded kids in front of one of the stores.

"Pretty much." Avery tapped Addisyn's arm. "When you come back from Whistler, we can do some more fun stuff, okay?"

The conversation continued, river-flowing easy, as they passed Skyla's store, heading toward the other end of the River Walk. Once they approached the second wooden bridge, the open-arms scent of coffee beckoned to Addisyn from the little shop on the corner where she usually bought her Cubans. Not today, of course. Not with Avery beside her.

The River Walk was quieter here, the stores behind them. "You haven't seen this." Avery pointed to a brushed silver xylophone just off the sidewalk. She twirled one of the mallets over the keys, then pointed ahead. "And the best part is up here."

They scuffed down a steep hill toward a short tunnel where the sidewalk burrowed under the road, and Addisyn gasped. "Wow!" The concrete portal to the tunnel was covered in small tiles, each one glazed with a child's crayon-bright drawing.

"The elementary schools made those for display when the tunnel was built. But that's not what I wanted to show you." Avery grabbed Addisyn's hand, tugging her forward into the shadows. "Check it out."

Blinking, Addisyn waited for sight to emerge from the dimness. The darkness was giving way to—"No way!"

Like a living kaleidoscope, dozens of multicolored lights swirled on the floor of the tunnel, each pattern flowing into the next. Addisyn's squeal echoed off the concrete walls. "Avery, this is awesome!"

"You like it?" Avery's face was silhouetted against the tunnel opening, but her grin wrapped around her words. "You know what it reminds me of?"

"Of course. The bowling alley when we were kids." Addisyn held out her hands, cupping the color. "It had all those lights on the floor when you walked in, just like this."

"Yes. And you thought it was magic." Avery gave a soft laugh. "How old were you then, ten maybe?"

"Nine, I think." These images had slept so long in the back of her brain, but now they were waking up. "I would beg you to walk me down there just so I could see the lights."

"Every day. Especially during the summer." From Avery's tone, she was as caught in the memory as Addisyn was.

Addisyn's throat pinched unexpectedly. "You always did it, didn't you?"

"Yeah. It made you happy." Avery shrugged. "It was a small thing."

One day, she'd find the words to show her sister the astronomical sum of all those small things.

Avery was still reliving the story. "And we would walk down there and stand in the lights, and then if nobody was around—"

"We'd dance." Addisyn grinned. "So let's do it again."

"What?" There was surprise in Avery's laugh, but not hesitation. "Right here?"

There was nobody else in the tunnel. Not that she would have cared anyway. "Absolutely." Addisyn punched her phone for "Fireflies," her favorite Owl City tune, then leaped into the lights. The colors showered over her like confetti. "A, you coming?"

"Wouldn't miss it." Avery was already bouncing next to her, arms overhead, her eyes shining in the light that splashed her face. "Now, you know I can't dance like you."

"Are you kidding? You're way better than me." The words were chopped breathless. "Remember some of those moves we made up?"

"You mean like the Dandelion?" Avery pinwheeled her arms, her hair floating around her face.

"Right!" She shouldn't have been surprised Avery remembered. "Or the Buffalo!" She gave an exaggerated sideways kick.

"Yes!" The chorus picked up, and Avery slapped her hand in a high-five. "Hey, we should go on tour!"

By the time the last notes of the song spilled, the dance had dissolved into giggles. Avery bent over her knees to catch her breath. "Start the song over."

"Start it over?" Addisyn raised her eyebrows. "Excuse me, but aren't you the one who thought this was crazy?"

"Changed my mind. I'm having too much fun." Avery flipped back upright and grinned. "Come on, Ads. Surely you're not tired already."

Addisyn laughed, pure golden joy tingling through her heart. This, *this*, was how it was supposed to be—the story they were always meant to live. The one where they weren't just sisters, but best friends.

She started the song over, the music lifting them both, and grabbed Avery's hands. And there in the lights that surprised the darkness, in the colors that drenched them in delight, they danced.

CHAPTER 12

First was a predawn drive to Denver, sleepy streetlamps blinking in the drowsy dark. Then a four-hour flight over a carpet of clouds that erased her sister's mountains within moments of takeoff. Now it was a jostling crowd spilling out of the skyway like beads from a broken string.

None of it could dampen Addisyn's enthusiasm. She inched along in the security lines with a smile so uncontrollable that her cheeks hurt. As she scanned her passport, she couldn't resist a celebratory fist pump. She'd made it to Vancouver! Less than two hours from Whistler. The bilingual signs that jutted throughout the concourse felt like a homecoming.

"Addisyn!"

Sparks shivered through her at the familiar voice. Before she could turn around, Darius was at her side. "You made it!" He hugged her, but her bulky carry-on pressed between them.

"Yeah…" Addisyn stepped back and fidgeted with a strand of her hair. She'd spent a large part of the flight preparing bright and witty remarks for this moment, but apparently she'd forgotten them in the overhead bin. "I'm here."

Well, obviously.

But Darius just smiled and reached for a Styrofoam travel cup perched on the railing next to him. "I brought you a Cuban. Not as good as yours, obviously, but still."

The cup glowed warmth within her hands. "Thank you."

"Let's get your bags." Darius's hand on her shoulder guided her through the crowds. "Then, you wanna grab something to eat?"

How could his touch always make her feel so completely protected? "Absolutely."

Baggage claim was a hassle, but twenty minutes later, they stepped outside, into the concrete puzzle of airport parking. A spatter of light rain stung her face.

"Yuck." Darius pulled his beanie a bit lower. "Rotten weather. If you want to wait here, I can bring the car around."

"Thanks, but it's fine." It would take far more than a little rain to dampen her spirits.

At his car, he opened the door for her. "You get in. I'll load your bags."

"Darius, I can help with—"

"No, no." The low ceiling of sky spit a bit more rain, and he shook his head. "Just sit in there where it's dry, okay? This will only take me a minute."

"Well…okay." No man had ever made her feel this special, and she savored the bliss of it. The passenger seat was as familiar as a gentle embrace. Darius even had that little maple leaf still swinging from his rearview mirror. But what was that on the dashboard? A photo. She leaned closer and blinked. A photo of—*her*. And him. Together, that day at Lost Lake…

"All loaded." Darius burst into the driver's seat. "It all fit in the trunk, except one bag, so I put that in the backseat where—" He froze with his seatbelt halfway across his chest. "Oh, uh, you noticed the picture."

"Yes." All this time, that picture had been taped to his dash? She watched the expressions play across his eyes. "I remember that day."

"It was a good day." Was it just the cold making his cheeks red? "I didn't want to forget it."

The rain whispered across the roof, lost in a silence that was begging for her to act. To reach for his hand and tell him that she'd forgotten nothing about their time together, that she was—

"Well, anyway." He clicked his seatbelt and turned the key. "Ready to go?"

"Oh. Yes." Addisyn swallowed down the intensity.

The rain hovered fitfully as they made their way through town, the wipers squeaking across the windshield. "So what's next?"

"Well, we're taking the Sea-to-Sky Road to Whistler." Darius tossed her a grin. "I mean, I guess you probably took it before, but I thought you might still enjoy it."

"Actually, I don't remember much about it. I was on an overcrowded bus both times." And both times she'd been drowning in distress—not appreciating scenery. But today…

"Great, then. I can show it to you. But first—" The rain was muddling the windshield, and Darius dialed the wiper speed up. "Lunch."

Addisyn's idea of *lunch* was sandwiches from a drive-through, but instead Darius parked in front of a trendy restaurant. As she climbed out of the car, the wind whipped the wonder around her. "Oh, Darius! That view!"

"Pretty spectacular, huh?" He shrugged on a windbreaker, clearly enjoying her reaction.

"More than spectacular."

The restaurant perched on the brink of a high rocky promontory leaning over an unrolling ribbon of river. A majestic suspension bridge spanned the water, turrets swooping toward the block-stacked buildings of Vancouver. And back of that—

"The mountains!" The profiles were captive curves, not yet the sharp etched peaks of Whistler, but still.

"Yep. The foothills, of course." Darius pointed at the bridge as they started for the restaurant. "That's Lions Gate Bridge. We'll cross it when we leave."

"And this river?"

"That's no river." Darius chuckled as he held the restaurant door for Addisyn. "That's the Burrard Inlet. A fjord that becomes Vancouver Harbor."

Embarrassment colored Addisyn's laugh, but her discomfort vanished inside the restaurant. They were seated at a table by a floor-to-ceiling window like a gateway to the breathtaking view. The place was warm and homey, a welcome refuge from the gray day outside. As they ate their Pacific grilled salmon, Darius gave her more details about the Sea-to-Sky Road. "It should take an hour and a half from here. I thought you might like to stop at the Nch'ḵay̓ viewpoint too."

"Yes, definitely." She didn't know where that was, but with Darius at her side, it didn't matter. She gazed across the inlet again. The wind was tugging on the treetops now, the rain pelting the windows more urgently. "Will it be raining in Whistler?"

"Probably." Darius reached for his coffee. "In fact, we might get our first snow while you're here."

"Really?"

"Yeah." He smiled. "Ski season is only three weeks away. It's time."

Once they finished eating, Darius went to pay for their food, and Addisyn wandered outside to the balcony area, empty on a day like this. The air was heavy with humidity, the rain once more a sullen drizzle. She drew in a deep breath, tasting the ocean-tang. An hour in Canada, and she already felt more at home than she had in over two months at Estes Park.

Her phone buzzed in her pocket. She pulled it out and glanced at the message on the screen.

Hey, Ads. Just checking on you. Haven't heard anything and it's long past your ETA. Flight ok?

Avery! Addisyn winced. How could she have forgotten her promise to text? Because Darius had absorbed all her thoughts, of course. Her thumbs flew through her response.

A, I forgot to text. I'm so so so sorry!!!! I'm good. Flight was fine. Darius picked me up. We're getting lunch then driving on to Whistler. I love you.

She snapped a picture of the bridge with the mountains behind it and sent the message. Two minutes later Avery's reply zoomed onto the screen.

Whoa!!! Scenery is beautiful. I see mountains. :) Be careful. I love you too.

The door creaked open. "Ready to go?" Darius's boots echoed across the boards.

Be careful. If there was a secret message in Avery's words, Addisyn didn't want to decode it. She slipped her phone back into her pocket. "Yes."

They crossed the Lions Gate Bridge with the gray sky pressing against the windows and the inlet wrinkling below, and then they were following the coastline north, on a curvy road fringed by evergreens that knew every secret. "Darius, this is gorgeous." A picnic area blurred by, huddled in a hollow of the forest. And then the road swung to the left, and the inlet once more flashed into view. "I definitely don't remember it being this pretty."

"It's a nice drive." Darius's hands were relaxed on the wheel. "Not passable all year round, though. I guess you saw my snow tires."

"Snow tires? No, I didn't notice."

"Yeah, it's the province law." Darius braked slightly to maneuver a particularly close curve. "No driving Sea-to-Sky without snow tires after October fifteenth."

"Really?" Addisyn raised her eyebrows at the scowling sky. "So we're going to get caught in a blizzard?"

His laugh wrapped her in warmth. "Hardly. But it's still going to be wet, I guess. Sorry the weather isn't better today. Not much of a welcome."

"Oh, it's okay." With her spirit so bright, who needed the sun?

It took about forty minutes to reach the Nch'ḵaẏ viewpoint. The rain had faded to mist, enabling them to wander around the small gravel parking area, but the views were completely blotted out by the clouds.

"The Native people named this place. Nch'ḵaẏ means 'haven.'" Darius pointed to their right. "They say a great flood swept this land, and up there on the mountain they were safe."

Safety on the mountains. It sounded like something Avery would say. "I like that story." Addisyn blinked away the mist that settled on her eyelashes.

"Too bad about this weather." Darius propped his hands on his hips, the lines of his profile strong against the wooded hillside, the ends of his dark hair curling with the humidity. "The view's not the best today."

His eyes were the color the inlet would be on sunny days. Addisyn glanced away. The view was the best anywhere to her.

Back in the car, Darius turned up the heat and rubbed his hands together. "Brrr. Getting colder out there." He winked at her. "Maybe your snow will come after all, yeah?"

She laughed. "I hope not."

"You might be snowed in all winter. Then you couldn't leave."

Darius's tone was airy with teasing, but something more serious lay in his eyes.

"Hmm." Addisyn watched the trickling trails of rain inch across the windows. "Might not be so bad."

The conversation faded to a comfortable silence, the road sweeping curve after curve, the wipers squeaking softly against the glaze of rain. Darius had turned the radio to '80s hits at a subdued volume, and now he began to sing softly.

Addisyn had never heard him sing, and she sank herself into stillness. He sang with a question in his voice, his emotions weighing out—as if he were singing to the mountains, or maybe to himself. The road curved and the rain swished silver and still he sang, thoughtfully, his soul unwinding with his voice, soothing her into a security she hadn't felt since childhood.

The moment cracked with a touch on her arm. "Addisyn? Hey. I didn't mean to startle you."

She blinked back to reality. The road looked different, and her neck was sore. "Wait—did I fall asleep?" She sat straighter, fumbling for her bearings.

"Yeah, for about thirty minutes."

Good grief, what awful manners! Heat squirmed across her face. "Wow—I didn't mean to."

Darius laughed. "Hey, I don't blame you, as early as your flight was. I just turned the radio off and let you sleep. There wasn't much to see anyway, with the clouds the way they are. Anyway—" he pointed—"I thought you'd want to be awake for this."

Snatches of buildings peeked from the trees ahead, like puzzle pieces fitting into finality. It looked like—

"Whistler!" She bounced in her seat, toddler-joy tingling through her. "Darius, we're here!"

"We are indeed." He grinned. "Welcome to Whistler."

Even huddled in the rain, the town still opened its arms to her. Her soul swelled with the love of this perfect place. *Nch'ḵay̓. Haven. Place to go when the flood rises.*

"So, it's 3:17." Darius glanced at the dashboard clock. "Where do you want to go?"

She'd planned on heading straight to her hotel when she arrived. But with Whistler welcoming her home… She grinned at Darius. "How 'bout the rink?"

The look on his face told her he'd hoped she would ask. "All right, then." The streets unrolled before them, the lights of the shops spilling golden carpets onto the sidewalks. "The rink it is."

△△ △△ △△

ADDISYN WASN'T PREPARED for the gut-punch of the memories. She froze on the threshold of the rink door.

"Just like you remember?" Behind her, Darius's voice was gentle.

"Yes." She forced her feet forward. The air still had the same smell of dedication and dreams. Nothing had changed since she'd trained in this rink before—as a nineteen-year-old at an elite skating program.

With Brian.

The eerie déjà vu toyed with her mind as she sat with Darius on the first row of bleachers, pulling on her skates. For a moment, a strange sense of panic breathed across her heart, as if the ghost of the girl she'd been was standing somewhere in the shadowed corners, in this place where—

No. She was imagining things. Of course this was not the same. Not even close. Everything was different now, just as Darius had said. Brian had no hold on her anymore, regardless of what idle threats he made or how many times he flickered through her nightmares.

"Addisyn?"

Darius's expression was expectant, and suddenly she realized he was waiting for her reply. "I—what?"

"I just asked if you were ready."

Why did she suddenly feel like stalling? She stared down at her still-unlaced skates. "I don't know—maybe it's not a good idea to practice tonight—I mean, I'm pretty stiff from the flight and the car ride and—"

"I'm not planning for us to practice tonight." He grinned. "For starters, I don't know the steps perfectly yet, and I'm not about to embarrass myself in front of America's top skater."

"Oh, Darius." Heat glowed in her cheeks with her hesitant laugh. "I

176

am not—"

"Come on." Before she could protest, he slipped to his knees in front of her chair and reached for her skates. "Hey." His voice was soft as he threaded the laces with an expert familiarity. "It's okay to be nervous."

The tenderness that tempered his strength would always take her breath away. "It's—you know. The last time I was here—"

"I know. But it's different this time." He tied the last knot and rested his hands on her knees. "I'm here. You're here. Everything is okay."

"I know, but—"

"No, don't overthink it. Let's just go out here and have fun." He stood and held out his hand.

He was only being gentlemanly, of course, but as she allowed him to pull her to her feet, the feel of his fingers between hers made all her doubts dissolve. And as soon as her skate blades met the ice, the painful memories splintered in the blaze of joy—the ecstasy that only came from this place.

Darius kept her hand in his as they glided around the rink. After a couple of laps, he pulled her to a stop. "Okay?"

The gentle skating felt wonderful, loosening muscles that were tight from the flight and the drive and the weeks of tension. "Yes. Better than okay."

The bright lights of the rink made his eyes look even bluer. "Good."

They continued with simple crossovers across the rink while Darius talked more about the program and choreography. "So the jumps are really basic, and there are only two that have to be synchronized. I think you'll be able to hear it in the music, though. It's right with the beat."

"I'm sure I will. And no more than two rotations?"

"Right. Lenny didn't think anything more was good for my back. Not yet, anyway." He squeezed her hand. "This will be easy for you. But I hope it's fun."

Addisyn leaned into his shoulder as they rounded a turn. "It will be so much fun."

The conversation continued as they practiced some choreographic steps and even attempted a couple of the jumps. "Way to go!" Addisyn cheered as Darius landed a toe flip.

He waved off her praise. "It was sloppy. But I'm getting better all the time."

"Sloppy? It looked great." It was hard to remember that Darius hadn't skated in so long. He had a natural grace and rhythm on the ice that attested to how deeply it throbbed in his soul, and how diligently he'd been working to return.

"So—" he skidded up beside her with a mischievous grin—"ready to take it up a notch?"

"Oh no." Addisyn shook her head in mock doom, but she didn't try to hide the sparkle in her eyes. "This can only be bad."

He laughed. "Thought we might try a lift."

"Um—" Addisyn narrowed her eyes. "What about your back?"

He shook his head. "This is fine. It's just an armpit lift. Lenny didn't put anything harder than that in the combination."

"I've never done lifts. I don't know what to—"

"All you need to do is hang on." Darius grinned. "For a lift like this, you're basically just letting me carry you. Super easy."

The excitement drowned out her nervousness. "Okay."

"So we start skating backward—" Darius took her hand and talked her through each step. "Now, put your left hand on my shoulder, and take my other hand with your right."

The movements were awkward, especially going backward. Addisyn reached with the wrong hand the first time and stumbled on the second. There was more frustration than humor in her laugh. "Darius, I can't make it work."

"No, you're good. You've got this." His patience was infinite. "Think of it like dancing, okay? Opposite hands, opposite arms. Just reach back for my shoulder and across for my other hand, and I'll do the rest."

"Okay." Her heartbeat was taking flight. Maybe from the thrill of being on the ice, or the challenge of learning the new move, or the proximity of Darius. Or all three. "Let's try again."

It took a few more attempts, but finally their hands connected at just the right moment. In a single fluid motion, Darius swept her up off the ice. Addisyn squealed and clung to him. "Darius, I'm going to fall!"

"No, no, that was good!" He set her down and leaned back to study her eyes. "How'd it feel?"

"A little scary." She laughed, the cool air of the ice rink tingling against her cheeks. "But exciting. Let's do it again."

Fifteen minutes later, they'd practiced the move several more times—enough that Addisyn was beginning to catch the natural cadence of it. "See? That's all there is to it." Darius swung her around again and nodded as she landed. "You're getting the feel of it."

"Yes. I think I am. One more time."

"One more."

Again, the backwards glide, hands connecting, Darius's arm strong under her shoulders. Then the upward lift, swirl above the ice, so close to him she could feel his breath on her face. Her feet found the ice again, but this time instead of stepping back, he wrapped her in his arms.

"How do you feel?" His voice was low, soft in the quiet rink.

The way it felt to be in his arms, she could have still been in midair. She closed her eyes and allowed herself to lean into his chest. "Good. Really good."

"Thank you for coming." He stroked her shoulder. "I mean that."

She leaned back just enough to lose herself in his eyes. "I'm glad I did."

There wasn't another man like Darius, another guy who would sing her through the rain and dance with her on the ice and hold her heart with gentle hands. He was leaning closer now, the depth in his eyes drawing her in—

And he stepped back.

"You know what we need?" His tone was lighter, the moment crumbled to powder all around them.

Cold-water disappointment splashed her, but she couldn't let it steal her breath. "What?" She found her ice-rink smile. "What do we need?"

"Ice cream." He held out his hand again.

"Ice cream?" She gripped his hand and glided with him toward the edge of the rink. She could back away from the moment, find her way once more to the safe ground of teasing. "It's about to snow outside, and you think we need ice cream."

"Oh, yes." He was already snapping on his skate guards. "There's a place down on Red Leaf Road. If you haven't had a waffle cone from there, you haven't lived." He looked up at her and grinned. "Ready?"

"Ready." For the ice cream, and the skating, and the adventure.

And for all that might happen in the two weeks ahead.

△△ △△ △△

LIKE A KEY in a lock, she was back where she belonged.

The crisp autumn air tingled in Addisyn's lungs as she strolled the sidewalk into the Whistler Village. Was any other little town so magical and inviting? Just walking under the Whistler flags on the lamp posts made her feel like the truest version of herself.

Mist rose from the mountains like fairy dust in the liquid morning sun. The gift shops were opening one by one, and an enticing aroma of something delicious wafted from the café on the corner.

Nch'ḵay̓. Haven…

It always had been. Especially when she'd visited the last time. She'd been so broken, so frightened, so helpless—yet even then, the Canadian town had wrapped its arms around her.

When she arrived at the rink, she flashed her ID at the door and headed to the practice area. Darius would join her once his shift ended at noon, but until then, she could practice alone for a couple of hours.

She glided onto the ice, into the movements that were their own kind of magic. She was deep in her own world when she heard her name.

"Addisyn Miles? Is that you?"

Addisyn snapped her head up to see a girl leaning against the railing around the ice. A girl who looked like—

Addisyn blinked. "Nikki? No way!"

"It's me." Nikki's laugh held an uncomfortable strain. "What a pleasant surprise."

The surprise part she could agree with. Addisyn forced a smile and skated up to the railing. "I never expected to see you here." The nicest thing she could say without overtly lying.

Nikki gave Addisyn an awkward hug, the railing rising between them. "Same. It's been too long."

"Yeah, I know." Addisyn flicked a hand through her hair and studied the girl who'd been her fiercest competition at most of her events. The girl who was probably even now sizing her up. "You, uh, training here?"

"Yes." Nikki brushed a fingertip over her eyebrow. If she added any more makeup, her face might crack. "I'm here for the Next Wave conference."

"Oh." Addisyn gripped the railing. She'd attended that very conference here. Before—well, everything.

"I received the Rising Stars sponsorship this year, did you hear?" Nikki tilted her head to one side with a decidedly feline expression.

The same sponsorship she'd lost. Addisyn wouldn't allow her face to show the pain of the soul-slam. "Nope. Hadn't heard."

"Isn't that the same sponsorship you—"

"Yep." This conversation would soon devolve into a full-blown catfight unless she relocated it to safer ground. "So, do you like it here?"

Nikki scrunched her delicate features. "Not really. It's so out of the way up here in this one-horse town." She brushed an invisible speck from the sleeve of her hot pink jacket. "Can you recommend any good places to hang? Clubs or anything?"

The question made the ice tilt slightly under her skates, but of course. Nikki still knew her as the girl she'd been—the one who'd frequented the nightlife scene with Brian. "Uh—no." She blinked back the disorientation. "Not much into partying these days."

"Good for you." Nikki's tone stopped just short of patronizing. "Probably better for your performance."

"Yeah, I think so." No need to let her rival know she wasn't exactly performing at the moment.

"I should follow suit."

Why did people say things like that? Self-deprecating comments with which you weren't allowed to either argue or agree? A vague smile seemed like the only safe response.

"It's just, you know, Ty likes to party." Nikki examined her lime-green fingernails. Were they really two inches long, or were those fake? "He'll be joining me day after tomorrow."

"Oh. Gotcha." Nikki's coach worked at an agency in Buffalo, but Addisyn had met him at several competitions. She'd never pegged the reserved, detail-driven guy as a club hopper. But then, she'd been wrong about Brian too.

"Speaking of coaches—" Nikki glanced around the rink—"where's Brian? Don't tell me he sent you up here by yourself."

"Uh—" Addisyn fiddled with her ponytail. Did Nikki truly not know? "We broke up."

The look of shock on Nikki's face couldn't have been contrived. "No way. Really?"

"Yep."

"Oh."

Addisyn scuffed her skate blade against the ice twice before Nikki spoke again. "Sorry." For the first time, she almost looked sympathetic. Almost. "I didn't know. I mean, I knew I didn't see you at Regionals this year, but I thought—"

"It's okay." Addisyn injected a breeziness into her tone. The last thing she wanted was crumbs of pity from Nikki. "It was the best thing for both of us."

"So—" Nikki narrowed her eyes. "Was he cheating, or—"

"It was a mutual decision."

Nikki twisted her lips to the side in her irritating *I-don't-believe-you* face. But just as Addisyn was seriously considering slapping her, she changed the subject. "So, someone said you were with Team Unlimited now."

"No." Addisyn fiddled with the zipper on her jacket. "I had a tryout over the summer, but I ended up not—uh—not taking that route."

"Oh, I see." Something unpleasant crept into Nikki's tone. "Well, I hear the competition there is stiff, so don't feel too bad." Although her voice suggested she rather hoped Addisyn did.

So now Nikki thought she'd been dumped by her boyfriend and rejected by a potential sponsor? Addisyn bristled. "I had an offer from them, Nikki. I just didn't take it." Well, technically she'd walked out on her audition—but had she stayed, she would have had an offer.

"You gave up Team Unlimited?" Nikki folded her face into some annoying mixture of disbelief and condescension.

"Yeah, well, I had a better opportunity." The words flashed out before she could stop them.

"Really?"

No. She'd gone too far. But when she opened her mouth to retract her ridiculous statement, her competitive teenage self was still speaking for her. "It's—uh—well, I can't say too much. All I know is it's going to be huge."

If Addisyn hadn't been so alarmed by the lie she'd just unleashed, the look on Nikki's face would have been funny. "Um—okay." She paused, her mental wheels clearly spinning. "So—you won't be back to skate with Brian?"

Addisyn smiled and shrugged. "No." That, at least, was true.

"Wow." Nikki laughed uncertainly and brushed her hands down her size-zero legs. "Bigger and better things, huh?"

Before Addisyn could respond, the rink door gave a soft creak behind her, and Nikki's gaze shifted past her shoulder. "Who's that? He looks familiar."

Addisyn glanced back just in time to see Darius wave at her and sit on a bench to lace his skates. Satisfaction curled through her. She couldn't have timed this better. "Oh, him? That's Darius Payne."

"Payne—" Nikki's jaw hung limp. "Darius *Andrew* Payne? From Vancouver?"

"Yes."

"Whoa. I didn't know he was still training. He's an icon, you know?" She propped herself into a more sultry pose. "And hot. Look at that hair...and those eyes..."

Addisyn watched Nikki out of the corner of her eye and prepared to relish the revenge of a lifetime. "He's my skating partner."

"Your—" Nikki's gaze swung to her with a respect Addisyn had never seen on her face before. "Girl—better opportunity is right." She leaned across the railing. "Come on. What are you two practicing for?"

The needling of her conscience was a small price to pay for the satisfaction of this moment. Maybe now Nikki would quit thinking of her as some poor had-been who'd been dumped by her boyfriend and abandoned by her agency. Addisyn just tipped her head to the side with her best mysterious air. "You'll have to wait and see." The event coordinators hadn't done any advertising yet, and Nikki would be back in

New York before she could discover that the big opportunity was nothing more than a benefit performance. In the meantime, maybe she could entertain herself with some far-flung speculations. And maybe she could whisper them to a few friends back in New York. Let everybody know that Addisyn Miles wasn't hiding somewhere licking her wounds.

"Addisyn!" Darius glided up beside her and wrapped his arm around her shoulder. "Who's your friend?"

"Hey, Darius. This is Nikki Stelles. I know her from skating." She couldn't have kept the smugness out of her voice even if she'd wanted to. Which she didn't. "Nikki, this is Darius Payne."

"Nikki, nice to meet you."

Nikki's eyes were enormous behind her fake lashes. She shook his hand as if in a trance. "Darius Payne." Her breathy laugh was almost a snort. "This is so cool. I want you to know, I admire your skating so much. I mean—you are just such an inspiration to me—to everyone, really—"

Nikki was getting ready to go into full-on fangirl mode and embarrass all of them. Addisyn grimaced, but Darius just nodded politely. "Well, thanks. It's a real joy to skate with Addisyn. We're getting ready for the—"

Oh no. "Darius!" Addisyn caught his elbow. "We need to practice." She smiled sweetly at Nikki as she herded Darius away. "Been great catching up, Nikki. See you around."

CHAPTER 13

"So we're just gonna take this jump, and then a glide." Darius studied Addisyn's face, but he saw no hint of hesitation. "Ready?"

"Ready." The total trust shining from her eyes knocked his breath away.

He wrapped his arm around her waist and drew her closer. Did she not feel it every time they touched? A pull stronger than gravity? He nodded to Lenny, and the music started. "Five…six…seven…eight."

With the ice under him and the music carrying him forward, Darius let himself be caught in the intricate fluid grace of skating, the beauty of the sport that had threaded through his entire life. He tried to focus more on the steps than on the feel of Addisyn in his arms.

The music was building. Time for the lift. Darius caught her hand and glided backward. "And…now." At his whispered signal, Addisyn gripped his shoulder and opposite hand, and he swung her gracefully up and around, as if they were dancing at an enchanted ball.

"Hold on, right there!" The music cut with Lenny's call, the delicate magic of the moment shattered. "Beautiful, guys. Let me check these notes, and you can start back from the toe flip."

"Whew." Addisyn sagged over her knees for a moment, then straightened with a laugh. "Is he always this much of a drill sergeant?"

"This is nothing. You should see him in the gym."

"I don't even want to imagine." She made a face and shook her head. "But I don't care. This is the most fun I've had in forever."

"It's fun for me too." If only she would see through his words to his heart. "You're the best skating partner I've ever had."

She just smiled and tapped his arm. "You must not have had too many."

"All right, guys, back at it!" The music started again, closing the conversation. And as they continued through the sequence, Darius fought against the familiar frustration.

Every day was pulling him deeper and deeper into her magic. Every day convinced him more and more that he never wanted to let her go. Yet every time he tried to tell her how he felt, the words twisted in his throat.

Like the night they'd arrived. He'd almost kissed her, right here on this ice. And a dozen times since then he'd been handed the ideal moment to open his heart. But he was so afraid—afraid of moving too fast, of going too far, of scaring her all the way back to America.

Part of his hesitation came from the sense that she was hiding her heart behind sparkling armor. She kept their conversations light—witty banter or chats about the surroundings or details of her life back in Colorado. Sometimes he was able to convince himself he saw longing in her eyes. But most of the time, he was sinkingly sure she only saw him as a good friend.

The thought hit him so hard he missed a step and stumbled.

"Break!" Lenny clapped his hands. "Darius, what happened?"

"Nothing. Just tripped." His laugh was weak.

"Okay." Lenny flashed a thumbs-up. "No problem, man. Take five."

Darius glided over the ice to where he'd left his water bottle on the railing. Addisyn came up beside him as he took a drink. "Are you okay?"

"Yes." He swallowed his feelings along with the rest of his water. "Just had a moment."

"We all do at times." Her smile pulled the rope around his heart even tighter. "Ready to try it again?"

That was another thing that made Addisyn wonderful. Her technique was faultless, and she'd mastered her part of the lifts in no time. Yet she was nothing if not encouraging, never showing frustration when Darius missed a step and always ready with some self-deprecating joke when he referred to her skill.

Thirty minutes later, they'd finished the workout, and Lenny tossed them each a towel. "That's great, guys." His smile was brighter than the arena lights. "You two are perfect together."

Perfect together. Darius rubbed the towel over his face. If only he could convince Addisyn of that.

"As a matter of fact—" Lenny folded his arms. "I have a proposal for the two of you."

A glance at Addisyn showed she was as surprised by this as he was. "A proposal?"

"Yes." Lenny hesitated. "This isn't something I normally tell clients, but—well, you two are special." He looked seriously between them. "The chemistry between you is incredible."

If only Lenny knew.

"You're doing a basic program, I mean, not even competition level, and I'm blown away. And I just keep thinking, you know—this could be bigger."

"What do you mean?" Addisyn spoke first.

"Well." Lenny hesitated. "Darius, you've heard me talk about my pal Brett Hart. You know, he coaches the pros here."

"Right." Of course Darius knew of Brett. The man's name was a legend among skaters.

"I want him to see you two perform. Either at the benefit, or an audition beforehand. I think he'd be mighty interested."

Addisyn spoke first. "You mean—he might recruit us?"

"If you skate like you're skating right now, no *might* about it."

"You're kidding." Darius studied his usually playful friend, but bedrock seriousness was in Lenny's eyes.

"No, dude, I'm not." Lenny shook his head. "You two are incredible together. And you can go farther than this." He shrugged. "Of course, you've got months till then. I just want you to know."

"Wow." Darius tried to clear the wad of cotton from his throat. "Thank you. For having faith in us."

"Always have faith. It moves mountains, y'know." Lenny gave a knowing smile and glanced upward. "And may I point out—a lot of mountains have already moved to make this moment possible."

WHEN BRIAN JERKED open the door, the irritating rhythm of jazz music spilled onto the sidewalk. He cursed softly as he headed through the shadowy club for the bar. Of course. He'd forgotten Friday was jazz night at Club Cinco. Could nothing go right for him?

He slumped onto a leather stool and yanked at his tie in a sudden burst of frustration. These days, it might as well be a noose around his neck.

"What'll it be, sir?" The bartender's thick mustache curved upward in a hopeful smile. "Perhaps a vodka cocktail? The Moscow Mule is popular tonight."

Brian flicked the suggestion away. Vodka screaming through his veins wouldn't help his stress levels in the slightest. "An old fashioned, and make it quick."

"Coming up." The man nodded and turned to the backlit bouquet of bottles behind him.

A woman's laugh tinkled, and Brian glanced over his shoulder. There were plenty of folks here tonight, collected in twos and threes at the confidential corner tables, but no one he recognized, which was a relief. Nothing said *pathetic* like drinking alone on a Friday night. He'd almost stayed home rather than risk humiliation, but these days, the upscale atmosphere of Club Cinco was the only place he could find a measure of calm.

"Here's your old fashioned, sir." The waiter clinked the glass onto the granite countertop. "Cheers."

The word was bitterly out of place. Brian just nodded and took the first sip, allowing the fruity flavor to swirl on his tongue for a moment. But instead of slinking away, his frustration pulled out a seat and perched next to him. How could a glass or two really help? When all his problems were tangling around his neck like a cursed constrictor?

The items stacked up on his mental list. None of the girls he'd met in Denver had been worth signing. Barmilli was watching his every step. And of course, there was the issue of Addisyn.

If she was competing again, and if Barmilli found out, there'd be no undoing the fallout. As Brian had done a hundred times since he'd seen her in Denver, he scanned back through their encounter, analyzing each word, each look, each detail of the conversation. Searching for the clues that had to be there.

The whole event was full of discrepancies. She'd claimed to be living with Avery, first of all. Brian took another sip of his drink and shook his head. After all the ways Addisyn had betrayed her, why would Bible-thumping Avery give her a second chance? But then, weren't religious people into forgiveness and all that? So maybe Avery saw this as her Christian duty. Redemption or whatever.

And then Addisyn had claimed to be *just practicing*. She had to realize how ridiculous that sounded. Skating at the center in Denver was a privilege reserved for USFS members, athletes with purposeful professional objectives. And anyway, Addisyn was a competitor. She'd always been. She wouldn't be hanging on the fringes of the world she left behind—unless she was planning to reenter it.

But if she really was competing again, why hadn't he heard about it? She hadn't been at Regionals. Her name wasn't tossed about by media or mentioned in sponsorship circles. And she wasn't on the client list of any of the elite agencies he worked with.

The whole situation was a puzzle he couldn't solve. But sooner or later, the pieces would slide into place. And he'd be left staring at a picture he already knew he wouldn't like.

"Hey, Felding."

Oh, man. He'd been seen. Brian forced a smile as Ty Burke slid onto the neighboring stool. "Ty. Hey. What brings you to town?"

"Client auditions. Just flew in from Buffalo."

"Good luck with that." Ty coached at an upstate agency. Nice place, but not nearly as big as Brian's.

"Drinking alone, man?" The dim lighting couldn't hide the hint of antagonism gleaming behind Ty's smile.

Brian twirled his glass and considered his response. "Just winding down, you know?"

"Gotcha." Ty chuckled in a way Brian didn't find funny. "I bet you've got a lot of winding down to do." He snapped his fingers for the waiter and watched Brian with a sideways gaze.

"Meaning—"

Ty shrugged. "Well, it's no secret you kind of lost your golden girl."

So everybody in the skating sphere was talking about him? Pitying him? He wanted to wipe that stupid sneer off Ty's face, but he had to choose his words carefully. Ty might not be as talented as he was, but he was just as ambitious. Very likely he was watching Brian's position—already angling for it. "Well." He took another sip of his drink. "It was for the best."

"Hmm." Ty nodded at the bartender as the man slid a martini across the counter. "Bad deal for you, though."

Brian didn't care to be reminded of how bad the deal was. He lifted his glass again.

"Whatever happened between you two? Thought you kind of had more going on than just coach and athlete." Ty gave a particularly irritating wink.

"She was ready to retire." He was sick of singing this song to every inquiry. "Decided she was done with the whole thing."

"Really?" Ty cocked his head. "That's not what I hear."

What? Brian studied the wineglasses dangling above the bar. Ty could be baiting him. Best not to appear too eager. "What did you hear?"

"You know Nikki Stelles?" Ty cleared his throat. "My, uh, client?"

Brian nodded. Everybody in the Mid-Atlantic Region knew about Nikki and Ty—another duo who often made skating headlines. And who were also suspected of blurring their professional and personal lives.

"So…" The pianist finished a song amid a smattering of applause, and Ty leaned closer as if divulging a state secret. "Nikki's out of town right now for a training conference. I'm flying out to meet her there tomorrow morning."

"And what does that have to do with Addisyn?" Impatience sharpened his tone.

"Because Nikki saw Addisyn at the rink yesterday."

His heart rate doubled, but he forced his poker face. "What rink?"

"Whistler Olympic Centre. Nikki's at that Rising Stars conference, you know."

Whistler.

He almost choked on his drink. Whistler, of course! He set his glass down and stared at Ty. "Is Nikki sure?"

"Very sure." Ty nodded. "She mentioned it on the phone last night. She talked to Addisyn and everything."

"What did Addisyn say?" Maintaining his indifferent act was becoming more difficult.

Ty took a long pull of his martini, watching Brian over the rim of his glass. Finally he set his drink down and wiped his mouth. "She said she was there to practice for an event. According to Nikki, it was some big opportunity. Something so huge Addisyn wouldn't tell her too much about it."

Fury crackled through him, his heartbeat throbbing in his ears. So Addisyn had been lying to him. Just as he'd thought. Retired in Colorado with her sister? What a joke. No, she was planning to perform again. And then Barmilli would see her name, and he would—

"And she was skating with some guy." Ty rubbed his chin. "She introduced Nikki to him. I forget the name, but he was somebody famous—you know, uh—"

In Whistler, there was only one guy Addisyn would have been with. "Andrew Payne?" The name scorched the inside of his mouth.

"Yes! Andrew Payne." Ty took another drink. "Oh yeah, and Nikki asked her where you were, 'cause Nikki didn't know about—you know—and Addisyn told her you two had broken up."

So on top of everything else, she was bragging about their breakup? Great. Just great. Ty was waiting. He had to say something. "Wow." He realized his hands were fists. He shook them out and tried to snatch a deep breath. "That's—interesting."

Ty cocked his head. "So—did she dump you? Or the other way around?"

"I was done with her." Brian coughed out a laugh. "She turned out to be as crazy as her sister."

"Didn't know she had a sister." Ty frowned. "I never saw her at the competitions or anything."

"She didn't support Addisyn's skating." That was putting it mildly.

"Is that why she quit?"

"Uh—" It was a good enough story, and it took the heat off him. "Yeah."

"Man." Ty looked almost sympathetic for the first time. "Seems like she should have at least had to finish out her contract. You know, I was just talking to my buddy the other day about how—"

Ty's mouth was still moving, but Brian's mind had frozen on the beginning of his statement.

Her contract.

That was it! The perfect solution. The trap Addisyn couldn't escape. How had he not thought of it before?

He drained the last of his drink and stood. "Gotta go. See ya, Ty." He slapped the guy's shoulder, a little harder than necessary.

"Hey, where are you—"

Brian didn't pay any more attention to the chattering fool. Instead, he yanked down his sleeves and marched purposefully toward the door. The heady sense of power was more intoxicating than alcohol could ever be.

△△ △△ △△

SOMETHING WASN'T RIGHT.

Baylie had known that for a long time, of course. Probably since the first day she agreed to work for Brian Felding. But this—this was a whole new level.

She bit her bottom lip and tried one more time. "Mr. Felding—what I'm saying is that I know you need this client schedule by the end of the day. I don't have time to take on another project before I can finish with—"

His hand smacked the top of her desk with a crack that made her jump. "It can't wait!" He scowled at her, an odd, almost feverish brightness to his eyes. "Look, this is urgent. Put the client schedule aside for now."

There was no use arguing. Baylie had at least learned that much in her six months of working for Mr. Felding. She closed the file on her computer and nodded. "Yes, sir. Can you please tell me what information you'll be needing?"

"All of it! Audition notes, training records, registration. And her

192

paperwork file, of course. You got it?"

"Yes, sir." Could she chance another question? "I'm sorry, sir—but why do you need all of this? Especially for a skater who's no longer—"

His curse burned roughly through the air. "That's not your problem, okay?" He ran a hand over his hair and seemed to gather some shreds of calm. "Look, I just need to clear out some old data. Just send me what you've got so I can decide what needs to go."

Nothing about this made sense. Especially when paired with his almost manic intensity. But satisfying her curiosity wasn't worth hazarding her already tenuous job security. "Yes, sir. I'll have it for you by lunch."

"Before lunch." He was already walking into his office, the words tossed carelessly over his shoulder like litter from a car window. "You've got time if you're not lazy."

The door of his office slammed shut like an exclamation point on his statement. Baylie gritted her teeth and rotated her shoulders, trying to shake off the stress of the encounter.

Moments like this made her long for the days when she'd worked downstairs in the receptionist area, alongside Mrs. White. When she'd been given this so-called promotion, the chance to work as Mr. Felding's private secretary, she'd been eager for all the supposed advantages—her own office, increased pay, and the chance to escape from grouchy Mrs. White's constant glass-half-empty mentality. Little had she realized that her new boss would be far worse than Mrs. White, even at her most cantankerous.

Well, she had to keep going. Only one more year at this snobby-nosed agency, and she'd finally have enough money saved for design school. Then someone else could sit under the thundercloud of Mr. Felding's wrath all day.

She clicked the folder on her desktop computer, searching for the name he'd scribbled on the office memo. Michaels, Rachael…Milburn, Tara…Miles, Addisyn. There.

She opened the file and waited while the computer loaded. The first item to appear was Addisyn's photo. Baylie's eyes widened. Oh! So that's who that was!

She hadn't known Addisyn personally, of course. But from her station behind the receptionist desk, she'd often seen Addisyn breezing in and out of the agency. Unlike many of the other skaters, Addisyn had always been kind, calling a cheery hello to the receptionists on her way to the elevator.

Baylie had always waved and called back. It sounded silly, but she had just had this feeling that she and Addisyn would have been good friends, if there hadn't been a wall between their worlds.

Mrs. White, on the other hand, had never acknowledged Addisyn's greetings. One day Baylie had asked about her stoic silence, and the older woman had cleared her throat with a sour expression. "Miss Miles is involved in some, well, inappropriate activities."

"Inappropriate?"

Mrs. White had removed her eyeglasses and punished them with the hem of her sweater. "Tabitha in the mail room told me that she thinks Miss Miles is *involved* with Mr. Felding." She said the word as if it were a federal crime.

"Do you know that for sure?"

"Of course not. But Tabitha said she saw them leave together the other day." Mrs. White had replaced her eyeglasses and reached for a stack of files. "And a pretty young girl like that?" She'd firmed her mouth. "I wouldn't be surprised. She always did seem like a floozy to me."

If anything, Mrs. White's dour gossip had only increased Baylie's interest in Addisyn's life. At the time, Mr. Felding was the heartthrob of the agency, and imagining a relationship between him and Addisyn seemed wonderfully romantic. Of course, that was before she'd gone to work for Prince Charming herself and found a toad instead.

Now she tapped her fingernail thoughtfully on the mouse and studied Addisyn's picture. Funny, she'd forgotten all about that conversation until now. Addisyn had left the agency sometime in February, and Baylie had been reassigned to Mr. Felding shortly thereafter. The demands of her new boss had left her with no time to wonder about Addisyn's departure. But now...

Baylie opened a blank email to Mr. Felding and dropped in Addisyn's practice logs, awards summary, and sponsorship notices. She clicked open the scores sheet before attaching it. Wow. She didn't know that much about the technical side of figure skating, but Addisyn's sheet had some of the highest scores she'd ever seen.

Here was an emergency contact release. Surely Mr. Felding didn't need that—especially since it was over five years old—but she'd attach it anyway. There was only one name: Avery Miles, sister. No telephone number, just an apartment address in the city.

So Addisyn had a sister. Another connective line threaded between them. Baylie had always wanted a sister, but her parents had saddled her with two irritating brothers instead.

She hit SEND on the email and slid the file of hard copies into Mr. Felding's mail slot, then went back to work on the client schedule. She was deep in the data when a woman's three-inch heels tapped into the room. "I'm here to see Mr. Felding, please."

"Um—" Baylie glanced up to see Ms. Reeves, the agency attorney, with a snakeskin purse and red lipstick like war paint. Baylie shuffled away the papers on her desk until she unearthed the intercom button. "I'm sending Ms. Reeves in."

Before she could end the connection, the office door opened, and Mr. Felding appeared, flush with all the charm he could conjure like a magic act. "Ms. Reeves! Happy to see you. Thanks for agreeing to meet on such short notice."

He herded her into the room, and Baylie's suspicions doubled. Why would he be meeting with the attorney? On the heels of asking for the data dive on Addisyn?

Long after Ms. Reeves left, even into the afternoon, Baylie wondered. As she put the finishing touches on the client schedule, she considered the situation. The whole thing felt weird. Should she—

Design school. You're only here till design school.

As she often did when the pressure became unbearable, she picked up her ballpoint pen and began doodling across the back of her junk mail stack, curves and lines and angles flowing into each other. One more year, and the pen would be a draft pencil and she'd be on her way to—

A shadow fell over her. "Well, well. Looks as if I'm not giving you enough to do."

Baylie jumped, the pen clattering to the desk. "I—I'm sorry, sir." She cringed at the scowl on Mr. Felding's face, an assortment of her own lines and angles. "I was just—taking a break."

But instead of yelling or cursing or threatening her job, he just shrugged, preoccupation glazing his words. "Fine. As long as you get everything done by the end of the day. Listen, I need you to shred the documents in here." He dropped a file folder onto the corner of her desk.

"Yes, sir." Shredding documents was kind of a pain, especially when she had to empty the little filter thing, but Baylie was too relieved to complain. After Mr. Felding's door was safely shut once more, she flipped through the file. The usual suspects—outdated release forms, rough drafts of contracts, old invoices.

She flipped on the shredder and stuffed three sheets into the slot, only to see the fussy red light glaring at her. Oh, brother. Some days the shredder turned obstinate and required her to feed the pages in one at a time. She stuck out her tongue at Mr. Felding's office door and began slipping page after page after page into the slot. She'd shredded nearly twenty-five pages when she reached one that looked…different.

It was a letter of resignation, printed in black ink on cheap copy paper. But it was the signature at the bottom that grabbed her attention.

Addisyn Miles.

The weird feeling was back, and it was getting stronger. Baylie swiveled her chair away from the shredder, squinting at the document in her hands. It was an original—that much was obvious. And it was dated February sixteenth.

Well, this had to be a mistake. No way would Mr. Felding want to shred an original resignation letter. She crept toward his office door and knocked tentatively. "Sir?"

There was a sigh, then heavy footfalls, and the door flung open. "Yes?"

She held out the letter like a white flag. "I—I found this in the file to be shredded. I thought it must be a mistake since—"

"A mistake?" His voice was a slap. "It's not a mistake. Now am I paying you to second-guess my work or to take care of your responsibilities?"

He didn't understand. "But sir, this is an original letter of resignation, and—"

"I know what it is. Just shred it, okay?" His tone abruptly turned almost conciliatory. "Look, I realize it seems strange to you. But actually, it's a duplicate."

"A duplicate?"

"Yes. I just didn't want two versions. That gets confusing." He gestured toward his file cabinet. "I have the real one in here." He closed the door on her next question.

A duplicate copy? That made no sense. The signature on this was real, no question, and the paper was folded in obvious envelope lines. And why would the *real* paper be in his office? The final documents on all the skaters were kept in their individual files. She'd been schooled on that procedure the very first day.

Forget it, Baylie. Mr. Felding was right. She wasn't being paid to be his watchdog—thank goodness. So she'd keep following the rules: ask no questions, cause no problems, and keep her head down. The only way to survive this stuffy place and escape to design school.

She turned back toward the shredder and finished the job, but even when she left work that night, she was still wondering about Addisyn Miles.

The girl who might have been her friend—and the girl who was definitely his enemy.

CHAPTER 14

It was going to be the most exciting afternoon.

Addisyn leaned back in the car seat, watching the Sea-to-Sky Road curve before them. "So tell me again where we're going."

"Brackendale. The bike trails are epic. And this time of year, there's another little surprise." Darius winked. "Trust me, you'll love it."

"I'm sure I will."

An easy silence fell over them, and Addisyn turned her attention to the scenery. The fall weather was gorgeous, mellow sun and shifting winds and silver clouds hovering over the rugged profiles of the rocky cliffs that lined the inlet. Across the mountainsides, threads of gold weaved through the green like veins of precious ore.

So far, Addisyn's experience in Whistler had held the vibrant glory of those fall leaves. Already she'd been there eight days—plenty of time to perfect their skating routine. Darius had been right—it was simple. It hadn't taken Addisyn more than two or three days to nail down the basics, accustomed as she was to the high level required for competition. But despite its simplicity, the routine was designed to appear difficult, and it would certainly impress the audience.

And while practicing together was fun, the adventures off the ice had been even better. They'd driven to neighboring Pemberton for a farmer's market, hiked the trails at the climbing center, and visited Bear Creek Park in Vancouver.

"I didn't even ask what you were up to while I was at work." Darius chuckled a little. "Did you behave yourself?"

Addisyn laughed. "Surprisingly, yes. I just walked downtown and did some shopping. I found Avery's birthday present."

"Really?" Darius guided the car around a curve. "When's her birthday?"

"In about three weeks. I'm a late shopper."

"So what'd you get her?"

"Well, I have to show you later. It's perfect, though. And then I went by the coffee shop."

"Really?" Darius grinned. "I bet Chelsea was excited."

Addisyn laughed. "Oh, yes."

Chelsea had run from behind the counter and grabbed Addisyn in the kind of hug usually reserved for troops returning from war. "Addisyn Miles! You're back!"

"Chelsea, hi!" She hadn't expected to be this glad to see the girl who'd often annoyed her when they were coworkers. "Yeah, I'm back." She'd bitten her lip. "Well, for a couple of weeks, anyway."

"Omigosh, this is so cool!" Chelsea had bounced in place with an effervescent energy. "What's going on? I've missed you!" She'd grabbed Addisyn's hand and towed her toward the counter. "I'll get your coffee and you tell me all about it!"

As the coffee maker hissed, Addisyn had leaned against the counter and filled Chelsea in on everything—her new life in Estes Park, and of course, her invitation from Darius.

"You're skating with him? In January?" Chelsea had sighed dreamily as she stirred milk into Addisyn's coffee. "Girl, that is absolutely the most Hallmark thing I ever heard. Didn't I always say you two were, like, the cutest couple?"

The heat in the coffee shop had turned Addisyn's cheeks red. "We are not—"

"Uh-huh, sure." Chelsea had laughed and bumped Addisyn with her elbow. "Right. And that's why Darius Payne went all the way to America to ask you to come here and be his skating partner for the event." She'd batted her eyelashes. "Lie to yourself if you want, but it doesn't get more romantic than that."

"What are you grinning about?" Darius's voice broke into her thoughts.

Addisyn blinked back to the present and sighed. "Oh, nothing really." Only in Chelsea's imagination was there anything more than friendship between her and Darius. She was there to skate with him, not fall in love with him.

If only her heart would get the memo.

"Let's stop here for a minute." Darius pulled off the road into a wide gravel area, then jumped out of the car and jogged around to open Addisyn's door. "What do you think?"

"Oh, Darius…" The view snatched her breath away. "This is amazing."

The river sprawled lazy here, cobalt glass rippling gently across the valley. A coppery crowd of frost-dried bushes leaned over its banks. And across the valley were the mountains, clouds snagging on their rough edges, sun striking a match on the snowcapped peaks.

"You like it?" Darius's arm brushed hers.

"It's gorgeous." Addisyn was just pulling out her phone to take some photos when she heard a strange squawking noise overhead.

"There they are!" Darius grinned and pointed into the clouds.

Addisyn glanced up to see an enormous bulky bird swaying on the tip of a pine tree. "That's—what is that?"

"An eagle." Darius waved toward a sign she hadn't noticed. "Welcome to the Brackendale Eagle Dike."

"What?" Sheer amazement slipped through her laugh. "No way!"

"Yes." Darius nodded toward a kiosk at the other end of the gravel area. "Come on. There's a display over there."

Interpretive panels told the story of the Brackendale eagles, but Darius seemed to know more than the signs did. "This is the eagle capital of the world." He gestured to a map on one of the displays. "Right now, the rivers up north are freezing over, and at the same time, the salmon are swimming inland. So that combination draws big flocks of eagles down south every year."

"And they end up right here." Addisyn tapped a statistic on the sign. "Three thousand eagles seen last season?"

"Yep." As they stepped out of the kiosk, Darius nodded to some studious-looking people clustered near the river, binoculars slung around their shoulders. "Volunteers. They come daily to count eagles."

A shadow swept the river, and Addisyn grabbed his arm. "Darius, there's another one! We've seen two!"

He laughed. "We'll see a lot more."

"This is the most amazing thing!" Oh, wouldn't Avery just love this place? Addisyn would have to send her sister photos later. "And here you said we were just going bike riding."

"We still are." Darius settled his hand at her elbow, guiding her back to the car. "Hop in. We're going to the bike trails at Mamquam River Park. Ready to see more eagles there?"

There was nothing she could do about the way his grin made her feel. "Definitely."

THE LONELY LOVELINESS of the Mamquam River drew Addisyn in as soon as they arrived. "Darius, this is unbelievable."

"I'm glad you like it." He hefted their bikes from the rack on his car.

"I love it." They were in a valley here, pressed against the knees of the mountains. The air was cool, heavy with the dampness of the river that threaded its wandering way into the trees.

"We'll be heading that way." Darius pointed to a gravel trail that burrowed between the evergreens. "Because it's so close to the river, we should see lots of eagles."

It felt good to be back on a bike, following Darius deeper into a place so magical, it might as well have been their own mythical land. Sun splashed off the river, but the trees collected their own knowing dimness, saturated in silence.

Addisyn ducked as they passed under a leaning tree trunk that dripped with moss. "Do you come here a lot?"

"Not a whole lot these days." Darius glanced over his shoulder at her. "My dad and I came here quite a bit when I was a teenager, though."

Addisyn smiled at the image of Darius as a boy, riding alongside his dad. "I bet that was fun."

"Yeah. We'd compete with each other to see who could spot the most eagles." A note of mourning crept into his laugh. "We always lost count, though."

"Because it wasn't really about who won."

"Right. It was about the—the joy. The peace." The trail was wider now, and Darius dropped back to ride beside her. "Coming here always made me feel closer to God. This—" his gesture took in the river and trees—"reminds me who He is. Who I am. Don't you think?"

How could she tell him she wasn't sure about either of those? "I—well, Darius, I don't know yet how I feel about God."

"That's okay." He leaned into a turn. "You'll find out."

He made it sound so easy. The trail veered into the shadow of the mountain, and Addisyn shivered. "I don't know, Darius. I just—I just don't know if faith is for me."

"Why not?"

The tumble of the river sprayed them with a fine mist as they rounded the next bend. If only her memories could drift downstream. "Well—I'm not—I've never been the good girl." A bitterness she hadn't known was there leaked into her words. "Not like Avery."

"So?" Darius's voice was still patient, no speck of judgment. "Haven't you heard that God meets us where we're at?"

"Yes, but—" She bit her lip, trying to navigate around all that she couldn't tell him. "I went to Colorado for a second chance, Darius. A new start, you know? But sometimes—sometimes I feel like it's all just the same."

"What do you mean?"

Clouds were collecting themselves overhead, colors muting out. She forced Brian's face from before her eyes. "Just—memories and stuff. And there are still things that—that hurt to think about."

"I don't think a new start means you forget." Darius's words were slow, soft, each coming from a sacred place in his heart. "It means you learn and you grow and then you move forward. Remembering."

"But that's just it." Addisyn blinked against sudden tears. "I feel like I can't move forward."

"You have to walk one day at a time, Addisyn. But first you have to make sure you're walking the right direction." Darius's voice was rich with compassion. "That's where faith comes in. Faith doesn't wait until you're where you want to be, you know. Faith takes your hand and walks you forward even when you're lost. Especially when you're lost."

Would he still tell her that if he knew how desperately her past was chasing her? And what about Skyla's painting and her talk of people being given new hearts? How did that fit in?

She was about to ask another question when his gaze jerked up. "Did you hear that?"

Addisyn slid to a stop next to him and lowered her head in concentration. At first she only heard the murmur of the river, the soft sighing of the trees. Then there it was—a squawking cry. "Yes!" She met his smile with her own.

"Eagles." He breathed the word and slid off his bike, propping it against a tree. "Come on."

They stumbled down the bank toward the wide gravel margin of the river. Away from the sheltering trees, Addisyn shivered as a sudden gust of damp wind whipped down the river corridor.

"Do you see them?" Darius kept his voice low, his hand poised on the binoculars around his neck.

Addisyn scanned the sweeping curve of the water. The evergreens crowded so closely along the borders that their thickness screened any movement. "I don't see anything."

"They've got to be around." Darius pointed to a splashing in the middle of the river, where something silver flipped against the current.

"What's that?"

"Salmon."

Salmon, struggling upstream in their epic migration. She'd heard of the phenomenon, but she'd never witnessed it. Suddenly, a shadow on a bleached limb upstream caught her eye. "Darius, there! On that dead tree leaning over the river. Is that an eagle?"

"Yes! He's watching the salmon." Darius lifted the binoculars from around his neck and handed them to her. "Here."

Addisyn peered through the lenses, fumbling with the controls, but the bird stayed blurry. "I can't—"

"Here." His fingers were warm over hers, and then the bird sprang into clarity. "Better?"

"Yes. Thank you." She could see every detail of the eagle's ancient white head, read the secrets in his eyes. The wind tugged at his feathers. "He's magnificent."

"Pretty amazing, right?" Darius was still close behind her, his presence tugging at her thoughts.

"Amazing." A sudden shyness pulled her focus from the eagle. She handed the binoculars back to Darius.

"Your hands are cold." Before she could respond, he slipped his fingers between hers. "Are you warm enough?"

The air had changed between them, and whatever was happening, she didn't want it to end. "Yes."

Her feelings surged toward him in an aching pull, and she tightened her grip on his hands, struggling to anchor to the moment. Mist was rising from the river, tangling in the trees, wrapping them in their own enchanted world. The world of the eagles and the salmon and the mountains.

"So, there was something my dad always said." Darius's voice mixed with the wind and the wonder.

"What was it?" Addisyn was savoring the feel of his hands on hers.

"He said that the eagles were a reminder."

"A reminder?"

"Just think about it." Darius glanced at where the eagle still perched on the stump, then found her eyes again. "They fly so many hundreds of miles to follow their course." His thumbs traced gentle circles on the backs of her hands. "My dad said it would remind me that nothing could hold me back. That no fear and no failure could clip my wings."

His words settled into the deep places of her soul. "Really?" Hope trembled in her whisper.

"Really." His voice was a bedrock of reassurance as reliable as the mountains themselves. He trailed his hands up her arms to her shoulders and pulled her closer to him.

"Only you can hold yourself back, Addisyn." He cupped his hand against her face, his words a gentle breath. "Let yourself go forward. Stop being so afraid to fly."

She couldn't move, couldn't speak, not when the merest breath might brush the magic from this precious moment. Darius was searching her eyes. Could he see her holding out her heart?

"Addisyn—" He bent toward her, and she closed her eyes. In another heartbeat, his lips were on hers.

After a long moment, he drew back and framed her face in his hands. "I—I didn't ask—" His face flushed, and he gave a breathless sheepish laugh. "I'm sorry—"

She shook her head. Her smile might split her face, yet there were tears in her eyes too. "Don't be sorry." The tears made the river shimmer in an otherworldly way. "I'm not."

And with that she ignored the voices of fear and failure. She tuned out the shadowed memories. She closed her eyes to all the past, and she did what she'd wanted to do since the moment she'd stepped off the plane. She looped her arms around his shoulders and kissed him in a way that she hoped would tell him everything she felt.

"Addisyn—" Darius breathed her name like a prayer.

"Mm?" She kept her eyes closed, memorizing the shape of him in her arms.

"We can't lose this." He brushed his hand through her hair.

"I know." She rested her head against his shoulder, breathing in the aroma of pine trees and salt-soaked air.

"Your new start—" He cleared his throat. "It could be here."

Here in Whistler? Addisyn drew back just enough to meet his gaze. "I—I couldn't do that, Darius."

"You could. We'd work out the details." He brushed his thumb across her lips. "I don't want to let you go."

Her heart swooped again at all that lay in his eyes. "I don't want to let you go either."

"So stay. We'll figure out the details." He kissed her one more time, a gentle kiss like an open door. "Forget the past. Let me help you remember how to fly again."

Addisyn pressed into his shoulder once more. He was so strong, so solid. Safety from everything she longed to outrun. "Darius—"

A sudden squawk made them both turn. With a single leap, the eagle was airborne, wings pulsing powerfully down the river. "Darius, look!"

"He's following his course." Darius's arms were still holding her close.

"Yes." A powerful and pounding hope beat its wings inside her soul. "We are too."

△△ △△ △△

THE DARKNESS IN her bedroom was heavier every night. Avery pulled the quilt closer around her shoulders and glanced at the wall of shadows outside her window.

She had always gone to bed early. Mornings were the richest part of the day, when the sun first kissed the mountains with alpenglow and the elk bugles quavered through the frosty stillness. Why stay up late in the darkness and be too tired to welcome all the beauty when it first appeared?

But with Addisyn gone, things were different. Avery still went to bed early, but the shadows soaked themselves with a bristling silence and the house muttered with creaking boards and settling beams. After the first weary night, Avery had relaxed her *no-dog-on-the-beds* rule, inviting Mercy to stretch out across her feet.

But tonight, the darkness prickled with an unease that even the dog's soothing presence couldn't dispel. Odd. Avery had survived a thousand solitary nights during Addisyn's rebellion. Yet after having her younger sister back for only three months, she couldn't reclaim her own sense of independence.

Avery shoved the quilt down and sat up, glancing at the inky pool of Mercy across her feet. The dog gave a slight snore, her paws twitching as she dashed through a dream. The glow-in-the-dark hands of the little wooden clock pointed to five till eleven. A full hour since Avery had gone to bed, and seven hours till sunrise.

Avery flopped back down. *Think of something else.* How many laps did Isaiah need to do tomorrow in the flight cage? He'd worked his way up to ten laps twice a day, but at his second evaluation three days ago, Chay had pronounced him still unready for release. Maybe when Addisyn returned, she could help Avery exercise him.

Addisyn. What was her younger sister doing right now? Not tossing in bed, certainly. Addisyn had always been a night owl. She'd be awake, relishing every moment of her vacation.

She seemed to be having a great trip. She'd called Avery every couple of days and texted her often with glowing updates. She and Darius had had a beautiful drive up from Vancouver. She and Darius were having lunch in Whistler. She and Darius had visited the farmer's market that morning and taken fresh vegetables back to his house to cook.

It was great—really great—that Ads was having such a good time. It was ridiculous to feel left out, silly to worry about her, and downright petty to resent her constant mentions of Darius. And it was nothing short of pathetic to be watching the darkness at eleven o'clock just because her sister wasn't in the room down the hall. How absurd. What did she expect? That Addisyn would forever be content to huddle under her wing?

It was just so crazy to think that Ads was in Canada. Canada! A whole other country, over a thousand miles away. And she could just up and go to these places, without anyone along to hold her hand. It felt all wrong.

Mercy suddenly jerked her head up with a listening look. Goosebumps crawled along Avery's arms, but the next moment she heard it too—the faint strains of "Rocky Mountain High" floating up the stairs. Only Addisyn would be calling this late.

Flinging back the covers, she scrambled for the doorway, Mercy bounding off the bed behind her. She fumbled for the light switch but gave up and scurried down the steps as fast as she could in the darkness. In the doorway of the living room, she paused in the glow of the lamp she always left on. Her phone had stopped ringing. Where had she put it?

There it was, on her desk. She scooped it up and tapped the screen. Yes, it was Addisyn. There was a voicemail, but she didn't bother with that. A ring and a half, and her sister's voice was on the line.

"Avery! Hey, I didn't think about the time zone difference till after I hung up. Did I wake you up? I know it's past your bedtime."

"No, not at all." No reason to mention that she couldn't sleep for worrying about her sister.

"You sure? I can call you tomorrow or—"

"No, really. I'm definitely awake." Her only hope of sleeping tonight lay in hearing that Ads was okay.

"Well, I just wanted to tell you what happened today." Addisyn's words were shaped by her smile. "Oh, A, it was just so cool."

The happiness in her sister's tone made Avery smile herself. This was much better than suffocating in her dark bedroom. "Tell me all about it!" She flicked on the wall switch, splashing light into the room.

"Okay, so Darius and I drove down to Brackendale this afternoon." Addisyn's voice lilted with a special joy. "We went biking on this trail through the mountains, beside the river. And it was gorgeous. All these big trees."

"Really? That sounds incredible." Avery sank into the couch and tucked her knees under her. Mercy flopped on the rug at her feet.

"Oh, it was. But the best part is, there were eagles everywhere."

"Eagles?" Avery gasped. "That's unbelievable."

"Yeah—like, hundreds of eagles. They come through there to catch the salmon." Excitement skipped across Addisyn's words. "Brackendale is called the eagle capital of the world. We saw so many."

"That sounds amazing. I would have loved to have seen that."

"I figured. You're the bird person." Addisyn laughed. "I took a bunch of pictures. I'm texting you some, okay?"

"Okay. I'll wait for them." Avery put the phone on speaker and watched the screen for Addisyn's message to appear. "Oh, Ads! Those are great pictures." She swiped through a few. Eagles in flight, eagles on the water. "Beautiful."

"It was the most fun thing. We watched the eagles, and we—we talked a lot. And then—uh—well, then we walked around some more."

Avery came to a shot of Darius on his bike. She swiped on past that one.

Addisyn was still describing their outing. "So then we drove back up here, and we went and got something to eat, and then Darius brought me to the hotel. And as soon as I had a shower, I wanted to call you and tell you all about it."

"I'm glad you did." She flicked to the last photo and paused.

"Yeah, it was amazing." Her sister's voice still rang with joy.

A joy that wasn't there in Estes Park.

They talked for a while longer, but when the call ended, Avery leaned back and stared at the gray ashes of the last fire she'd built.

It was cold in the living room, but she didn't feel like trudging back up the dark stairs right now. She tugged the heavy woolen throw off the back of the couch and draped it over her lap, then looked at that last picture again.

Addisyn and Darius were standing in front of the mountains, hope reflecting from their faces. Avery studied every detail—the protective curve of Darius's arm around Addisyn's shoulders, the way her sister leaned into his embrace with the confidence of belonging. But one thought rose above all others.

How could Addisyn be so—so—*grown?*

She put the phone down and rubbed her eyes. She'd known Addisyn wasn't a child any longer. Of course she had. Over the last three months, she'd been reminded constantly that the turbulent teenager who'd left three years ago was a clear contrast from the self-assured young woman who'd returned.

Through it all, though, she'd still seen her sister as the younger one, the fragile one, the one to be guided and guarded. But now the truth of the photo mocked her attempt to ignore the obvious. Addisyn looked beautiful—sparkling—independent. A grown woman—a woman with her own life to lead and her own story to explore.

A woman who most definitely did not need her older sister's guiding hand.

A hollow ache swelled behind Avery's heart and burned within her throat. Only one thing could keep her from breaking down right then and there. She tossed aside the blanket and hurried to the photo in the dining room. The cheap white frame that held the image as familiar as her own face.

Avery gripped the picture with knuckles stretched white. This was the picture she'd carried—always. The reminder of the time when Addisyn readily reached for Avery's hand.

She touched her sister's face gently. Ads had been so young, so small, so hungry for Avery's love and guidance. And Avery had willingly laid all else on the altar just to hold her close, to keep her safe.

Ironic. In this image she was pushing her sister forward on the swings, helping her fly farther than she could have on her own. Now she was the one pulling Addisyn back, begging her not to soar quite so high.

She was losing her. All over again. A thread of panic knotted itself around her heart. How could she possibly compete with the dazzling adventures Addisyn had in Whistler? Pacific mountains and eagles on the river and a handsome man who clearly adored her. Hiking trips and pizza nights must pale in comparison.

Somehow when Addisyn had come back to her, she'd held on to the inane expectation that they'd pick up right where they left off—two sisters against the world. But she was fighting the inevitable, as doomed as those salmon struggling upstream in her sister's picture. *Oh, Ads. Don't grow up and go away. Don't leave me behind.*

Still clinging to the photo, Avery returned to the couch and burrowed under the throw again. Forget trying to sleep in the dark and ominous second story, where her sister's soft breathing wasn't coming from the room at the end of the hall. The house was as empty as a cracked shell from which the bird had flown.

Mercy's warm tongue swiped her hand, and Avery closed her eyes to trap the tears. What was the matter with her? She should be happy, because Addisyn was happy. That was what mattered, right?

But she still had the sinking sense that something precious and irreplaceable was being slowly and inexorably wrenched from her unwilling hands.

And that was more than her heart could take.

CHAPTER 15

Light was reaching for her, tugging her insistently from sleep. Avery blinked her eyes open. Why wasn't she in her room?

The brief swirl of disorientation settled. Of course. She'd come down to talk to Addisyn, and then she'd slept all night on the couch. And now the sun was peering in through her picture windows, and it almost looked as if—

She swung her legs off the couch, nearly stepping on a slowly-waking Mercy, and rushed to the window. The sun was laughing at a world draped in fresh snow, throwing back a brightness that pricked her eyes.

The darkness of the night dissolved into a swoop of joy. The morning gleamed like a gift, the mountains glittering, snow sparkling on every limb.

This first snow wouldn't last, of course. It was wet and clumpy, and there couldn't have been more than four or five inches. Already Avery could hear it dripping from the eaves of her house, dwindling in the sunshine that was bright for November. But she would enjoy it while she could.

She dashed to her mudroom, Mercy on her heels, and pulled her boots and coat on over her pajamas. A clump of snow plopped to her deck when she opened the door. "Mercy, look! Snow!"

Mercy sprang from the deck and dashed off in a wild uproarious circle, powder scattering around her. Avery laughed, the joy rising into the crystalline blue sky.

El Shaddai—thank You for this day. She breathed in the holiness of the moment, the snow like a promise of perfection. *Thank You for leading me to this beautiful place. Thank You that You make hearts as white as this snow.*

A Steller's Jay made a pompous landing on a pine branch, sending a shower like confetti to the ground. Avery gave one last smile upward. *You are beautiful, Lord. Help me serve You well today.*

Elk tracks dented a zigzag across her yard toward the road. She followed them, reading the story in the snow. From the size of the tracks, she'd guess at least one bull, and a heavy one at that. And two or three cows. How long ago had they passed through?

Snow was sagging along the beam of her gate. She unlatched it and stepped out to examine the road. It was a little slushy, but nothing that would prevent her from making it to work just fine. In fact, there were already tire tracks, veering by her mailbox.

Her fingers were tingling numb, so she pulled the wad of mail from her box and whistled for Mercy. "Let's get ready for work, girl!"

It was going to be a good day.

Back inside the cabin, Avery shivered and rubbed her palms together. Mercy trotted into the kitchen and perched patiently by her food bowl.

"One second, puppy. I know you're hungry." Avery kicked off her boots and flipped through the mail. An electric bill, a Cabela's catalog, and a flyer for a fundraiser at the library next month. She tacked the flyer to the refrigerator with an antler magnet, thumbed through the catalog—she could really use some new hiking pants—and set the bill on her desk to be paid that evening.

Oh. She'd missed something. Under the bill was an envelope addressed to Addisyn.

A strange sense of foreboding crinkled over her. Other mail had come for Addisyn in the last two weeks, of course, and Avery had simply piled it on the counter in the mudroom, where it waited for her sister's return. But this carried a more forceful feel. Bold letters across the front ordered **OPEN IMMEDIATELY.**

Mercy was back beside her, nosing Avery's hand impatiently. Automatically she patted the dog's head. "Wait, girl. We'll get your food in a minute."

She turned the envelope over, and the return address seemed to leap from the flap. **REEVES LAW FIRM, 110 CAVENDISH BOULEVARD,**

NEW YORK, NEW YORK.

An attorney? In New York City? Fear wadded itself inside Avery's stomach. Why would Addisyn be getting mail from an attorney in New York City? And why was it so urgent?

If Avery opened Addisyn's mail, her sister would be furious. But what if this couldn't wait?

Another moment balanced on the edge of indecision, then she fished her pocketknife out of her coat, flipped the blade, and slit the envelope as warily as if a phantom might emerge. Instead, there was only a single sheet of paper, dated four days earlier. Austere black font on white paper. Standard stark business form. Under the date was a subject line: "Re: Notice of Breach of Contract."

Breach of contract? The trembling began, the envelope unsteady in her hands. Her eyes darted along the lines.

Dear Miss Miles:

Please be advised that I have been retained by Brian Felding of the New York Figure Skaters' Agency to assist him in dealing with an alleged breach of contract on your part.

Brian Felding.

Avery's heart jerked. No. It could not be that Brian would once again lay his filthy hands on her sister's life.

As I know you are aware, you and Mr. Felding entered into a contract in which you agreed to perform certain services, which included but were not limited to him being your sole agent as it relates to your skating career. Mr. Felding was to receive compensation based upon your activities as a skater. In exchange, he was to provide skating opportunities to allow you to fulfill your career.

It has been brought to my attention that you have failed to comply with the terms and conditions of this contract. Specifically, Mr. Felding has reason to believe that you have sought other performance opportunities without his permission or consent. In the event you sought to terminate this agreement, one of the primary responsibilities placed upon you was to provide written notice to Mr. Felding before termination of the contract. Since you failed to do this, you are in breach of this agreement. If you continue to violate the terms and conditions of your contract, Mr. Felding has instructed me to inform you that he will initiate all legal proceedings available to him in order to force you to comply with the terms and conditions of your agreement.

Please contact my office within ten days from the date of this letter so that we may discuss your continued compliance with this contract. You may contact me at the address contained in this letterhead. If I do not hear from you within ten days from the date of this letter, Mr. Felding has instructed me to initiate legal proceedings immediately. This could include a verdict against you for compensatory damages, possibly punitive damages, attorney's fees, prejudgment and post judgment interest, and court costs. Your immediate attention to this matter is imperative.

Avery's disbelief dashed over the words three times before slow-plodding reality could catch up. Then she sagged limply into the doorframe like a fighter against the ropes.

Her lungs were tight, each breath pitched high and hard in her chest. A jagged rockslide of memories pounded through her mind. Brian had marred her sister's life with misery. He'd preyed on her weaknesses and profited from her strengths. He'd spun an elaborate web of woe and enticed her right into its heart. And now he was trying for a reprise.

Avery had fought the bitterness for years, struggling to overcome the way his name burned in her soul. But now, it all surged back, riding the wave of a fierce protectiveness that stung strength back into her spirit. She wouldn't let him do this. He couldn't hurt Addisyn this way. Her precious sister who had worked so hard to escape the pain he'd inflicted.

Oh, how by the High Peaks would she tell Addisyn about this?

There was a scraping sound on the roof, and a chunk of snow and ice slid past the window. Avery stared outside, where the white was whittling itself away. Dark, wet grass poked up across the yard. Only shrunken patches of snow remained.

Hadn't she known all along it wouldn't last?

△△ △△ △△

A CATCHY TUNE was invading her dream. Caught on the fringes of consciousness, Addisyn burrowed further into her pillow until the noise stopped, then slowly slipped back toward sleep.

And it started again.

Addisyn groaned and shoved herself onto her elbows, dragging herself toward alertness. The tune ended again. It was…her ringtone.

She glanced at the clock on the wall of her hotel room. 6:10? Seriously? Who was calling her this early?

A text bleeped through. Someone was really insistent. She rubbed her eyes and sighed. Fine. She'd check to make sure it wasn't an emergency, then she'd go back to bed and grab another half hour of sleep.

She stumbled out from beneath the warm covers. The hardwood floor in her hotel room felt as cold as the rink. She warmed one bare foot over the other as she dragged her cell phone out of her bag.

Two missed calls. Both from Avery. What in the world? Addisyn flicked to the text.

Addisyn, there's a problem. It's urgent. Call me the minute you get this. I love you.

An urgent problem? Panic submerged Addisyn's irritation as she hit the callback button. Avery answered halfway through the first ring. "Addisyn. There you are. I thought you might still be asleep."

"I was. The phone woke me up, but it's okay." She had no patience for pleasantries. "Avery, what's wrong? I saw your text."

Silence stretched, uncertain and uncomfortable. Addisyn pressed the phone closer to her ear. "Avery?"

"I'm here." Each word sounded as if it were being dragged out unwillingly. "We have a problem."

"What do you mean?" Her foreboding tripled. If whatever this was had shaken even her unflappable sister—

215

"I don't know how to tell you this."

"Are you hurt? Sick?" The panic that accompanied the possibility caught her off guard.

"No, no, nothing like that." Avery sighed. "A letter came for you this morning. It said it was urgent and to open immediately, so—so—I did."

"You read my mail?"

"Addisyn, just listen, okay?" Avery's tone slammed her annoyance back. "It was from an attorney in New York."

An attorney in New York? "What? That has to be a mistake. There's no reason that—"

"Addisyn." Avery's voice turned dull, heavy with pain. "Brian hired an attorney. He's—he's threatening to sue you."

Brian again.

The floor dissolved beneath her feet. Addisyn sank to her knees on the cold, slick hardwood. "Avery—what?"

"I'm so sorry." Pain still tore at her sister's words. "I hated to have to tell you. I knew how upsetting—"

"Wait." Avery was wrong. She had to be. None of this made any sense. "What did the letter say?"

"It says you're in breach of contract."

"What does that mean?" Addisyn scrubbed at her eyes. It was too early for this. She could barely remember her own name when she first woke up, let alone deal with legal technicalities.

"Uh—" Avery didn't sound sure herself. "It means you violated your agreement with him."

Violated her agreement? "How?"

"He said—well, here." Paper rustled. "I'll read it to you." Avery cleared her throat. "'Dear Miss Miles: Please be advised that I have been retained by Brian Felding of the New York Figure Skaters' Agency to assist him in dealing with an alleged breach of contract...'"

So Brian was still fighting, now with words as his weapons. *Failed to comply. Initiate all legal proceedings. Compensatory damages.* Every phrase ripped another gash in the hopeful happiness she'd built, the fragile freedom she'd found disintegrating like a spiderweb.

"So...that's it." Avery's voice was barely above a whisper. "What do you think?"

She couldn't answer, not yet. Not when she was watching all that she'd overcome rising against the blank hotel room walls.

"Addisyn? Are you still there?"

"I'm here"—but really she was there, with him, and he was telling her all over again how stupid she was to believe she could escape him—

"What gave him this idea?" Avery's voice was stronger now. "Come on, Addisyn. Stay with me. We've got to think this through."

Avery was right. Addisyn stood and began pacing, the reality dogging her steps. No use hiding anything now. "I talked to him. He told me—"

"What?" Horror stretched her sister's voice. "You talked to him?"

"Yes." Her teeth were chattering. It was getting colder in the room.

"So—he called you? What did he say?"

Avery thought he had called her? Addisyn paused. Maybe she could just go with that for now instead of shocking her sister with another bombshell. She focused on the second question. "He was—mad. And he said that—that—I was a problem to him." The last words were nothing more than a hoarse whisper. "He said—that he would blackmail me, make me pay." She swallowed down the sick taste.

"He threatened you?" Avery's voice bordered on panic. "And you didn't tell me?"

She wanted a deep breath, but there was no air in the room. "I thought he was—you know, being Brian. Blowing smoke and bluffing."

"You should have told me! How long ago was this?"

"I didn't want to worry you." How had everything spun so out of hand? "About a month."

"He can't threaten you like that." Avery's words pinched through gritted teeth.

He could. He had. He would do it again. "You're holding a letter that says he can."

"No. No way." Her sister's voice turned cold, words rattling against each other. "I am not having that—that *jerk* sending letters and making phone calls and threatening you. Now this has gone on long enough. If I have to fly to New York and face him myself, I swear by the granite peaks of the High Country that he will not—"

"Avery." Her sister's tirade was as futile as a paper tent in a hailstorm. "Don't you see? He's right." The nausea hit harder. "I can't get away from him—I won't ever be—"

"No, Addisyn!" Avery's tone meant war. "You can't think like that. You are not going to live under his shadow for the rest of your life." Avery paused. "Okay. Think. What does he mean, 'failed to provide written notice'?"

"I don't know." Addisyn dropped her throbbing head into her hand and fumbled through what she remembered of the details of her contract. Goodness, she'd signed it years ago. "We were supposed to send a letter in writing if we wanted to quit."

"That's what this says." The question gathered itself for a moment before Avery spoke again. "Ads—when you left—did you send that letter?"

"Yes." Of that she had no doubt. "I typed it on my laptop the morning I left."

"And then what happened?"

Avery sounded like an attorney cross-examining a witness. Addisyn bit back exasperation. "I put it in a stack of all these things I needed to mail. And then I took them all by the post office on my way to the airport."

"Um—" Avery was tiptoeing into this. "Are you sure it was in there?"

She was sure, wasn't she? "Well—I mean—it was in the stack. I just dumped everything in the blue box outside."

"So—he didn't get it."

Addisyn tilted her head. "Or he's claiming not to have."

"Either of which is equally unprovable." Avery was quiet, the thoughts screaming through the silence. "Maybe you have a copy here at home?"

"Um, I might. It could be in with my skating stuff." She didn't remember printing her own copy, but it was worth checking.

"And then what's this part?" The paper rustled again. "Uh—seeking 'other performance opportunities.'"

Addisyn rotated her shoulders. "He—he had this idea that I was signed with another agency." There was no reason yet to divulge what had given him that notion. "I guess he's still believing that."

A thought struck her. Was it possible Brian knew about Whistler?

True, it wasn't a competitive event, but could he have heard about it somehow and misunderstood? Of course not. How would he have found out?

"You have a copy of your contract, right?"

"Yes. In my files at home." Addisyn bit her lip. "What—what should I do?"

"We need to look at your contract. And we need to find a copy of that letter. And then we need to talk to a lawyer."

That was Avery all over. Always the one following the stepping stones, the plan unrolling before her.

"We'll take care of this together." Avery was obviously finding her equilibrium again. "I'm with you all the way, okay?"

"Okay." Addisyn squeezed her eyes shut. Avery was indeed with her. Standing in the crosshairs of Brian's plot. And Addisyn had dragged her there.

"Brian will be sorry he tangled with us, right?" Avery's laugh fell flat.

Addisyn gulped and tried to buoy her tone. "Right. Absolutely."

They couldn't talk much longer; Avery was already late leaving for work, although she assured Addisyn that Laz would understand. So already Avery was suffering the fallout. And the real trouble hadn't even started yet.

When Addisyn hung up, she smacked her hand against the hardwood. How had she been that stupid? Had she really thought Brian would let her go that easily? She should have seen this coming. Should have known that Brian never made idle threats. She'd dared to believe during these wonderful days with Darius that she wouldn't always live in the shadow of everything she'd been.

But not so.

Darius. She wanted to call him, run to him, hide in his arms, but the news wedged itself between them. How could she untangle all the explanations and throw the knotted ends into his hands? Where would she even begin?

No, she couldn't tell him. With his sterling soul, he'd insist on standing by her. But she wasn't subjecting Darius to all that Brian could dish out. The fewer people she dragged into this war, the better. For all of them.

She still couldn't cry. Still couldn't feel anything besides an aching emptiness. Mechanically she stood and began opening drawers, unzipping her suitcase. She'd leave this morning, for two reasons.

First, she wouldn't be able to skate now. No event planners would allow a participant who was facing potential legal action. That opportunity was over.

But more importantly, there was no sense in deluding herself into believing that it was possible to escape her past. No sense in spending another day living out some pretend perfection with Darius. No sense in seeing all she could have, only to have it yanked away. No sense in trying to move forward with Brian constantly dragging her back.

A gust of rain sheeted against the hotel window. Addisyn gazed out where the clouds hung low and remembered Darius's words from their first day. *Nch'ḵaÿ. Haven. Place to go when the flood rises.*

Well, the flood had found her here.

△△ △△ △△

DARIUS GLANCED AT his watch as he threaded through the downtown traffic. He didn't have much time before work, but Addisyn had texted this morning and asked him to come by the little coffee shop at the Gold Aspen.

He couldn't wait to see her again, especially after the day they'd had yesterday. Rain spattered in his face as he opened the car door, but it would take more than the weather to dampen the joy she brought him. He jogged through the entry and glanced around. There she was, at a corner table, her back to him.

He walked up behind her and squeezed her shoulders. "Hey, pretty girl."

She turned, but the expression she gave wasn't quite a smile. "Hey."

Concern slammed into his soul. "Addisyn? Is something wrong?"

"Well—yes."

He slid into the chair across the table from her. "What's going on?"

She tucked a strand of hair behind her ear and bit her lip. Her features were tight. He could see that now. And her eyes were—terrified.

He leaned forward and touched her hand. Even her fingers felt cold. "Addisyn, you're scaring me. What's wrong?"

"I need to go home." Her words were flat, detached.

"What?" It was the last thing he'd expected. "Like—now?"

"Yes." She stared into her coffee.

Breathe, Payne. Don't panic. Darius ran his hand over his face. "Okay. Start from the beginning."

"Avery called me this morning." Still her voice was drearily matter-of-fact. "Something's come up at home."

He waited, but she didn't elaborate. "What's come up?"

Her eyes held a silent, desperate pleading. "I—it's just something I need to handle."

Nothing about this seemed right. "But is everything okay?"

"It will be. When I get home." She returned her gaze to her coffee. He hadn't seen her take a single sip.

He couldn't force her to open her hand and show him the secret she was holding tight. It must be something between Avery and her. "All right." He choked back the disappointment. This wasn't the end of everything. She'd go home a little earlier now, but she'd still be back for the event. "Could you—could you maybe come one more time between now and the event? Mid-December or—"

"That's the other thing." Her words tumbled out. "I don't know if I can do the event."

What? The air ripped from his lungs. "You're not going to skate in January?"

"I—I don't know." Uncertainty fractured her words. "I have to see. Once I figure out what's going on at home."

"Addisyn." He struggled to keep his voice from sounding whiny and desperate. "You've already signed the agreement—Lenny—"

"Darius, I know." Her voice was trembling now, her words more fragile every moment. "And maybe—but I don't know. I'm so sorry. Please, try to understand."

"How can I understand when you won't tell me what's going on?" His confusion spilled into a half laugh that held no humor. "Last night we were—everything was fine. Now this morning, suddenly, you're leaving and not coming back."

"I'm sure—I mean, you can still skate without me even if—"

"I'm not skating without you." That much he was sure of.

"I'm sorry." Her shoulders sagged lower.

What had happened? If her heart had been an open door yesterday, now it was padlocked tighter than Fort Knox. And she'd left him not one toehold to try to scale her walls.

She stood and slung her purse over her shoulder, then glanced at the clock on the wall. "You need to get to work."

She was right, but he couldn't let her walk out of here. Not with things like this. "So, can we talk again after work, or—"

"I won't be here. I've already packed everything." She tossed her still-full coffee into the trash. "I'm taking the eleven thirty bus to the airport."

Just like that? She would be gone in less than four hours? A raging tide was carrying him down the river, and Darius was struggling to keep his head above water. "If you'll wait, I'll drive you down to Vancouver after—"

"I can't wait. I've already told Avery what time to pick me up in Denver." Her voice, her face—all were as distant as if she were already a thousand miles away. She held up her hand in a weak wave, then turned for the door.

"Addisyn, wait!" He leaped up from the table and caught her elbow.

For a heartbeat he thought she'd pull away. Then she turned back to him, tears glistening on her face.

His own frustration melted away at the sight of her obvious pain. "Hey." He brushed his thumbs across her cheeks. "Come on. Please talk to me." He caught her hands in his and drew her closer to him.

Instead of melting into his arms the way she'd done yesterday, she held herself stiff, her hands limp in his. "I told you. I have to go home. I'm sorry."

"But—there's something else going on. Isn't there?" He gentled his voice and looked past her walls. "Come on, Addisyn. Tell me what's wrong. You know you can trust me."

For a minute she held his gaze, that desperate plea still behind her eyes. Then she looked down. "It's just—something at home. That's all."

That's all? He clenched his jaw. She wasn't being truthful. She was in some kind of trouble, or she wouldn't be acting this way.

Unless...

The thought was a barbed arrow, swift and merciless. "Is this—because of yesterday?"

"Yesterday?" Addisyn stared at him blankly. "What do you mean?"

"The—" Heat rose to his face. "You know. The eagles and—everything."

"Oh."

"I mean—when I—" He cleared his throat. "Did I make you uncomfortable? Or—"

"No." Her answer came quickly. Too quickly? "It's nothing like that."

But the pieces were fitting together now. He'd moved too fast, just as he'd told himself not to do. Her kiss must have been nothing more than a reaction to the moment, an emotional response that she'd now had time to consider. And regret.

He pulled his hands away and stuffed them in his pockets.

"Darius, please." For the first time, her emotionless facade seemed to be slipping. "It's nothing to do with—with us."

But of course it was. He'd come on too strong, and he'd scared her all the way back to America. "Forget it." The disappointment forced the words out more roughly than he'd intended.

She blinked. "No, Darius, I mean it. It's just that—I can't honor our agreement now, and—"

Honor our agreement. Such an impersonal phrase. Such a clinical way to describe their time together.

"Never mind." He didn't want to hear any more excuses, couldn't bear to take any more of this. "You don't owe me an explanation."

"Darius—"

"You're right. I have to get to work." Mostly he just had to get away before he broke down in the coffee shop. "Have a safe trip home."

And with that, he walked out of the warmth of the shop, into the pelting of the November rain.

CHAPTER 16

The morning sun slanted directly in her eyes, shafts poking through the lattice of the flight cage. Addisyn gripped the wooden slats and squinted against the glare. Why was she out here, anyway?

She'd been supposed to meet Avery at Live Bigger for lunch, but when she'd arrived, her sister had been on the phone with a supplier. So, for whatever reason, she'd wandered out here while she waited.

Strange. She'd never paid much attention to Isaiah before she left for Whistler. He was her sister's project, not hers. But today, she'd been strangely drawn to him.

Probably because she just needed an escape. A way to pretend that all the walls she'd thought had fallen weren't really rising around her again.

She pressed closer to the slats of the flight cage and stared at Isaiah. There hadn't been much action from him in the ten minutes she'd been watching. He was roosting, head hunched downward on his perch. A defeated posture that probably matched her own.

How had she ended up in this situation? Where was the wrong turn that had landed her here? She had no job. No purpose. No dream. Nothing, in fact, except the ever-hungry past.

Of course, her sister still insisted that everything would be fine, shoving confidence against the reality of their situation. She'd faced up to the threat with her typical systematic approach—poring over Addisyn's contract, rereading the letter a dozen times, even acquiring a recommendation for a lawyer from Laz's extensive network of acquaintances. The man was in Fort Collins, an attorney with over four decades of experience in entertainment law, and Addisyn had an appointment with him next week.

Isaiah fluffed his feathers, burrowing his beak farther under his wing. Avery had said that when he'd first been moved to the flight cage, he'd been eager to fly, even in a wobbly way. So what had happened since then?

"Hey." She kept her whisper soft. "Isaiah."

The hawk didn't even raise his head. Addisyn frowned. There was something achingly familiar about his dejected pose.

"Maybe you've given up." Were the words for her or Isaiah? "Maybe you don't like the cage, but you don't see a way out."

"Are you speaking to the bird?"

Addisyn quickly blinked back the stinging in her eyes and turned to see Skyla walking up with her easel. "Hi, Skyla. Yeah, I am." She tried for a laugh. "He's not very talkative today, though."

Skyla propped open the easel and glanced into the flight cage. "Yes. I see."

"How is he doing?" In all the turmoil, she'd forgotten to ask Avery for the latest update.

"Doing well, but still off in his flight." Skyla moved the easel a couple of feet, feeling for flatter ground. "He failed his second flight evaluation while you were gone."

"Oh…so what does that mean?"

"Chay tries the birds three times. If they fail all three, then they are unable to be released."

Unable to be released. The phrase had an ugly edge. "And—and then what happens?"

"Well." Skyla paused, her hands on the easel. "He would become what we call a species ambassador. He would live at the center and travel to events with us. Schools and festivals and everywhere we are sharing about the birds."

The wrongness of the idea caught in Addisyn's chest. "But he'd never get to be—where he was supposed to be. Never get to fulfill his purpose."

"He must be able to fly without friction before he can be released. The risk of reinjury—"

"Maybe he'd rather go free and risk getting hurt than stay in a cage and be safe his whole life."

The words were louder than she'd intended, slapping at the air between them. But Skyla offered no reprimand, only a curious tilt to her expression. "Addisyn, this seems strong in you."

What could she say? That she knew how it felt to be trapped in a cage? That the desperate defeat in Isaiah was something she recognized? That she longed to see something, anything, take wing again?

Any of those statements dragged too many explanations alongside, so she reached for the most basic version. "I—I just want him to be able to fly. That's all."

"Yes. A bird on the wing is sacred. Do not give up. We will pray for the healing power to flow into his wings. And perhaps he is gathering strength even now. My grandfather used to say that to fly again after injury, birds need double courage." Skyla stared at her easel for a moment. "Kaka was on the tribal council at the Pine Ridge Lakota reservation."

"Wow! That's so cool."

"Yes. Kaka worked for peace. And for moving forward without forgetting."

"He sounds like a wise man." Addisyn raised her hand to block the sun. "What else did he say about hawks?"

"Well—" Skyla brushed a hand through her hair. "He used to tell an old fable. About a girl who tried to climb too high and ended up in the sky-world, above the earth." Her voice relaxed into a new rhythm, the storyteller's melody. "She was kidnapped by an evil man who made her his slave."

The story peered at her with a knowing familiarity. "An evil man?"

"A sky-spirit, Kaka said. One of the wicked ones." Skyla shrugged as if that explained everything. "He kept her from her family, and she was trapped in his world by her own foolishness with no way to go back home."

The back of Addisyn's neck was prickling now. "What happened?"

"The hawk." Skyla's rare smile pierced the gloom of the tale. "He came to her rescue when she was helpless. She rode on his back to return to her loved ones."

"Oh." Addisyn choked back a surge of emotion. "I—I like that story."

"As do I. It is truth, you know. Not the events, perhaps, but the lesson. Always, always, there is a way of escape. A way of return."

Clearly Skyla had never met anyone like Brian.

Skyla peered at Isaiah again. "He is still fearful, I see. Do not worry. He will grow brave as he grows strong, and when the time is right, he will fly." She gestured toward the store. "My other supplies are in my car. Walk with me, please."

Addisyn nodded and fell into step beside Skyla. They were almost halfway back to the store when Skyla spoke again. "There was something else Kaka always said about hawks."

"What was it?"

"He said that because they dwelt in the sky, they protected the earth from the attacks of evil spirits. That they were always warrior birds, fighting off the darkness. Even now, they are somewhat of a sign for me."

"A sign?" Addisyn cocked her head.

"A reminder that in the world above, the forces of light and love are fighting against all that would overthrow that."

"Hmm." Addisyn glanced up to where the sun gleamed gold over the mountains. "That's neat."

But as they approached the store, tears stung at her eyes. Because the darkness that threatened her was something she herself had created.

And no hawk was coming to rescue her from that.

△△　△△　△△

HE HAD HER, and he wasn't letting go.

Addisyn struggled against his grip, but it was no use. Brian's hands clenched around her wrists like manacles.

"Time to go, Addisyn." With a vicious yank, he pulled her one step closer to him. One step farther from safety.

"No!" She flung the word against him. "Brian, you can't take me!"

The sneer stretched across his face. "What do you mean? I already have."

"Addisyn!"

Avery's voice! Relief spilled through her. She glanced over her shoulder to see her sister, only a few feet away. "Avery, help!"

Instead, Avery crossed her arms, a scowl darkening her face. "Really, Addisyn? You're going down this road again?"

"Avery!" Panic clawed at her words. "I don't want to! Help me!"

But the sister who'd always been her rescuer didn't step in this time. "This is your fault, Addisyn." Her shrug dismissed the whole situation. "You made your choice."

Pain pounded her lungs. "Avery, please—"

"See?" Brian's grip crushed her arms. "Even your sister agrees."

With that, he kicked at the ground, and a chasm split the dirt between her and Avery, a jagged rip that widened wickedly with every moment. Until a canyon loomed between them again.

Brian's grin gave her goosebumps. "Now—"

She was tilting on the edge of the chasm, her head spinning. Black rocks reached up like teeth, waiting hungrily for her to fall. "No—Avery—"

But the ground plunged away, and she was swirling down. Wind screamed past her ears. The rocks leaped toward her and she was helpless and she was—

She was awake.

Addisyn shot to a sitting position, breath heaving hard, heartbeat choking. Her mind fumbled frantically to tease apart fiction and reality.

Even in the darkness of the room, the familiar landscape of the furniture held reassurance. A dream. Was that all?

Just a dream?

No cliff—no Brian—?

No.

She gripped the plaid quilt and pulled in a shuddering breath. Okay. She was in bed. She was safe. And the terrifying sequence of events was nothing more than a nightmare.

The floorboards in the hall creaked under hurried footsteps, and then the door to her room cracked open. "Addisyn?" Avery's whisper was heavy with concern. "Are you okay?"

She was far from okay. "Did I wake you up?"

"Yes, but don't worry about that." Avery sat on the edge of the bed, the mattress squeaking softly, and flipped on the lamp. The gentle light showed the worry in her eyes. "You were crying, calling out." Avery smoothed her hand over Addisyn's hair. "You're sweating."

Avery was right. Her pajama top clung damp around her shoulders. Addisyn lifted her hair off the back of her neck and squinted at the clock by her bed, but it was too dark to read the hands. "What time is it?"

"A little after four thirty." Avery swung her legs onto the bed and rubbed a soothing circle on Addisyn's back. "Was it a bad dream?"

Her throat tightened. "Yes." The events were a dream, but the threat wasn't. "About—about Brian."

Avery's hand froze mid-circle. "Oh, Ads." She pulled Addisyn into a comforting hug. "Do you want to talk about it?"

"No. It was just a stupid dream about him." Well, and about Avery. She wanted to tell Avery that part, wanted to hear her assurance that such a thing would never happen. But at the same time, she didn't want to name the fear at all.

"Hey. It's all going to be okay."

Avery's perpetual refrain. "A, you don't know that."

"Of course I do." Avery's voice vibrated with confidence. "I promise you. We'll figure this out."

Addisyn didn't respond. What was there to say? Avery didn't understand the guilt she carried, the weight that groaned and creaked against her heart.

"Remember, you're seeing the lawyer on Monday." Avery angled herself so she could hold Addisyn's gaze. "I'm sure he'll know what to do. I just wish I didn't have to work so I could go with you."

"I'll be okay." Her smile felt weak. "When I get home, we can talk over whatever he tells me."

"Yes." Avery was nodding, executive mode fully engaged. "We'll make a plan."

Addisyn didn't point out that no plan could thwart the one Brian had already set in motion. Avery had taken the whole thing much better than she had. Maybe it was her personality—she'd always been the steadier, more practical one. Or maybe it was her faith. At any rate, she seemed completely unfazed by the whole situation, with a poise Addisyn envied.

"So?" Avery raised an eyebrow at her. "What else is bothering you?"

"Avery—" She cleared her throat. This was so embarrassing, but she'd put it off long enough. "I don't—I don't have the—the money. For the lawyer, I mean."

"I know. I'm paying for that." Avery's voice was still unconcerned. "I'll send a check with you."

"No. I can't let you do that." A thought struck here. "I still have the account you helped me set up for emergencies. I could pull the money from there." Her laugh was shaky. "This definitely qualifies."

"No, I don't want you to touch that account. Don't worry about it." Avery flipped her hand dismissively. "Please, just let me do this."

"Um—okay. Thanks." She had no other choice. Humiliation squirmed through her. If she had listened to Avery, she would have gotten a solid job, kept tabs on her finances, and never been involved with Brian. Instead, here she was, begging her older sister for money to bail her out of her mistakes. "A?"

"Yeah?"

Addisyn whispered the words so the darkness in the room wouldn't hear. "What if he sues me and wins?"

"He won't win."

"But what if he did?" Terror tangled around her voice. "You saw the letter. He's suing me for court costs, attorney fees, everything. Where would we get the money if he—"

"Now, hold on a minute." Avery tapped her arm. "*If* he sues you, and *if* he wins, which are both highly doubtful, we'll get the money. Don't worry about that for a second."

"H-how?" Addisyn wiped her cheeks on her wrist.

Even in the dim lamplight, she could see the expression on Avery's face. The same granite-grit resolve she'd worn when she'd told Addisyn they were leaving their father. "I'll sell the house."

The shock slapped her back. "A, no! You can't do that!"

"I can and I will. I've already been thinking this through." Avery's voice was still calm, her words undergirded by a bedrock certainty. "This house and this land would go for top dollar. I can move into something in town."

Everything was crumpled up, twisted together, and Avery's

selflessness was another two-ton weight on Addisyn's chest, crushing her into the mattress. How much more guilt could she take before she collapsed under its weight? "That's not a solution. You can't give up—"

"Listen, Addisyn." Avery's determination had a flint-sharp edge. "I would give up anything to get him out of your life and off your back. We'll do whatever we have to do."

"But—"

"Ads." Avery squeezed her shoulder. "Please, try not to worry. We'll figure it out. Together. Now, you need some rest. I can sleep in here till morning if you think it would help."

Nothing would help. Nothing except getting both of them out from under this threat. Nothing except finding a time machine and rewinding everything to the hour before she met Brian. "Thanks, but that's okay." Addisyn lay back and tried to project a peace she didn't feel. "I'm tired. I'll probably go right back to sleep."

"Well, okay." Avery hugged her, flicked off the lamp, and headed for the door. On the threshold she paused. "If you need me, I'll be here."

If you need me, I'll be here.

The one constant in her life. "I know. Thank you."

"Of course." Avery hesitated a moment longer, but then she was gone, back down the hall toward her bedroom.

The darkness in the room was a heavy, hostile presence. Addisyn closed her eyes, but she could still feel it watching her. For a moment she wanted to run after Avery and curl up in her sister's bed, the way she had when she was a little kid scared of thunderstorms.

If only she'd listened to Avery. Why had she been so desperate to disobey? Why hadn't she heeded her sister's warnings? If she had, then none of this would have ever happened. To either of them.

Images from the dream clicked through her mind like a highlight reel. She'd had nightmares about Brian before, of course. But this was the first night she'd dreamed about something else. Something more frightening than Brian's anger and sharp rocks and yawning chasms.

Avery's rejection.

This is your fault, Addisyn. You made your choice.

She was being ridiculous. She'd never hear those words from

Avery—never. It was just her subconscious scaring her with a stupid dream. It would never play out in real life. Avery would never hate her.

Not even if she has to pay for all your attorney's fees? Not even if she loses her house because of you?

She couldn't imagine Avery selling this cabin, couldn't imagine her moving to some boring place in town. Avery had come to the mountains to escape all the pain of her past. After everything she'd been through, she deserved at least that much. And here Addisyn was threatening everything she'd worked for.

She rolled onto her side and drew the covers up tighter. *Relax, Addisyn. Pull yourself together.* Avery was right. They'd face this together, and they'd find a solution.

No nightmare could rip them apart.

△△ △△ △△

AVERY WAITED WHILE the hands on her bedside clock dragged with an agonizing slowness around the next hour. Then she pushed the covers back and crawled out of the bed as quietly as she could. Mercy raised her head sleepily, but Avery patted her back. "It's okay, girl." She kept the whisper soft. "Go back to sleep."

Mercy sighed and dropped her head between her paws again. Avery rubbed the soft fur on her pup's ears. She needed to reinstate the *no-dog-on-the-beds* rule, but with all the turmoil in her life, she wasn't ready to relinquish Mercy's warm comfort across her feet every night.

She crept to the window and looked up. The moon was almost full, a lopsided golden disc spinning through a starless sky. The light was so intense she could see the outlines of the pine trees, the shoulders of the mountains, even the shimmer on the creek at the bottom of the hill.

How were her hands still shaking, an hour after Addisyn's nightmare? She leaned against the window and tried to breathe calm. But like a ghost in the moonlight came the image of Addisyn, eyes wide with terror, awakening from one nightmare only to enter another one.

Just like when their father was alive.

She couldn't do this, couldn't stay one more minute in this sinister silence. With a cautious glance down the hall toward Addisyn's room, she tiptoed down the stairs to the living room and sat at her desk. The lamp was glowing, of course, and she stared at the papers scattered under it. A few to-do lists for the store, an article about best flight cage practices for raptors, and a dog-eared trail map of Wild Basin area hikes. But it was the document in the middle that caught her attention. The copy of Addisyn's contract.

Since she couldn't sleep anyway, why not do some research? Avery powered up her laptop and typed "breach of contract" into the Google search bar. Immediately a dozen different websites leaped at her. Legal definitions and case stories and at least five law firms that specialized in this type of case.

She clicked on the first link and started wading through the legal jargon, comparing the verbiage in Addisyn's contract with what she was unearthing online. An hour later, she leaned back and rubbed her eyes. It was just as unpromising as she'd suspected.

The bottom line was that Addisyn had agreed to perform exclusively for the agency and fulfill all engagements contracted by them on her behalf for the period of five years. She'd been not even three years into the contract when she left Brian.

And the contract specified that for Addisyn to be released from her obligations, she had to send a notice in writing. Addisyn continued to insist she'd done that, but of course, it was her word against Brian's.

According to everything Avery was finding, this was a classic breach-of-contract case. The fact that Addisyn's leaving had been prompted by abuse and manipulation from Brian apparently didn't matter at all. Not unless they wanted to initiate some mess called a countersuit.

The only part that didn't fit in was this weird line about *other performance opportunities*. She still didn't know where he'd come up with that. Her sister hadn't skated for anyone except him.

The brightness from the computer was hurting her eyes. Avery closed the laptop and buried her face in her hands. The wolf pack of fears nipped at her heels, howling through her thoughts, and it was taking all her willpower to stay one step ahead of their teeth. But for Addisyn's sake, she had to outpace the panic.

Her heart squeezed at the memory of how small and defeated her sister had looked tonight. And with the image came a flare of protectiveness that ignited into white-hot anger. How could Brian *do* this? Just when Addisyn was finally, finally, starting to heal?

Her fury at Brian was matched only by her frustration with her own helplessness. Long before she'd engineered their escape from their dysfunctional childhood, she'd already been the rescuer, the one her sister counted on to shore up the sagging timbers of their life. Whether it was a skinned knee or friendship drama or ornery math homework, Addisyn had run to her for comfort, advice, guidance, resolution.

But now, she sat immobilized in the middle of a rockslide, watching the boulders tumble toward them both.

Addisyn is suffering, and I can't stop it. Addisyn is in danger, and I can't help her. Addisyn is sad, and I can't—

Her lungs were tightening, her throat closing in. *Stop it!* If she didn't find a way to calm herself, she'd have a panic attack right here at her desk. And she wouldn't allow herself to break down, wouldn't allow a single crack in the wall of confidence she'd built. If she couldn't stop the rockslide, she could at least keep Addisyn from hearing the rumble of the threat.

She pursed her lips and exhaled, longer than normal. There. That was better. She took another deep breath. Then another, and another.

She glanced around the living room, the familiar comfort of her sanctuary. What if she lost her home? She'd been serious about what she told Addisyn. If she needed to sell her cabin, she'd do it in a heartbeat. She'd gladly give up every square foot of her land to rescue Addisyn from that monster. But still, the thought of losing this home ripped inside her soul. It was her gift, she'd always believed—her blessing from El Shaddai.

El Shaddai, Who had always come through for her, Who now refused to reach into the whirlwind and show His strength again.

She looked up, past the rough-hewn timbers in the roof of her cabin. "El Shaddai." The whisper was the empty ache of her hurting heart. "Where have You gone?"

She waited, but there was nothing she could construe as an answer. No gentle feeling of calm, no soft voice in her soul, no reassuring knowing.

When was the last time she'd had a knowing, anyway? Not since that day in La Junta, which was a puzzle in and of itself—Addisyn had clearly been fine. But since that day, she'd had no feelings, no words.

Why?

Facing this was terrifying enough. But the thought of facing it without El Shaddai was unbearable. Avery rubbed her eyes. The fault was hers, probably. She'd been busy and tired and stressed, and she'd let the connection between them falter. Fear had suffocated grace, and her soul was feeling the ache.

More from desperation than desire, she reached into the drawer of her desk and pulled out her dilapidated Bible—the same one she'd bought for $1.75 at a Goodwill store the year she'd found the Lord. She flipped it open at random. A verse halfway down the righthand column caught her eye.

But I wait with hope for you...

Avery sighed and set the Book down. Wait? There was no time for that. She needed action, not waiting. Fighting, not surrendering.

She stood and clenched her fists, steeling herself for battle. She wasn't powerless. Not at all. They had options, didn't they? She'd found the lawyer. He'd be able to help.

It would all be okay. She would make it so. Because just like always, it was up to her.

△△ △△ △△

EVIDENTLY LAZ AND Avery were still playing catch-up at the store. Tonight, Avery had called Addisyn to let her know they were having trouble balancing the accounts.

"Okay." Addisyn had glanced at the wall clock. "I'll wait dinner."

"No, go ahead and get something. There's some of that vegetable quinoa in the refrigerator." Avery's voice had sounded beyond weary. "I'm not that hungry anyway."

So now Addisyn was sitting with her cold bowl of quinoa, staring at the gathering darkness beyond the window. Her own watery reflection gazed back at her, superimposed over the shadows outside.

It was the worry, not the work, that was fraying Avery's voice with fatigue. Just as it had been in New York.

Without warning, the memories rushed in, the frenetic whirling circus of that world. Avery had been only seventeen when they'd moved there. Four years younger than Addisyn was now. At the time, Addisyn had accepted her sister's accomplishments unquestioningly. Now she couldn't begin to believe all that Avery had done.

Sitting in their cheap apartment, staring at the budget with her expression pulled tight. *No, Ads, don't worry. We've got plenty of money.* Coming in from her second job at ten o'clock at night, the smell of fast food still clinging to her clothes. *Did you eat, honey? Good. No thanks, I'm not hungry.* Holding Addisyn's hand, protecting her from the perils of their new world. *Don't ever open the door if I'm not here. Yes, of course you're safe. But just keep the door locked.*

Avery had done everything, and Addisyn had only been a burden. And were things so different now? It was her fault they were facing Brian's threats. Her fault that Avery sounded so trapped. Her fault…

But there was one important difference between the past and the present. Yes, she was still a burden, still dragging Avery down. But now, she had the power to do something about it. And she'd been collecting the courage to try.

She didn't give her fear another chance to handcuff her resolve. Instead, she grabbed her phone and punched the still-familiar number with cold fingers.

"Hello?"

"Hello, Brian." The sound of his voice ripped a jagged hole in her spirit.

"Well. Addisyn." A mocking triumph undergirded his words. "To what do I owe the honor of this call?"

"I got your letter." She gripped the edge of the table until her knuckles stretched white.

"Ah, yes." Smugness oiled his tone. "The letter. I thought you should have received it by now."

How could she have ever loved this man? "Brian, what do you want?" She'd shoot straight, the way Avery would. "Why did you send me this letter? I'm living in Colorado and working temp jobs. I'm no threat to you."

"No threat?" Brian's tone tilted up, showing the hard edge underneath. "When you've walked out on me to compete for some other agency?"

When would he get off that? "Brian—I told you. I'm not—"

"Yeah, you told me, and you were lying!" His curse flicked like a whip across the face. "I know what you've been up to, Addisyn."

"Brian, I'm not up to anything!" Time was draining away. A few more minutes, and Avery would be home. "I swear I—"

"Don't play innocent with me." His voice was rising in the terrible gathering fury Addisyn knew. "You've been in Whistler skating. Nikki Stelles saw you."

Nikki Stelles.

The room swung around her, waiting for her response. "How—"

"Ty told me all about it. I ran into him the other day." Brian huffed. "Evidently you've got big plans, Addisyn. Plans so big you can't even discuss them with a friend."

All her empty boasting puffed into the room like a cloud of toxic gas, suffocating her. Why hadn't she considered the possibility that her stupid showboating would make its way to Brian? How could she have been so—

"Brian—" The confidence had fled from her tone, leaving her words wobbling. "I—I was fibbing to Nikki. I'm not actually—"

"Oh, Addisyn, do you really expect me to believe that?" Sarcasm brittled his voice. "Especially since I understand your hippie lover boy is part of those plans."

Heat pounded in her chest. "Brian, don't you dare talk about—"

"Addisyn, you're wasting your time." His words were rough, cutting through her defense. "Look, you can't fool me anymore, okay? But guess what? It doesn't matter who you're training with or what your plan is. A lawsuit like this could put a damper on you for years, baby. Nobody wants to sign an athlete facing legal action, you know. Especially one that broke her contract." He clicked his tongue with exaggerated condemnation. "That's just plain unethical, Addisyn. And there are consequences for that. Very serious consequences."

She didn't have to take this. She could scream at him. Or hang up. Or throw the phone through the window. She closed her eyes, picturing

Avery again, worry weighing her face. *Come on, Addisyn. Do it for her.*

"Okay." She took a deep breath, squaring up to the dreaded question. "So what can I do to get you to drop this?"

"Want to strike a deal, huh?" His laugh was anything but funny.

"Yes." It turned her stomach to kowtow to a bully like him. But to erase her guilt, she was willing to crawl over the broken glass of her mistakes. "What do you want from me?"

"You know what I want." His tone returned to center. "I want you to come back to the agency. Finish out your contract."

The answer she'd expected. The answer she'd feared. "Brian, you can't possibly think that I would ever come back to that agency."

"Just to finish your contract." He sounded rational, reasonable, as if he were brokering any normal business deal. "Not with me, of course. You'd have a different coach, different agent."

"No." She didn't have to consider the answer. "No way."

"It's your choice. You had the option of coming back on good terms." He sighed elaborately. "But you wanted to do it the hard way, didn't you?"

Addisyn straightened her shoulders and tried for her best imitation of Avery's big-sister tone. "I'd sooner walk off the end of the world than come back to that life." She smashed her free hand into a fist. "You won't get away with this. You'll be hearing from my lawyer. And Avery is helping me find—"

"Ah, yes. Avery. Always running to your rescue, isn't she?"

Her heart was throbbing so hard now she could feel it in her shoulders. "What do you mean?"

"Just wondering how she's taking this news." His chuckle rubbed fury all over her. "Has she gotten tired of putting up with you yet?"

His words scattered, and there was the dream. The frost in Avery's eyes. The gash between them like a wound in the earth. She yanked her mind from the image. "Brian, don't you dare bring Avery into this."

"*I* bring her in?" His voice was hardening again. "*You* dragged her in this time, Addisyn. Right into the middle of everything."

"Brian." Her mouth was so dry she could barely shape the words. "Stop."

"I bet this is raining on your happy little reunion, huh?" He paused, but she couldn't chase down her spinning thoughts enough to answer. "Sooner or later she'll get her own life, you know. She'll quit bailing you out all the time."

Avery, help!

This is your fault, Addisyn. You made your choice.

Nausea rocked her insides. She wanted to hang up, but the venom of his words had paralyzed her.

"And what about you, Addisyn? What will it take for you to see that you can't run far enough?" Again, his nasty laugh. "A new start? Isn't that what you said? As if I don't know exactly what you are."

A surge of rage and pain finally snapped the spell. "That's enough, Brian." Addisyn spit the words into the phone. "You know what? Just forget I called."

She hung up and flopped forward over her knees. She suddenly realized she was shaking, the terror and trauma twisting their way through her. His voice, his face, his anger—it was all wrapping around her, choking off her thoughts, strangling her words—

She jerked upright, melting the memories with the fire of her anger. Bringing Avery into this? How dare he? How *dare* he?

But wasn't he right?

Avery would never have been involved in this—if not for her.

Headlights glanced against the opposite wall. Avery was home. Addisyn retreated into an irrational relief. She tucked her phone into her pocket and hurried to the door to greet her sister.

She wouldn't let the conversation haunt her. She lifted her chin, allowing the anger to congeal into resolve. Brian was wrong. Avery would stand by her. She always would. Sure, they had their tense moments, but the bond between them would never be broken again.

But most importantly, no matter what happened, she would never go back to her old life.

Not ever.

CHAPTER 17

Forty thousand feet. Brian glanced down at the clouds rolling beneath the wings of the jet.

He had always appreciated the view from the top.

He tapped his pen on the edge of his notepad. The ninety-minute flight from New York to Montreal was supposed to give him time to respond to his email backlog, dictate three memos for Baylie, and watch some film on the potential clients he was going to interview. However, already halfway through the flight, he'd spent the whole time doing nothing but trying to figure out Addisyn Miles.

He had to hand it to her—the girl had more guts than he'd realized. Frankly, he'd expected her to cave by now. He'd been sure that when spooked by the terrifying threat of legal action, she'd be more than willing to surrender to his demands.

When he'd seen her number flash on his phone screen last night, he'd taken a moment to enjoy smug satisfaction. But instead of acknowledging defeat, she'd been stubbornly defiant. Even his jabs had only seemed to harden her resolve.

She had always been spirited—far too much for his taste—but given enough pressure, she'd never failed to crumple. So where was she finding the strength to resist this time?

He'd pondered the question all the way from LaGuardia, and he finally had an answer. There was only one possible explanation. Only one reason Addisyn had suddenly developed such dogged endurance.

Avery.

As much as he despised Addisyn's older sister, Brian had to grudgingly admit that she had access to a reserve of mysterious power he'd never fully understood. He glanced out the plane window, where the clouds rolled through the sunlight in a way that looked otherworldly.

Brian didn't believe in all the hocus-pocus around psychics or prophets or whatever they called themselves. But if he did, he'd have pegged Avery as one. Whatever the explanation, Avery somehow knew a lot more than most people. Sure, on the surface she seemed quiet and unobtrusive, but then out of nowhere she could reach into a person's soul and hold up whatever she found. All tinged with religious fanaticism, of course, but still enough to make someone—uncomfortable.

And to top it off, she had always harbored a blind affection for Addisyn. She had sacrificed for her younger sister in stupidly selfless ways, and even now, apparently, she'd overlooked Addisyn's rejection and welcomed her back with open arms.

So that was it, wasn't it? Brian could subdue Addisyn when she was isolated. But now, Addisyn had Avery at her side. And her sister had more than enough strength for them both.

Anger ripped through him. He really hadn't wanted this to explode into a big legal deal. He was fully prepared to take Addisyn to court, but he'd been hoping the threat alone would convince her to back down and save all of them the expense and headache. He refused to glance at the fact that his record of, well, indiscretions was another reason he'd prefer to avoid the courtroom scene.

But now, court was right where they were headed, because the two sisters had practically formed a coalition against him. Just as they had all those years ago.

He stared at his notepad, watching the memories shape themselves against the blank paper. At sixteen, Addisyn had been ridiculously naive, so innocently ready to fall in love that she'd nearly swooned over the corniest compliments. The path should have been simple, really. The girl had few friends and no parents, only a vague "big sister" she'd referenced frequently.

He grimaced now to recall how he'd initially pictured Avery as an older version of Addisyn—just as unsuspecting, just as easy to manipulate.

But instead, meeting Avery for the first time had introduced him to a woman who combined an uncanny ability to see through his facade with a definite protective streak.

Looking into her eyes had made him feel—well, weird. Addisyn had described her sister with words like *intuitive* and *sensitive*, but she hadn't prepared him to face off with a warrior. He'd had this creepy sense that Avery could see right down to the rock bottom of his soul. And she'd definitely let him know that she wasn't impressed by whatever she'd found there.

But in the end, he'd outsmarted her—because he'd known there were cracks in the sisters' relationship. A rebellious teen and an overprotective older sister? Tension was ready to boil over.

All it needed was someone to stir the pot.

So he'd set to work on Addisyn—dropping a comment here, inserting a criticism there. Slowly, he'd watched her attitude toward her sister deteriorate. And his big chance had come after Addisyn made the regional championships. Avery had promised to be there, but at the last minute she'd had to work, or something. Addisyn had been devastated.

Brian had made full use of the moment. He could still remember his conversation with Addisyn the next day. "Avery says she's sorry. She says she couldn't get off work." Addisyn had turned troubled eyes to him. "But this was so important to me. Couldn't she have tried harder?"

He'd known that attacking Avery outright wouldn't get him anywhere; Addisyn was still too loyal to her sister. But a more circuitous route had done the trick handily. "It does seem like she could have done something. I mean, this was such a huge moment for you." He'd shaken his head regretfully. "I can't imagine her not being there."

Rebellion had flared in Addisyn's eyes. "Sometimes it just feels like she wants me to be her obedient little sister my whole life. Like I don't have any identity away from her."

Brian had hidden his jubilation at hearing some of his own criticisms echoed in Addisyn's words. "Of course. I mean, she's obviously very controlling." He'd pulled a solemn face. "I'm sorry you've had to put up with that. I'm sure she's hard to live with."

Addisyn's face had twisted uneasily, and for a moment he'd had the fear that he'd pushed too far. "Well—" She'd spoken slowly, the words rising through the turbid water of her emotions. "I wouldn't say that. I mean—sometimes—but she's—she's really cool. She can be pretty fun." Her expression had softened to something almost like longing. "We used to have good times together—when we were little. But—we haven't in a while. We're just—it's not the same." Her laugh trembled. "I guess—I guess I'm growing up. I'm not sure I like it."

Brian had smiled sympathetically. "Well, things change when you grow up. You get to decide who you want to be. Not who everybody expects you to be."

He smirked now, remembering how totally trusting Addisyn had been. Ready to swallow his every word. It had only taken a few such conversations to reshuffle her whole worldview.

Strange, wasn't it? In the end, his success with Addisyn had been based less on making her love him and more on making her hate Avery.

Interesting. He leaned back in his seat. Yes, it was coming between them that had scored his victory before. If only there were some way to again drive a wedge and exploit those cracks. And surely, just as before, there were cracks. Big ones this time. Two strong-willed sisters thrown back together after years of hostility? Yeah, things couldn't be as smooth as Addisyn let on.

No matter how holy Avery thought she was, the pressure of the situation had to be taking its toll. Stress would trump spirituality at some point. And Addisyn was probably turning difficult and defensive, the way she always did in a bind. Toss in some lingering resentments from the past, and their newfound bond was likely as tenuous as a spiderweb.

The possibility grew, but there was no way to initiate it. By the time the plane banked over Montreal, he'd examined a number of options, but none seemed right. He shrugged as he fastened his seatbelt. He wouldn't become discouraged. Instead, he'd trust his signature good luck. Maybe the perfect chance would drop into his hands.

After all, he reminded himself as the plane began its descent, he was, and always had been, the one on top.

△△ △△ △△

"ALL RIGHT. LET'S get to it." Avery pointed to the pink zip portfolio in the center of the table. "Everything is in there?"

"Yes." Addisyn pulled out the chair across from her. "All the papers and anything else I had from skating. They're not really organized, though."

Well, that was no surprise. The real shock was that her scattered sister had kept any paperwork in the first place. "All right." Avery slid a notepad and pen across the table to Addisyn. "You make a list of everything we find that might be useful."

"Okay." Addisyn regarded her skeptically. "And what, exactly, are you thinking we'll find?"

"Well, I mean—" She wasn't sure herself. "I don't know. I just don't want to leave a stone unturned."

Addisyn nodded. "I'm hoping we'll find a copy of that letter. But I don't think I made one."

"Yes. That would be nice." Avery was still amazed that her sister had sent a letter of that importance without making a copy. Or using certified mail. Or doing anything remotely responsible. She pushed away her frustration and unzipped the case. No need to create further tension. "Who knows. Maybe it's in here."

The first clump of papers was as jumbled as Addisyn had warned. A flyer for a vitamin supplement was next to a registration form for a skating camp. Avery moved both of those to uncover a birthday card signed in smeary purple ink. Well, this could take all night.

"Here." Addisyn collected part of the chaos. "I'll go through this half."

"Okay." It seemed best to begin by just sorting the items into categories. Avery was making three stacks when Addisyn held out something. "Here's another copy of the contract."

"Great. Let's see it again." As if she really needed to. After a week of replacing sleep with fretting and online research, she'd practically memorized the document. Still, she flipped through the stapled pages.

There was Addisyn's salary. The number of zeros never failed to steal Avery's breath. If Brian sued Addisyn for her salary—and damages— She stopped herself before she could calculate the number again. Which meant more to Brian—the money, or the revenge?

She forced herself to cling to concentration, raking the pages for any clues. On the signature page, something she hadn't noticed before caught her eye. "Hey." She tapped the paper. "Who's Mitch?"

"Mitch? Oh, Mitch Shapiro." Addisyn leaned back. "He's the director of Rising Stars. Where my sponsorship came from."

"So why's he on the contract?"

"Because he was part of the agreement. Mitch paid Brian's salary, through the sponsorship, and Brian coached me."

Hmm. That could be important. Avery pointed at the notepad. "Write down to ask the lawyer about Mitch. Find out if he would have any say-so in this since he's on the contract. Maybe you could try to call him."

"That's not a bad idea. At the very least, he might have clout with Brian." Addisyn scribbled down a note. "See? Progress." Her smile looked forced.

"Progress." Avery set the contract aside and shuffled through some more papers, the puzzle pieces of the situation spinning through her mind. There was still one angle that made no sense at all. "Hey, Ads?"

"Uh-huh?" Addisyn was unfolding some origami-like program.

"Brian's letter." Avery tapped her fingers on the table. "He said you had breached your contract by seeking other opportunities. Where would he have gotten that idea?"

Addisyn shrugged vaguely. "No telling."

"But you haven't skated anywhere since you left him." This was the part that just couldn't fit. "Think, Ads. What could have given him that idea?"

Addisyn hesitated. "Maybe—somebody said—I don't know, maybe a rumor went around or something."

"Could it be something to do with Darius?"

"Darius?" Addisyn snapped her head up. "What do you mean?"

Avery blinked. "I just meant, maybe a rumor started because of you being friends with him, and him being a skater. Maybe someone got the idea you two were skating, or something."

Addisyn studied her for a moment, then seemed to relax. "Oh. Maybe." She rolled her eyes. "Who knows where Brian gets his ideas."

That much was true. He could have fit together some half-baked suspicions. Or concocted the idea himself.

The conversation shifted to questions for Addisyn to ask the lawyer. "Tell him about Mitch for sure." Avery wrestled more papers from the portfolio. "And ask him why Brian would have put that about 'other opportunities' in the letter."

"Uh—okay." Addisyn rolled the pen between her fingers. "What about next steps? Don't we need to find out what to do if Brian actually sues me?"

Avery couldn't bear to think that far ahead, but Addisyn was right, of course. "Yeah. I guess so." Again she wished she could go with Addisyn. There was no way she could trust her sister to get all this information straight.

"I'm going to ask about my letter of resignation too. Like, what recourse we have since Brian's lying about not getting it."

Avery glanced at the portfolio case. Did she dare bring this up? "Addisyn. Are you—are you sure about mailing the letter?"

Addisyn looked at her in puzzlement for a moment before realization soured her expression. "You mean—you think I didn't?" She gripped the edge of the table. "Of course I did."

"But—" Avery bit her lip. "Look, Addisyn, every scrap of everything is in that case. We've been through nearly all of it, and we haven't found anything."

"I know. I didn't make a copy, and I should have. But I mailed it."

"You had a lot going on. You might have thought you did and actually—"

"What, you don't trust me to take care of a big thing like that?" Addisyn's eyes narrowed with hurt.

Avery held up her hands like a white flag. "Addisyn, don't get mad at me. I just—I just wanted to make sure."

"I mailed it." Addisyn clipped each word short.

"Okay." Avery would believe her. She didn't really have a choice.

She flipped through some more papers. An email chain between Addisyn and Brian, complete with an absolutely sickening amount of heart emojis. A printout of a strength-training regimen. A program from a skating event in Missouri. She flipped that one open to see Addisyn's name near the top.

The next item felt heavier. Avery glanced over it and raised her eyebrows. A certificate of accomplishment from Addisyn's local league—back in Syracuse, before they'd even moved to New York City. "Ads?"

"Hm?"

Avery held up the certificate. "This is—from the local league? In Syracuse?"

Addisyn shrugged, her gaze avoiding the paper. "Yeah. It was the year I went to state." She tilted her head. "Don't you remember? When I was in the Northwestern State Tour?"

Avery studied the certificate, then set it aside. "No—I mean, I do remember you being in some competition that year. I guess I didn't realize it was such a big deal."

Addisyn cleared her throat and concentrated on her stack. "I was the youngest competitor from the league to make state."

"Really?" Avery glanced at the date on the certificate. Addisyn would have been twelve; she would have been sixteen. Why didn't she remember this?

Avery flipped through a few more papers before her sister spoke again. "Hey, look."

Avery glanced at the photo her sister held up, and guilt burned along her spine. "Oh. Yeah."

It was the same photo that had been in Addisyn's album. The media shot. Avery looked down at her stack again. "I remember that picture."

"It was my first regional championship." Addisyn's next words were too soft to hear.

Avery glanced up. "What?"

There was a challenge behind Addisyn's eyes. "I said you weren't there."

All Avery's breath escaped. "Addisyn." She studied her sister's face. "It wasn't my choice. If I could have been there, I—"

"I watched for you. The whole night. You had promised me you'd be there." Addisyn gazed at the photo again. "And then you weren't."

Addisyn still resented that? All these years later? Avery searched the empty air between them for words. "I—I'm sorry. I told you, I had to work."

"You could have asked off." Addisyn flicked the photo back into the stack.

"I did!" Frustration frayed her voice. This was ridiculous, apologizing for a years-old offense. "I asked off weeks ahead of time. And then that very afternoon, Mr. Holt asked me to work late. I told him I couldn't, because my sister was performing, and he told me I could work late or find a new job."

"Oh." Addisyn's face shifted slightly. "I didn't know that."

"Right." Avery heard the irritation rubbing at her tone. "Because you never gave me the chance to explain."

The silence no longer fit well between them. It stretched over unsaid words for a few misshapen moments before Addisyn spoke again. "You never liked me skating, did you?"

Avery's heart rate doubled. "Why would you ask that? I came to your performances and—"

"Not that one."

Avery took a deep breath, shrugging off the sting of the words. "Addisyn. You're not being fair." She worked to keep her tone reasonable. "I missed that performance. And I'm sorry. But the rest of the time I supported you, and I made sure you had every opportunity."

"That's not the point!" Addisyn's voice was climbing an unsteady staircase. "Skating was my *world*, Avery. My whole world. And you never—" Hurt colored over the anger in her voice. "It's like you had no interest in that at all. Like, there was this whole part of me that you didn't care about."

So there. Addisyn had splashed her emotions across the table, and now she was looking to Avery to clean up the mess. But what could Avery say? That she couldn't follow her sister into a world she knew nothing about? That she resented skating for taking Addisyn away? That there wasn't a single picture of her in Addisyn's photo album?

The whole conversation—the whole *night*—was asking for energy she couldn't spare. Avery rubbed her eyes and glanced away from her sister's held-out heart. "Look—can we talk about this later?" She gestured to the papers in front of them. "When we're not working on a battle plan?"

Like that, the door behind her sister's eyes swung shut again. "Sure. Okay."

Avery lowered her head and shuffled through some more papers. So Addisyn was still upset with her over a single incident years ago? An incident that really wasn't her fault, anyway? And weren't the years of sacrifices and love and support enough to outweigh that?

A wave of frustration suddenly knocked her emotions sideways. If Addisyn had listened to her even once, they wouldn't be marooned in this mess. She'd warned Addisyn about Brian. She'd cautioned her sister a hundred times about his darkness. Yet Addisyn hadn't listened. She'd rushed into one stupid choice after another without ever slowing down.

And now her choices were catching up with both of them.

⁂

ADDISYN'S THROAT WAS crammed with cotton as she parked in front of Mr. Graves's office. She gripped the file folder they'd assembled last night and shot Avery a quick text.

I'm here. Talk to you this evening.

A bell jingled as she stepped through the door into a rather fussy lobby. A secretary with dangling eyeglasses peered over the sleek desk. "May I help you?"

"I'm here to see Mr. Graves." Her fingers were sweating. She shifted the file folder to her other hand. If only Avery had been able to come.

"Your name?" The woman balanced her glasses on the bridge of her nose and squinted at a clipboard.

"Addisyn Miles." Just confirming her identity felt like an admission of guilt.

"All right. I'll let him know you're here." The secretary tucked a phone to her ear, and Addisyn perched on the edge of the slick leather sofa. A text vibrated through her phone. Avery, of course.

Okay, sounds good. Don't forget to ask him all our questions. Write down his answers and we'll talk about it tonight.

Addisyn didn't have time to respond before a balding man with a bright blue tie peeked through the doorway. "Hello there! Addisyn Miles?"

"That's me." Although right now, she would rather be anyone else. She stood and accepted his outstretched hand.

"Nice to meet you." Mr. Graves led her down the hall to his office, an ornate cave of law books with diplomas staring from the walls. "Now, tell me what you can about your situation."

Addisyn sat in the wingback chair across from the desk and sighed. In the tangled mess, which loose end should she pull first? "Um—I'm a professional figure skater. Well, I was a skater, I mean. And I'm facing legal action from my former coach."

The threads were fraying now, the details wrapping around the story. How she met Brian. How she received a scholarship. How she signed a contract with the New York Figure Skaters' Agency. How she left because of his abusive behavior.

"Did you seek to terminate the contract at that time?" Mr. Graves had listened quietly, his look at once intent and detached.

"Yes, but I don't have proof of that." She flicked the edge of the file folder nervously. "I sent a letter before I left, stating my intentions. But now Bri—Mr. Felding says he never received the letter."

"Did you send it certified mail or—"

"No." If she heard that question one more time, she'd bang her head against the mahogany desk. "I know I should have. I was just—I was focused on getting away from him. I didn't think about the consequences." Consequences. Exactly what Avery always accused her of ignoring.

"Did you have any other contact with him after that?"

"Yes. He arranged an audition for me in Chicago, but I passed on that." Her head was starting to ache. "And then I saw him a couple of months ago in Denver, at an ice rink where I was practicing."

"Did he speak to you at that time?"

"Yes." Addisyn bit her lip. "He told me I would regret leaving the agency. Next thing I know, I received a letter from him threatening legal action."

Mr. Graves's eyebrows arched slightly. "May I see this letter?"

"Here." Addisyn slid the file folder across the desk. "My contract is in there as well, in addition to a timeline of events my sister and I prepared."

"Perfect." He scanned through the documents attentively, silence peering over his shoulder. Addisyn slowly traced the swirl patterns on the chair's upholstery.

Finally he looked up. "Hmm. Yes, yes…and so this Mr. Felding is, or was, your coach, correct?"

"Yes."

"Now, I see a mention here of Rising Stars." Mr. Graves tapped the contract with his pen. "Could you clarify that for me?"

"Rising Stars was the foundation that awarded my sponsorship. They paid Brian's salary also." Something she hadn't known until later in her relationship with him.

"Were you still under their sponsorship at the time you left?"

"No. They terminated their sponsorship back in January due to my failure to meet performance goals." The words were still sour. "I had a bad season due to injury."

"So at the time the breach of contract allegedly occurred, you were not under the sponsorship."

"No." She couldn't tell if that was good or bad.

A few more questions, a few more responses, each one leading along a path she couldn't see. Finally Mr. Graves sat back and sighed. "Unfortunately, Mr. Felding does have good grounds here. Without evidence that you mailed the letter, we have no proof that you attempted to end the contract in good faith. Therefore, we have no legal grounds for a defense."

"But—I know I sent that letter." Addisyn leaned forward in her chair, her words reaching desperately for his belief. "I promise, I wouldn't have forgotten something that important. I remember typing it and putting it in the envelope and taking it to the post office on my way out of—"

"Miss Miles, while I don't doubt your word, you must understand that something more—substantial—would be needed in a court of law."

Like a copy of the letter. Or a mail receipt. As Avery had said.

"But—Mr. Graves, I left Mr. Felding because he was controlling and manipulative. I was—I felt I was in danger." The shadow of the words fell over her. "Shouldn't that count for something?"

Mr. Graves hesitated, staring at his shelf of legal books as if the answer might be scribbled across their spines. "It does, and it doesn't. While it might glean sympathy from jurors—"

So he was already expecting this to go to trial.

"—it won't justify the breach legally." He toyed with his pen thoughtfully. "Of course, you could file a countersuit to claim—"

"No." She couldn't add another loose thread to this knotted mess. "I don't want to be in a courtroom at all."

Mr. Graves nodded. "I understand. Not an uncommon attitude, certainly." He hitched his eyeglasses higher and peered at the contract again. "Now. I also see something about 'other performance opportunities.' Can you shed any light on this?"

"No." Addisyn shook her head. "I only performed at the agency-designated events. Bri—Mr. Felding arranged all that."

"You haven't skated or made plans to skate anywhere since you left the agency?"

What? Addisyn stared at the lawyer. "Why would that matter?"

"Because as far as we're concerned legally, you're still bound by this contract. At least until we can prove otherwise."

"I don't understand."

"Let me clarify." Mr. Graves pressed his fingertips together. "In your contract, you are bound by an exclusivity clause, in which you agreed to participate only in agency-sponsored events."

Of course she knew that. After the nights she and Avery had spent poring over the document, there wasn't much Mr. Graves could tell her about the terms of the contract.

"And from a legal standpoint, this clause is still binding. Your contract is not considered as dissolved because, according to the plaintiff, you did not adequately provide notice of your intent to withdraw. Thus, entering into partnership with any other entities to participate in any event would be in direct violation of your contract."

No. No, this wasn't happening. Addisyn dug her fingernails into the fabric on the chair. "I—I agreed to participate in a charity event with my—my friend. In Canada." She swallowed. "I didn't realize—I never thought the contract was still in force."

"Oh." Mr. Graves's face set grimly. "That's going to make this harder."

The walls were looming over her, the law books bared like so many teeth. "So then—I mean, can't I fix this? I don't have to skate. I can tell them that—"

"Have you already signed an agreement?"

Addisyn closed her eyes, blocking out the way the truth leaned over the desk. "Yes."

"Well, then, Mr. Felding can very well claim anticipatory repudiation."

Addisyn opened her eyes again. "Antici—what?" What was it with lawyers and their big words?

"Anticipatory repudiation. In other words, when a party makes their intention to violate the contract clear, they can be sued even if the violating behavior has not yet taken place." He paused and lifted the first page of her contract. "Although, your contract states that you will not 'seek to enter into other agreements.' So in your case, the breach has in fact already occurred."

"I—I never thought about that being wrong. I thought the contract was nullified because I sent the letter."

He sighed. "Well, there may be some ways we can work around."

From his tone, Addisyn doubted any were coming to mind for him.

"We could have attempted to argue that leaving the agency was necessary for your well-being given your coach's actions. However, it will be much harder to defend a more, uh, deliberate breach such as this."

The despair surged like a rising tide, and she was drowning. She'd been so stupid. In every way, she'd played right into Brian's hands. And now—

"I'll study the case law on this in the coming days. In the meantime, I'll draft a letter back to Mr. Felding explaining that you disagree with his allegations."

"He hasn't actually sued me yet." Addisyn clung desperately to the last shred of hope. "Do you think he might back down?"

"Maybe." Mr. Graves's mouth twisted. "But from the way you've described him, I'd say you should prepare for battle." He stood, sweeping away the conversation. "Thank you for coming in, Miss Miles. I'll be in touch. You may make your payment to my secretary out front."

She was getting ready to pay over three hundred dollars for some of the worst news of her life. "Of course. Thank you."

Alone in the hallway, she pulled out the check Avery had given her. The sight of her sister's handwriting clenched the fist of failure even tighter. As awful as the appointment had been, the worst still lay ahead.

Because she couldn't hide any longer. The time had come. Avery would have to know everything—tonight.

△△ △△ △△

UNPACKING A BOX of hiking shirts, Avery caught herself glancing at the clock on the wall again. Four forty. Seven minutes later than the last time she had checked.

Addisyn's appointment with Mr. Graves had been at four. Surely she was almost done by now. And as soon as the store closed, Avery would be able to go home and find out what the lawyer had said.

But something told her it wouldn't be encouraging news.

After all, what could Mr. Graves really offer? Without that letter, Addisyn was caught squarely in Brian's trap. From a legal viewpoint, she'd breached her contract. It was that simple.

So there was really no recourse…except for one possible solution.

Avery had been toying with the idea for three days, ever since it had first struck, lightning-sizzle, during one of her sleepless nights. And the longer she considered it, the more convinced she became that it was the only option that could still hold out any hope. Even if she would rather jump into the freezing waters of Lake Haiyaha on a subzero night.

Four forty-eight. She'd finished unpacking the shirts, and the customer stream was slow this afternoon. Now was the time to do it, before she lost her nerve. Before she had to go home and face Addisyn's despair. She found Laz behind the register. "Laz, may I have ten minutes for a phone call?"

"Of course." He waved off her question. "You know you don't hafta ask."

"Thanks. I'll make it quick." She hurried out the back door of the shop. The cold air struck her like a slap, but she didn't care. For this call, she needed to be able to see the mountains.

While she dialed, she kept her eyes on the place where the sun touched the peaks. Three rings, and a voice answered with robotic perfection. "New York Figure Skaters' Agency."

Fear sucked her words away. *Come on, Avery. You can do this.*

"Hello?" The voice sounded annoyed.

Addisyn. For Addisyn, she would face any dragon. "I need to speak with Mr. Brian Felding, please."

"One moment." A click, and some posh classical music tinkled over the line. Avery made a fist with her free hand, fingernails digging into her sweaty palm.

The music stopped. The phone clicked. But a hesitant female voice answered. "Um, hello?"

"Hi." Had she reached the wrong place? "I need to speak with Brian Felding."

"Oh, yes. Okay." The girl sounded young, and definitely inexperienced. "This is his office. Uh, who can I say is calling?"

"Avery Miles." Avery watched her name turn to a cloud in the chilly air. "Please tell him I'm calling about my sister."

"Your sister Addisyn."

The words caught her off guard. "Yes." Wariness slid suddenly around her soul. "How did you know that?"

"I handle the files. I just—the other day—well, never mind." The girl gave a sheepish laugh. "Hang on a minute. I'm transferring you."

Avery didn't have time to wonder about the mysterious exchange before Brian's voice cut over the line. "Hello, Avery."

A rush of darkness slammed against her soul with his words. She hadn't realized how many shadows the sound of his voice would raise. "Brian."

His laugh held an uncomfortable tone. "Well. This is a nice surprise. What's up?"

She wouldn't back down. "You know what's up."

"You mean the lawsuit?" Brian sighed. "Addisyn left me no choice. She had to realize that backing out of a contract with no warning would have repercussions."

The phone was slick in her sweaty hand. "She claims she sent you the letter of resignation."

"It's not in her file."

The wind whipped up, stinging against her cheeks. "Brian, why are you doing this? What do you want from her?"

"You mean you have to ask me?" His voice dripped with sarcasm. "Here I thought you had some kind of superpower that told you everything. What, is it not working too well right now?"

She'd raised her younger sister, survived New York City, and built a life in the Rocky Mountains, but not hating this man took more effort than all of those combined. *El Shaddai…* "Brian. I'm not here to spar with you." She forced a cold detachment into her tone. "I want to talk business."

"Business?"

Addisyn. For Addisyn. "What do I have to do to get you to drop this?"

"Oh. I should have seen this coming." His laugh wasn't funny. "Going to battle for little sis, huh?"

"Yes." *Always.*

"Did Addisyn ask you to call?"

"Of course not!" Avery began pacing, the tension driving her in circles. "She would have never asked me to do that. She doesn't even know I'm calling you."

Silence. Avery could almost hear Brian's mind spinning through the ramifications before he spoke. "Look, Avery. I get where you're coming from. I really do. And your dedication is—touching. But this is between Addisyn and me." His tone darkened. "I don't think you really want to get in the middle."

"I already am." The mountains nodded at her encouragingly. If only she could inhale their strength. "Brian, this is my *sister*, you realize that? If you want to go after her—you have to deal with both of us."

"Oh, Avery." Exasperation shoved past his words. "Do you never learn? I would have thought you'd have given up on Addisyn a long time ago."

"I'll never give up on her." The bedrock of the mountains was underneath this truth.

His tone turned caustic, acid-bathed. "Always the rescuer, aren't you? Always there to swoop in and save the day. Well, this time you can't, okay? Addisyn broke her contract fair and square. She didn't send the letter of resignation, and now she's competing again for another agency. I can't let that—"

"Wait a minute." If nothing else, she could rout this rumor. "Brian, I don't know where you got that idea about Addisyn competing. She hasn't been back on the ice since she left you."

"Avery, don't lie to me!" Brian's anger was pulsing through the phone line, a terrible force like gathering storm clouds over the High Country. "Look, you can't fool me. A friend of mine saw her in Whistler not three weeks ago."

"That's easy to explain." Why wouldn't he believe her? "She went to Whistler to visit a friend. She was there two weeks. I don't know what you're thinking, but Addisyn is not competing again. I can swear to that."

Silence again while the mountains listened and Avery watched her breath puff into nothing. Brian's next words came slowly, with an undertone like the shadows that trickled across the valleys. "So…you really don't know, do you?"

Foreboding crinkled across Avery's shoulders, but she shrugged it off. No. She would not be intimidated by Brian. "What do you mean?"

He hesitated for the first time. "I know this guy, okay? This fellow coach. I ran into him at a—well, in town, and he told me that one of his girls had talked to Addisyn in Whistler."

She was still pacing, boots crunching over the gravel. "So?"

"So Addisyn was practicing at the rink when they talked."

The world tilted so oddly that Avery stumbled backward and shoved a hand against the wall of the shop to brace herself. Brian was crazy. He had to be.

"Was she—" She could barely form the words. "Was she with a coach?"

"She was skating with that hippie dude from Vancouver." Disgust huffed through Brian's tone. "What's-his-name Payne."

Darius. Addisyn had been practicing with Darius on an ice rink in Whistler. Avery forced herself to peer through the panic, searching for the logical explanation that had to exist. "So maybe they were just skating for fun, or—"

"Don't think so. That's the pro rink. They would have had to have credentials to be there."

Avery's legs felt as unreliable as if she'd just hiked ten miles. Addisyn could not have deceived her. Not this time around.

"And—" There was an odd exultation in Brian's voice. "Addisyn told Nikki, that's the girl, that she was in a competition." He paused, allowing the sentence to slam into Avery's soul. "A competition so big she couldn't say much about it."

"No." The word was instinct, slapping back the idea that Addisyn had been hiding the truth all this time. The possibility was more than Avery could process. "Brian, you're lying. No way."

"Avery!" For once, his voice was serious. "I'm not lying. Really. Shoot, I saw her myself at the rink in Denver. That was what first made me suspicious."

In Denver? Avery's world righted itself a little. Now he was definitely wrong. Addisyn hadn't been to Denver. Her sister lived with her, for crying out loud. She would know if—

Wait.

"When—when was this?"

"Back in September." If he was lying, he was doing it with confidence. "A Sunday near the end of the month."

The time of the expo. She'd been in La Junta.

Where had Addisyn been?

The knowing. El Shaddai. She'd had the knowing…

"I—I don't believe you." But the words didn't come out with the conviction she'd intended.

"Wow. So she didn't tell you any of this?" Smugness smeared itself across Brian's tone. "Guess she'll have some explaining to do."

The ground dissolved beneath Avery, and she melted to the cold earth, shudders working through her. Addisyn had lied to her. No, Addisyn had *betrayed* her. She had trusted her sister—again—and Addisyn had been going behind her back.

Just like before.

"I—" The fingers of her free hand dug into the gravel, struggling to ground herself in the moment. "I'm sure there's a good explanation—"

"A good explanation? Of course there is." His laugh was laced with sarcasm. "The explanation is that she's been lying to you. She's sneaky, and you're trusting. What a perfect pairing."

Avery didn't realize she was crying until the mountains blurred in a twisted distortion. Her teeth were chattering, but she worked to inject her voice with steadiness. "This doesn't change anything, Brian."

"Are you kidding? It changes everything." His voice sounded almost gleeful. "Because now you know. She's not worth fighting for. And whatever truce you thought you two had reached—well, she doesn't think enough of you to even be honest." He chuckled. "I'll bet she's been laughing behind your back this whole time."

"That's enough." Avery had to escape, had to end this nightmare of a phone call. What had Addisyn been doing? How many lies had she spun around them both? "I have to go."

"Fine." That odd victory was back in his voice. "I guess you two do have a lot to discuss. Oh, and tell her hi from me, Avery. Tell her I'll see her in court."

CHAPTER 18

Addisyn had tried on a dozen different ways of telling Avery, and none of them fit.

Avery, we need to talk about what the lawyer said.

Avery, there's something I should have told you.

Avery, please don't be mad, but—

Who was she kidding? She slumped deeper into the chair and rested her elbows on the dining room table. It didn't matter how gently she tiptoed up to the sleeping subject. When it awoke, everything would come undone.

She'd been stupid. So stupid. Avery was going to be more than upset—rightly so. And then what? Would this be enough to snap the fragile thread between them?

And she had no solution to serve as a peace offering. Again and again since arriving home, she'd sifted through the situation, but she'd always come up empty-handed. She'd even tried to call Rising Stars and talk to Mitch. But his bored-sounding secretary had let her know he was out of town, and she had little hope that the woman would deliver her message to him when he returned.

No, facing the truth was like trying to scale a sheer rock wall. No cracks or crevices offered a way of escape.

The crunch of gravel under tires made her stomach flip. Avery was home. But why was she driving so fast?

The truck shuddered to a stop in the yard, and the door banged open more quickly than she would have expected. "Avery?" She looked up just as her sister appeared in the doorway.

Her sister's face was as unyielding as the bedrock of the mountains. She shrugged off her coat and tossed it at a chair. Addisyn blinked. "Avery! What's wrong?"

Mercy trotted up, prancing around Avery eagerly, but her sister brushed the dog aside. "Addisyn Grace Miles." Her words were unusually tight, emotions straitjacketed. "We need to talk."

She hadn't heard her full name from Avery since her teenage years. Addisyn gulped down the knot in her throat. "Okay…"

"Why were you in Whistler?"

The last shreds of normalcy drained from the room, leaving only the question that would splinter the bridge between them. Somehow, Avery had beaten her to the punch line. Still Addisyn clung to the words that were not lies. "I went to see Darius—I—"

"And to skate, right?" Avery took a step toward the table, into the widening space between them. "You went to Whistler to skate. And you did not tell me."

What could she say? What she should have said a long time ago—the truth. "Yes."

A strange silence filled the room—the kind that hung heavy over the mountains before a storm rolled in. The unnatural calm held its breath for a few moments before Avery spoke again. "So it's true." Her words were more unsteady now, balancing on the edge of disbelief.

"But—" Frantically Addisyn ducked beneath her explanation, like a leaky umbrella in a downpour. "I mean, I told you I went to see Darius, and I did, so it wasn't a—"

"You were skating with Darius in Whistler." Avery's expression was changing, her disbelief slowly hardening into certainty. "I can't believe this."

Addisyn stared at a knothole on the table. If only she could crawl through it and disappear. "How—how did you hear that—"

"You want to know who told me?" An odd fire glowed in Avery's eyes like heat lightning on the horizon. "Brian!" Her laugh was more like a cry. "Brian told me. Because I called him to try to help you."

This couldn't be happening. The storm was rushing toward them both at a pace that left her no time to react. "I—I'm sorry—I should have said something."

The silence balanced uneasily between them again. Still hovering hopefully, Mercy glanced between them with a whine like a question mark. Then Avery sighed and melted into the chair across the table from Addisyn. "Don't you realize, Addisyn? This changes everything."

"But, Avery, it's not like Brian is saying. It's not a competition, it was just supposed to be a charity event. Just a one-time—"

"What did the lawyer say about it? Or did you keep it a secret from him too?"

The accusation stung, but she deserved it. "No. I told him."

"And?"

The question carried the warning of distant thunder, but she had nowhere to hide. "I thought it would be okay since my contract was over. But he says—he says it's a definite breach. Because, without the letter, my contract was still binding. Is still binding, I guess."

Avery's face dropped to her folded arms for a moment. When she raised her head, the corners of her mouth were unsteady. "So is this where Brian got this whole idea in the first place?"

"Yes." Another *yes*, another weight in the groaning scale of her sins. "I—I sort of—well, I kind of exaggerated. About the event, you know. To a friend—someone I knew from skating. I guess—I guess she started a rumor—and so he heard and thought—"

"Please tell me you are joking." Avery gripped the edge of the table. "So you're getting ready to be sued because you lied. To me—to this *friend*—to Brian. All the way around, you were deceptive and—"

"Wait a minute." Why was her sister trying to make her feel worse? Addisyn pulled hard at her emotions. She would not get drawn into a fight with Avery, would not weaponize words she'd later regret, but frustration was flicking at the edges. "I feel bad enough about this, Avery, so can you cut all the—"

"I just can't believe you would do this!" Avery's tone was rising, gale-force. "You lied to me. Straight-up, in-your-face, lied to me."

"But I did go to see Darius!" The tension shoved her to her feet, her chair scraping away from the table. "Once and for all, I did not lie. I just didn't tell the whole truth."

"Right. Your specialty." Now Avery was on her feet too, her expression blazing with something stronger than frustration.

Her specialty? "Now what is that supposed to mean?"

"What I said. This is your pattern—every time. You scheme and plot behind my back while I think everything is okay. You twist these half-truths and—"

"Now hold on." Anger struck like lightning. "You act like this was some horrible thing I did. What's so wrong with a simple skating event?" Old wounds stretched, scars itching. "Why have you always hated my skating?"

"Maybe because of this right here." Avery waved her hand at the wire-edged words stacking between them. "Skating brings out the worst in you, Addisyn! Just look at what's happened!"

She'd known Avery felt that way, hadn't she? But to hear it out loud— "Avery, don't you realize that skating is my life? And you never tried to understand." Again she was back on the rink at Regionals, searching a thousand faces for one who never came. "You never showed an interest. You never asked me about it or even—"

"Because I saw what happened. Every time." Accusation slanted from Avery's narrowed gaze. "Skating is bad for you, Addisyn. And then add a guy into the mix, and you lose all your common sense."

That's how Avery saw Darius? As just *a guy*? A clone of Brian? "Leave Darius out of this." The words could barely squeeze between her teeth. "What are you accusing him of?"

"Pulling you astray, for starters." Avery was using her most irritating big-sister voice, the tone that she knew rubbed Addisyn's soul backward with annoyance. "He's a bad influence, and I'm really wondering why he thought it was okay to sneak around with you behind my back."

"Really, Avery? You're going there?" Her heart thudded with a pounding urgency. "What do you think this is, one of your peer-pressure lectures? He had an invitation, and he asked me to—"

"How involved are you two?"

"We are not *involved*." She couldn't spit the word out of her mouth fast enough. "What is it with you and guys, anyway? Every boyfriend I have you're determined to dislike." Okay, so there had only been two, one of whom was crazy, but this was no time for details.

"Boyfriend?" Avery's tone was a clap of thunder.

"Friend, then!" Addisyn flung her arms. "Acquaintance! Whatever!"

"You told me he was just your friend. So you lied about that too?"

"Avery, stop it!" The anger was blurring her vision. "Darius is a good guy. He's kind and gentle and—and—*trustworthy*. But we're not—" Tears caught in her voice. "We're not—a thing."

"But see, that's the problem!" Avery folded her arms, a barred gate. "I don't know whether I can believe you, Addisyn. And—I *trusted* you." Her words wobbled. "Don't you see that? Good grief, I let you go to Canada to visit a guy I've spent less than twelve hours with, and I didn't even ask questions. Obviously I should have, but I didn't."

I let you go. Like she needed Avery's approval for every little thing? "Okay, so I didn't tell you. You wanna know the real reason why?" The storm was within her now, the clouds that had loomed for so long finally bursting. "Because, news flash, you don't have to know everything, okay? Like, I can have a life without your permission."

"Oh, Addisyn, seriously." Avery rolled her eyes, a cardboard cutout of the classic older sister. "How come *I'm* the bad guy just because I happen to love you and want to make sure you're okay and not doing stupid stuff?"

"Avery, it's my life!" The turbulence in her soul was forming itself into the tempest of a lifetime. "I'm twenty-one years old, okay? So you can quit doing your high-and-mighty big-sister act and—"

"Being twenty-one hasn't made you grow up." Avery's words sizzled in the air between them. "You're going to be in a lawsuit because of your failure to think of consequences! Do you realize that? I'm getting ready to lose everything—the house, the land—" Tears glazed her eyes for a moment before she blinked them away. "And the worst part is I was ready to let it all go! I stood beside you. I supported you. I loved you unconditionally! After everything you did to me, I still, *still*, made the decision to trust you again." Avery shook her head. "And look at this. I should have known better."

The words stung, flaring her emotions further. "Well, *I* should have known not to trust *you* again! You were always the perfect one, right? Big sister can do no wrong." Something deep inside winced at the acid in her tone, but she shoved it aside. "I didn't leave home because of skating or Brian, Avery. I left because of *you*!"

Shock slapped itself across Avery's face. "Because of me?"

Now was the time to step out of the storm, to backtrack the trail of damage, but instead she pushed forward. "Yeah, you, Avery! You've always done everything you could to keep me in your cage. Just like you're doing now."

"Addisyn, listen to yourself!" Tears were glittering on Avery's cheeks. "I made sure you had a new start. I'm letting you live here in my cabin. I found your car for you. I encouraged you to take the job with Skyla. Everything I've done—everything I've *always* done—has been about helping you!"

Help, help, help. Help was heaped on her, and she was sick of it. Addisyn swiped her hand at the shrinking cabin. "This is about control, isn't it? You don't want me to get out of the precious little box you put me in. You don't want me to do anything that you haven't approved! And no matter what I do, it's not what you want!"

"What *I* want?" Avery's hands were shaking, the way they always did when she was losing her grip on her emotions. She took three quick steps and grabbed the picture from the sideboard, thrusting it at Addisyn. "*This* is what I want. I want you to be who you were here. Happy and open and—and full of light."

Would it always come back to this stupid photo? Would she always have to compete with her childhood self? "Of course this is what you want, Avery." Sarcasm sliced her words. "Because you want me to be a kid forever. Right? I'm supposed to be the obedient little girl. Just following you around and doing whatever you want!"

The crash fractured the air around them before she realized she'd thrown the frame to the floor. It gave way on impact, glass spinning away in shards, cheap wood splintering.

"Addisyn!"

The horror in her sister's voice only doubled her anger. So this was what it took to get Avery's attention? Addisyn yanked the photo from the mess on the floor, pinching it in furious fingers.

"Addisyn, give me that this instant! Don't you see? The picture. Us together." Avery's breath was jagged, as if she'd been running up the peaks. "That's what—that's what we're losing. I gave you a second chance, Addisyn. And you—you just threw it away!"

"I didn't throw it away." She was sick of the photo. Sick of Avery standing right behind her, telling her exactly how high she could fly. "You tried to lock me up!"

"And you told me you were different now!" Avery's tone was a wagging finger. "But you're exactly the way you always were."

Exactly the way you always were.

The words knocked the breath from her lungs, and rage rushed in to replace it. "Well, you know what?" Every word was lightning, burning bolts like weapons. "You're exactly the way you always were too!"

And then she was yanking at the cheap photo paper, and their faces were flying apart, and the rip sliced through the turbulence. And then Avery's cry was soaring into a wail. "Addisyn, what have you done?"

What had she done?

There were two jagged halves in her trembling hands.

And now, just when she needed it most, the anger was draining out of her. Leaving nothing but a huge and horrible hole. Anguish soaked through the walls of the moment, reaching for them both.

No! Had she really—

She felt the desperate plea in her eyes when she stared at Avery, but her sister's pale face was stretched with suffering. No wonder. She'd carried this photo next to her heart for twelve years. Right beside the place that believed in Addisyn no matter what.

And in a single instant Addisyn had destroyed them both.

"Avery—" The word was a drowning gasp. If she could start over, if she could go back, if she could—

But with the single word, her sister's countenance crumpled, pain creased into every corner. She spun away, snatched her coat, and dashed toward the door. Mercy scrambled up from her bed in the corner.

"A-Avery!" Addisyn's teeth were chattering. Uselessly gripping the torn picture, she ran after her sister. "Avery—wait—oh, Avery—"

Freezing air blasted her words away as she turned the corner into the hall. The front door was open, still swinging. She dashed onto the porch just as she heard Avery's truck growl to life, and then with a grinding of tires on gravel, her sister was driving away, her headlights flicking over Addisyn for the briefest blinding moment.

She spun, almost colliding with Mercy as she skidded back into the house. She had to apologize, had to do something—she'd call Avery, she'd—

The light glinted off her sister's phone, tossed haphazardly on the countertop.

Okay, then she'd go after her. She snatched her car keys and ran back outside. She was nearly to her car when rationality finally overtook her. How could she go after Avery? She had no idea where her sister might be. And anyway, what would that accomplish? All Avery wanted right now was to be away from her.

Understandably so.

The sick feeling curled around her stomach until it forced her to her knees. The grass was sharp, spiky with frost. A warm breath panted near her ear, and Mercy's tongue swiped at her neck.

It was then that the sobs began, the great choking ones that wrenched themselves out of her and drowned in the darkness while she gripped the torn photo in futile fists. Their younger faces stared accusingly at her as she gazed with horror at the giant rift between them.

The rift she had torn with her own hands.

△△ △△ △△

AVERY HADN'T PLANNED her course before she'd scrambled into her truck. Everything had been shrunk to a single goal: *get away*. Away from the house. Away from the gashed photo. Away from the dead end of her second chance with her sister.

So she'd made the turns without thinking, chasing her headlights forward into the dark. But now she suddenly realized where the lights were leading. As if her body had taken over for her when her mind and heart were dazed with pulsing pain. She was on Fall River Road, taking the back way into Rocky Mountain National Park.

Of course. Where else would she run but to her mountains?

The entrance booth was sleeping, shuttered in the darkness, but the gate was open. Ghostly trees blurred by her windows, and Avery glanced at the speedometer. She was pushing fifty—not safe on these curvy mountain roads, but she couldn't slow down, couldn't let the pain catch up.

A hard ache was swelling in her chest, but like a wounded animal, she needed to reach a safe place before she could give in. The curves stacked upon each other, and then she was in the unrolling meadow of Endovalley, the pull-off for Sheep Lakes just ahead.

Perfect. She flipped on her blinker and parked the truck. Once the headlights flicked off, the deep darkness spread its wings over her. A lopsided gibbous moon barely blinked through the murky sky. Its light trickled feebly over the landscape, hardly enough to make out the square shadow of the little ranger station or the unflinching profiles of the mountains.

The heavy wings pressed harder, darkness draped, and in a sudden overflow, Avery smacked the steering wheel. "No!" The cry was torn from her, a wrenching wail that sounded nothing like her voice. "No, no, *no!*"

She'd been too numb to cry, the tears trapped within the pain in her chest, but now they were coming, sobs shaking her like a giant fist. How could Addisyn have *done* that? How *could* she?

Everything had unraveled, and the loose ends were more than she could untangle. But one thing was mercilessly unmistakable: Addisyn had lied to her. Even now, even in their second chance, Addisyn had been hoarding secrets like poisonous seeds, waiting to bear bitter fruit. She'd tossed Avery's trust aside as if everything they'd gone through meant less than nothing.

But this time, it was even worse. Because now, Addisyn's lies had set off a rockslide for both of them. And what else was coming? Avery couldn't begin to predict the depth of her sister's deception, the weight of all that might still be unsaid.

Avery couldn't spend another moment in the truck, breathing the cramped air of regrets. She threw open the door, the cold wind scraping her wet face. Burrowing her hands into her pockets, she began walking.

Back and forth, back and forth, shoving forward into darkness and disaster. The length of the parking area and back. Again and again and again.

But the pain walked with her, step for step, dangling the torn photograph relentlessly before her eyes. Avery had carried that picture, in that frame, for a dozen years. It had sat in her bedroom in Syracuse, in the apartment when they ran to New York City, on her desk in Colorado while she waited for Addisyn to come home. And for all those years, it had been in her heart. A reminder of the bond between her and the person she loved most in the entire world.

Now in a single night the rift had been torn. And nothing would ever be the same.

Her boots clomped against the pavement like a panicked pounding on a locked door. Her breath was jagged, loud. "El Shaddai!" The Name was a wail into the night, a cry against the prevailing darkness and the watery moon and the sun that was so far from rising. "Help me!"

No answer came. No answer did, these days. She swiped her sleeve across her face and kept walking.

An elk bugled down in the valley, the sound floating upward in the clarity of the cold air. Avery paused and glanced up, where the stars hung low above the sharp ridge of the mountains. Even at night, the air smelled fresh, exciting—the tang of the altitude and the adventure.

Another bugle answered from the tree line. Avery reached for her first deep, shuddering breath. The raging storm was slowly ebbing, the tide flowing back and leaving a dreary, empty shore. Maybe she was just worn out from crying. Or maybe the mountains were soothing her, the way they always did. She could flee to them broken and bleeding, and they would never fail to reach maternal arms around her.

The cold air crackled in her lungs, her breath swirling toward the patient moon. She wasn't giving up. Not on Addisyn. Not on their relationship. She never could.

El Shaddai—God of the mountains—hear me. She held out her hands, cupping starlight and wind and a desperate bankrupt hope. *Help me. Help me bring right from all these wrongs.*

Another bugle. Avery waited until the last note floated into silence, then she turned back to her truck. Whatever was next began with talking to Addisyn.

She stayed under the speed limit this time, taking the long way home through Estes Park. When she saw Addisyn's car still parked in front of the cabin, some unacknowledged fear crumbled to ashes. She let out a deep breath and trudged across the yard to the house.

The lights were off except for one in the living room, but the door was unlocked. Avery crept into the hallway warily, as if a mountain lion might spring from behind the couch. "Addisyn?"

The stillness swallowed her voice. Avery locked the door behind her, the click of the bolt sealing in the tension. In the kitchen, claws clicked across the slate floor, and Mercy nudged her hand. For some reason, the tears threatened all over again.

"Mercy." She rubbed the dog's ears, tracing the confusion on her pup's wrinkled forehead. "I'm sorry, girl. Tonight was—unusual."

She tiptoed upstairs to Addisyn's room. Moonlight and shadow colored contrast through the space, patching themselves together over a tumble of bedsheets and Addisyn's face against the pillow. Avery waited for two slow rises of the quilt, then three. Addisyn was assuredly asleep. Somehow the clatter of the truck and the disturbance of Avery's entry hadn't awakened her.

Avery sat softly in one of the inky patches on the side of the bed and studied her sister's face. With the restless, rebellious expression she usually wore softened by sleep, she looked much younger. So like the little girl who had needed her big sister to love her. There were salty tracks of tears on her cheeks.

Tonight had been hard on them both.

Avery hung her head and exhaled the last of her anger. Addisyn couldn't carry all the blame, not when she herself had gripped the whole situation by the wrong end.

Her tone, her words, her emotions—all of them had come from a place far from center. Had she really done that? Come in swinging, making accusations and pointing fingers and riding over her sister's every attempt at defense?

And why was it always this way?

El Shaddai— What could she say to Him, here in the blurring shadows where nothing was clear? *I keep pushing Addisyn away, and I don't understand how and why. It's the very last thing I want to do. I love her so much—I would do anything for her.*

Memories bubbled up from the secret spring of her heart, carrying their own bittersweet flavor. Her little sister had curled up next to her on the couch to hear stories and begged her for piggyback rides around the yard and delighted in trips to the mall. And she, in turn, had shielded Addisyn from their father's tirades and reassured her after bad dreams and spent several harrowing weekends teaching her how to drive.

But the single string of their lives had frayed into nothing more than tragic turmoil and repeating resistance. And now, they might as well have been standing on opposite sides of the Continental Divide.

Sorrow was stinging at the corners of her eyes. How could she love her sister so much and still not be able to reach her? How could she want so badly to keep Addisyn close yet push her away at every turn?

△△   △△   △△

DON'T MOVE.

Addisyn kept her eyes closed and pulled each breath rhythmically. Feigning sleep was ridiculous—a juvenile avoidance tactic that solved nothing. But at least it could keep her from seeing the destruction she'd wreaked tonight.

The mattress creaked slightly as Avery shifted position. Her sister had been sitting silently on the side of the bed for what felt like ten minutes by now. What was she thinking? That she hated Addisyn? That she wished her prodigal younger sister had never come back?

"Help me, El Shaddai."

Even the soft whisper seemed loud in the listening dark. Avery was praying. Of course. The privacy of the moment prickled over Addisyn.

"I need—" Her sister paused, no doubt sorting through the unspoken requests dangling all around them both. "Strength. Wisdom. Guidance."

The shadows pressed against them for a few seconds before Avery spoke again. This time her whisper was stretched crooked, pain pulling at every word. "I can't do this."

271

Another creak of the mattress, Avery's hand smoothing uselessly over the wrinkles in the quilt. And then her sister's footfalls followed each other out of the room and down the hall.

She still wouldn't open her eyes, wouldn't let the darkness see her cry. She'd sobbed the whole time Avery was gone, turned inside out by the regret. More tears wouldn't help now. What had her sister said?

Help me, El Shaddai.

I need strength.

I can't do this.

Couldn't do what? Couldn't cope with Addisyn, most likely. Couldn't keep moving forward through all the turmoil Addisyn had brought to her life. Addisyn's soul sliced at the realization that her sister had to beg for supernatural strength just to deal with her each day. But she couldn't blame Avery. Not when she was just as disgusted by herself.

The dull ache behind her ribs was worsening, pressing more insistently against her breath. She was tired of watching the same movie play on the insides of her eyelids—the paper ripping between them, the sharp shredding sound, the pure pain on Avery's face. Over and over and over until she had to open her eyes, had to sit up.

The room was drenched in darkness, but the pale blur of her reflection stared at her from the dresser mirror. Addisyn looked away from the hopeless face of the girl in the mirror and glanced out the window instead. The snow on the mountains gleamed, as if the whole Front Range were a white-capped wave riding across the dark sea of sky. A world that locked itself against her—but flung every gate wide to her sister.

This land was Avery's great love, a sanctuary that had protected her soul. Hadn't Addisyn noticed—at least when she first came—the peaceful joy in her sister's countenance? And no wonder. For the first time in her life, Avery had finally been happy and free. She'd awakened to the sunrise every morning and hiked mountain trails and listened for elk in the evenings. And then once again, Addisyn had crashed back into her world and destroyed it all.

It would have been better for both of them if she'd never come home at all.

The moon was lower now, a bobbing balloon sinking toward the earth. Addisyn sank forward over her knees. Brian had been right all along. And Skyla's endless assurance of grace and healing and new beginnings was—well, it was for people like Avery.

No, it was stupid to think Addisyn could ever escape her past. It would follow her and walk beside her and twist every single thing about her future. It would be the dark shadow over her sun, the raincloud on her horizon. And it would continue to hurt not just her, but the people she loved the most. Like Darius. Like Avery.

There was only one way she could stop it. One way she could keep her past from poisoning everyone. One final choice she could make—one decision that would protect Avery from being hurt by her again.

It was the last thing she wanted to do, but it was the only thing that made any sense. Her thoughts bounced backward and forward, filling in the outlines of the new plan until certainty grew. Then, quietly, she swung her feet over the edge of the bed and headed to the closet—to the bags she'd never completely unpacked.

The bags that must have expected this all along.

CHAPTER **19**

Avery had fully intended to talk with Addisyn first thing that morning. Before the cracks between them could harden any further. But the whole time she dressed, let Mercy out, and made toast, Addisyn hadn't come downstairs.

Finally, when she couldn't wait any longer before leaving for work, she'd crept up to her sister's room. Addisyn was still tangled in the quilt, her hair splashed across the pillow.

No surprise that Ads was still asleep, given the turmoil of last night. Avery had weighed her options but finally turned away. Dragging her sister from sleep was an unwise way to kick off a conversation like this.

The reasoning was valid, smoothing over the truth she would barely glance at—the idea that maybe, just maybe, she was putting the conversation off. Probably because she had no idea of where to begin sifting through the rubble of the argument. Or of how much had been lost in the detonation.

She'd manufactured a smile for Laz and busied herself with a variety of chores all morning. But now, on her lunch break, she'd left Mercy at the store and headed back home. She and Addisyn needed to talk. Untangle the lies. Exchange forgiveness. And figure out what kept going wrong between them.

She glanced at the dashboard clock as the truck groaned up her rutted driveway. Twelve fifteen. A good forty-five minutes before she needed to be back at the store. She pulled up to the house and coaxed the stubborn gearshift into park after only a few tries. Absorbed in crafting different beginnings to the conversation, she was halfway to the house before she noticed.

Addisyn's car was gone.

A shock jerked her soul. Like the time she'd been hiking and stepped into a hole she hadn't realized was under the leaves. She shook her head and fought her way back to the solid ground of rationality. So what? Addisyn was probably at the gym. Or downtown. At the grocery store, even.

Her boots thumped loud on the porch. The door was locked. Of course. Addisyn wouldn't go off and leave the house unlocked. It didn't mean anything more than that.

She jogged back to the truck for her keys and let herself in. Dark. Empty. A house holding its breath.

"Ads?" Her voice startled the air in the cabin. No response—naturally. It had been silly to call for her sister. Clearly she wasn't here.

But she was at the gym, right? The store? She'd be back soon. Very soon.

Her feet unwillingly followed each other up the silent stairs, fear slithering behind her. The door to Addisyn's room loomed at the end of the hallway. Avery clung to the knob for just a moment before she pushed inside.

Another hole, another stumbling step to yank her off balance. The room was spotless. Every shred of her sister's personality swept up and taken away.

The truth stood with folded arms in the center of the room, but she could still dodge it, still peer around and see some other logical answer standing behind it. She raced to the dresser and ripped open the bottom drawer.

Empty.

She yanked open another drawer, and another, and another, until the whole dresser gaped openmouthed. The truth was standing over her now. She was forced to look at its face.

For a moment, she was the girl in New York City, the one watching her sister ride away in Brian's BMW, the one sobbing out her soul on the cold tile floor of her apartment. She spun away from the empty drawers, flinging off the disorienting merge of past and present. Something on the bed snatched her notice. Some object propped on the pillow.

The photo.

Her heart dropped as she lifted the picture. Someone with careful hands had gently smoothed glue over the tear, merging the two halves once more. But still, the fault line that ran between their faces was impossible to overlook.

Under the photo was something else—a folded paper. Her hands were shaking as she opened the words.

A,

I'm so sorry about last night. I don't know why things are always like this between us.

Oh, Addisyn. Avery closed her eyes for the briefest moment. *I don't know either.*

Anyway, I just need to be away. Don't worry about me. I'll be fine.

Take care of yourself. And Mercy and Isaiah. I know I don't act like it, but I love you.

Ads

Her sister's signature warped behind tears. She barely had time to lay the photo and letter down before the first sob shook her.

How could this have happened? How could the rewritten story still have ended here, with the same painful plot? *El Shaddai—El Shaddai—El Shaddai—* His Name, over and over, but the storm was blowing harder. Her lungs were too full. No room for air. She grabbed for oxygen, but it was just out of reach.

No! She shook her head. *Stop. Stop. Breathe. Come on.* She forced the fullness from her lungs, found a shuddering breath. *That's right. Keep breathing. And find her.*

Find her. Yes. Addisyn couldn't have gone far. She was somewhere close. Right?

But Avery had left for work almost five hours ago. Ninety minutes would have taken Addisyn to Denver. And from Denver, she could have booked a flight to anywhere in the world.

Again, the wind whipped up, but she refused it. She stumbled downstairs on unsteady legs and grabbed her phone from her bag. The call skipped straight to voicemail without even ringing.

"Ads…" This conversation would have been hard enough in person, but pouring out her soul to a blank machine was far more difficult. "I…you're gone. Please come back." She couldn't keep the frantic from fraying her words. "Just come back and—and talk to me. Please. I'm sorry. Or call me. Please call me. Or text me. Or—"

Would Addisyn hear her heart? Or would she delete the message without even listening to it?

"I love you. I'm sorry." Futility swept over her. These words were too small to bridge the rip between their faces. "We need to talk. We can't—it can't be this way."

She hung up without saying *bye*. *Bye* was a period on the end of the sentence. *Bye* was permission to disappear. *Bye* was not a word she was going to say.

Not now.

Not ever.

△△   △△   △△

THE ROAD WAS steep and curvy, a heartbreaking downhill plunge out of the mountains. Addisyn rode her brakes around a curve and bit her lip.

She'd been going down long before she took this road.

She hadn't shed any more tears. Not since she looked over her shoulder and tucked away her last aching glimpse of Avery's house, snuggled safely in the trees. Peaceful and protected—the way it had been when she came.

The way it would be again, now that she was gone.

She'd been driving less than an hour at this point, having left long after she'd planned. First she'd overslept, and then she'd had a dozen loose ends to knot. Finish her packing. Mend the photo. Find a way to fit *goodbye* into a note. Fill the car with gas, plan her route, and pick up breakfast at the diner. She hadn't passed the Estes Park city limits sign until eleven forty-five.

Still, that gave her almost six hours before Avery would come home and find her gone. Not that it mattered when Avery found out. Her sister was still furious, no doubt, and for good reason. She'd likely be glad Addisyn was gone, relieved that Addisyn's problems could no longer infect her. Or maybe she'd be upset at first, but she'd quickly come to realize— this was the only way Addisyn could prevent the shrapnel of her past from taking out both of them.

Even if Avery wanted to track her down, she'd have no idea where Addisyn planned to go. And with the lawsuit looming, New York City was the last place Avery would think to look for her.

The land was leveling somewhat now, the rock cliffs opening up as Addisyn drove through the little town of Lyons. At a stoplight, a sudden uncertainty hit her. Now which way was it here?

She'd taken this same course to Denver before. She should remember. Highway 36 to Lyons and Longmont and then the interstate. I-25, right? A straight shot south.

But did she turn or go straight to reach the interstate?

She glanced for her phone, intending to check GPS, before she remembered it was turned off and buried inside her purse. The light blinked green, and the Jeep behind her honked. Addisyn flipped the decision like a coin and made the righthand turn. She was fairly sure she'd come this way before. Anyhow, all roads led to Denver, most likely. Taking the quickest or easiest route wasn't a priority today, as long as she got there.

The radio was on some stupid talk show, the host yammering about the latest political controversy. Addisyn fiddled with the dial while she drove, but all the other channels were just static. Figured. Nothing was clear anymore.

She switched the radio off and concentrated on the scenery. But the craggy mountains, sweeping vistas, and evergreen trees only pressed more painfully against her. She was leaving behind so much.

A thought struck her. What would she do with her car when she reached Denver? She couldn't very well abandon it at the airport. Why hadn't she considered that complication? Maybe she could call someone and let them know where it was. Laz, perhaps. He could take the car back to Estes, and Avery could sell it and get some payment for how much Addisyn had cost her.

In money, anyway.

Addisyn numbly followed the road for half an hour before uneasiness began to prickle over her. Where was she? Shouldn't she have been in Longmont by now? Before, it had seemed that Lyons and Longmont were close enough to hold hands. But now, the road seemed to be burying itself deeper and deeper in the heart of nowhere.

Addisyn was just about to pull over and turn her phone on for the GPS when she saw a sign peeking through the trees. Finally! Only—it wasn't a typical highway sign. Her wariness returned, and she squinted until she could read the weather-worn lettering.

WELCOME TO ELK CREEK.

Elk Creek?

She had no idea where that was. But it wasn't Longmont.

She'd taken the wrong turn, no doubt. She squeezed into the next narrow pullout, then turned her phone on and went straight to her maps app. For a few irritating seconds, the colored loading symbol spun, then the typed words smacked at her.

No connection. Cannot retrieve route.

No cell service! Addisyn flopped back into the seat. Seriously? *Seriously?*

Options flicked frantically through her mind. She could try to drive on into the supposed town—if *town* was the right word—and ask for directions. Or she could backtrack to Lyons—where she'd have cell service.

Yes. Lyons was the better option. Addisyn tossed her worthless phone into her bag and maneuvered onto the road again. As the car swooped around the curves back toward civilization, she fought down the exasperation. It was okay, really. Annoying, yes, but no big deal. She had the whole day to reach Denver. She'd just go back to Lyons and then—

The boom erupted from under her hood a split second before the car jerked wildly. The seatbelt yanked her back as the engine's thrum deteriorated to a heartrending grinding noise.

No. No, no, this was not happening! Addisyn gripped the wheel and wrangled the car to the roadside, the motor rattling with a dying cough. She screeched onto the cramped shoulder just as the car gave a final shuddering gasp.

Long moments slipped by while the motor clicked gently a few times, then flatlined. The shock kept Addisyn slumped in her seat. An old memory floated through her mind. A teenage Avery, grease-stained hands fiddling with something in her truck while Addisyn watched with a cautious curiosity. "A, when I'm old enough to drive, how will I know what to do if I have a problem?"

"Oh, that's easy." Her sister had tossed a grin over her shoulder. "When something goes wrong, just focus first on stopping. You've got to stop before you can fix things. Then somebody can help you with the rest."

Well, she was stopped, all right. But nobody was coming to help.

She shook herself back to the moment. She probably needed to get out of the car. For all she knew, the whole thing was getting ready to blow up or burn down or do something equally dramatic. It would be in keeping with the rest of her life. She climbed out into the chilly day and examined the car with a fearful expectation, but there was no sound except the wind rustling through the dry leaves.

What next? Look at the engine. That's what Avery would do. Addisyn walked to the front of the car and studied the hood. She knew how to open it because of watching Avery with her truck, but her secondhand knowledge fizzled out once she was peering at the mass of blackened apparatus underneath. She knew nothing about cars or whatever mysterious wizardry made them go, so what had she expected? That she'd be able to spot the problem and fix it with no tools or experience?

Panic was slowly rising, and it was becoming harder and harder to hold her head above the tide. Each truth was another crashing wave. She was alone on a desolate mountain road. She had no cell service. And her car was, for all she knew, irreparably damaged.

She was shivering by now, the cold slowly working its way through her. She couldn't stand here all day, and she'd yet to see another car while she'd been driving this desolate road. But she hadn't been that far from the Elk Creek sign yet, had she?

She found a heavier coat in her bag, slung her purse over her shoulder, locked the car, and started walking, sneakers scuffing crumbling asphalt back toward Elk Creek. She tried to calculate distance from her driving time and speed. Three miles? Four?

Frustration and fear twined around her legs with every step, and the wind stung tears to her eyes. By the time her car was out of sight, her emotions had twisted to a raw rebellion. "So what's the big idea?" She flung the question toward the low-hanging ceiling of sky. "I ruin everything, and I can't even manage to leave? Is this Your idea of a joke?" The frustration faded to something more tentative. "What do You want with me?"

She paused, waiting for something she couldn't see. A bird sang loudly in a tree nearby. A few pines creaked in a fresh gust of wind. But the sky remained insolently aloof. Of course.

Avery would have received an instantaneous answer to her prayer. But then, Avery would have never buried herself in this mess to begin with.

She gave in to the tears now, swiping them with her coat sleeves as she trudged farther down the vacant road. She was crying because she wanted to be in Darius's arms, his hands on her face and his whisper in her ear. She was crying because she wanted to run to Avery and hear her sister's soothing voice. But mostly she was crying because she wanted to escape from this embedded pain—the sharp edges of her story, the ones that would always leave her stranded on lonely roads.

Suddenly she heard it. Or was it only the wind? No. It was a motor.

She waved her arms frantically just as a car veered around the hairpin turn. Brake lights flashed, and the driver's window rolled down. Addisyn trotted to the car as a woman's voice called to her. "Do you need help?"

"Yes, I—" She glanced into the car, and the rest of her sentence blew away in the wind. *No way.* "Skyla?"

Skyla's lips quirked slightly upward. "Addisyn Miles."

So now humiliation could be heaped upon all her other woes. "What—what are you doing here?"

"I am spending a few days in Elk Creek." Skyla glanced in her rearview mirror. "Was that your car about a half mile back? The brown Accord?"

Addisyn nodded limply, watching the story piece itself behind Skyla's eyes.

"What brought you to this road, Addisyn?"

"I'm on my way to New York." Okay, that sounded stupid even to her.

"New York?" Skyla's eyebrows headed north.

"I got lost." She heard the edge to her words, but she couldn't help it.

"Well, now you are found." Skyla put the car in park and gestured to the passenger door. "It is not safe to stay in the middle of the road. Get in."

⋀⋀　⋀⋀　⋀⋀

LESS THAN TWO weeks from the start of the ski season, and the climbing center was whirling with activity. Darius was unpacking boxes of mountain harnesses when his phone vibrated in his pocket.

He didn't bother to pull it out. It was probably one of the guys asking about the plans for watching the next hockey game. Or maybe it was Lenny, still trying to figure out why he'd canceled their sessions.

The one person it wouldn't be was the one he wanted to talk to the most.

When Addisyn first left, he'd still been determined to reach her, driven to scale her walls. But his calls and texts went ignored. Finally he'd realized: no matter what had gone wrong between them, she didn't want to talk to him.

So he'd taken on extra hours at work, letting himself be caught in the current of busyness and pulled downstream from the situation. It couldn't lift the dark clouds from his sky, but at least it reduced the number of hours he sat with his gloomy thoughts in an empty house.

He grabbed the next case of harnesses just as his phone vibrated again. Balancing the box with one arm, he slid his phone from his pocket and glanced at the screen.

Avery Miles?

An internal alarm bell clanged. Why would Avery be calling him? "Hello?"

"Have you talked to Addisyn?"

The abruptness of the question sucked his heart through a siphon. "No." He dropped the box to the floor and sank onto it. "Avery, what's going on?"

"She's gone." The words were a trapdoor to a reality he hadn't considered. "And I need to know if you were involved."

Darius was snagged on the first part. "Gone? What do you mean, gone?"

"Just that." Avery's tone was ragged with emotion. "I came home from work on my lunch break, and she has packed all her stuff and taken off." Something else crept into her voice. "Did you know about this?"

What was Avery saying? "I'm not sure what's going on, but—I haven't talked to Addisyn since we—since she left Whistler."

"Darius, I need to know." She was trying to sound firm, that much was obvious. But the tremble in her voice showed how much the situation was straining her. "Did she tell you she was coming up there? Or was this your idea?"

"You mean, did I talk her into running away from home?" Avery hadn't been super friendly in Colorado, but now there was a challenge behind her words. Darius fought down his indignation. "Look, I can tell you're upset, but—"

"Upset?" The word warped under the weight of emotion. "Yes, I'm upset. She's my *sister*, Darius."

"Where would she have gone?"

"To you." Again, her tone was pointing a finger at him. "Are you sure you haven't talked to her?"

"Of course I'm sure." There had to be something bigger going on here. Some reason he was so obviously in Avery's crosshairs. He couldn't ignore the frost at the edges of her words any longer. "Look, Avery, if I've offended you somehow, I'm really sorry. You seem like—"

"Well, I'm just very—concerned." Her pause wasn't long enough for him to reply. "Darius, I feel that you have been—that you have lied to me."

"Lied to—"

"I found out last night that your inviting Addisyn to Whistler was a— a cover-up for some skating event. And I think it was very presumptuous of you to lure my sister into some scheme to—"

"Whoa, whoa, whoa. Hold on." If he didn't stop this train now, it would hurtle much too far down the wrong tracks. "Back up. You mean— you didn't know about the skating?"

"No." Avery's voice lowered several more degrees. "Addisyn just told me she was going to Whistler to visit you. She never mentioned that you had asked her to skate."

Disbelief throbbed its way through him. "Oh—wow." The words sounded as weak as he felt. "I thought—oh, man. I received an invitation to skate for a charity event. And so—and so I asked Addisyn to partner with me, because she's the most talented skater I know, and—you know, I thought it would be a cool opportunity for her. But I told her—I told her to ask you about it."

"Well, she didn't." Avery's tone was rising, the train leaving the station once more. "She never mentioned a word about it, and now we're all in trouble, and she's—"

Darius stiffened. "What do you mean, *in trouble?*"

A pause stretched over the phone line. Avery's next words came slower. "You didn't know about Brian?"

Brian? What did he have to do with anything now? Darius shook his head. "Avery, please, start from the beginning. I—I know you think I had something to do with all this, but I promise you, I'm in the dark."

"Oh." Avery's tone backed down slightly. "I thought she would have told you."

Something uneasy prickled at the base of his neck. "Told me what?"

"Well—" Defeat dragged down Avery's words. "While she was in Whistler, a letter came here to the house. I—I opened it. And it was Brian. He's claiming she breached her contract with him and threatening to sue her." She sighed. "Things have been—difficult here."

"Breached her contract?"

The edge was back to Avery's voice. "By skating with you."

"What? How? We didn't even—"

"Her contract prevented her from entering into any other

agreements. I won't get into the legal details, but trust me, she is in serious trouble."

So it was his fault? He'd unknowingly led her into Brian's trap? A rock slid to the pit of his stomach. "Avery—no way. I never meant—I never would have done anything to hurt her or put her in a bad spot." An ache spread behind his ribs. "You have to believe that I didn't mean to—"

"The fact remains that she *is* in a bad spot, Darius. And you have to understand my perspective." Avery's tone was freezing over again. "I worked so hard to keep her safe. To help her heal. And then—and then she got involved with you, and everything came undone."

The sick feeling was burning more bitter every moment. Avery was right, wasn't she? It was his fault. And there was nothing he could do to fix things now. "Avery—look—I—"

"Darius, you came to Estes Park and went behind my back. You invited my sister to do something that has now come back to get her into legal trouble. And you two kept it all a secret from—"

"Now, hold on a minute." Frustration joined the gang of emotions playing tug-of-war with his heart. "I don't know what she was thinking or why she didn't say something to you. But I told her to get your permission before she came. And I do know that when I first talked to her about the invitation, she told me she was worried to talk to you about it."

"Worried?"

"She said you disliked her skating."

Silence for a beat. "That's—that's not true. Well, I mean—but it's just that I know that skating has led to poor decisions for her. First there was Brian, and now this deal with you."

Avery was lumping him with Brian? Darius flinched. "Avery. I'm not Brian, okay? I'm not perfect, yeah. But by the grace of God, I try to live in the light. And I never would have done anything to hurt Addisyn. I swear it."

He braced for a comeback, but instead Avery sighed. "I—okay." Grudging, maybe, but a start. "I'm just—" Her voice crumpled slightly. "I'm very worried right now, with her gone, and I don't know what to do or—or anything."

"I understand." His frustration softened slightly. "What would have made her leave?"

"She's—she's very stressed over all this, and then we had a, well, a disagreement."

A disagreement. So Addisyn had pulled away from all of them. Darius bit his lip. "I haven't heard from her at all."

"If you do, will you please let me know?"

"Sure. Of course."

After the call ended, he hung his head, the guilt settling its dark wings over his shoulders. How had his good intentions led to this place? He'd only wanted to help Addisyn heal. Instead, he'd put her right back in the clutches of the man who'd wounded her in the first place.

He glanced up at the narrow walls of the storage room. The pieces fit together now, the painful puzzle resolving. No wonder Addisyn had left so abruptly. But why hadn't she told him? Hadn't she known he would stand beside her, help her take on the fight?

Well, he wouldn't stand back any longer. Resolve built within him, chasing back the shadows of the guilt. Yes. He'd find her, and he'd undo the damage he'd caused with his clumsy hands. And then he'd make sure she knew the most important thing.

There was no threat that could drive him away.

△△ △△ △△

APPARENTLY MECHANIC SHOPS hadn't yet found their way to the wide spot in the road that was Elk Creek. Instead, Skyla explained, the locals relied on Larry. She touted the fact that his truck had a tow winch, as if that were the only criterion for one's ability to provide expert mechanic services.

"Here we are." Skyla's confidence appeared still unshaken as she pulled up in front of a tired-looking house with peeling paint itching from its walls. "Larry has hands for this work."

Addisyn just nodded and gazed at the chaotic zoo of dilapidated vehicles jumbled in the dead grass around the house. She considered asking if these were the cars Larry couldn't fix. Or how much he might charge for his doubtful expertise. In the end, she bit the questions back.

This was what that emergency bank account was for, and it wasn't as if any other options were presenting themselves.

"Greetings, Dirk." Skyla nodded at a lanky guy shambling toward them. "Is your father here?"

"No, ma'am." The kid was a cornstalk—tall and skinny and topped with silky blond thatch. "He's gone to Crested Butte with Uncle Frank. Bear huntin,' y'know. Comin' back tomorrow."

"Tomorrow?" The outburst shot from Addisyn's disbelief before she could stop it.

Dirk glanced at her, then back at Skyla. "Got a car problem?" His bony shoulders lifted in an angular shrug. "I'm not as good as Pop, but I can sure take a look for ya."

It took every bit of an hour for Dirk to follow them back to Addisyn's car and hook it to the famous tow-winch truck. As they followed the diesel-belching vehicle back to Elk Creek, Skyla cleared her throat. "So you were heading to New York City."

"Denver first. To get a flight."

"I see."

A long quiet spun between them while Skyla drove with an impassive face and Addisyn focused on the feathered dreamcatcher dangling from the rearview mirror. Finally she couldn't bear the stretching silence any more. "You said you were spending some time in Elk Creek." She couldn't imagine this as much of a getaway destination, even for a person like Skyla.

"Yes. I have a house here. I lived in this town before I married Chay." Skyla braked slightly, keeping her eyes on the red taillights ahead. "I come back here at times when I need a few blank days. I listen to the quiet and read the stars. And paint."

"Oh."

"I am glad I was here for you today."

Addisyn was glad too. She guessed.

By the time they pulled up in the muddy patch of ground that was both shop and backyard, the kid already had the car's hood up. He turned as Addisyn and Skyla approached. "I dunno what Dad would say, but it looks like the fannin' belt to me." He pointed at some indistinguishable detail in the engine. "Right there, see? Looks like it done tore right in half."

Like the picture. The jolt took her breath, but Addisyn pushed it from her mind. "Why?"

"Prob'ly been gettin' ready to go for a while." Dirk tinkered with another element in the engine while he talked. "Sometimes somethin' starts wearin' under strain, and then it only takes a little thing to make it snap."

He was talking about motors, nothing more. She had to remind herself of that.

"Us'ally they make a kind of clickin' sound for a while. That's your signal to get it fixed."

A clicking sound. Addisyn wanted to bang her head against the metal hood. "My sister—she mentioned that." She bit her lip. "I never heard anything."

"Driver's us'ally too close to hear it." Dirk nodded. "Typic'lly it's the person standin' outside that can hear the problem."

"Rather like life." Skyla ran her hand over the hood.

And who asked her opinion? "I guess." Oh, why hadn't she trusted Avery? Her sister had coaxed compliance from a beaten-up truck for years. If anyone could have been trusted to sense a potential problem, it was her.

But of course, Addisyn hadn't listened. Why was she always tone-deaf to warnings? "So, can you fix it?"

"No, but Dad can." The cornsilk bobbed confidently. "Of course, he'll hafta find a new belt first. Make some phone calls, check with his guys. Will you be leavin' it here?"

"Yes." Skyla was steering the conversation now. "We will come by tomorrow and speak with your father." She pressed her palms toward him in a bow that would have seemed out of place for anyone but Skyla.

He smiled and tapped his brow as if saluting. "Anythin' for you, Miss Skyla."

Skyla said nothing as she started the car and turned back onto the narrow road. Once the rusty heap of cars disappeared from the rearview mirror, she flexed her fingers on the steering wheel. "Your sister does not know you are here." The words were not a question.

"Right." Addisyn clipped the word short. None of this was Skyla's business. "Um, where are we going?"

"To my house." Skyla's look indicated that this should have been obvious. "Where you'll be staying."

What? "No." The word sprang out before she realized how rude it sounded. "I mean—I can stay at a hotel."

"A hotel? In Elk Creek?" Skyla's lip twitched. "You are staying at my house."

So again, she didn't have a say. Addisyn supposed she should tell Skyla *thank you*, but she hated the way everything today had conspired to rob her of all choice. "Are you going to tell my sister I'm here?"

"I do not paint on the canvases of others." Before Addisyn could decipher that remark, Skyla pulled up in front of a small white house and opened her door. "Here we are."

Addisyn stayed in her seat. "You could give me a lift to Denver. I would pay you, of course. Or you could take me into Lyons and I could get a hotel there. If it's easier for you, I mean."

If Skyla heard her, she gave no sign. She just walked purposefully toward the house with her crinkled skirt swaying. Addisyn sighed and followed.

The outside of the house was weathered, but in a kind and grandmotherly way—as if it watched the stories within its walls with an infinite patience. Addisyn was somewhat expecting Skyla's taste to match Avery's, but when the door swung open, she was greeted with a very different flavor. Wood-paneled walls were hung with Native American art and paintings that had to be Skyla's own creations. The furniture was faintly retro, a leather couch stacked with southwestern pillows and cane-backed chairs circled around a coffee table overflowing with some luxurious houseplant. The calming aroma of something herbal and soothing—incense, maybe—hung in the room like a blessing.

"This is a beautiful place." Addisyn trailed her finger along a beaded lampshade. "Did you decorate it?"

"Years ago. It was my sanctuary." Skyla pointed down the hall. "The guest room is small, but it will do. The bathroom is next to it. Dinner has been in my slow cooker for a while. It will be ready when you are."

"I can pay you for—"

"My Kaka always said to never cheapen a gift with money." Skyla reached beneath a bamboo end table and plugged in a cord. A lumpy salt lamp hummed with a rosy glow.

Addisyn glanced around the room tentatively but couldn't bring herself to sit down. The whole day had been too disorienting. "Skyla, I don't want to sound rude, but…why are you helping me like this?"

Skyla tilted her head and gazed at the ceiling as if searching for the words. "Working with the birds, one learns the signs. I am called to bringing the hurting to safe places."

"I'm not your project, Skyla." Addisyn knew the edge to her voice was childish. "I'm not hurt. I'm fine."

"There are shadows in your eyes, so I do not need to know the story." Skyla adjusted the crystal pendant around her neck. "Years ago, I was also lost and shadowed. Ever since, I have tried to do for others what there was no one to do for me."

And with that, she brushed a rattling bead curtain aside and ducked into the adjoining room. Addisyn sighed and slumped onto a chair with a grudging acceptance. Okay. One night in this place wouldn't kill her. And tomorrow she'd be back on the road for Denver.

CHAPTER 20

She was getting tired of constant turbulence.

Jostled in the back of Chayton's SUV as it bounced along the dirt roads, Avery rubbed her temples and fought for focus. They were flying Isaiah in open country today for the first time—an occasion that deserved her attentive, watchful presence.

But how could she concentrate, with the urgency of Addisyn's disappearance beating at her brain? It had been nearly twenty-four hours since her sister's departure, and she'd still heard nothing but screaming silence. Her thoughts sprinted in endless circles. *Where is she? Is she safe? Why do things always have to be so—*

"Miz Avery? You with us?"

"Yes!" She snapped herself back to the present and nodded at Laz. "I'm sorry."

"I was jes' tellin' you that we're almost there, but the road ahead is a little rough."

"Okay." If Laz hadn't considered the road thus far to be *rough*, what lay ahead must be barely passable. Avery gripped Isaiah's cage as the SUV lurched through ruts that seemed more like sinkholes. Leaning from both sides of the narrow road, trees dragged their fingers along the windows of the car.

After ten more bone-rattling minutes, the road dead-ended in a sudden surprise of meadow. Chay cut the engine and grinned over his shoulder. "All right. Let's see this bird fly."

"Waalll, yer drivin' an' that road done give me arthritis." Laz grudgingly climbed out of the car, stubbornness etched into his face. "Wish I hadn't come today. I got stuff at the store, and—"

"Laz." The message in Chay's tone was gentle but unmistakable. "You need to be here." He slung the bag of equipment over his shoulder and pointed to the top of the meadow, where the land swept itself into a gentle rise. "We'll try from up there."

The brush was knee-high, dried grasses and shrubs like the meadow's tangled hair. Laz fell into step beside Avery and cocked a shaggy eyebrow. "So?"

She tunneled her hands into her coat pockets. "So, what?"

"Yer thinkin' too much again."

"I know." Avery sidestepped a prickly bush. "Laz, I'm terribly worried. I don't have any idea where she is." The panic she'd tried to submerge was rising, bobbing its head above the waters of her spirit. "I've called her probably ten, twelve—well, I don't know how many times. It always goes straight to voicemail. So how can I find her if I can't even get her to answer the phone?"

"Hmm." Laz kicked at a splintered log. "You sure yer not just—"

"You two coming?" Chay's call floated down the hillside.

"Yep, it's jes' not ever'body likes to pretend they're runnin' a race all the time!" Laz glanced back at Avery. "I'll talk to you later, Miz Avery."

Chay's eyes held an uncharacteristic gravity as they joined him on the small rise. "Okay, let's do this. Do you think he's ready?"

Laz's look tossed the responsibility of answering to Avery.

"I—I think so." She forced herself to make the shift, to step from the everyday into Isaiah's world. Her personal catastrophe still pounded at the door of her thoughts, but for now, she wouldn't answer. "The main thing I've noticed in the last few days is that he looks smoother. He was listing a bit on his turns last week, but he hasn't done that for a few days now. His landings are solid too."

"That's good." Chay nodded, the wind tugging at his hair as he unrolled a length of thin cord. "No margin for error if he's ever going to be released. He's got to be able to fly well enough to dodge predators and catch food."

"I know." The unspoken weight of the occasion settled itself over her shoulders. "So, can you tell me again how this works?"

"Well, I'm sure Laz told you it's called creance flying." Chay motioned to the crate. "Can you hold him?"

Isaiah's weight fit naturally into Avery's arms now. She kept her gloved hands around him as Chay fastened some kind of leather straps to the bird's ankles. "So, these here are called jesses, okay?" He snapped the cord to a ring on the anklet. "Now, what we're going to do is basically like the flight cage, yeah? Just run him down the field and back. Only holding the cord. Sort of like a kite."

"So it gives him more practice?"

"Yeah, it just helps us see him flying in a more natural environment. Helps us know if he's ready for the next steps yet."

"Creance flyin'—it takes skill." Laz's words leaked with the same stale pain that always seemed to rise when he was around Isaiah. Avery glanced at him, but he was studying the place where the pines poked against the sky.

Chay's lips tightened with an uneasy compassion, but he directed his words to Avery. "If the bird really takes off and flies to the end of the line, they can injure themselves. Even crash, sometimes, if they jerk too hard."

Avery blinked. "So—this could hurt him?"

"It won't, Miz Avery." Laz swung back toward the conversation. "The trick is to keep the line slack, work with the bird." Again, something ached behind his eyes. "And to know when to let 'em go."

"So, when you've had the chance to work with more birds, you'll be doing this someday." Chay smiled and took Isaiah from her, his gentle hands wrapped around the squirming bird. "For now, just run beside me and see how it's done, okay?"

He squatted slightly, a man ducking under the wind, and then his hands came up and the wings rose and Isaiah was flung free against the sky.

"Come on!" Chay was running, boots crunching through the dry grass, and Avery sprinted with him down the mountain meadow. Isaiah's wings dipped strong and sure, like a rhythmic heartbeat, and then he glided into the outstretched arms of a pine at the foot of the field, the moment over in a blink.

"Yes!" Breathless joy hung in Chay's voice. He slapped Avery's palm in a high-five, then glanced at where Isaiah balanced on the swaying branch. "Now that's how it's done!"

Avery laughed, his exhilaration spilling onto her. "So—he did well?"

"Did well? Oh, he was perfect. Just perfect. Let's take him back up." Chay jostled the tip of the branch, and Isaiah sprang free, sliding low this time, skimming just over the grass. Again Avery was running, breath beating, brush yanking at legs, eyes on Chay who held the line that bound them all. And then they were back atop the rise, and Isaiah fluttered to a landing on his old cage and gave a satisfied squawk.

"Isaiah, good boy!" Avery laughed with the wonder of it, the rightness of seeing Isaiah back where he belonged. "Laz, did you see him?"

"Sure did." Something shadowed still tugged at the edge of Laz's expression, but his grin was undoubtedly pleased. "He's lookin' perfect."

"All right, then." Chay rubbed his hands together and smiled at Avery. "Ready to go again?"

Twenty minutes later, after Isaiah had crisscrossed the meadow a dozen more times and Avery's legs were beginning to burn from sprinting over the steep terrain, Chay pulled on his gloves and gathered the hawk into his arms. "Let's give him the chance to rest. We'll try him again in a moment. But he was absolutely magnificent so far."

"No problems? Nothing holding him back?" Avery hovered as Chay poked Isaiah back into the box.

"None." He straightened and slapped his gloves against his thigh. "He's ready to be released."

Released.

The word punctured the fragile bubble of peace that had protected the moment, and all her unthinking happiness leaked out. Released. Of course. Hadn't she known this time was coming? Or had she simply celebrated each milepost without glancing at the destination they foretold?

Released. So like *goodbye.* Words of ending. Words of loss.

"Avery, we'll be right back." Chay gestured to Laz. "We need to grab some more stuff from the truck. Can you wait here with him?"

"Sure. I'll stay with him." But soon she wouldn't be able to, would she? He would pierce through her protection, fly from her outstretched hands.

Tears stung at her eyes, but that was ridiculous. Wasn't this the goal? She'd worked hard for this, hadn't she? He was only in exile in that cramped cage, but this was the kingdom he was heir to. It was good—truly good—that he was ready to once again climb the clouds.

Leaving her behind.

Isaiah stirred inside his cage, eyes bright as he peered at the meadow. For the first time, seeing him in his cage looked…wrong.

Was this how Addisyn had felt? Caged and contained, far from her waiting world? Had Avery blurred the line between safety and suffocation?

But what about her?

The sorrow would no longer be denied. She dropped to the ground, among the bowed heads of the dry grasses, and watched the tears drip onto her faded canvas pants. How many more treasures of her heart would be pried from her pleading hands? How many more times would she taste the tears of being left behind?

"Hard to let things go."

Avery snapped her gaze up just as Laz lowered himself to the ground beside her with a noise between a grunt and a sigh. "I tole Chay he could carry his own stuff. I'm gettin' too old to climb this hill, much less totin' all that garb he thinks we need." He squinted at her with his disarming compassion. "Looks like it's a good thing I came back up here."

"Yes—I—" Avery's breath caught, her lungs stuttering behind another sob.

"You 'member right off the bat, I done tole you not to hold wild things too tight."

"I know." The tears on her face were cold in the wind. "I didn't listen."

"Hard lesson to learn." He picked at the frost-faded grass. "Sometimes we forget about healin' and start jes' holdin'."

"I always wanted him to be healed." Avery worked her words past the lump in her throat. "But I wanted—I wanted to keep him safe."

"Safe. Yep. We all start thinkin' that way sometimes. But then when we see 'em in the sky—well, we know what they're meant for. Cain't clip those wings."

"I—I've given so much." But love didn't give her a lien on the hawk's life. Or on Addisyn's.

"Don't forget that we ain't the ones healin' 'em, Avery girl. That's their own bidness to work out with Somebody much bigger'n us. All we gotta do is jes' step out of the way. Give 'em some love and some time and some space."

"But—it's our job to—"

"It's our job to let Him do His."

The wind shuddered past the pine trees, searching for something hidden in the grass. Avery watched a cloud curl itself around the edge of the mountains before Laz spoke again.

"One time I didn't listen either, Miz Avery. An' a bird went down 'cause of it."

Avery turned toward him, but he was staring at the mountains. She bit her lip, sealing the questions inside, waiting for his story to unspool.

"He was a Ferruginous Hawk. Purty darn uncommon here." His face creased with a bittersweet smile. "Jonah, I called him. I got too attached to him, I'll be the first to admit. I'd just come from—well, I'd had a rough patch. And he was my buddy, sorta. I didn't wanna say goodbye. I flew him on the creance long after Chay tole me to quit. Long after I shoulda let go."

Already foreboding had laid its fingers on the story. "What happened?" Were those tears in his eyes? Surely not.

"One day I had him on the creance, and he made a break for it." Laz sniffed and scrubbed at his eyes with his sleeve. "He—he flew to the end. Faster'n I could keep up. And then the line jerked him—and he fell."

The words lurched, and she was the one at the end of the rope, slamming against the ground. "And—"

"And he was hurt bad." A rough pain rubbed itself over Laz's words. "I called Chay—he did all he could, but that bird had to stay at the center in Fort Collins. Species ambassador, they called it. What they meant was, he'd done broke his wing too bad to be released again."

"What did you do?"

"Walll, first I did some swearin'. And some cryin'. And then I did what I shoulda done first. Some prayin'. I asked the Good Lord to remind me to keep these big ole clumsy hands open." The clouds reflected in his eyes. "It's hard. But it's the only way we keep from hurtin' more'n we help."

Addisyn's face floated behind the story. "I only wanted to help." Sorrow draped dark over each word. "I wanted to—to make sure everything was okay."

"Not our job. Our job is to get 'em back to the skies." Laz glanced upward. "We work an' cry an' sweat an' pour our whole heart into 'em, all so's we can toss 'em into the clouds again. Into God's hands."

"God's hands." The curling cloud was smaller now, sunlight igniting its edges. "Laz, I've held everything in my own."

"Haven't we all at times." There was never any judgment from Laz. Just the real, raw ore he'd mined from a life in the mountains. "We gotta wait on God. Let Him do what He does. Quit steppin' in His way." He cocked his head. "But trust me, we need reminders. Why d'you think I named this bird Isaiah?" He must have read the blank confusion on her face. "Isaiah chapter forty. Verse twenty-eight. When you go home, read that verse again."

Footsteps crunched behind them, and then the creance rope dropped into Laz's lap. "Hey, buddy." There was a smile in Chay's words. "Time to take that bird back out."

"So?" Laz snatched up the rope and scrambled to his feet, his bluster back in place. "What's that got to do with me?"

"Because you should be the one to take him this time."

Avery watched Laz's hands tighten over the rope for three long heartbeats before he spoke. "Waalll. All right. If yer tired of runnin' up and down this meadow, I guess I could." He blinked back the shine in his eyes and raised his eyebrows at Avery. "As long as Miz Avery goes with me and makes sure I don't forget to let go."

MAYBE IT WAS the fact that the bed was extremely narrow. Or that the room watched her with unfamiliar eyes. Or maybe it was the bizarre designs on the beaded wall hanging. Regardless, Addisyn had snatched her sleep in intermittent bites, each soured by disorienting dreams.

As a result, she was sleep-starved, exhaustion raking her up and down, by the time she and Skyla returned to Larry's. But she wasn't so tired that she couldn't recognize a setback when she saw it.

"Good news is I found a belt and ordered it." Larry was a burly guy with a week's growth of stubble and perpetually squinting eyes. He gnawed on the end of a toothpick as he talked. "Bad news is it's at my buddy's shop in Casper."

"Casper—"

Skyla cleared her throat. "Wyoming. Casper is in Wyoming."

"Wyoming?" Addisyn's voice stopped just short of a shriek. "You can't—there's not one closer?"

"Nope. And that one was hard to find. This is kinda an older model." He jabbed the toothpick toward the Accord. "I told him to overnight the belt. If it comes in soon enough, I can have this car fixed in the morning."

Another night in Elk Creek? Addisyn looked to Skyla for help.

Skyla, however, simply spread her hands. "Sometimes a delay is the gift of time to consider."

Well, easy for her to say. She wasn't the one whose relentless past was chasing her into an ever-narrowing future.

Addisyn wallowed in the frustration of the situation all the way back to Skyla's house, but as they stepped inside, she determined to shake off her sulking. "What are you getting ready to do, Skyla?"

"I am going to work on Isaiah's painting." Skyla was already heading down the hall toward the room Addisyn knew was her studio.

"May I watch?" Addisyn paused on the threshold of the window-wrapped room. After her prickly mood, she might not be welcome.

"Of course." Skyla was collecting colors, squeezing different hues onto a wooden palette. "I am only forming outlines. There is not much to see yet." She brushed her hand over the canvas. "Rather like life, do you not think? The Spirit moving before He can be seen?"

"I—I suppose so. Can I see what you have so far?"

"Certainly, if you wish."

Addisyn paused a respectful distance behind Skyla and studied the canvas. The faint outline of a hawk held in a pair of hands seemed to hover above the blank space. "Wow." Addisyn cocked her head, imagining the way the painting would grow. "May I ask a question?"

"Yes."

"Whose hands are those?"

Skyla dabbed her brush in a dot of paint the color of sunset. "What do you think?"

Addisyn squinted at the watery lines. Even at this stage, she could tell the hands were those of a man, strong and sure. "Chay's?"

"No. But I think you will know soon. When you are ready."

Addisyn shrugged and stepped back, perching on a three-legged stool. She watched the paintbrush move from palette to canvas for several minutes before Skyla spoke again. "Where are you going, Addisyn?"

"I told you." That had come out more snappishly than she'd intended. "New York."

"Yes, but why?" Skyla flicked her brush at some detail on the canvas. "You do not want to go there, so how are you being called?"

The whole story was too long a road to walk, so she searched for a shorter route. "Do you remember when we talked about healing? When you were painting that day out at the store?"

"Of course. I always remember what I discuss while I am painting."

"Well, you told me that healing is a process. And it sometimes hurts."

"Yes."

"What if that process doesn't work for you? And what if—what if it doesn't just hurt you? What if it hurts everyone around you?"

Skyla squeezed a few drops of blood-red onto the palette, then added a single squirt of a tawny hue the color of the dry grass. "Is this why you are running away from Estes Park?"

"I'm not running away." Defensiveness slanted her words. She sighed. "Okay. So maybe I am. But it's complicated."

"Complicated." Skyla swirled her paintbrush in a glass jar half full of water. "Most of life is. And most people who use that term simply do not wish to face it."

"Are you saying that's a cop-out?" Her defenses were rising now.

"Yes."

Okay, then. If Skyla wanted to hear the story, fine. "All right. I used to have a very different life." She watched Skyla's face, but her expression didn't waver. "And then, I got away from—from that place. And I came to the mountains to be free from what I left behind." A lump she hadn't expected lodged itself in her throat. "But it came after me anyway."

"A bird with a broken wing cannot fly anywhere."

Even given Skyla's philosophical style, the comment was unbelievably random. "What?"

"Healing must come first." Skyla laid down her brush and turned toward Addisyn, conviction crackling in the depths of her gaze. "It is not your location, Addisyn. You are wounded. And with your wound, you cannot fly."

So Skyla was saying it was *her* fault? Indignation bristled within her, but a glance at Skyla's unapologetic face told her she might as well argue with the mountains. She fiddled with the hem of her shirt. "I don't know what you mean."

"Yes, you do. Or you would, if you would empty yourself." Skyla's smile crept across her face. "You are one such as I was. So very stubborn, aren't we?" She pushed up her sleeve before Addisyn could reply and tapped a thin white scar that threaded across her wrist. "I received this scar years ago. A Barred Owl sliced me with her talon as I was freeing her from a hunter's trap. Strange still how the birds fight. They thrash and work as if they never need my help."

The analogy stuck an accusing finger at her. "And—you think I do need help."

"Of course. As do we all." Skyla was mixing color again, blending the hues together. "We are allowed such privilege, yes? To choose life instead of death. Newness instead of oldness. Victory instead of defeat. All in one choice."

"And what choice is that?"

"The choice for release and renewal." A light lapped at the edges of Skyla's words. "The choice to hold hands to Heaven and say, 'Help.'"

The stool was harder than she'd realized. Addisyn shifted her weight. "The choice for God."

"This makes you uncomfortable?"

"Yes."

"Discomfort sits on the threshold of truth." Skyla shrugged and turned back to her canvas. "But I believe that any wound can be healed if we are willing to allow ourselves to be held. If we allow Someone higher to lift us and bind the wounds."

"But, Skyla—there are things—there are people—" Addisyn sighed. "It's not that easy."

"Easy?" Skyla's eyebrows leaped to attention. "Who said it was easy? No, healing is the hardest work there is." She glanced out the window, where pine trees tapped against the glass. "But that is why I love working with the birds. They come in so broken, you know. So fragile. But really, it only takes love and care for the power to return to their wings. Once they submit to healing, it is quite smooth. And such a miracle to be present and testify to the healing. No matter how broken they are, they do not stay that way."

There was a tug in Skyla's words. A beckoning like a half-open door. For just a moment, Addisyn considered reaching for the knob.

But then the black-and-white facts sliced across the moment, fraying the fragile threads. Addisyn clenched her jaw and watched the door swing shut. She wasn't going to find deliverance anywhere—not in Skyla's eccentric philosophy or the power of her paintings or even in Avery's footsure faith. Not when she had a letter from a man who hated her—and a contract that lashed her to him like a choking chain.

She slid off the uncomfortable stool and turned for the door without another word. Tomorrow, she'd be away from Skyla's stories and the mountains her sister loved and the promise of those rising wings on the canvas. And the day after that, she'd be in only one place.

The past—that would once more be the present.

△△ △△ △△

DARIUS HAD NEVER expected Addisyn to come to Whistler.

The destination was simply too easy. A girl hoping to disappear would surely not select a town so obvious to her well-meaning friends.

Still, in deference to Avery's certainty, Darius had checked with the rink last night. Today on lunch, he'd even driven to most of the nearby hotels. As he'd expected, his search returned nothing.

It was the evening of the second day since she'd left. By now, even

Avery would have to agree that Addisyn wasn't coming to Whistler. Or would she simply think Darius was lying to her?

Regardless of Avery's feelings, Darius needed to expand his search. And while at work, he'd dropped a pin on his mental map. A place that just might make sense.

A few snowflakes sprinkled his sleeves as he hurried out of the climbing center and hopped into his car. He turned the heater on full blast, rubbing his hands together. The lights of Whistler sparked against the indigo dusk. The town was whirling to life the way it did every year, the tourists streaming in with the snow.

His phone rang just as he was backing out of his parking space. He glanced at the screen on his dashboard.

Avery.

He tapped the TALK icon and cleared his throat, walls firmly in place. "Hello, Avery."

"Darius. Hi."

Her tone was different today. Calmer, softer, maybe even—friendly? He wouldn't lower his defenses yet. "I was planning to call you tonight, actually. I don't think Addisyn is coming here. I haven't heard from her."

Avery sighed. "That's what I figured, when I didn't hear from you. Is she maybe there and just hasn't contacted you?"

"I don't think so." A brief gap appeared in the thickening traffic, and he pulled out of the parking lot. "I've gone by the rink, and I've checked with all the hotels."

"Thank you." The words sounded more like an apology. Avery cleared her throat. "I really do appreciate that."

"Of course." Maybe ultimately Avery would realize he wasn't a sister-stealing monster. "Do you know anywhere else she might have gone?"

"I've tried and tried to think. The only other place where she spent any amount of time is New York City, of course. But there's no way she would be there, especially with the lawsuit. Other than that, there's nothing I can come up with. But, I mean—" An ache crept into her tone. "I missed three years of her life, so—yeah, there's a lot I don't know."

"Well, I was wondering about Denver." Taillights blinked red eyes in front of him, a centipede of cars creeping through downtown.

"Denver? What about Denver?"

"It's a figure skating hub, so it seemed logical to me. I think Addisyn trained there for a bit at some point, actually." Better not to mention that Addisyn had visited that rink recently. He wouldn't risk pulling the pin on another potential secret.

"Do you think I should drive down there and check?" Hope hurried Avery's words. "I can leave first thing tomorrow morning, get there by—"

"No." But he recognized her feeling, the need to be making waves instead of riding the current. "Here's the thing. It would be difficult for you to get much information without skating credentials." He didn't have time to worry about how Avery would respond to his latest plan. "So, I'm going down there tomorrow. It was the soonest I could get off work."

"You're going to Denver?"

"Yes." The stoplight blinked from yellow to red, and Darius locked his jaw. *Go on, Avery, try to tell me no.* "I need to find Addisyn."

"You would go all that way to find her?"

"Absolutely." He didn't have to think about that answer. "I did it before."

"What do you mean?"

Had Addisyn not told Avery this story? Darius leaned back in his seat awkwardly. "Well—when she got in trouble before—you know, with Brian—I found out she was in Chicago, and I went there to help her. To stop her from, you know, making a mistake."

A few moments of silence dripped by before Avery spoke again. "That's how she got away from Brian? Because—because of you?"

"No." He ducked under the embarrassment. "Addisyn made the decision. I was just there to—to support her. Well, and to intervene when Brian became—unpleasant."

"I had no idea." Avery's words were slower now. "I didn't—I mean, I never asked her what actually happened."

The green light nodded at him reassuringly. Darius pulled forward again.

"Darius, will you answer a question for me?"

His guard snapped back into place. "Uh—sure."

"Are you in love with my sister?"

What? The question crashed into his heart like a head-on collision. "I—uh—I mean—" His face was throbbing. "She's very—very special to—"

"But do you love her?" Avery's voice was still level, but it was as unyielding as the mountains. "Tell me, Darius. I need to know."

He was out of downtown, onto his lonely side street, and his headlights cut the path forward to the truth that had been bottled within him for so long. "Yes." The word uncorked his emotions, and all that he'd been too scared to say unrolled like the road ahead. "She's—she's amazing, and she's sweet, and she's so smart, and—and I've wanted to tell her for a long time, but I didn't know—I just worried that maybe she didn't want me to—but—" He swiped his arm across his forehead. He was flailing now, stumbling and staggering through his own sentences, but on one truth he could stand tall. "Yes. I love her. Very much."

He pulled up in front of his house and writhed in the emptiness that stretched between them. If Avery had disliked him before, she'd detest him now. Would she scold him? Hang up on him?

"Thank you. For telling me that."

Darius blinked. "I—"

"She loves you too."

Avery hadn't seen Addisyn's stone-carved expression the day she left Whistler. "I don't know if she—"

"Darius, please listen." There was a slight tremble to Avery's voice, but her words were bedrock firm. "She's my little sister. She can't hide her heart from me. Not really. And—and I can tell her compass is set to you. And that's been hard for me to accept, but—"

Stepping into the pause seemed like a bad idea. Words could get a guy in trouble in a moment like this. He waited until Avery spoke again.

"Darius, I called today to apologize. What happened the other day—I shouldn't have jumped on you like that. I should have given you a chance to tell me your side instead of believing the worst."

Now he had to say something, even with awkwardness tangled all over his tongue. "Oh—well—hey, it's okay."

"No, it's not." The intensity in Avery's voice beat back his feeble words. "When you said that I was judging you, that it wasn't fair of me to compare you to Brian—you were absolutely right. I was wrong. I've been wrong about a lot of things." Regret hung from her words. "I'm truly sorry."

Apologies were always hard to handle, like a lumpy package that didn't fit quite right in his hands. Darius rubbed his palm over his face. "Well—thanks. Like I said, it's okay. I mean, I get it, about thinking I had—" *Wrong road.* "But, anyway, I never intended to hide anything from you. Really, I told Addisyn to get your blessing about skating."

"I see that now. But she only told me she was going to visit you." Avery's words were measured. "So when I found out, I felt very—deceived."

He couldn't blame her. The reasoning made sense. "That's not— that's never what I had in mind. I wouldn't ever want to do something underhanded. Especially where Addisyn is concerned. I know how close you two are. I never wanted to come between that."

"We are. Well, we were." There was a soft sniff from the other end of the phone. "I only wanted to keep us that way. That's all I ever wanted. And I—I failed."

"No." Darius shook his head, as if Avery could see his conviction. "She loves you, Avery. She's just—hurting."

"She's got to be. She wasn't honest with either of us." Avery paused. "That's why we have to find her."

The Denver skyline traced itself across the night. "We will."

"You know something, Darius Payne?" Avery's tone lightened. "I think Laz was right about you." She paused long enough to give her next words meaning. "You're one of the good ones."

"Well—" Darius bit his lip, but his grin stretched anyway. "I try to be. With God's help."

The smile in Avery's voice made her sound almost like Addisyn. "So—can we maybe start over? Friends this time?"

"Oh, yes." Darius closed his eyes and breathed in a future he could finally imagine. "I'm counting on it."

△△ △△ △△

THE TRAIL CARVED its way from the valley to the very summit of Deer Mountain—three steep, sharp miles upward. The route was demanding,

305

but Avery had always loved it. She never failed to lose her breath at the sweeping views, and she delighted in climbing through each new layer of forest—mountain meadows that unrolled themselves across the slopes, then subalpine forests full of brooding pines and sifted sunlight, then the last stretch above tree line, where only a few stubby and twisted trees still clung stubbornly to the stones. And finally, of course, this reward—the rocky summit itself, where she could perch on a sun-warmed boulder and see all the way to the High Peaks on one side and nearly to Allenspark on the other. The town of Estes Park itself dabbled dots of buildings and landmarks in a green valley just underneath her.

The trail was usually a popular one, but today, on a blustery afternoon in the middle of November, she was alone. She'd only passed two other hikers the whole time, both of whom had been descending.

The weather was surely responsible for that. The wind was whipping today, the mountains bearing the heavy clouds on their shoulders. The town was scrambling with the news of the season's first serious snowstorm, expected before the end of the week. Another few days, and the autumn— so brief, so bright—would be overtaken by the throes of winter. And for the second year, Avery would take pride in standing shoulder-to-shoulder with the mountains to face the most brutal season—remaining *"from ice-in to ice-out,"* as Laz always said. She'd hoped that this year, she wouldn't be alone. But now…

Cloud shadows laid their gentle fingers on her, and she shifted position on her boulder. She drew a deep breath, throwing open her heart to the cold mountain air and allowing it to clear the cobwebs from her soul. The few twisted trees answered the wind with a strange sound, a cross between a whistle and a moan. Avery wasn't frightened. These were her mountains. She spoke their language.

For the last few weeks, her normal hiking routine had dwindled, what with the store's demands and Addisyn's drama and Isaiah's healing. Now, sitting here, all that she'd been missing was as obvious as the stenciled sky. She'd needed this, needed to plunge into the mountains and immerse herself in their peace. It always called her back to center.

No wonder her life had limped off-balance these last months.

Her backpack was slouched against the stone. She unzipped the top pocket and slid out the one thing she'd been carrying with her each day. The item that hadn't left her side since Addisyn had vanished—the picture.

She swallowed down the burning in her throat. It was obvious that Addisyn had tried her hardest to repair the damage. But still, the focal point of the image was no longer their smiling faces, but rather the crack between them.

Avery flipped the picture over and brushed her finger over the scrap of paper taped to the back. It was Laz's familiar scrawl, the paper he'd slipped into her hand yesterday at the conclusion of Isaiah's flight session.

Isaiah 40:28

A fresh gust of wind slapped against her, and she closed her eyes. She'd come here for answers, for guidance, maybe even for peace. But nothing had quite settled. Not yet.

Isaiah 40:28

Still gripping the picture, she reached into her backpack and pulled out her dog-eared Bible, the little one with the faux leather cover that accompanied her on every hike. The pages flopped readily to Isaiah. It was one of her favorite books, after all. She flipped past the prophecies of the One to be called Wonderful, the rhythmic rune of the virgin conceiving, the song of the Suffering Servant. At chapter forty, she dragged her finger down the page, struggling to catch the words even as the thin sheets flailed in the wind.

Don't you know? Haven't you heard? El Olam, Yahweh, the Creator of the ends of the earth, doesn't grow tired or become weary.

El Olam. Yahweh. Avery closed her eyes and listened to the winds, the ones both inside and outside herself. El Olam, the Everlasting God. More constant than the mountains. More faithful than the sunrise. More patient than time itself.

And Yahweh. The Self-Existent One. The One Who needed no other to hold Him up.

In all her work and worry, had she forgotten His Names? Had she believed, by some preposterous pride, that she was the one responsible for shoring up the timbers of her life? That her plans for her sister were better than His?

His understanding is beyond reach.

Yes. Avery let her eyes find the far point of the horizon. Understanding beyond reach. An understanding that filled the heavens like an endless sea of light. An understanding that saw where she was blind and worked where she was helpless and knew where she was ignorant. She looked back at the Book.

The strength of those who wait with hope in Yahweh will be renewed. Power vibrated through the promise. *They will soar on wings like eagles. They will run and won't become weary. They will walk and won't grow tired.*

On wings like eagles. The words crackled with their own jolt of meaning, and understanding spread across the page. A hawk named Isaiah. Of course. The freedom and power and exultation of a raptor in flight were right here, in the pages of Scripture—promised to her.

If she would wait with hope in Yahweh.

Wait.

With hope.

In Yahweh.

Had she ever done that?

Not when it came to Addisyn. No, there she'd put herself in His place. She'd shouldered the burden of them both, and she'd believed it was her solo duty to keep Addisyn safe. To take care of her and protect her and shield her the way she always had.

But over and over again, the weight had crushed them both.

She'd blamed so many external culprits for causing friction between her and Addisyn, pointing fingers at a dozen different excuses. The pressure of their life in New York. Her own exhaustion and trauma. The difficulty of being Addisyn's parent instead of her sister. The lure of skating and the deception of Brian and the rebellion in Addisyn's soul.

But it wasn't really Brian or New York or even skating that had come between them, was it? Because here she was—in a whole new place, a whole new season, and still, she'd gripped her sister too tightly. And so they had both fallen back into the broken story.

She still believed that standing with Addisyn was a sacred trust, that El Shaddai had bound their lives together with His mysterious cords of love and loss. But she'd stepped beyond the bounds, blurring the lines between His responsibility and her own. Had she even prayed for her sister in the recent months? Or had she only lectured, worried, advised, questioned?

What would have happened if she'd chosen instead to trust? To free her sister's future. To release her own snatch for control. To know with glowing faith that no matter what trail opened before either of them, it would lead ever upward.

To the High Country.

Sorrow dragged at her soul. She'd never granted El Shaddai space to stir in Addisyn's heart. Never given her sister the opportunity to find the promise of this verse.

No wonder neither of them could fly.

On wings…

Those who wait with hope…

The pages flapped eagerly in the wind, as though the Book itself had wings. Avery felt the smile in her soul before it came to her lips. How glad she was that these worn pages never held any condemnation. Only the conviction that led to courage.

We toss 'em into God's hands…

She lifted her face to all that was higher than she. *El Shaddai—* She could strive and struggle, but she always came back to Him, to the God Who had molded these mountains, the Eternal One Who was above and beyond all time, the Self-Existent One Who would never need her help. *Help me—*

The words welled up from the deep places of her spirit, rising into the same wind that held the hawks. By the time she lowered her head and blinked back the cleansing tears, she realized that she'd been gripping the photo tightly as she prayed, so tightly that she'd creased the edge. She held it in front of her once more, forcing her gaze to focus on the light on their faces, not the jagged rip between them. And then she knew exactly what to do. With careful fingers, she slipped it between the truth-soaked pages of her Bible. Right there in Isaiah's chapter.

The clouds were sinking downward, but her spirit was rising up. She closed the Book firmly on her fears and frustrations and tucked it back into her bag. When she hoisted her backpack to her shoulders, it was surprisingly lighter than it had been on the way up.

She gazed over the view one last time—the town that had welcomed her and the peaks that were her home and the valley below where she and her sister had heard the bugles not so long ago. Then she picked her way through the rocks—down the path home.

The wind was still whipping, but the mountain held firm. There was a long trail ahead, but by the grace of El Shaddai, she would learn to walk it.

CHAPTER 21

Addisyn kicked her toe against the tire and turned to Larry. "Thank you for getting this fixed."

"My pleasure." He flicked through Addisyn's cash with grease-blackened fingers. "Filled it up with gas too."

Sliding onto the stiff leather of the driver's seat, Addisyn adjusted her rearview mirror and caught sight of her bags slumped in the backseat. She'd already transferred them from Skyla's Bronco. There were no more reasons to delay. "Skyla, thank you for everything."

"Of course." Skyla had been unfailingly polite all morning, but disappointment hung around her like a mountain mist.

"Drive safe." Larry frowned at the flat gray sheet of sky. "We're due for a winter storm."

"Winter storm?" Addisyn's fingers tightened on the wheel.

"It is due to arrive tomorrow." Skyla too glanced at the clouds. "Estes Park will have at least a foot."

"Snow for Estes." The idea coiled sadness in her soul. "Avery loves snow."

"It will be a blessing for her." Skyla took a step closer. "Addisyn?"

"Yes?"

Skyla reached through the still-open door and gripped Addisyn's shoulder. "Please, do not be in such a hurry that you do not hear."

No, she couldn't handle the way Skyla's words forced open her defenses. She couldn't take this now, not when she needed to be putting the walls up, armoring herself for the future ahead. "I promise you that this is for the best."

"You took a wrong turn, but you have the choice for a better one."

"Yes, I know." Addisyn reached for the door handle.

Skyla's lips pursed in defeat. But she stepped back, out of the decision between them. "One choice, Addisyn. One choice, and the wings will rise."

The wings will rise? Addisyn wouldn't allow herself to try to decipher that last remark. "Thank you, Skyla. I appreciate it."

And with that, she closed the door on everything that lay behind and pulled away from Larry's house without glancing in her mirror once.

The distance back to Lyons was covered in a swoop, her tires eating the road with an eagerness she couldn't share. She made the right turn this time, but it had never felt more like the wrong way. By Longmont, carsickness was squeezing her stomach. Maybe from the winding road. Maybe from the emotions wrestling inside her. She paused at a gravel pullout. A few moments of fresh air might be just what she needed.

She paced back and forth beside the car, drawing slow, deep breaths into her unsettled soul. The air was crackling cold, with the strange charged heaviness that preceded storms. She'd be gone by the time the winter weather arrived, but Avery would enjoy it. Would she still have to work? Or would she go for a hike? Addisyn pictured her sister tromping through some winter forest, eyes bright with the wonder that she always wore in the mountains.

Probably thanking God that her troublesome younger sister was gone.

Addisyn forced her mind away from the idea and glanced around. The land was much flatter here, the wide valleys stretching into farms. A rusty barbed-wire fence stitched its way beside the road, cattle dotting the pasture behind it.

Still, though, if she looked to the west, the High Peaks were visible—even higher and holier now. As always, far too high for her to reach.

She slid back into the car before the tears could come. For the rest of the drive, she focused on pulling into herself, sorting all her memories from the last three months and locking them in the basement of her heart. And she didn't cry again—not as she arrived in Denver, not as she trundled through security, not as she boarded the east-bound jet.

She spent the first hour of the flight gazing out the window, watching the wrinkled quilt of mountains and fields and towns drop away beneath the plane. Sunset kindled behind her, but she was soaring into the shadows.

We are always one choice from healing…

Skyla's words buzzed uncomfortably around her seat, but Addisyn shooed them away like a pesky insect. That wasn't true for her, couldn't be. She didn't have a choice now.

No, she'd made it long ago.

She glanced at the bag that held her phone. During her layover in Chicago, she needed to make the call that would wave her white flag. And at some point, she would have to contact Avery—let her know that she was okay, and that the legal threat was over. But that wouldn't be for a while.

A sudden spasm of something like panic ripped through her, but she gritted her teeth and rode it out. True, this was far from the best option, but it was the only choice. Because Brian had been right all along. She couldn't escape her past.

Or him.

Still, the tears didn't come. Not until she glanced again at her ticket, and the date leaped accusingly to the forefront. She'd lost track of her days, and the realization slammed a final fist onto her beaten soul.

Tomorrow—her first full day back in New York—was November seventeenth.

Avery's birthday.

△△　△△　△△

IT HAD WORKED, of course. Just as he'd known it would.

Brian leaned back in his chair and kicked his feet onto the corner of his desk. Oh, moments like these made everything worthwhile. "So when will you be here?"

"I told you, I had a layover in Chicago." Background noise garbled behind Addisyn's voice. "I'll be there sometime this evening. I'll come by the agency tomorrow morning at nine o'clock."

So she expected him to conform to her schedule? There was an authority in her voice he didn't like. "Nine o'clock?" He hedged as if considering. "Well, I don't know if—"

"Nine o'clock, Brian." The razor edge on Addisyn's voice sliced his pretense to the bone. "Take it or leave it."

"Okay, okay." She'd been around Avery too much, and her sister's annoying independence was rubbing off on her. Well, he would take care of that. "Nine o'clock. In my office?" He hated himself for putting a question mark on the end.

"That's fine."

"I'll have the papers ready. Your waiver, all that."

Her tone was flat, final. "All right."

He couldn't wait to see Barmilli's face. Couldn't wait to hit Club Cinco next and swagger in front of the other agents. "You're making the right decision, you know." He forced a serious note into his tone. "Fulfilling the rest of your contract is the honorable—"

"Don't you *dare* talk to me about honor." Her hiss burned his ear. "And don't patronize me. I'll see you at nine o'clock." With that, the phone clicked dead.

Well, she was in a whole mood. Not that it mattered. She'd be better when she got back to the city. Back to who she really was.

He pressed the intercom and waited until he heard Baylie's voice. "Yes?"

"Put an item on my calendar for tomorrow morning. Nine o'clock, meeting with Addisyn Miles." The words tasted strongly of victory.

"Addisyn Miles?" Baylie hesitated. "She's meeting with you?"

"That's what I said, isn't it?"

"So—she's coming back?"

It was none of her business, but he wouldn't pass up a chance to spread this news. "Yes. She's coming back here to finish out her contract because she recognizes the error of her ways." Sarcasm worked through his words. "And the threat of legal action, of course. Just write it down, will you?"

He clicked off the intercom and laced his fingers behind his head. Clearly, the seeds he'd planted during his conversation with Avery had taken root. Now that had been a lucky break—just the opening he had needed to drive his wedge. He would have loved to watch the discussion they undoubtedly had later. Avery had probably kicked her younger sister out of the house. And into his hands.

Yes, it was all working out. Tomorrow, all the pieces would finally align. He'd prove his value to Barmilli. He'd have his revenge on Addisyn. And he'd show everyone the truth.

Nobody could bring Brian Felding down.

⩓ ⩓ ⩓

BAYLIE'S BAD FEELING was getting stronger.

9 a.m., Addisyn Miles. The reminder she'd scribbled on Mr. Felding's calendar had tattooed itself across her thoughts. All afternoon, while she arranged client schedules and updated files and now processed applications, the words tapped her on the shoulder. *9 a.m., Addisyn Miles. What are you going to do about it?*

Baylie sighed and scanned the last application in the stack. Traci Sharm, age nineteen, Pittsburgh, Pennsylvania. Height five foot six, weight far below what belonged on a frame that tall. Baylie entered the data dutifully, watching the details arrange themselves into a portrait. A snapshot of another girl who didn't know the truth about Brian Felding. A girl who probably trusted him the way Addisyn had.

Someday, somebody needed to put a gate across Mr. Felding's path. And she'd really thought Addisyn might be the one to do it. First there was the call from the older sister—Avery, wasn't it?—in a tone that absolutely meant business. And then a letter had come yesterday from an attorney in Colorado. Baylie had skimmed over it as she stamped it received. It was crammed full of legal jargon, but even the words she didn't know had a rock-hard ring. *Refuses to accede to your demands...denies allegations of past misconduct...sees no basis for your accusations.*

But now, the calendar. *9 a.m., Addisyn Miles.* Mr. Felding's voice had rung with victory. The battle was over now—Addisyn was down for the count, knocked out by Mr. Felding in a fight with no referee. Clearly, he'd bullied her to nothingness, the same way he bullied Baylie and his clients and anyone else who tried to stand in his way. There was no way to stop him.

But what if there was?

315

Design school, Baylie. Design school. She had to keep her focus straight, couldn't allow her sympathy for Addisyn to cloud her judgment. This job was a link in the delicate chain of her future. Without it, the whole sequence would crack. Nothing was worth risking that for.

She reached for her pen. Only on the blank page was life easy and decisions uncomplicated. Only at the end of her pen did shapes line themselves in predictable patterns and beauty arise from disconnected doodles. But today the shapes squished lumpy and the patterns wouldn't play and the pen staggered with uncertainty. From behind every line and curve, one phrase peered out. *9 a.m., Addisyn Miles.*

She ripped the page loose in a burst of frustration and tossed it into the trash. She needed to talk this through with someone, anyone. Not her dad—he usually only called on holidays, anyway. Not her mom—she'd be busy grading papers from her classes at NYU, workload as bloated as always. What about Kim? She could meet her friend after work and get her take. Kim loved dispensing advice. At the very least, she could examine the situation from another angle.

As soon as Baylie could escape from work, she darted down the stairs, waved at Mrs. White—who didn't wave back—and caught the subway downtown to the A & O Diner. Funky electronic music invited her inside when she opened the door.

"Baylie!" Kim waved from their usual table—front corner, next to the window. As Baylie slid into the booth, Kim grabbed her arm. "Are you okay? You said you needed to talk."

"Yeah, it's just—I need advice."

True to form, Kim immediately folded her features into a guru-like expression, delight dancing in her eyes. "Advice?" She tapped the menu. "I've got grilled cheese sandwiches coming for us both. So spill it, girlfriend."

Baylie plunked her chin into her palm and began. How Addisyn had mysteriously left. How Mr. Felding had asked her to shred the letter. How everything had kept getting weirder since then, and how she suspected the net was larger than what she could see.

"And now, she's going to be here tomorrow morning." Baylie nodded her thanks as the waiter slid two plates onto the table, then peered at Kim.

"So what should I do?"

Kim shook her head, hoop earrings bouncing. "Baylie, it's none of your business."

"I know, but—it doesn't seem right. What he's doing."

"No, I agree. He seems like a total jerk and a half." Kim took a bite of her sandwich before continuing. "You know, I used to see them all the time."

Baylie blinked. "Them, who? Mr. Felding and Addisyn?"

"Yeah. They came to Club Cinco a lot when I was waitressing there. Remember that job? Last year, when I was still thinking Dylan and I could make it work?"

"Oh, yeah." Kim had worked at the posh joint for a few months before she and her bartender boyfriend parted ways. "So what did you think of them?"

"She was nice. Beautiful girl, super sweet. Smart. You could tell by talking to her." Kim flipped a hand under her glossy dark hair. "I sort of thought her ID was fake, but hey, it wasn't my job to check that stuff. Now, he was a different story. A real piece of work."

"What do you mean?"

Kim twisted her lips. "Just kind of—possessive, maybe? Like, he would order for her and stuff. And stayed glued to her elbow the whole time they were there. I always pegged him as the male chauvinist type. You know, keep the woman under lock and key." She took another bite of her sandwich, then grinned. "But also, he was an NTG."

"NTG?"

"My personal restaurant slang. 'No-tip guy.'" Kim laughed. "And I never have good opinions of NTG's. So I might be biased."

"No, that's about how he is at the office." So even back then, Addisyn hadn't been happy. Yet she'd still managed to smile at Baylie every day. Baylie stared at her untouched sandwich. It was probably getting cold, but she wasn't hungry.

"Baylie, look." Kim pushed her plate aside and leaned forward. "It's not your problem, okay? Let them—" she waved her hand vaguely— "work it out, or fight it out, or whatever. But I don't want to see you lose your job and your chance at what would make you happy, just because you were trying to save the world."

"I'm not trying to save the world." Baylie fought down the defensiveness in her tone. "But—if I know something isn't right, shouldn't I say something?"

Kim shrugged. "I mean, I guess everybody has a different opinion on stuff like that. Me, I just say go along and keep your head down, you know? I think most of us have enough problems without adopting some more from other people." She must have read the uncertainty on Baylie's face. "Okay. Think about it this way. If you decided to intervene tomorrow, what would you actually do? Even if you tell this girl you shredded the letter, then what happens? You realize it's just your word against Mr. Felding's."

"So it might not do any good anyway?"

"Exactly. And then you've thrown away your job for no reason." Kim smiled and bumped Baylie's shoulder. "Don't worry about it, Bay. I promise you, if this girl is still like she was at Club Cinco, she can take care of herself."

Kim was right, of course. Baylie told herself that all the way home and even late that night, when she stared at the ceiling in her dingy apartment instead of sleeping. Everything her friend had said was stitched with good sense. Logical. Impossible to refute.

But there was one detail Baylie hadn't shared. One detail she hadn't been ready to bring from possibility to reality. And that detail was the one that floated above her bed now, poking insistently at her thoughts.

9 a.m., Addisyn Miles. Baylie glanced at the clock on her bedside table. In less than ten hours, Addisyn would face her greatest enemy. And she would lose.

Unless.

⩓⩓ ⩓⩓ ⩓⩓

DARIUS'S OVERNIGHT BAG had already been riding shotgun when he'd driven to work on Thursday morning. As soon as his shift was over, he'd headed to Vancouver and caught the next flight to Denver. His plane touched down in the Rockies around eleven o'clock that night.

In some ways, the city was like Vancouver, stacked skyscrapers and the smearing headlights of busy boulevards, but the air was foreign. Even in the darkness, he could feel the breath of the mountains, sense them sleeping on the horizon. He'd grabbed dinner at a drive-thru and checked into a hotel near the airport. As he'd sunk into sleep, he'd comforted himself with the certainty that Addisyn was so close, right here in the same city.

But now, as he drove to the rink under an uneasy sky, doubts crammed themselves into every corner of his rental car. What made him think he'd find Addisyn in Denver? Was it logical to assume she'd come here just because it was a figure skating hub? Wouldn't she seek to put more distance between herself and Avery?

The elaborate sports complex sprawled before him, and as he crossed the parking lot, he reached for reassurance. His reasoning was valid. If Addisyn were considering a return to skating, Denver was a logical first step. She had come here before, so she could be seeking to anchor to the familiar. And even if he didn't find her here, he might locate clues, or people who knew her.

The glass door slid shut behind him as the guard behind the front desk glanced up. "Hey." He gave his best *I'm-not-a-dangerous-person* smile. "I'm looking for a friend of mine."

What the skinny guard lacked in brawn, he compensated for in bravado. "I'm sorry, sir." He folded his arms and swelled his narrow chest. "We can't divulge personal information about our athletes to the public."

Okay, that had been the wrong approach. "I'm not the public. I'm a skater from Vancouver. This athlete is my competition partner"—it wasn't a lie—"and I believe she trains here."

"A skater from Vancouver?" The man's wariness lifted slightly, and he narrowed his eyes, as if trying to fit Darius into a mental box. Suddenly he brightened. "Say—I know you. You're the one who medaled in the Vancouver Olympics—Andrew, uh—"

"Payne." Darius nodded. "Andrew Payne."

"Yes!" The man snapped his fingers in recognition. "Payne. I knew you looked familiar. Well, Andrew Payne! Looking for your training partner, you say?"

If he hadn't been choking on urgency, the guy's pivoted personality would have been funny. "That's right. Hoping to surprise her. Could you check for me?"

"Absolutely." Compliance overflowed from the man now. "Name, please?"

"Addisyn Miles." Darius paused to spell out Addisyn's first name. "She's a figure skater."

The man scrolled through a directory on his computer, then shook his head. "I'm sorry. She hasn't checked in here since September."

September. When she'd come to practice before. His hopes snapped in half. "Are you sure?"

"She's not in the database." The man flipped his computer screen around and gestured to the list of names. "But I can go ask the coaches just to be certain. If you don't mind waiting, sir."

For Addisyn, he'd wait the rest of his life. "I don't mind at all."

The man bustled away, and Darius glanced around the lobby area. Chairs marched rigidly down the hallway, but he leaned against the wall instead. It was always cold in places like this. Cold and expensive-looking.

His phone vibrated in his pocket. He pulled it out just enough to see a text from Avery. **Have you gone to the rink yet? Is she there?**

He slid the phone back into his pocket. He wouldn't text her until he knew for sure.

"I'm sorry, sir." The man hurried back, draped in an apologetic grimace. "She hasn't been here. None of the administrators in that department remembered her or saw her on training schedules."

Well, the hunch had been good, but it hadn't played out. Darius swallowed his disappointment. "Thanks anyway. You've been very helpful."

Back in the parking lot, the sky was even more foreboding, the flags overhead snapping in the chilly wind. He dialed Avery. "She's not here."

"Oh." Disappointment leaked from Avery's words. "I had hoped…"

"So had I." He rubbed his hand across his beard. "I'm going to check with some of the skaters here this afternoon."

"Okay." Avery paused. "She went farther than Denver, didn't she?"

He wouldn't let the possibility invade his purpose, not yet. "We don't know that. At the very least, I might find clues. Maybe someone she was friends with."

"I don't even know who her friends were." Avery's tone cracked, pain spilling through the words. "I—there's so much I don't know. So much. And here in Estes Park, she really didn't have anyone she spent time with. I mean, Skyla, of course, but she was her boss, so—"

This was a name he hadn't heard. "Skyla?"

"Skyla Wingo. Addisyn worked for her in September and October. But they weren't close or anything. Skyla isn't very—open."

Darius frowned. Of course it would be just another dead end, but still, leave no stone unturned, right? "Could I have Skyla's number?"

"Oh—well, I mean, sure. But I really don't think she will know anything. Addisyn didn't even see her after the job ended, except sometimes here at the store."

As Darius finished the conversation with Avery and ducked back into his rental car, he had to agree with her logic. But the truth loomed over him as he dialed the number she sent him. If Skyla didn't know something, he had no leads left.

"Hello?" A woman's voice.

"Skyla Wingo?"

"Yes."

Not a talkative sort. Avery had been right. "I'm—I'm Darius Payne. I'm looking for Addisyn Miles."

Silence. He glanced at the phone to make sure the call hadn't dropped. "Are you there?"

"Yes—" Her word stretched slow. "How do you know her?"

"I'm—her friend from Canada." Okay, that sounded sketchy. He searched for a way to establish validity. "Her sister gave me your number."

"Canada? You are the friend she went to visit, then?"

"Yes."

"I did not expect this as part of the pattern."

"Excuse me?"

Another silence, longer this time, and then Skyla spoke again. "Addisyn was here with me."

As the conversation unfolded, Darius couldn't believe what he was hearing. Addisyn had been far closer than any of them realized, and now, she had gone east.

"New York City?" He shook his head. "Why would she go back there?"

"I do not know. But she left for the airport only a few hours ago."

"The lawsuit." He grabbed at the idea. "It has to be something to do with the lawsuit."

"Lawsuit?" Skyla sighed. "I do not know about a lawsuit, but I do not think that is what is drawing her back either. Perhaps that is indeed the story she tells herself, but it is not the pull."

"What do you mean?"

"I have seen it before." Her voice was rich with wisdom. "It is sometimes so with the birds as well. They take flight in the same place they were wounded."

Darius didn't know how birds related to this conversation, but he had the information he needed. "Well—thank you."

"You are going to find her, is this so?"

"I'm going to try, yes." He put the car in drive.

"This is good. Perhaps you can help her find the path." Skyla hesitated. "You are placed in the pattern, Darius. Hold Addisyn with care."

His throat tightened. "Yes, ma'am. I promise I will."

He thanked Skyla again and ended the call, battling the downtown traffic back toward the airport. So, somewhere in New York, Addisyn was being held hostage by the very fears that had torn them apart. It had to be the lawsuit. And Brian.

The thought of Brian being anywhere near Addisyn made his heart rate lurch into overdrive, hurry nipping at his heels. But an hour later, he'd checked out of the hotel, navigated to the airport, and returned the rental car only to learn that all the flights to New York were booked. His cell phone rang just as he sank into one of the uncomfortable plastic chairs at the airport. He snatched at it and answered without looking.

"Darius?"

Oh, thank God. "Addisyn!"

The tone dipped in apology. "Sorry. It's Avery."

"Avery." He dropped his forehead into his hand as the relief leaked away. "You two sound so much alike."

"I saw I missed a call from you earlier."

"Yes. I'm at the airport now." He sketched the outline of Skyla's information, but when he finished, the phone held only silence. "Avery?"

"I'm here." Avery sighed. "I should have called Skyla. She was the one person—but I just never thought. I mean, she and Addisyn had nothing in common."

"Well, I guess she was with her over the weekend, at least." Darius glanced at the flight board again. "I need a flight to New York, but I can't get out of Denver. Everything's booked."

"They might start grounding flights soon anyway. Did you know about the winter storm?"

"Winter storm?" Darius shook his head. How many more obstacles could be piled on his path?

"The snow has started on the mountains up here. They've already closed Trail Ridge Road over the pass." Worry tightened Avery's voice. "It's not snowing in Estes yet, but we're supposed to get a foot here before tomorrow morning."

"What can I do?" The question was more for himself than Avery.

"Addisyn is in the hands of El Shaddai, Darius. I—I have had to put her there. To stop trying to be everything." Avery's words ached, but they stood strong. "Not easy for me. But I have to trust that He is good and right and holding my sister in His hands. And so—and so I will wait. And pray."

Wait and pray. Darius didn't have time to respond before she spoke again. "Darius—I need to ask you something."

Her tone spilled a shadow over him. "Okay."

"When you find Addisyn—" again a struggling pause, war waging between her words—"tell her that I am very sorry. And that I want her to—to go to Whistler with you."

The meaning behind her words knocked him off guard. "Avery—"

"I'm serious, Darius." Tears trembled in her voice, but there was no denying her conviction. "I've been thinking this through. She will not want to come back here to Estes Park, not after—well, after everything that happened. And I want her to be where—where she is safe. And—and loved." Her voice shrank to a whisper. "It would be best."

"I still think—"

"Please, Darius. Promise me that you will tell her."

"Okay." He wouldn't argue with her further, not when the weight of the words was obviously crushing her. "I'll tell her, Avery."

Long after they ended the call, Darius still sat on the metal chair, Avery's words ringing.

I have to trust…I will wait…and pray…

Maybe it was time for him to do the same thing.

Right there and then, with his options closing and Addisyn missing and his heart breaking, Darius bent his head and prayed. Because neither he nor Avery could protect Addisyn or guide her or stand beside her through whatever lay ahead. There was only one person who could still reach Addisyn now.

God Himself.

CHAPTER 22

New York was exactly as it had always been—streams of blank-faced people and skyscrapers that sealed off the sky and unending noise that shoved its way across Addisyn's soul. The city was a circus, especially compared to the peace of Estes Park. Even the air was heavy, drenched with the odors of car exhaust and asphalt and the spicy food sold in the corner stands. Nothing like the crisp, clean winds of the High Country.

Addisyn checked her watch as she clambered into the backseat of the dingy cab. 8:21. She had thirty-nine minutes before her scheduled surrender.

The driver punched his meter and glanced over his shoulder. "Where you want to go, miss?"

Home. Addisyn crossed her arms, folding her emotions back into herself. "New York Figure Skaters' Agency."

Healing is one choice away…

Skyla's words struck her soul with a force greater than if they'd been audible. Addisyn flinched, startled. The next moment, surprise gave way to sorrow. One choice? Not for her. Not anymore. But—

"Wait." The word tumbled out on its own.

"Yes, miss?"

Now she was acting like Avery, with words and warnings and whatnot. She needed to get to the meeting, needed to push past all this nonsense. But suddenly she knew exactly where to go. "Um, the corner of Fifth and Thirty-fourth, please."

"Sure thing." The taxi driver threaded his way through traffic, and

Addisyn slumped against the slick vinyl seat. What was she doing? Nothing good could come from revisiting that place.

As she stepped out of the taxi, the wind slapped her face like an insult. She paid the man's fare with unsteady hands and then crossed the hectic sidewalk.

The bench was still there. Empty. Waiting.

It was just as elegantly Victorian as always, still resembling something snipped from a Dickens novel. When Addisyn had first visited this spot years ago, she'd thought it the most beautiful seat in the city. It had taken time and truth for her to realize that rust lurked in the wrought-iron corners and that the copper veneer was only cheap paint.

She gripped the arms, the metal throbbing cold beneath her fingers. And then she was sitting on the unforgetting bench. Right next to the ghost of the girl she'd been.

She'd been so young, so naive. So stupid. She'd been running wide open, already scrambling over the protective safeguards Avery had tried to set. Otherwise, she would have never been sitting on this bench.

Next to Brian.

A fresh gust of wind tugged at her jacket. She shivered and forced herself to look at the memories without flinching. She couldn't remember all they had talked about that day. Skating, surely. Competitions, training, performances? Whatever it had been, it had all dissolved when he'd kissed her. For the first time.

The wonder of the kiss, the intensity in his eyes, the feel of his hand on her face—all of it pulled her through a hidden doorway to a world she'd never imagined. She'd stepped across the threshold without ever looking back, never dreaming that what she thought was a fairytale love was actually a bondage that would haunt her for years.

She closed her eyes and let the past come, swooping in on the bitter winds. And the years peeled back, and she was once more the rebellious girl, ready to run. And Brian walked beside her, and she knew the ground was shaky, but she couldn't find a single saving *no*. Not when her lies to Avery weaved more elaborate, more frequent. Not when Brian began inviting her to his house. Not even the first time he told her to...

Addisyn shuddered and forced herself forward.

And then she was saying *yes* to Brian, over and over, even when every time scraped her heart just a little more raw. And then she was driving away in Brian's BMW, a stack of suitcases in the trunk and her sister discarded.

And she was changing her number, the very next day, so that Avery could never find her again. She was submerged in Brian's schemes, the swap of her old and new lives complete. But then she was rising to the surface, gasping for her breath, and she was finally stumbling onto dry ground. And Avery was there, reaching out a second chance, and Addisyn was believing that all the guilt, all the past, would stay right here. On this bench where it all began.

But it hadn't.

It wasn't until she opened her eyes and saw the tears dripping onto the metal that she realized she was crying. Every terrible choice had unraveled from that moment here on this bench. This was the story she'd run a thousand miles west to escape. The one that kept pulling her back to this place, this pain.

And in every real way, she was exactly the same girl who'd sat on the bench. She'd deceived Avery and put herself first and fallen back into Brian's schemes. Just as she always had.

A sob shattered her soul, and then another, and another. The weight of all she had been and still was and had hoped she'd never be groaned like granite upon her shoulders. Skyla had been right. It wouldn't matter how far she ran. Not when she carried the brokenness inside herself.

"It was always me. All along." The wind whipped the words away, but it couldn't take the truth. She'd made the choices that paved the path, and then she'd walked it.

Every single sad step.

And then, through or above or underneath the roiling tumult of the city, she heard it. A single cry. A cry she'd heard—in Colorado. She glanced up just in time to see a whoosh of wings and a regal creature floating to a landing on an office building across the avenue.

A hawk? Here in New York?

She blinked back her tears, peering through despair. The hawk clung to the crown molding over the door of the building, its gaze twisting up and down the street. When it finally settled itself, Addisyn could have sworn it was staring at her.

Goosebumps unrelated to the cold prickled along her arms. She was being ridiculous. This was a coincidence, nothing more. But what had Skyla said?

Messenger birds—carrying warnings from the other world—

"Hey." Addisyn whispered the word. For a fleeting instant she wondered just how crazy she looked, sobbing on a bench and talking to a bird. But the urgency of the moment drowned out concerns for appearances. "Do you—do you have a message for me?"

The moment suspended itself between them, the connection stretching across the street—her with her irrational breathless hope, him with his piercing gaze that willed her to remember.

The hawks are warrior spirits—they fight the darkness—they rescued the lost girl and brought her home—

So maybe the hawks didn't do all that. But if Skyla and Avery were right, there was Someone else Who did.

She'd felt Him, hadn't she? He'd been there when she found Avery again. When she threw her gaze across the sweeping vista of the ice-edged mountains beyond Beaver Meadows. When she stood in Skyla's store and poured out her limping prayer. When she'd kissed Darius beneath the eagles' rising wings. And most certainly when she'd watched Isaiah search for strength.

What if, through every awful moment, His arms had been around her, His hands cradling her heart? She'd resisted and rebelled and run, yet the forces of light that Skyla talked about had invaded her very darkest times.

There is no wound that cannot be healed…if we are willing to be held…

She hadn't been willing. But now, the disjointed harmonies were singing a seamless song that took her breath. Yes, she'd been broken. Yes, she'd been wounded. But all along, healing had indeed been closer than she realized.

She closed her eyes, and it was Avery's face in her mind. Her sister's gentle hands around Isaiah, her shining face cheering him on as he flew. Was that Who God was, after all? The Healer Who salvaged the broken and bound their wings and once more released them into far-flung skies?

One choice.

Even now?

Always one choice.

Always?

The choice to lift hands to Heaven and say…

"Help." The word was a whisper to the sliver of sky over the city. "Help me."

It was all she said, but she somehow knew it was all that was needed. The One her sister called El Shaddai, the Almighty One, could hear her heart. And the simple syllable—confession and consecration and commitment rolled into one—snapped some frozen chain that had pressed against her heart. The wind was still cold and the city was still chaotic and the future was still uncertain. But inside her heart was a growing center of power and peace and purpose. And here on this bench where her life had ended, it was now beginning again.

She was crying once more, but these were quiet tears, healing tears, the overflow of the release. She looked up just in time to see the hawk leap with powerful wings and soar away from the madness of New York, into the gathering clouds.

The wings will rise.

And suddenly she knew exactly what Skyla had meant.

She pulled in her first deep breath and swiped her hand across her cheeks. She wanted to sing or laugh or pray or soar into the clouds beside the hawk. But first, there was something she had to do.

She brushed her hand one more time over the bench as she stood. Then she walked with the straightness of the hawk's flight down the street toward the New York Figure Skaters' Agency.

△△ △△ △△

THE MARBLE BUILDING rose before her like a portal to the past. The carved lions still guarded the entrance, staring sightlessly forward. Addisyn looked away from their curling fangs and stepped through the door.

The receptionist was the same angular woman who'd been there for years. Her gaze didn't rise from her computer screen. "May I help you?"

Addisyn willed the woman to keep looking down. The last thing she wanted was to be recognized. "I have an appointment with Mr. Brian Felding."

"Fourteenth floor." The woman glanced up and blinked. "Hey, aren't you—"

"Thanks." Addisyn shot her a nervous smile and scurried for the elevator. She pressed the button for the fourteenth floor with sweat-slick hands. Her stomach jumped as the elevator began to rise. But her determination didn't waver.

Healing is one choice away…

This was her choice. If Skyla could see her now, she'd be proud. So would Avery.

The elevator dinged. Addisyn headed down the carpeted hallway, trying to steady her breathing. She stepped into the office underneath Brian's stenciled name.

"Hi." A girl about her own age glanced up from behind a paper-piled desk. Brian's secretary, obviously, although not the one he'd had when Addisyn was with him. Her eyes widened slightly. "Um, can I help you?"

"I have an appointment with Bri—Mr. Felding."

The girl's gaze flicked over her face. Addisyn frowned. "Is something wrong?"

"Uh—no. Not at all." The girl picked up a pen, then laid it down again. "He hasn't come in yet this morning. I think his meeting downtown ran long."

"Oh." Part of her was grateful for any reprieve. But the bigger part simply wanted to fast-forward through this whole encounter. "Okay."

"You can have a seat right over there." The girl gestured to a pair of uncomfortable-looking chairs in the corner.

"Thank you." Addisyn perched on the one farthest from Brian's office. Words chased themselves around her mind. What would she say? *Brian, I've changed my mind. Brian, I won't let you do this. Brian, you're not—*

Every option doubled her pulse. She glanced out the window, once again picturing the beating wings. *Help me.*

She didn't know how she would frame it or how he would respond or how she would handle the legal battle that now undoubtedly lay ahead. But no matter what—

"Um, may I ask you something?"

Addisyn glanced up. Had the girl been staring at her the whole time? "Sure."

"You're Addisyn Miles." The girl cleared her throat, unease stretching her words.

Wariness stepped between them. "Yes."

"You, uh, you probably don't remember me." Her smile was tentative. "I worked in the lobby when you were here."

Worked in the lobby…oh, yes. Sure enough, the girl was the same perky receptionist who'd waved to Addisyn each day. "That's right. I do remember." What was her name? Had Addisyn even known?

"Really?" The girl's laugh was still nervous, disjointed. "Well, I, uh, I—" She paused and seemed to swallow down her hesitation. Then she stood abruptly. "Addisyn, I need to talk to you about the whole legal thing. With Mr. Felding."

No. Addisyn's guard slid back into place. Even she knew better than to discuss the lawsuit with a third party. "I really shouldn't—"

"No, please listen to me." There was a pleading in the girl's eyes now, words colliding with each other. She threw a fearful glance toward the door, then locked her gaze onto Addisyn again. "Please, I know it sounds weird. And maybe it doesn't mean anything, but I really think you need to see this."

The temptation tugged at her, but Addisyn stayed in her chair. "If Brian has something I need to see, I'm sure he'll—"

"He won't. Not this. Please, just trust me." Again the girl slid a glance at the door.

Well, could it hurt to see what this girl was so desperate to show her? Addisyn shrugged and crossed the room to the desk. "Okay."

"He'd be furious if he knew I had this." The girl's voice was muffled now as she flicked through a pullout file drawer. "He told me to get rid of it, but—" She slipped out a file and flipped it open. "Here."

The air around Addisyn shattered, shards of disbelief pelting her heart. No! It couldn't be!

"Isn't that your letter?"

Still she couldn't speak, couldn't force any words through the shock. She reached for the paper, and it rustled reassuringly in her hands. Of course it was her letter. There was her signature at the bottom. There were the words of release she'd typed on her little laptop the morning she'd stepped out of Brian's world. And there was a red stamp—received, February 16.

"Maybe it doesn't mean anything." The girl watched Addisyn's silence uncertainly. "But, I don't know, about a month ago, he brought me that letter in some stuff to be shredded. He told me it was just an extra copy, but it didn't seem right to me. I didn't know what to do, so I just put it in that drawer. Then when I heard you were coming in, I thought…"

The letter. Her precious letter. She wouldn't cry here in the office, but she was teetering on the brink. She laid the paper down and impulsively squeezed the girl in a hug. "Thank you."

"Will it help you?" Hope lit a lamp in the girl's expression.

"Will it help?" Addisyn's laugh snagged on a sob. "Yes. It will most definitely help." Relief was breaking over her like a warm wave. She handed the letter back to the girl. "Can you make me a copy of this? And can you make sure the original gets back to my file?"

"Sure." The girl ran the document through a little inkjet on her desk and handed her the copy, the paper still holding a faint warmth. She smiled. "I'm glad I could—"

Footsteps tapped in the hall, and the door flung open. Addisyn felt Brian's presence behind her even before she heard his hard-edged voice. "Addisyn."

Her chest pounded painfully, but she pulled herself straighter. She had nothing to fear from him. Not anymore. "Brian."

"Right this way." He ushered her into his office as if this were a royal reception. Addisyn could feel the girl's gaze on them as Brian stepped in behind her and closed the door.

A wave of shadowed familiarity rose from it all—the mahogany desk, the chevron rug, the beige-striped armchair in the corner. This had been headquarters, when she'd believed they were a team.

The view of the city blinked in the window like a familiar face.

Addisyn walked to the glass and scanned the sharp-stacked skyline. She didn't turn even when she heard his footsteps on the floor behind her. "This is a good call. I've already notified my lawyer. We'll be contacting your attorney on Monday."

The view from the fourteenth floor was dizzying, the ground a long way down.

"Bet it's good to be back in the city. Back home."

New York would never be her home. Her home was riding in Avery's rickety truck, both of them singing along off-key with John Denver. Her home was enfolded in Darius's arms, hearing his heart beat strong and sure for her.

"Well. Here are the papers. You ready?"

She was completely ready. Ready to make her one choice. The fear that had driven her to New York had fled, and the paper was power in her hands. She turned.

"Brian, I'm not signing anything."

His expression rippled with confusion. "What?"

"I am not coming back to this agency. To you. To any of it." Odd, how looking at him now brought no fear, no anger, just a distant detachment.

"Are you crazy?" The expression on his face might have been funny if the stakes weren't so high. "What are you saying?"

"I'm saying you can't do this to me." Every word stood fearless in his face. "You're my past, but you're not going to be my future."

"So you want to do this the hard way? You want to drag this all through the courts?"

"If that's what you think you need to do." She kept her voice even. "But it probably won't get you very far."

"What do you mean?" He stepped toward her, but she didn't back up.

She lifted the paper, her one-way ticket out of his world. "I have a copy of the letter I sent, Brian. I left this agency fair and square." She paused, watching shock chase itself across his face. "I did not break my contract. And I don't owe you anything."

"How did you get that?" He tripped over his mistake. "It's false. I can prove it. I'll take you to court and make sure everybody—"

"But other things could come up in court, you know." The playing field had finally tilted. "Like the fact that you were controlling and manipulative. Or that you pushed me into a wall. Or maybe that you didn't acknowledge receiving my letter of—"

"Are you threatening me?"

His anger was the same grenade it had always been, but finally she wasn't afraid to pull the pin. "No." She shrugged. "Just thinking out loud."

"You're not going to get away with this." He spit the words in her direction. "I won't let you think that you can—"

"Do what you like, Brian." The wings were rising, carrying her far above his ground-level life. "But I've made my choice. I'm going home to the High Country."

"Home to the High Country?" A harsh laugh jerked loose. "Addisyn, don't you hear yourself? You're starting to sound like your sister!"

Her grin probably infuriated him further, but she couldn't help it. "Oh, I hope so."

He slammed his hand against the desk, his curse ripping through the air between them. The next instant, the office door opened, and the girl peered around the corner. "I'm sorry, but—is everything okay?" Her eyes were on Addisyn.

"Everything is fine." Addisyn sidestepped Brian and walked toward the door. "I was just leaving."

"You've lost your mind." Brian hissed the words after her.

No, she had found her wings. Addisyn paused with her hand on the knob and glanced at the girl. "Thank you."

The secret glowed in the girl's smile. "Have a *very* nice day, Addisyn Miles."

Hallway, elevator, all of it leading her out, every step part of her way forward. As she crossed the lobby for the last time, the receptionist called to her. "Hey, I remember you now! You're Brian Felding's girl."

"No." Addisyn shook her head, the truth still buoyant in her heart. "Not anymore."

She stepped past the stone-eyed lions into the wind where the wings soared. She didn't see the hawk again. Of course not. His message had already been delivered.

There was so much to be done, so much to be said, in a future that would be shaped by the same merciful hands that appeared in Skyla's painting. But there was really only one way to start. Addisyn pulled out her phone and punched the number. One ring, two rings, and there was the magic of his beautiful voice. "Addisyn?"

"Darius. It's me." The smile began deep in her soul. There was nothing holding her back now. No wounds to work their way between her and this man that she loved more with every sunrise.

"Addisyn." Fear and relief wrestled in his tone. "Are you okay? I've been trying to call—"

That was Darius, every time, and Addisyn basked in the caress of his concern. "I'm okay. Really and truly okay."

Silence, and then he released a long breath. "Thank God. You're— where are you?"

"I'm in New York." She looked up at the sliver of sky between the skyscrapers. How high would that hawk have flown by now? "But I'm coming home."

⩕ ⩕ ⩕

ADDISYN ALREADY HAD the text typed on her phone. Once she made it through security at Denver International Airport, all she had to do was press SEND on the two words that had been waiting on her screen.
I'm here.

She pocketed her phone and stood near the wall, watching the river of humanity from the shore, waiting for a familiar face in the current. And then she heard her name, and Darius was shouldering his way to her.

Her heart jerked at the sight of him. What had she done to deserve a guy who cared so deeply for her? How could she have let him go? She wanted to run to him, but awkwardness chained her to the wall.

He stopped inches from her, his smile shielding the deep emotions that stirred in his eyes. "You're here."

She swallowed down the nervousness, wringing the words from her soul. "Darius—I'm sorry. For letting you down and for not telling you about the lawsuit. And Brian." She studied the floor between them. "I was—really embarrassed. And afraid. But still, I shouldn't—I mean, that's no excuse for—"

He stepped forward, and then his arms were around her, safe and strong. Her explanation died as she relaxed into his embrace.

"Addisyn, you don't have to apologize." He brushed his hand over her hair. "I just wish I had known so I could have helped you."

"I didn't want you to be pulled into my mess." She clung to him more tightly, as if the memories might tug her away. "I didn't want to be a burden, or for you to feel like you had to—"

"Hey." His voice was soft, every word soothing the tender places of her heart. "You could never be a burden. And nothing you could tell me would ever chase me away." His tone lifted slightly. "So next time, maybe let me know before you run off to New York, okay?"

The laughter washed the tension from the moment. She lifted her head to meet his eyes. "Okay. But I'm not going back to New York."

"I'm glad." He was searching her face for the story. "What happened?"

"Well, a hawk happened. And a letter. And God." Addisyn laughed again at the question marks in his eyes. "I'll tell you everything later."

"Then I'll take a rain check on the details." Darius stepped back but kept his arm protectively around her shoulders. "For now, we need to figure out where we're going to go before everything is socked in."

"Oh, the winter storm!" With everything else that had happened, the snow threat had slipped between the cracks of her mind. "Is it still coming?"

"Any time now. When I talked to Avery earlier, she told me it was already snowing in the High Country."

Avery. Her sister's name settled across her shoulders. "So—when you talked to Avery—how is she?"

"Worried, mostly."

Of course she was. Leaving had been a selfish move. Addisyn bit her bottom lip. "Does she know where I am?"

"Not yet. I thought you might want to be the one to tell her that."

Shame prickled against her, pushing her farther from her sister. How could she tell Avery anything? Before she could respond, Darius spoke again. "She told me earlier—she made me promise to tell you something. If I found you."

Addisyn's stomach flipped. What message had Avery sent? Judgment? Warning?

"She said that she'd handled some things badly, and she was sure you wouldn't want to go back to Estes Park." There was a serious slant to his tone. "So she said she wanted you to go to Whistler. Where you would be—safe." His arm tightened around her shoulders. "Protected. Cared for."

"Avery said that?"

"Yes."

The options tugged at her from opposite angles. She could catch the next flight to Vancouver with Darius and never again have to face the relationship she'd ripped. Or she could retrace her steps to the mountains and this time, bring healing instead of hurt.

"So what do you want to do?" Darius was watching her, waiting to catch her response.

Only one choice felt right in her hands. "I want to get my car." Addisyn glanced out the concourse window. The mountains were cloud-covered, but she knew where they rose. "And then I want to see my sister."

△△　△△　△△

THE CLOUDS PRESSED lower the farther north they drove. Somewhere just before Longmont, the first snowflakes spattered the windshield.

"Guess it's starting for the Front Range now." Darius turned on the windshield wipers. He'd insisted on driving, and Addisyn had yielded with no reluctance.

"Can we make it?"

"I think so." Darius's hands were still relaxed on the wheel.

"But what about the mountain road?"

"Hey." He tossed her a reassuring grin. "You have a pro driver, remember? A little bit of snow can't stop us."

"Pro driver?"

"You bet." He switched the windshield wipers to a higher setting. "Canadians know how to do snow, girl."

"Well, I guess that's true."

When he reached a hand across the console, she gladly slipped her fingers between his. Really, she couldn't worry about the weather, not when Darius made her feel so safe. And anyway, it was rather beautiful driving in the snow, watching the whiteness tangle in the treetops and smooth every sharp edge. Like grace, Avery might have said.

Grace. Addisyn let herself rest in the warmth of the car and the wizardry of the snow. It was still amazing—that divine hands were willing to bind her wounds, that Love Himself was gathering her broken wings.

How much had she missed trying to fight her own way forward? She'd pushed away Skyla's wisdom and Avery's faith and Darius's love. She rested her gaze on the sight of their linked hands. It was a mistake she prayed she'd never make again.

"Lyons." Darius's voice scattered her thoughts. He nodded at the town sign. "How much farther?"

"Half an hour, but it's Highway 36. The worst section." Addisyn reached for her phone. "We have cell service here. I'm going to call Laz, let him know we're coming."

One ring. Two rings. What was that crazy old man doing? Three rings, and then Laz's familiar drawl came through the line. "Live Bigger Outdoor Supply, Laz speaking."

"Laz." Addisyn grinned at Darius. "It's Addisyn."

"Addisyn?" His voice hollowed with disbelief. "Good Lord, girl, what's going on?"

"I'm on my way back home."

"Back home? Back here to Estes?"

Addisyn laughed. "Yes." For the first time, the mountains didn't seem out of reach. "So, um, is Avery working today?"

"She asked for the afternoon off. Her birthday an' all, y'know. I think she went hiking."

Well, that fit Addisyn's plan even better. "She went in the snow?"

"She left earlier. It didn't start here 'til 'bout thirty minutes ago. Anyhow, you know yer sister, Miz Addisyn."

Yes, her sister, the mountain girl. "Then I'll see her this evening."

"She loves you, y'know." Laz coughed. "Remember that the next time you wanna go traipsin' off somewhere."

"I know." Addisyn's throat pinched. "I love her too."

"So where you been?"

"Oh—all over. New York City, most recently."

"New York—"

"I'll tell you the story later." She would rapidly reach the end of the unspooling cell service. "We're driving back now."

"*We?* Who's *we?*"

"Me and Darius."

"Darius? The boyfriend?"

Addisyn laughed self-consciously. "Well—"

"Yes." Darius leaned closer to the phone and winked at Addisyn. "The boyfriend."

The flutter that tingled through her nearly drowned out Laz's next question. "In this storm?"

"Yes." *The boyfriend,* he'd said. *The boyfriend.* Darius was her—

"Now, hold on. That ain't safe. That clicking sound—"

"I got the car fixed." The hard way, but it was still true.

"You don't have snow chains."

"We can make it before it gets too bad."

"You are a stubborn one, y'know that?" Laz huffed. "Yer sister is a saint to put up with yer shenanigans."

Addisyn laughed. "Yes. She is. Now, I'm almost out of cell service, but I'm going to need your help when I get back." Darius nodded at her encouragingly. "I have a plan."

Five minutes later she'd explained the details to Laz, and he was as excited as she was. "That's perfect. I'll be there. Now, be careful. I ain't comin' to dig you two out of a ditch somewhere."

"We'll be careful." Addisyn gripped her seat as Darius made the turn onto the narrow, cliff-edged highway that soared straight through the mountains to Estes Park. Finally, after all these years, she was going up. "Bye for now, Laz."

The snow was more intense now, the flakes flinging themselves at the windshield, but the little car held its footing. "Hey, Addisyn." Darius didn't take his eyes off the road, but his voice held a smile.

She turned in her seat, savoring the sight of him. "Yeah?"

"So, there's this girl I like."

"A girl?" She could play along. "What's she like?"

"Beautiful. Sweet. Caring. Brave." Every word was like a kiss. "She's something else."

"You know, I think I met her once." Addisyn leaned back into the seat. "But I don't remember her being any of those things."

"Hmm. Maybe you don't know her like I do." Darius raised his eyebrow at her. "Oh, and she has a real thing for coffee. She drinks way too much of it."

Addisyn laughed. "Cuban lattes?"

"Now would I like a girl who didn't drink Cubans? Dealbreaker right there." He hesitated, the laughter fading to something deeper. "I've got just one problem."

"What's that?"

A pullout appeared in the whirling whiteness. Darius maneuvered the car next to the protective rock cliff, then leaned over the console, his heart reflected in his eyes. "Well, see, I'm in love with this girl. But I don't know for sure how she feels about me."

Snow wrapped its silence around the moment, and Addisyn searched for a deep breath. Then she gently took his face in her hands. The face of this beautiful man who had never given up on her.

"She likes you. A lot." She rested her forehead against his and closed her eyes, holding out the truth she'd harbored for so long. "She thinks—she's in love with you too."

"Really?" His hands covered hers. "That's the best news ever."

This time when he kissed her, the moment held a promise deeper than she'd imagined. When he finally pulled back, she shook her head, tears stirring with her smile. "Darius. How am I so blessed to have you?"

His eyes were shining too. "Seems like I'm the blessed one." He kissed her one more time, then brushed his thumb over her cheek. "Now. Let's get you back to the mountains."

"Yes." She laughed, the rush of joy sweeping her upward. "To the mountains."

The snow was continuing to strengthen, the wipers chasing each other at high speed. Outside the window, the white blurred the landscape into blankness, the only visible elements the stretch of road just ahead and the ghosts of the hillsides on each side. In twenty minutes, they were at the top of the pass, and the wind howled around the corner of the mountain. Addisyn sucked in her breath as the car skidded slightly. "Darius!"

"It's okay." His voice was still calm. "I'm going to get you there."

But she could see his hands tightening on the wheel. The road was beginning to crust over. "I think there's ice in this now."

"There may be. But Canadian snow powers, remember?" A reassuring smile shaped his words. "Just trust."

Trust. She drew a deep breath. *Help us get back home.*

Surely they were close. Any minute now—

The car crept around a curve, and then she could see it, like a sentry in the snow. The rock-hewn sign. ESTES PARK.

She squealed in excitement as Darius laughed and slapped the wheel. "Yes! We made it!"

In the valley below, the town spread out like a fairy world, the lights twinkling through the snow. They were almost home now. All they had to do was follow the light.

CHAPTER 23

It hadn't been much of a birthday so far.

Even with her heart wrung dry, Avery had forced herself to move forward with her plans for the day. She'd taken the afternoon off from the store and started hiking from Glacier Gorge. She'd planned to climb all the way to Timberline Falls, nine miles roundtrip. But at the spur trail for Mills Lake—not even halfway to her destination—the wind had felt damp, the air pressing down with the strange weight that came before a storm. The first flakes had landed on her shirt only minutes later. She'd decided to turn around, but the snow had become uncomfortably heavy long before she reached the parking area.

And now the snow was intensifying, flocking the trees and shrinking the scenery and swirling in the old truck's peering headlights. Riding her brakes around a curve, Avery was thankful for her tire chains. Driving in weather like this wasn't something she loved about a Colorado winter.

She needed to focus on the positive. Even if she'd had to abbreviate the hike, it had still been good—and good for her. She was trying to once more find the rhythm that was healing to her heart. Hiking was cleansing, restoring, invigorating. A time for her to talk to El Shaddai. To pray for her sister. To make peace with her own soul. And to do the hardest thing, the one she'd been working at since her realization on Deer Mountain— to wait.

The truck skidded slightly on the winding road, and Avery realized she was gripping the wheel. She relaxed her fingers with a wry smile. Gripping would probably always be her knee-jerk response. Any time she felt her world tilting, she'd likely still cling with frantic fists. But at least now she knew she could choose a different reaction.

El Shaddai—get me home.

The wipers could barely keep up now, the snow smearing across the windshield. Avery turned her defroster on, squinting through the blurring white until she saw her mailbox, waving her home. Thank goodness. The house would be dark and empty, but at least it would be shelter.

A light blinked through the storm as she rounded the final curve of her driveway. Headlights? Someone else was out in this weather? As she drew closer, she could just make out the bulk of Laz's beefy truck parked by the porch.

Laz? Her heart rate shifted into high gear. Only a serious issue could have brought him out in this kind of weather. Something urgent. Or something he hadn't wanted to tell her over the phone. Was it Isaiah? *El Shaddai, no. Not today.*

She yanked on her parking brake and swung open the truck door just as Laz emerged from his vehicle. "Laz!" She snatched her still-damp coat from the passenger seat and shrugged into it. "What's going on?"

His face was a blank page, no emotions to read. "Been waitin' on you to drive up."

"Why?" The snowflakes were sticking to her eyelashes. She blinked and wiped the back of her arm over her face.

And then his grin, bright enough to cut through the storm. "Jes' got me a surprise for your birthday, Miz Avery." He looked over his shoulder at the house, then once more indulged in a knowing grin. "I think you'll like it."

A surprise for her birthday? Avery donned the best smile she could muster and brushed the snow from her coat. "Really?" The only thing she had wanted for her birthday was for her sister to come home, but she kept that thought to herself. "Well, let's see what it is."

"Come on inside first." He squinted at the sky. "Looks like the Good Lord's shakin' His down pillows out here."

Avery laughed, and together they waded through the snow into the house. In the mudroom, she peeled off her jacket and kicked her wet boots aside, then turned to Laz expectantly.

He brushed some snow from his beard and jerked his head. "Keep goin'."

Surprise burst upon her as she turned the corner to the living room. In front of the wall, a backdrop of balloons bobbed as if too excited to stand still. Streamers swooped from the antler chandelier. And a roaring flame was snapping its fingers in the fireplace.

Darius stood up from the couch, a sheepish smile on his face. "Hello, Avery."

"Darius—Laz—" What was going on? Confusion tangled in her laugh. "How did you get—"

"Well, they had some help."

Avery spun toward the voice just as Addisyn stepped out from the corner, holding a birthday cake and smiling with a tentative hope. "Happy twenty-fifth, A."

Joy collided with her soul, sending the shadows spinning away. "Oh, Ads!" Laz gave a knowing grin and took the cake from Addisyn, but Avery ignored him as she flung her arms around her sister. "You came back." She squeezed her eyes against the prick of tears and hid her face in her sister's shoulder, the tension in her soul uncoiling.

"I did." Addisyn's arms tightened around her. She cleared her throat and stepped back just enough to meet Avery's eyes. "I mean, obviously. Surely you didn't think I would forget your birthday."

The joy bubbled up in a healing release of laughter. Avery glanced around the room, then found Addisyn's eyes again. "And you did all this. It's beautiful."

"Well, there's a lot to celebrate." The glow was strong behind Addisyn's gaze. "Come on, A." She grabbed Avery's hand and tugged her toward the dining room. "Dinner will get cold."

"Dinner." Avery glanced at Laz and Darius, who were both watching and smiling from the corner. "Who cooked it?"

"Now, Miz Avery, we decided you'd been through enough without either Miz Addisyn or myself tryin' to do some kind of kitchen magic." Laz guffawed as they circled the table. "But as it turns out, yer sister's boyfriend is one mean chili cook."

THE BIRTHDAY DINNER couldn't have been better—chili and friends and easy conversation. And her sister. Finally Avery pushed back her chair. "The chili was great, Darius. I need a few minutes before the cake." Hesitation dragged at her words when she glanced at Addisyn. "Could we—would you mind talking for a minute?"

"Sure." Addisyn jumped up. "Living room?"

As soon as Avery sank onto the couch, Addisyn flopped beside her and leaned into her the way she'd done as a little girl. "A. I'm so, so sorry."

"Oh, Ads." Avery pulled her closer and sighed. "I'm really sorry too. You were—you were right. What you said—that night. I didn't know I was doing it, but I put you in a cage."

"Sometimes cages are good." Addisyn drew her knees up, tucking her feet under her. "Sometimes they make a safe space. A place to heal."

Addisyn was being gracious. Avery lowered her head. "I did want you to heal. I wanted to keep you safe. And close. But instead, I pushed you away. Just like before."

"No." Addisyn shook her head. "It's my fault. I wanted to—I don't know, do my own thing, I guess. I didn't do anything you wanted me to."

"But that's just it, Ads. Your life is between you and El Shaddai." The fire snapped, a shower of sparks swirling up the chimney. "So, I told Him finally—that I would give Him control. Wait for Him to work."

Addisyn's smile started in her eyes. "Well, I think He answered your prayer."

"What do you mean?"

"I mean—I had an—an encounter with Him." Addisyn shrugged shyly. "It was—it was pretty cool."

"An encounter?" Avery watched the light flicker over her sister's face.

"Yeah. I wanted so badly to have a new start, A. But after Brian—" She rolled her eyes and flicked her hand. "That's why I left." A shadow dropped over her expression. "I didn't want you to suffer because of me."

The realization splintered Avery's heart. All the times she'd thought Addisyn difficult or distracted, her sister had been carrying burdens bigger than what she'd comprehended. "Oh, Ads." She gripped her sister's hand.

"I'm so sorry."

"So, I thought if I went back to Brian, he'd leave you alone. But—" Addisyn grinned. "I don't think we have to worry about him."

"What do you mean?"

"I'll tell you the whole story later. It's incredible." The light was returning to Addisyn's face. "But the best part is I finally realized what you and Skyla were talking about. About how God makes people new." A holy kind of awe traced through her words. "I believe—He did that for me."

"Addisyn, that's wonderful!" Amazement and gratitude mingled in Avery's laugh. "See what happens when I get out of the way." She tilted her head. "So that's why you came back?"

"Well"—Addisyn's eyes sparked with a teasing glint—"no, actually I came back because I realized I couldn't spend the rest of my life without your pizza."

Avery laughed. "So I'm indispensable, is that it?"

"Something like that, yeah. I mean, that pizza really is incredible." Her tone was still teasing, but her eyes held something much deeper. "I kind of decided I didn't want to lose you."

The unspoken words made Avery smile. "You know something? I don't really want to lose you either." She shrugged. "Who else is going to remind me to have spontaneous sidewalk dance parties?"

Addisyn giggled. "Or beat you at Go Fish?"

"Exactly. Or go shopping downtown. Or listen to me talk about hawks all day." Avery slipped her arm around Addisyn's shoulders. "That's why El Shaddai made us sisters. He knew we needed each other."

"Yes." The fire crackled for a few more seconds before Addisyn spoke again. This time, there was a serious undertone to her words. "I don't want us to be separated again, A."

"Well—about that." Avery angled herself to meet Addisyn's worried gaze. "See, I kind of realized something while you were gone."

"Yeah?"

She spoke slowly, fitting her thoughts to words. "The only kind of distance that can really separate us is the kind that starts in here." She tapped her finger over Addisyn's heart. "If we stay close there—well, it won't matter where we are in the world." She grinned and leaned back, sliding a sideways glance at Addisyn. "Even if I'm, you know, chasing hawks in Colorado, and you're, say, in Whistler, with this really good-looking guy."

Addisyn flushed scarlet and glanced down, but not before Avery caught her smile. "Uh—well."

"He loves you."

Addisyn looked up suspiciously. "Thought you didn't like him."

"Yeah, well, that's another place I was wrong." Avery felt the sheepishness in her smile. "He's—he's not Brian."

"I know." Addisyn picked at a loose thread on her shirt and glanced over her shoulder toward the dining room. "He's great. But—I should have told you about us skating. I thought—I was sure you would be upset. I know you never liked my skating."

"No, Ads." Avery waited until her sister met her gaze. "I blamed skating for taking you away. It wasn't true, but it was how I felt. And I haven't been there for that part of your life. But I want that to change."

"Really?" Hope stirred in Addisyn's eyes.

"Definitely." Avery smiled. "You know, I'm getting ready to have a lot of free time. Off season at the store, and winter, and all that."

Knowing dawned in Addisyn's eyes. "And?"

"And I think I might like to go to British Columbia sometime this winter. Check out the hiking there. See some other mountains. Maybe visit my fabulous figure skating sister." Avery poked at her. "If she wanted me to come."

The light behind Addisyn's eyes had never been stronger. "I know she would."

"We can go hiking."

"There are some awesome trails there."

"I'm sure." Avery laughed. "We can take selfies from the top."

"Yes. And that reminds me—" Addisyn grinned and reached for a grocery bag on the coffee table. "Your birthday present. I've had it for a month."

"A month?" Avery dropped her jaw in mock amazement. Addisyn was famous for scrambling for gifts last-minute. "No way."

"Hey, Darius can vouch for me. I bought part of it in Whistler." She grimaced and tapped the plastic bag. "Ignore my wrapping job."

Avery laughed and reached into the flimsy sack. Something rough brushed her hand. What would Addisyn have—

Her breath fled as the plastic fell away. The photo frame was solid, hand-carved wood. Something that would last through the years. Avery brushed her finger over the mountain design.

And inside the frame—the photo from that day in Beaver Meadows. When they'd heard the bugles and hiked the trail. The two of them held in the arms of the mountains, laughing into each other's eyes.

"Look at the back." Addisyn bounced slightly on the couch.

Avery flipped the frame over, and from the cardboard backing, Addisyn's handwriting leaped out.

To Avery. Sisters Strong!
— Ads

Tears were spilling over the edge of her heart. Avery gently set the frame on the table and pulled Addisyn into her arms. "It's perfect, Addisyn." Her emotions drew the words to a whisper. "Thank you."

"I'm glad you like it." When Addisyn finally leaned back, Avery saw she was swiping at her eyes too. "I figured it was time for us to have a new picture." She gave a sheepish shrug. "I mean, I know it's not the same as the old one, but…"

Avery glanced from the photo to her sister's beautiful face. Her wonderful, courageous sister who was finally finding her wings. Again, the emotions swelled in her throat. "No. It's not the same." She gripped Addisyn's hands. "But you know something?"

"What?"

"I think it's even better."

"Gals?" Laz's voice made them both jump. He peered around the corner and coughed. "Sorry to interrupt, but if you two don't come on, Darius and I are gonna hafta eat all this cake ourselves."

"IT'S THE PERFECT day for this." Addisyn dug her hands into her coat pockets.

"Couldn't be better!" Avery's face had that mountain glow again, peace in her smile and a dream behind her eyes. "Clear and just a little bit of wind. Not much like last week."

"That's for sure." Addisyn squinted up at the watery winter sunshine. The snow from the storm had dwindled to patches under the trees, and the wind had tamed itself in the pines.

Yes, this week was nothing like the last. Because the storm was finally over.

"Just think. Almost three months from the time he came to us, and now Isaiah is going free." Avery peered through the slats of the flight cage. "I had a knowing when I met him."

"Yeah?"

"Yeah. I didn't realize what it meant for a long time." Avery leaned against the side of the cage. "But I think I do now."

"Well?" Addisyn grinned. "I want to know."

"I'll tell you. Later." Avery took a sip from the Styrofoam cup she held and tilted her head. "Hmm. You were right, Ads. Coffee's really not that bad."

Addisyn laughed. "I thought I was hallucinating when I saw a coffeemaker in my sister's kitchen. I guess I converted you."

"Not so fast. Hot cocoa is definitely better." Avery took another sip and smiled. "But I could get used to this."

Addisyn held out her own cup. "To Isaiah."

"To Isaiah." Avery bumped their cups and gazed toward the High Country. "May he have fearless flight."

"And winds in his favor." Addisyn glanced back toward the store. "Why isn't Laz up here yet?"

"He was still loading the SUV with Chay and Skyla. And Darius, of course." A smirk tugged at Avery's expression.

"What?" Addisyn bit her lip to keep her smile from peering through. "Why are you looking at me like that?"

"Oh, no reason." Avery's eyes rounded with mock innocence. "I just think it's so nice that Darius used his vacation time to stay in Estes Park for a week. All to help us with Isaiah."

The smile escaped before she could yank it back. "Avery, if you embarrass me around him, I swear I will—"

"Embarrass you?" Avery's eyes danced. "Good grief, Addisyn, I'm your sister. Embarrassing you is practically my job description."

"Well, as good a job as you're doing, you deserve a raise." The laughter was easy between them.

"It's just so wonderful to see someone be as dedicated to conservation as Darius is." Avery's giggles escaped between her words. "He's really developed a passion for raptors all of a sudden."

"Avery!" Addisyn forced seriousness into her features and lunged at her sister, but Avery sidestepped her, the fun sparkling in the air between them. "If you say one more word about Darius—"

"Did I hear my name?" Darius strolled up behind them.

Addisyn slanted one more glare at Avery, but her sister just raised her eyebrows and took another drink of coffee. She sighed and turned to Darius. "Hey. Is everything loaded?"

"Just about. Laz is finishing up the rest." Darius's usual beanie was blue today, bringing out the color of his eyes. He peered between the slats of the cage and whistled at Isaiah. "Avery, you did a great job with him."

"Not really." Avery smiled and shrugged. "I just gave him the space to heal."

An upbeat jingle invaded the moment. Addisyn jumped and reached into her pocket. "My phone? I never have service here."

"Do you need to take that?" Avery glanced at her.

An unknown number, from—New York City. Addisyn's stomach knotted itself. What now? "Um—yeah. Give me just a minute."

Avery nodded and turned back toward Darius. Addisyn paced to the edge of the trees before she swiped on the call. "Hello?"

"Is this Miss Miles?" The man's voice was thick with a New York accent.

"Yes." The trees bent over her, waiting for his next words.

"Miss Miles, this is Angelo Barmilli at the New York Figure Skaters' Agency. How are you today?"

"Fine, sir." Well, she had been until he called. She glanced over her shoulder at Avery and Darius, happily oblivious with Isaiah. What terrible timing. "How are you?"

"I'm well." His sigh dropped between them. "It has come to my attention that one of our coaches has been threatening potential legal action against you."

"Yes, sir." Her pulse throbbed in her neck. "Brian Felding, sir."

"Yes, so I understand. I was unaware of this—action—until yesterday, when I received a call from Mitch Shapiro at the Rising Stars Foundation."

Mitch?

"He informed me that you had reached out to him regarding this issue with your contract, but he had been out of town and didn't receive your communication until Monday. He was very—displeased—to hear of Mr. Felding's threatened action." He cleared his throat. "As a matter of fact, I may as well be blunt. He was so opposed to the idea of a former Rising Stars skater facing legal action that he threatened to remove his support from our agency."

Hope was peering between the trees, but Addisyn wouldn't look at it yet, not until she could read what lay under Mr. Barmilli's words. "Really, sir?"

"Yes. And following his phone call, I looked into the matter myself. As I said, that was the first I'd heard of it. I quickly came to the realization that any legal threats were completely groundless. Your letter of resignation is on record in your file—"

Yes.

"Thus, I hope you will accept my full apologies."

Groundless. The word swiped a sunrise across her heart. "Of—of course, sir. I appreciate your calling."

"Please be assured that I was completely unaware of Mr. Felding's drastic action and would not have sanctioned it had I known. He will be facing disciplinary action in the coming days."

"I see." She couldn't say any more and still keep the victory from her voice.

"I wish you all the best, Miss Miles." The man's voice took on an almost fatherly tone. "The agency will be sending you a letter in the coming days to formally recognize your amicable separation. If you should ever wish to return, you would be most welcome. Again, I'm sorry for any distress this may have caused you."

"Thank you." The last shadows were clearing, the relief ricocheting through her. "I appreciate this very much."

As soon as the call ended, she flung both arms in the air and screamed in a way that brought Avery and Darius scrambling out of the flight cage. The news nearly lifted her off the ground as she sprinted toward them.

"Addisyn!" Her sister reached her first, confusion and concern rippling across her expression. "What's happened?"

Finally, she had something wonderful to tell Avery. She gripped her sister's shoulders, the excitement shoving past her words. "Avery. That was Barmilli. He's the head of my old agency."

"What did he say?" Darius's hand rested reassuringly on her shoulder.

"He said—" Laughter slipped out instead of her words. She brushed at the springing tears and shook her head. "He said—he did an investigation. The legal threat was—groundless. He's sending me a letter saying so." Again, the laughter spiraled into the cold air. "And it sounds like Brian is going to be in some hot water too."

"What? Are you serious?" Avery waited for Addisyn's nod before she gave a whoop that could have been heard in Lyons and swung her sister off the ground. "Yes!"

"So there, A." Addisyn squeezed her sister in another hug, longer this time. "It's all good now."

"What's goin' on up here?" Laz's voice bellowed. "Miz Avery, are you tryin' to scare that bird to death by screamin' yer fool head off?"

"Laz!" Avery stepped back, tears and laughter tugging her in turns, and hurried toward him. "You've got to hear this!"

As Avery and Laz stood at the edge of the clearing, Addisyn smiled at Darius. "It's my new start."

"Yes." He slipped his hands into hers and pulled her closer. "But you already had your new start, you know. Whatever happened with this wouldn't have changed a thing."

The truth of his words soothed her soul. "I know." She looped her arms around his neck and let him pull her into the safe circle of his embrace.

"You know what else this means?"

"What?" She was watching the mountains over his shoulder. The snow caught the sunlight in a way that was nothing short of dazzling.

"You know that event isn't till January. Still two months away."

Addisyn drew back just enough to meet his eyes. "So you're saying—"

"I'm saying that as long as my skating partner could find time in her schedule, we could still make it happen."

If she were any happier, she'd be flying with Isaiah. "I think she could."

His eyes lingered on hers. "Would you be okay? To skate again, I mean?"

Addisyn turned the idea over and felt only peace. "Yes. Things are changing, Darius."

"They definitely are." He ran a hand over her hair, his words a warm breath against her face. "You know something?"

"What?"

"I think this is an extraordinary day for a new beginning."

"Hmm." The mountains laughed, and she did too. "I think you're right."

She tilted her face, and his lips met hers, the kiss born from the glittering mountains and the ice-edged air and the wings rising behind them both. Finally Darius pulled away and brushed her hair back. "There's your sister coming. But we will finish this conversation later."

Addisyn laughed and stepped back just as Avery and Laz walked up. Laz's smile was stretched into a knowing smirk, but he simply clapped Darius on the back. "Well, son, I think ever'thin' is ready."

As Laz made conversation with Darius, Avery raised her eyebrows and leaned over Addisyn's shoulder. "Like I said. Very interested in the hawk, isn't he?"

"Oh, honestly, A." Addisyn bumped her sister's arm. "You saw nothing."

"Right." Avery laughed. "Don't worry. I won't tease you. Can't answer for Laz, though." Before Addisyn could respond, she clapped her hands and headed toward the enclosure. "All right, everybody. We've got a bird to release."

ADDISYN SLID CLOSER to Darius as the SUV nosed down the rutted dirt road. She glanced over her shoulder at Avery and Skyla in the row of seats behind them. "How's Isaiah?"

"Restless." Avery grinned, then grabbed for Isaiah's crate as the car lurched through another pothole.

"He can feel the freedom." Skyla nodded at Avery, bracing Isaiah's box from the other side. "He is ready."

"Where are we taking him again?" Darius worked his fingers between Addisyn's.

She gripped his hand and smiled. "Lumpy Ridge." She peered through the tunnel of trees, but she couldn't see the rock formations yet. "Hawks love it there." She leaned forward as much as her seatbelt would allow. "Right, Chay?"

"Yes!" Chay swung the wheels to the left, and Addisyn caught a glimpse of the pothole they'd avoided. "Lumpy Ridge is a target area. Prime nesting habitat, too. We release a lot of our birds there."

"Only 'bout ten more minutes now." Laz grimaced and grabbed the dashboard as another jolt crunched through the car. "'Less, of course, Chay kills us all first on this here road."

It was under ten minutes when the road blurred into a mountain meadow fringed with pines. The bizarrely stacked rock outcroppings of Lumpy Ridge juggled themselves behind the trees. "Okay." Chay cut the motor and smiled expectantly over his shoulder. "Let's do this."

As Laz and Chay carried Isaiah's box to the center of the clearing, Addisyn moved closer to Avery and studied her sister. "Are you excited or sad?"

"Well—" Avery glanced at Darius, and then her eyes found Addisyn's again. "I want the very best for him. So I really can't be sad."

The unspoken truth beneath Avery's words squeezed her heart. "Really?"

"Really."

The wind was more restless now, tugging at the trees. Addisyn watched the pines scrape against the sky. "But what about him? Will he be nervous to go, A?"

Avery cocked her head. "What do you think?"

There were so many emotions to sort through. Addisyn shrugged. "I think—maybe."

"Well, he might feel a little uneasy. He's gotten used to a cage, after all." Avery draped her arm reassuringly over Addisyn's shoulders. "But I think he will be very excited. This is what he was born for, you know."

Her wonderful sister who had always been her wings. Addisyn worked the words past the emotion caught in her throat. "Thanks, A."

"Of course." Avery kept her arm around Addisyn's shoulders as they walked toward the rest of the group. "And I'm serious about coming to Whistler, you know."

"Definitely." Addisyn laughed. "Dance party on the sidewalk?"

"It's a date!"

Chay rubbed his hands together as they approached. "Everyone ready?"

"Isaiah is." Skyla raised the camera slung around her neck and snapped a shot of the cliffs, then smiled. "The wind is calling him."

"Well then, let's get to it." Chay glanced around the group. "First, though, I want to thank each of you. You've all played a role in this healing."

Beside Addisyn, Darius squeezed her hand.

"The ancients believed that we are surrounded by a holy temple. That love and joy and wisdom wait in every corner of the world." The mountains leaned closer, listening to Chay's words. "And I see that more and more clearly with every hawk we help. Each one has a story that mirrors our own. We've been blessed to live Isaiah's journey alongside him."

"Yes." Avery's whisper was soft. Addisyn glanced at her sister to see her nodding upward, as if sharing a secret with the sky.

Skyla stepped forward. "And now we must pray for the power. For us to open our hands, and for the wings to rise. And to be thankful for the blessing we are given, to receive the calling that compels us to look to the sky." She glanced at Laz. "The prayer should come from you."

"Me?" Laz's face colored a dull red. "I ain't much for prayin' out loud—"

"Please, friend." Chay put his arm around Skyla and nodded at Laz.

"Pray for the bird. Pray for us all."

"Waalll, then." Laz cleared his throat and swiped off his trapper's hat. "Lord God, we come here today lovin' this world You've made. We come thankin' You that healin' happens. That no broken wing goes unnoticed by You."

He paused and sniffed. Was he crying?

"And we thank You, God, for remindin' us of the important things. Like healin.' And hope. And the wings that carry us poor folks forward. Thank You for this bird, and thank You for these hearts. Amen."

He jammed his hat back on and cleared his throat. "All right, Miz Avery. Let's get this bird back in the sky."

Avery turned to Addisyn and grabbed her hand. "Come on."

"What? No, I don't—"

"Yes. We're doing this together."

She couldn't argue with the rightness of the situation, couldn't shake the feeling of the sacred, so she allowed Avery to lead her to where Isaiah's cage stood. Laz nodded approvingly at them both and then reached into the crate, pulling Isaiah from his ground-level life for the last time.

"Here." Avery slipped on her own leather gloves, then handed Addisyn an extra pair. "You hold him first."

"Okay." Addisyn reached for the hawk, awkwardly positioning his squirming weight. This was the closest she'd ever been to him, to the power that seemed to crackle through his healed wings. "Am I holding him right?"

"Relax your grip." Avery placed steadying hands over Addisyn's and shared a glance with Laz. "You can't hold wild things too tightly, you know."

A gust of wind swirled through her hair, and with the hawk in her arms, Addisyn glanced around the circle of friends—the ones who had lived the story of healing. Avery. Darius. Laz. Chay. Skyla. The wings had risen for them all.

"Now what?" She glanced at Avery, their hands crisscrossed around Isaiah's wings, but it was Laz who answered.

"Now you jes' open yer hands." His smile held the light of the mountains. "He knows what to do."

"I'll count for us." Avery grinned, the wind washing joy over her face.

"One…two…three!"

Opened hands and outstretched arms, and then the beautiful bursting of Isaiah's wings. A leap into air, a flinging of faith, and he was soaring forward, pulled by the invisible call, climbing the cold winter air to freedom.

A cheer rose in his wake, and then Avery grabbed her in a hug. "Ads, we did it!"

"We did!" Addisyn looked up to see Skyla's arms around them both. "Did you get pictures?"

"Many." Skyla smiled, the mountains reflecting in her eyes.

Avery bumped Addisyn's shoulder. "More for that frame, right?"

"Yes, definitely."

"Hey, he's still up there." Darius's voice cut over the swirl of excitement. He pointed to the spear-tip of the tallest conifer, where sure enough, Isaiah was balanced, a dark silhouette against the sky.

"And there he goes!" Avery clasped her hands like a prayer as Isaiah flapped free from his perch and soared toward the cliffs. He rose higher, power pulsing through his wings, and then he blurred into the fire-flung sunset kindling against the High Country.

"He found his wings." Avery's voice was soft, but there was a peace behind her smile.

"Yes." Addisyn watched the place where his wings had risen over the mountains' eternal shoulders. The pines would point him onward, and the stars would craft his course, and the wild wind would carry him ever upward. "He's flying now. And so are we."

KEEP READING!

Thank you for joining me on this journey, dear reader! I hope you were blessed by this story. If you enjoyed this book, would you please consider taking a few moments to leave a rating or review? Reviews are one of the best ways you can support my writing as well as help other readers find books they might enjoy. Thank you in advance!

Now, I have more exclusive content for you—"Free to Fly," a special bonus scene that takes place two months before *Where the Wings Rise*!

Along with her husband, Chay, Skyla Bluefeather Wingo works tirelessly on behalf of the birds who find their way to the couple's wildlife rehabilitation center. But when Skyla receives a cryptic call regarding an injured Red-tailed Hawk, helping this bird find healing might be costlier than she expects.

It was so much fun to delve further into Skyla's character and explore this scene, and I can't wait to share it with you! You'll find it in the official Climbing Higher Library on my website. This virtual library contains all the exclusive content from the Climbing Higher series—including a prequel scene from Addisyn and Avery's escape to New York and even a collection of gorgeous mountain-themed phone wallpapers. Just scan the QR code below or visit www.ashlynmckaylaohm.com/climbing-higher-library to download "Free to Fly," and the other special content, today!

Thank You!

Dear Reader,

Unlike *When the Ice Melts*, this story did not come to me as a single, cohesive concept. Instead, I began my planning process with a frightening scarcity of ideas. I knew I wanted to continue Addisyn's journey and that her relationships with Avery and Darius would be key in that process. But for a time long enough to terrify my productivity-wired brain, I had no solid ideas.

And then one day, while I was driving home under a storm-scudded autumn sky, the inspiration flashed so brilliantly that I slapped the steering wheel. "That's it!" I exclaimed to my startled mother, who was riding shotgun. "I need a hawk in my book!"

As family members of writers must learn to do, she smiled encouragingly without the barest notion of what I was referring to and gently suggested I wait to fully focus on the plot until I was no longer behind the wheel of a moving vehicle.

So why a hawk? Well, for many reasons. First of all, hawks are simply epic. I thoroughly enjoyed the research needed to write this book, and each new piece of information left me more in awe of these remarkable birds, and of the people who so selflessly work to protect their habitat, educate the public, and rehabilitate injured birds.

But there's another reason, one that's even closer to my heart: Isaiah's journey is one that is required of us all.

If you're like me, then pain has written itself across the chapters of your story. Fears and failures have broken your wings and left you languishing in a ground-bound life. And maybe, like Addisyn, you've tried to run from your past, or ignore it, or bury it so deeply under distraction that it can never again see the light of day.

But as Addisyn discovered in this book, we often can't go forward until we're brave enough to go back.

The choice, you see, is ours. We can stay on the ground, of course. We can accept our broken wings and try to convince ourselves that our life is fractured, but fine. We can go on pushing down our pain and stubbornly ignoring our failures.

Or we can choose the other path.

Like Skyla, we can learn to look upward, to watch the wings in wonder. Like Darius, we can call for strength, the uncommon courage to face what must be overcome. Like Avery, we can surrender, throwing all that we are into the hands of One Who gently holds our hearts. And like Addisyn, we can honestly face all the horrible history, all the late nights and wrong turns and dark days, and allow the God Who knows the sparrows to once more bind our broken wings and release us into the limitless future He has for us.

And that is my prayer for you, dear reader. May you never forget that You are loved, that His glorious heart beats strong for you. May you always stand with double courage, choosing healing over hiding. And most of all, may you feel the strength of His Spirit in the rising of the wings, and may You allow His healing to send your soul skyward.

— Ashlyn McKayla Ohm
August 2023

CLIMBING HIGHER

Don't miss the other two installments of the Climbing Higher series!

When the Ice Melts **(Climbing Higher #1)**
Losing her dreams may mean finding herself.
Competitive figure skater Addisyn Miles erased her older sister Avery from her life years ago. But when her dreams crumble and an old threat resurfaces, Addisyn must find Avery again…and the faith her sister followed.

Why the Mountains Stand **(Climbing Higher #3)**
Her darkest story might just be her greatest strength.
When a legend resurfaces in the Canadian mountains, Addisyn forms a reluctant alliance with Kenzie, a girl with a troubling link to Addisyn's own past. Now, they must move past the secrets that haunt them…and discover the purpose to their shared pain.

Find out more about the Climbing Higher series and read the first four chapters of each book for free by scanning the code below or visiting **ashlynmckaylaohm.com/my-writing/** today!

ABOUT THE AUTHOR

A worshiper of the Creator and a wanderer of creation, Ashlyn McKayla Ohm is most at home where the streetlights die and the pavement ends. She is passionate about shaping stories that weave together unfailing truths, vivid characters, and dramatic natural settings—bringing readers face to face with not only the mountains but also the God Who still moves them. If she's not daydreaming about her next book, you'll find her hiking, birdwatching, or otherwise getting lost in the woods.

Follow Ashlyn's writing at the links below!

Website: www.ashlynmckaylaohm.com
Instagram: www.instagram.com/wildernessashlyn
Facebook: www.facebook.com/WordsfromtheWilderness

Acknowledgments

A story may start as an idea tucked away within the author, but it takes so many hearts and hands to bring it to the light. It is with humility and immense gratitude that I acknowledge all who have helped me along the way.

For my friends who prayed for me, believed in me, and never laughed when I told them I was going to be a writer. If I began to list names, I could fill this entire book, but please know you are all so dear to me.

For my fabulous cover designer, Hannah Linder. Thank you for taking my sketchy vision and translating it to a cover that captures the spirit of the story.

For the experts who so kindly helped me gain the knowledge I needed to tell this story well: Julie Harbison, licensed physical therapist, and Carin Avila, executive director and board chair of the Rocky Mountain Raptor Program in Fort Collins, Colorado. Julie, thank you for lending your physical therapy expertise to help me write Darius's injuries and recovery in the most accurate way. Carin, I so appreciate all that you shared with me about raptor rehabilitation along the Front Range. This book, and its author, are indebted to you both.

For my extraordinary beta readers: Sonya Chittum, Ailsa Millar, and Alan Robinette. Thank you for the patient reading, the stellar suggestions, and the love for the story that bolstered my own.

For my amazing parents, Ralph and Derri Ohm. I would never be able to fly if you hadn't been my wings. You have given me strength in weakness, light in darkness, courage in the face of fear, and always, always, a love beyond measure. If I could count the stars or weigh the wind, I might be able to tell you how much I love you.

For my Savior, Jesus Christ. No words I could command would come close to describing the glory of Your infinite gift. Thank You for spinning this story in me and for guiding me through Your grace. On every night of *not-enough* or day of *don't-know*, Your love has never let me go. May You continue writing Your story on the pages of my life, and may Your fire fall on this altar where I offer it back to You.

www.ingramcontent.com/pod-product-compliance
Lightning Source LLC
Chambersburg PA
CBHW070602300726
48975CB00006B/1679